Flowers for the Dead

C.K. Williams

OneMoreChapter

One More Chapter an imprint of
HarperCollins*Publishers*
The News Building
1 London Bridge Street
London SE1 9GF

www.harpercollins.co.uk

First published in Great Britain by HarperCollins*Publishers* 2019

A catalogue copy of this book
is available from the British Library.

ISBN: 9780008354404

This novel is entirely a work of fiction.
The names, characters and incidents portrayed in it are
the work of the author's imagination. Any resemblance to
actual persons, living or dead, events or localities is
entirely coincidental.

Set in Birka by Palimpsest Book Production Ltd,
Falkirk Stirlingshire

Printed and bound in Great Britain by
CPI Group (UK) Ltd, Croydon CR0 4YY

For Thérèse
and for my parents

No coward soul is mine

Emily Brontë

The doorbell rings.

It sounds shrill in the small attic flat. The walls are slanted, lights turned off, the floral wallpaper barely visible in the dark. A small kitchen merges into a sitting room, an old dining table stuffed into the corner. The TV is on, but there is no one in sight. A pot of begonias is sitting on the windowsill. The flowers are drooping their heads. Outside, streetlamps cut stark shadows into the dark London street.

The doorbell rings again. Urgently, it resounds through the empty flat.

The bedroom door opens. A woman comes stumbling out. She must be in her thirties. She is dressed in floral sweatpants and a dressing gown, a little threadbare, the wool as dark as her eyes. Pulling it around herself, she stares at the front door. A shiver runs through her body, from the tip of her black hair to the soles of her bare feet, peeking out from the dressing gown. For a moment, she looks inexplicably frightened.

Then she takes a deep breath. Her lips are moving, although no words are coming out. *You can do this.*

Glancing at the windowsill for a moment, she then focuses on the door, rubbing the palm of her hand. It seems to be cramping. Her lips are still moving as she walks up to the door. Hesitantly, she presses the buzzer.

Through the peephole, the woman stares out into the hallway, cast in darkness. Someone is coming up the stairs. She can hear their steps ringing through the stairwell. Their laboured breaths. Their heavy boots.

The woman freezes. A drop of sweat runs down her neck, caressing her bare skin.

A dark figure comes into view. Distorted by the peephole. A man. Tall. Broad-shouldered, his face in the shadows. Breathing heavily. Raising a hand.

She takes a panicked step back.

The man's hand finds a light-switch. Suddenly, the hallway is flooded with light.

He is wearing a delivery uniform. Carrying a parcel.

The woman lets out a breath, relief softening all of her features. Just a delivery man. Her muscles relax as she opens the door and steps out onto the landing. 'Thank you for coming all the way up here,' she says. Her voice is melodious if soft. She gives him a shy smile, which he returns. She is closer to forty than thirty, but men still like it when she smiles.

'All right,' he says. He makes her sign for the parcel, then hands it over to her. They say goodbye as strangers do. She watches him retrace his steps, making sure he's left, then retreats into her flat.

The parcel is small, no bigger than a shoebox. She sets

it down on the dining table, making the wood creak, and leans against the windowsill. Absent-mindedly, she feels the soil of her begonias, making sure they want for nothing as she looks at the parcel, careful curiosity written all over her face.

Until she sees where the parcel is from.

The moment she notices the address, her pulse quickens. It's come all the way from Yorkshire.

The woman takes a step back. Her eyes race to the kitchen area, to the rubbish, the recycling bin. She could simply bury it deep, under carrot peel and the remnants of dead flowers. Her hands are shaking as she reaches for the parcel. Touches it. Hesitates. Looks back at the kitchen.

Again, her lips are forming words. *You can do this.*

She picks up the parcel and moves into the kitchen. For a moment, she is overwhelmed by an absurd urge to shake it. Hold it up to her ear and listen.

Then she turns away, forcefully, and reaches for a pair of scissors. Carefully, she cuts it open.

Inside the parcel sit only a few harmless items. Trinkets, really. A copper thimble, an old drawing of a wildflower, a few souvenir magnets from mountain villages all over Europe. A picture frame of an older couple, smiling into the camera, bearing an obvious resemblance to the woman. A letter sits on top.

As soon as the woman lifts up the letter, she sees it.

Underneath the paper lies a flower. Pressed and dried. Shaped like a bell, dark petals, black berries.

The woman recoils. Her breath is coming in hard, short

3

bursts. A memory sears through her, like a crack in the walls of a dusty room. Sweat on her skin. Saliva running down her neck. A shout ripped from her throat and the taste of leather on her tongue.

She takes another step back. Her mouth is forming the words *you can do this, you can do this*, but the memories keep driving her back. Back until her body hits the wall. She digs her nails in, tries not to slide down. To keep herself upright. *You have to fight it.* But there is no way she can fight this. The dark berries, the purple petals.

The woman knows what sort of flower this is.

Her hands begin cramping. The soles of her bare feet. Her chest, her lungs, her windpipe. She reaches for her throat, the clammy skin as she tries to push the memories away.

This is deadly nightshade.

She knows because she has had it in her mouth. Tasted its sweet, deadly berries, nineteen years ago. Nineteen years ago, on a night just as dark as this one. The night when she opened the door to her parents' house and let in her worst nightmare. The torn sheets. The shards of glass, the smell of lavender, the blood between her legs. Her raw throat and the taste of leather in her mouth.

The woman slides down the wall, silently, eyes fixed on the table. All you can hear is a soft swoosh as the dressing gown slithers along the wallpaper. The low noise of the telly. The occasional car driving by. Her finger, tapping on the floor.

It is only in the woman's memory that another sound can be heard. And this is a new memory. Something she had burnt out of her mind as utterly as possible. Something she has not remembered until this very moment.

It is a doorbell.

And it is ringing.

Ding, ding, ding.

I. Lies

Chapter 1

LINN

I am the reason girls are told not to trust a stranger. In the small town in the Yorkshire Dales where I grew up, the homes as lonely as the mountains, what happened to me is every parent's cautionary tale. They tell it to their daughters, their precious little girls, their nieces, cousins, sisters, mothers. *Don't open the door to strangers. Don't walk home too late at night. Don't wear that skirt.*

It has been nineteen years, and I've never been back there. It has been nineteen years, and I've never told anyone this story. That is why what I'm about to do is so utterly, breathtakingly stupid. Or brave. Maybe that's one and the same thing, anyway.

I am in our bedroom, packing the rest of what I will need. Listening carefully for any sounds from outside the bedroom, I'm stuffing my things into an inconspicuous shopping bag from Tesco. In a hurry, I put the parcel that I received last night into the bag, making sure it is stowed away safely. The dried flower of deadly nightshade now sits in my pocket. My movements are harried. Frantic. Energetic. As they have not been in many, many years.

I'm about to go back there. Drive from our London flat onto the motorway and ever further north into the dark autumn night. To the lonely house where I grew up and the High Street in the village where I played knock, knock, ginger as a child with my friends under the red boughs of the rowans. Where we always used the same code when we rang the doorbell, until all of the village knew it:

Ding, ding, ding.

I take the book I'm reading from my nightstand and throw it into the bag next to the parcel. Quickly, I tie the bag closed and hide it under the bed, covering it with the extra bedding we keep there. I can feel the pulse in my palms, my heart beating frantically.

For nineteen years, I believed the official story. The police said it, and I believed it. At seventeen years of age, still living with my parents in Yorkshire, one night I opened the door of our house to a stranger. My parents were not at home, gone to see a show in Manchester. By the time they came back, the police were already there. Their daughter had already been raped, and could not recall anything except the pain splitting her open, blood running down between her legs. She could not remember how she had got there, or who had done it.

I couldn't remember.

I straighten. Close my eyes. Listen to my heartbeat, trying to calm myself down. I am thirty-six now. For nineteen years, that is the story I believed.

But it is not the true story.

I turn to the dressing table, looking into the mirror, putting my hair back in order, strands that have come undone in my hurry. My face looks just the same as yesterday, but everything else is changed: when I looked at the dried flower in the parcel, a memory came back to me. Like a titan arum suddenly coming to bloom after years of nothing, the deadly nightshade made me remember.

It made me remember how the doorbell rang that night.

Ding, ding, ding.

That was why I opened the door in the middle of the night. Because I thought it was someone I knew.

I stare at my face in the mirror. The lines around my mouth and my eyes, on my forehead. For nineteen years, I believed it had been someone I didn't know, a stranger who'd made the most of their opportunity and had been long gone before I was found.

But no stranger would have rung the doorbell like that. Everybody in the village knew that that was my code. Our code.

It was someone I knew.

Even in the mirror, I can see that my shoulders are shaking, my chest, my hands. With fear, and with fury. That is why I am going back to Yorkshire. Back to the one place where I swore to myself I would never return. Back to where it all happened.

I am going to find out who did this to me.

Turning away from the mirror, I let my eyes sweep through

the bedroom once more. There is nothing else I need to pack. My suitcase is already downstairs in the boot of the car. I am ready. All I need is for Oliver to leave.

I can hear him puttering around in the kitchen, just beyond the bedroom door. He is setting the table for our farewell dinner. He is leaving for a conference tonight.

Taking a deep breath, I look into the mirror once more. I put on a smile, watching the corners of my mouth lift. Then I leave the bedroom.

Oliver smiles at me when I emerge, as kind as absent-minded. He whistles as he sets the table. If it can be called that. My husband pushes out air through his lips while he hums and calls it whistling. It would be infuriating if it weren't so utterly, thoroughly him – sweet and funny and a little bit awkward. His woollen sweater is orange and blue. I gave it to him.

I try and pretend that everything's normal. Water my begonias on the windowsill, however hopeless a case it might be, making sure they have enough to drink. I try not to look at Oliver, because the truth is, while he's here and doing that silly whistle, I will never bring myself to leave. Suddenly, I feel the need to tell him. Tell him everything. It's like a pull, or more like a push, like he's pushing me against the wall. I will tell and then stay here and keep living this life that we have got used to, but which can't give him what he wants.

Determined, I walk into the kitchen and turn off the stove where the mash has been simmering. Dinner's ready, nothing fancy, just mashed potatoes and pork pies from the supermarket down the street. Oliver doesn't mind that I'm not a world-class cook, and I like to think my baking makes up for it. I love baking. Made our wedding cake myself. That was also because money was a little tight – when isn't it, really, with the rent you have to pay these days? – but still. It was a feast of chocolate, almonds, vanilla and marzipan, decorated with edible flowers.

While I serve the mashed potatoes in small bowls on our plates with the pies next to them, Oliver reaches for the remote. 'You want me to turn off the TV, Linnsweet?' he asks.

'Thanks, Sweet-O.' The name jolts through me as I say it out loud. That's what I call him, Sweet-O. Have always called him that. It was a joke at first, because of what his mum used to call him. *My sweet Oliver. Sweet-O*, I used to tease him. He came up with Linnsweet in return. They stuck.

He's set the table nicely, I realise as I sit, with a candle and the cloth napkins his mother gave us for Christmas five years ago. After we had just moved here. It is our third flat. We've been together ever since we were seventeen. Went to school together. People sigh wistfully when they find out. Those are the most romantic stories, aren't they, they say, where you marry your childhood sweethearts.

Except the story that's told about me isn't one of romance. Except that I'm not good for him. I have always known this, known that he could have done so much better for himself than a traumatised high-school girlfriend who did not even manage to feed the fish regularly. That he deserves so much better. A real family, a proper partner. But I was never brave enough. Never brave enough to go, not even for his sake. When you love someone, you let them go, they say. But how could I let him go?

Until I received the doctor's letter, three months ago. The results were clear. Oliver is not going to have any children if he stays with me. He will never have a family.

Oliver digs in; he could never wait for anyone when it came to food. Nor can I, actually; for such a mediocre pair of cooks, we sure love good food. But not tonight. Tonight, I sit across from Oliver, clutching the fork in my hand, incapable of taking a single bite. My knuckles feel like they are about to burst through my clammy skin. *In sickness and in health, to love and to cherish.* I know he won't leave me. Not after he's stuck with me for nineteen years. He is too loyal. Too kind. But I cannot take that away from him, too. He has always wanted a family. He was so excited, that morning three months ago when we thought I might finally be pregnant. I had woken up to his hands on my body, to his lips on mine, the scent of a fresh bouquet of flowers and warm croissants on the dresser. The fit of nausea had been so sudden, I didn't even make it to the bathroom before I threw up. He thought it meant we were going to be a family. I thought so, too, so I went to the doctor's.

Turns out that's not what it meant. If there's one thing I can't get, it's pregnant.

I look at Oliver, watch him eat, talk, his soft face, his shaved head hiding that he's going bald and grey, that deep line on his forehead and his bright blue eyes, bright even after all these years. *Till death do us part.* It is so hard sitting here and saying nothing. Funny, because I thought I was good at lying.

I hope he won't look into the car on the way out, when he leaves for his conference. I hid the suitcase under a woollen blanket and bags of groceries. In case he looks into the boot, out of curiosity. I hope he won't realise. It would break his heart. My husband. *For better, for worse.*

But how much worse?

Finally, I also make myself take a bite. The mash turned out fine, actually. Then I ask him about the conference. It calms me down just to hear his voice. The corners of my mouth twitch into a half-smile. The conference will last for a week. He has been on the road more and more this past year to go to conferences, to workshops, but this is the first time he will be delivering a keynote. He has been so excited, so nervous, so busy, he's hardly had the time to think about anything else. To realise that I had become quieter. To think about what I might have been thinking about. To wonder about the fact that I never told him what came of the visit to the doctor's except to say we'd been wrong.

'Linnsweet?'

I look up at him. Maybe he made a joke. Maybe I missed it. There is a crease on his forehead – he's worried about me. Poor Oliver, always having to worry about me. Nineteen years of little else.

Again, I make myself smile. 'Sorry. You like the pies? They turned out quite nicely, didn't they?'

A grin flits across his face. 'Always so modest,' he teases.

'It was intended as a compliment to Tesco,' I insist, corners of my mouth twitching again.

This time, he laughs for real. I would love to laugh with him, but my throat constricts. He has sacrificed enough, I remind myself as I force another bite down my throat. Let him go.

Oliver smiles at me when dinner is over. Blows out the candle. This one's blue. They're always blue. Then he takes me into his arms, his strong arms, maybe not as strong as they used to be, but still a place where I can't move once I find myself in them. *To have and to hold.* 'Will you be okay while I'm gone?' Oliver asks. 'Doing anything nice? Go see a show, maybe? Bake something for me?'

Tell him. Just tell him.

I open my mouth.

'Sweet-O,' I say. He looks at me. His blue eyes and large pupils, blown wide from how we have been pressed against each other.

I swallow. He wants me so much. Even after all these years. All these years that he has taken care of me.

Now it is my turn to take care of him.

'Maybe I'll just stay in and wait for you to come home,' I say, every word painful, my mouth twitching. 'Keep the couch warm.'

'Do some laundry, maybe?' He laughs.

'That sounds crazy,' I manage.

'I know, right? Lock him up now, he's a nutter.'

'I'll iron your shirts,' I say, feeling that non-smile on my

16

face again. He needs his shirts, now that he's in management, and frankly, he's rubbish at ironing. When they offered him the promotion, from nursing to public health manager, he said, *Hell, yes.* That is why he's been going to all these staff training courses, all these conferences. I always knew he would be great at it. Oliver has always wanted to help people, told me so on our very first date. No matter how hopeless a case, he doesn't give up on anyone. Sometimes I think that's why he's stuck with me so long.

He laughs again, lets me go and grabs his travel bag. I breathe in, then out. Press my arms to my body, my legs together so that I won't pull him back towards me. He deserves to be happy.

When his cab has arrived, we go downstairs together. He is taking the late-night train to Cornwall. He likes trains. I put on my coat, my gloves and scarf and the hat I made for myself when I took up knitting for a bit. The front door needs a heavy push to open, then we step outside. It's a cold autumn night.

'I miss you already, Linnsweet,' he says and kisses me.

I kiss him back and try to tell myself to do the right thing, not to cave now. Not to be selfish. To let him go. He looks at me, so much want in his eyes and desire and regret. 'I'm sorry I've got to go,' he says, and I cannot speak.

Don't speak.

So all I do is nod.

Then I watch him walk to the kerb.

I watch him greet the driver, a friendly 'How're you, mate?' I watch him put his bag in and wave at me.

Then I watch him glance at our car.

He hesitates.

My pulse quickens. Slowly, he turns back to me. My throat goes dry. He looks at me, in my coat, with the gloves and the hat and the scarf, too. I feel perspiration in my armpits and my thighs and the palms of my hands, like sweaty fingers stroking my skin. Let me do the right thing.

He turns to the driver. Tells him something. Then he walks back towards me. 'Did you forget something?' I ask, my voice sounding normal even as my tongue feels like it is stuck to the roof of my mouth.

He takes my hand and kisses its back, making my insides twist. 'Don't you need help with the groceries?'

I shake my head, glad I'm wearing gloves. Otherwise, he might notice the sweat on my palms. The fluttering of my pulse, the shaking of my fingers. 'No, that's all right, Oliver.'

'No, come on, you don't have to carry them up on your own. He said he could wait. You should have told me, I'd have helped you when you got in.'

'No, really, you'll miss your train,' I say, laughing even, playfully pushing him towards the cab. 'Go, Mister Manager.'

Oliver doesn't budge. He does not like being pushed. 'You should've told me.'

'I'm sorry,' I say, rubbing my hand across my lips. There are so many things I should have told him. 'The only thing that'd make me even sorrier is if it made you miss your train.'

As he gets into the cab, I let out a relieved breath. I watch him until the cab has turned around the corner, towards the city centre, waving till I can no longer see him.

I wait five more minutes. Ten.

He does not come back.

I stare at the corner my husband disappeared around. The red-brick house, the bare tree on the corner, the blue light of a TV set flickering through the curtains. It takes me a moment to notice that there is something wet on my cheek.

Confused, I take off my glove and lift my hand. There are wet tracks on both sides of my face. Wiping the liquid away, I realise they are tears.

I don't know if they include this in their story. When they tell their cautionary tale about me, up in Yorkshire once night has fallen. Do they add, *And after it all happened, she decided it was safer to just stop feeling things? That's what trauma is, girls, not being able to feel anything, not even sad when you let the person go that you love. Don't open the door to strangers. Don't walk home alone at night. Don't wear that skirt.*

I hope they do. I hope they tell the true story.

Well. If we knew what the true story was.

I hesitate, car keys already in my pocket. I'm ready. If I only knew how to do this. I haven't gone anywhere without Oliver, except to the shops, in years.

Just take one step at a time.

Slowly, I start walking towards the car, hands buried in the pockets of my jeans.

Already in the driver's seat, I glance up at our flat one last time. It's then that I realise I've forgotten something. Two things, actually.

I rush back upstairs and unlock the flat once more. I'm leaving Sweet-O everything, of course, everything except what I need and he can't use, my clothes and my makeup and the last picture of my parents, taken two months before their deaths. It was one year ago that they left us.

I hesitate as I look at the CD rack; all my hand-signed records of The Dresden Dolls are already in the car, but there are still The Police's *Best Of*, Blondie's *Greatest Hits*. I take a deep breath, then I leave them. Oliver loves our music. And it may be selfish, but I want something for him to remember me by.

What I came back for aren't CDs. It's my bag with the parcel, *and* my begonias. The bag in one hand, I leave the bedroom and walk across the living room to the windowsill facing the busy street below. 'Left behind just because you droop your heads?' I whisper to my begonias, running a finger along the green stems. They are hardy begonias, *Begonia grandis*. I got them on a whim in the summer, when they were looking so sad and thirsty inside Tesco.

Wrapping them in a plastic bag, I look around the flat one last time. I reach into my pocket and take out the note I wrote for Oliver. That's all I am brave enough for. It says that I am fine, and that this is the best way, and that I don't want him to come looking for me. That he has spent too many years of his life taking care of me already. That I truly wish him all the very best and a real family with someone who can give him what he needs. Someone who will be good for him.

My hands are trembling as I put it on the table. Look at it, the innocent piece of paper, the blue candle on the table, blue like my husband's eyes. Feel him push me against the wall.

Stay.

The doorbell rings. I flinch. Then I remember it is past ten, and the drunks are starting to stumble out of the pub across the street. Some of them think it's funny to play a round of knock, knock, ginger with the pub's neighbours before going home. First time it happened to me, when we'd just moved here, it was the middle of the night. I woke up in panic, the cold sweat of fear leaving traces all over my body, like insistent fingers. With time, I got used to it, though. At least they usually don't piss in your doorway when they've rung all the bells.

Then it rings again.

They never ring again.

That's Oliver. It must be Oliver.

I rush to the door. Press the button. Nothing happens. I press again. Someone pushes against the front door, downstairs, I hear it echo through the hallway. It won't open. Jammed.

I dash downstairs to open it, carrying my bag and the begonias. If it's him, I'll stay.

When I open the door, it is not Oliver, not his soft, bald face. Instead, there is a delivery woman, red hair tucked under her cap. 'Bloke named Oliver sends you these,' she says unceremoniously. 'Hope he's not a creep.'

'We're married,' I say, shuffling my bag and the begonias

around so that I can take the large bouquet she hands me – autumn flowers, red and orange and yellow, so tasteful.

If only there weren't also stems of lavender tucked deeply into the bouquet.

'Doesn't answer my question,' she says and puts out her hand.

I stare at the bouquet; it is the same he bought a week ago, before I went to the doctor's. Then my eyes drop to her fingers. Her nails are polished blue. Behind her, two drunks are falling out of the pub doors.

Then I realise she wants a tip. I fumble with my wallet and press a few coins into her hands and watch her leave. I put the bouquet down as soon as she is out of sight. Now all I've got to do is walk out, unlock the car and drive.

I hesitate. Breathe in the scent of the flowers at my feet.

Then I push out. Out into the cold and the dark. I haven't wanted anything in a long time. But I want this.

I want to find out who did this to me.

THE NEIGHBOUR

It is early morning when I hear the engine roar, lying awake as I often do. It is barely dawn, the light outside white and grey. Must be an old car, the way it sounds. I saw lots of cars like that before I moved here. Now, not so much.

A country road leads past my drive, single lane, old stones piled up into low walls on both sides, grey during the day and black at night. It is absurd. Even after all this time, I still start when I hear a car. They come down this road so rarely.

Surrounded by starch-white pillows and sheets, I listen to the sound of the engine, trying not to be nervous. You can hear them coming a mile off, cars like that. Do not be nervous. And do not get up. It is an obsession, my therapist told me. You are obsessed.

The sound of the engine turns louder. I turn onto my back, fiddling with the bed sheets. They are clean and stiff. There are no other houses down this road, bar one.

Is that why you bought the Kenzies' home? my therapist asked me. *No,* I lied, *I needed more space.*

The windows are frail things. I feel the draft wafting in. When I heard the Kenzies were moving, when I saw the price they had put the house up for, I did not hesitate. I phoned up Mrs Kenzie and went round and signed the lease the following week.

The car is up on the crest of the hill now.

I do not have an obsession.

I get up, bare feet cold on the old wooden floor. The boards creak when I put my toes on them. The summer nail polish came off a while ago, only traces left, dark green like the forests where I was born. I pull back the curtains, white lace so that I can look out and watch the road even when they are drawn.

The house is situated off the dirt road; when it snows, you cannot make it out of here without a 4x4. Like in Gdańsk, but that feels very, very far away. It always smelled like salt there. I still wake up and miss the sea.

The car comes into view, headlights cutting through the woods.

It has the right colour. I have seen it on her social media.

A frisson runs through me.

You are obsessed, my therapist says, her voice very calm.

Aren't you? I would like to ask her back.

I see it, a white blur through the gnarly trees and their bare branches, a white blur in the heavy fog. I watch it.

My body is shivering.

It is the right make.

It could be her.

LINN

Mist thickens into fog as dawn approaches. I am heading along Grassington Road after I turned off the A59 at Skipton. The narrow road dissolves into a milky grey mass. Houses are turned into shadows, rising and falling by the side of the road as I pass them. Trees seem to suddenly appear, gnarled branches reaching across the road, as if they were reaching for me. The steep slopes of the peaks are familiar even in the dark. The grass, grey in the morning, is glinting with dew. I even recognise the old stone walls, black blurry lines climbing up the bare slopes. My fingers are clenching the steering wheel so hard my knuckles hurt. Have been ever since I passed the sign: COUNTY OF NORTH YORKSHIRE.

The fog thickens and thickens as I continue down the A684, on and on. I pass through Aysgarth and along the Ure. This must be Worton. Then Bainbridge, this sharp bend to the right, past the low houses and the roses climbing up their walls, sprawling like spidery fingers in the fog. I am so very close now. On and on I go, turning off the A684 onto the single-lane side road leading to our village. I thought it would make me nervous, these narrow roads, not wide enough for two cars. But it is not the roads I am worried about. Nor is it the shadows passing me on both sides, the silhouettes of trees and walls and roadside heath.

I do not slow down until I see the silhouette rise on my right: the crippled old oak tree by our village sign. The village I know so well, even when I cannot see it. The narrow old bridge across the brook, the High Street where I used to play, the farns growing thick on the steep slopes surrounding us. The Dresden Dolls are filling the car with their disturbing sounds, louder and louder the closer I get to my parents' old house.

It is far out of the village, sitting on a dead-end dirt road where farns and goatsbeard and marsh orchids grow, with only one neighbouring house, the Kenzies'. And even they lived a mile off before they moved away. They were friends, Mum and Dad and the Kenzies. Best friends. It was they who sent me the parcel – the Kenzies. In the letter that came with the parcel, they explained that they had moved out of their house, out of that village, not half a year after my parents' death. They said that they were now settled in their new home in the East Riding, by the coast, and that they wanted to send me a few things of my parents' they'd found as they'd unpacked their boxes. The dried nightshade, for example, which my mum had given to them for safekeeping. She hadn't said what they were keeping it for, only that she didn't want it to be thrown away, but that she no longer wanted it in her house, either.

That was Mum's thing, drying flowers. They were all over the house. Even this one. Deadly nightshade.

The fog is so thick that I do not see the graveyard, either. Thank God. I know I pass it on the left. Know where it is. Know whose graves I haven't been to see.

I do not slow down but drive on, drive on until the dirt road comes into view, sloping up into a forest before it leads to the two lonely houses. I turn.

At the crest of the hill, driving past the Kenzies' old house, I take a glance, but the fog is still too heavy. I only catch a glimpse of the sharp gable and the uppermost window, emerging from the white, milky mass.

For a moment, I believe I see someone standing there. A slim silhouette. Dressed all in white.

Watching me.

The car stutters. Quickly, I push my foot down on the accelerator. When I look back up, the window is empty.

The Kenzies never said whether they had found a buyer. My begonias bob their heads up and down on the back seat, peeking out of the plastic bag as I keep driving. They make me think of our flat in Leyton. Make me glance in the rear mirror. Just to check.

As if I had to. This is the last place Oliver would expect me to go. On our computer, I'd checked websites for a few cheap places to stay in Brittany, in Norfolk and Kent, just in case. But wherever he would suspect me to be, it wouldn't be here. Not after I didn't even return for my parents' funeral, twelve months ago.

My face turns hot as I think of it. There is something wet in my eyes. I blink rapidly as the road turns narrower and narrower, from a dirt road to a path in the woods, snaking its way back to the main road on the other side of the forest. It disappears amidst the pale stems of the sycamores and the winding branches of the ash trees, between the wych elms and bare rowan trees. I used to take my bike down that path, even when it was dark. It seems far too frightening now that I look at it, dwindling like a dying brook in the headlights ahead of me.

I nearly miss our drive even as the fog keeps clearing. At the last moment, I recognise the downy birch and the high hedge and derelict stone wall on my right. I realise my hands are shaking so badly that I cannot stabilise the steering wheel. As if there are climbing plants sprouting in my lungs, it is difficult to breathe.

Braking, I turn into our drive. Between the shreds of fog, the old house emerges: two floors, made of limestone, standing between hunched hawthorn and sharp holly and tall birches. There is an abandoned garden and a wooden front porch with a roof, damp and dark.

You can do this, I tell myself. *You have to do this if you want to find out what happened to you.* This house is a part of it. This house surrounded by woods, with a front porch and a set of chimes by the door that I gave to my mum when I was fifteen, the small bells still dangling in the wind when they left for the hike they would never return from.

The moment I come to a stop at the bottom of the drive, the moment I turn off the engine, I sink back into my seat.

I made it.

For a moment, all I feel is light. As if I am floating. I made it. I did the right thing.

A little unsteady on my feet, I get out of the car, the cold wrapping me into its cool arms. I open the boot and take out my suitcase. It's heavy. Then I fetch the begonias from the back seat. 'We made it,' I whisper to them. 'Well done, my darlings.' I'm a florist, and let me tell you, you don't pass your exams if you don't talk to flowers.

The pot in my arms, I walk up the front porch, a rather eccentric addition of my father's. I walk past the chimes on the front porch.

Wait.

I stop. Turn to the side, still on the wooden steps. I remember the chimes. Dangling onto the stairs, announcing every visitor. Remember their sound. Remember the doorbell. Remember the sweat and the noises.

But the chimes are gone.

Putting down the begonias carefully, I walk up and down the porch, then onto the dead meadow on both sides, looking for them. They must have been blown away by the wind. Or a cat came and … I don't know. The Kenzies told me in their letter that the chimes were still here. But I suppose that happens. No one has been here since my parents left.

A hiking accident. That's how they died. Here, too. Right here in the Dales.

Returning to the front steps, I take my begonias back up and look for my parents' keys in my handbag, blinking rapidly, trying not to think about the Kenzies' voices over the phone, stained with tears as they delivered the news. My hands are cramping, so are the soles of my feet. Instead, I think about having a bath, or a shower, after I have lugged the suitcase from the car into the house. A nap on the couch, even, once I've got the heating back up and running. Before I face my parents' bedroom. Before I make a battle plan.

Finally, managing to fish the keys out of my bag in spite of the cramp in my hands, I bend over to put them into the keyhole. It is a bit rusty, I think at first, when I do not manage to turn the key.

Then I realise that is not the case.

I cannot turn the key because the door is already open.

THE DETECTIVE INSPECTOR

Things get stolen here. Not often, mind, but it does happen. There is no such thing as 100 per cent security. Other than that, we are doing well. Break-ins, occasionally. This is an area where people don't exactly come from old money. Some, though. And the break-ins, they have become more frequent. It is a problem.

A set of chimes, though? To be honest, I think she's blowing things out of proportion a little, don't you? I don't want to say hysterical. It's not like she's shouting. But a set of chimes. You might think the wind has blown it away or some animal has come and torn it off. Maybe the Kenzies took it when they moved. Who would go all the way out there just to steal some chimes?

I look at her. Clutching that flowerpot to her chest and trying very desperately to smile. I haven't seen Linny in years. Recognised her straightaway, though, when she walked in, and what a shock that was. To see Linny back here, Linny of all people, after all these years. How long has it been, twenty years, nineteen? Hellfire! Nineteen years since I last saw her. I mean, not even at the funeral. Can you believe that? The only child not showing up to her parents' funeral? And that house of theirs just sitting down in that hollow at the end of that dirt road, all empty and nobody using it?

So, you know, a right shock, seeing her again. But shock's nothing new to a policeman, is it? So, when Linn shows up like that and tells me her parents' door was open, not just unlocked, I thought it was serious, I really did. But then we drove there together and went inside, and nothing had been stolen or damaged or even moved, and I looked at that rusty old thing of a lock and have to say I'm not surprised it didn't hold.

Didn't say that, though. We're back at the station now and I want to help her, I do. She's always been a darling of ours, Little Linny from Down-in-the-Dip. That's what we used to call her parents' house, Mark's and Sue's, because of how they built it right at the bottom of that hollow in the woods. It's the only house on that road except the Kenzies'. But the Kenzies don't live there any more. Mind you, it's none of my business whom they sell their house to. I only know, I wouldn't have picked that one. That's all I'm saying. But I guess they didn't want to stay after Mark and Sue were gone. Bloody hiking accident.

'You're in good hands here,' I tell Linny as I take out a form from the shelf behind me. The police station has been reno-vated. It's all white and modern now and there are neat lines on the floor telling people where to stand and where not to go. Not to come too close to the counter, for example, unless they've been asked to. That must be a London thing. Where they have shootings at police stations when someone from Tower Hamlets comes walking in. Or Leeds, at the very least. Here, I tell everybody to just come up to the counter. Right up.

'Come here, Linny,' I tell her. She's in ratty jeans and a worn coat that used to be quite nice, I think. Her hair has turned a little bit lighter. Thinned out, too. I remember her hair as black as the forest up by her house, and her eyes as large as a doe's, even when she was a teenager. Pretty girl, that. She moved away pretty early, right out of school. With her boy. Her man. Oliver. Good man, that one. Promising swimmer, he was, and I should know, I coached the team for a while. Shame he didn't go into swimming professionally. He could have really made it as a swimmer. Better than Jacob Mason, even. Olympics, absolutely. Gold for England, that would have been something!

So, we were sorry to see them go. Her parents especially, of course. But I did not blame them. How could I?

I knew it was my fault. Know it was my fault she never came back, not even to visit. I tried to do all I could to help, but she didn't want to stay after all that.

All the more reason why I want to help her now. That's why I don't say, *You know, the fair was in town a couple of months ago, may have been a few teenagers out for an adventure, or just time passing and wearing down that old lock, you know? Taking the chimes as a bonus, so to speak.*

Besides, I get it. Alone as a woman, you'd get flayed easily, wouldn't you? Scared, I mean, you'd get scared easily. So I hand her a form and when she's filled it all out, I fax it straight up to Northallerton (tried and true, a fax machine). Looks like it puts her at ease. She's smiling again, and that's all I want.

Let me tell you about all the ways this girl could smile. She had the most expressive face as a kid – you could always tell there was something going on in that bright mind of hers. Especially when she'd played a trick on you and you hadn't found out yet. There was that twitch in her face. She loved to play tricks, Little Linny did. Now, her smile's friendly, maybe a little shy. I walk around the counter to show her out, putting my hand on the small of her back to reassure her. Let her know I'm here.

'I'll keep you posted on any developments, Linny,' I say.

'Thank you, Detective.'

Something tugs at my chest as I remember her as a little child, coming to play knock, knock, ginger with her friends in the town centre, giggling behind the bushes on the other side of the street as I pretended not to see them. Ding, ding, ding, that's how they always rang the doorbell. Everybody in the village knew it.

'Please, Linny, call me Graham.'

There was that boy with them, too. A bit weird, wasn't it? Even as teenagers, they still stuck together. Linny and Anna and that boy. Teoman Dündar. He didn't play footie or go loitering around pubs with other young men his age, smoking cigarettes. Wasn't that what folks of his background did?

Instead, always trailing those lasses. Maybe that's what people do where he's from, though. Don't take women seriously, do they? Linny's parents were worried, in any case, I remember that.

I watch her leave, still trying to smile, dropping purple petals where she goes, watch her through the bulletproof windows (another London regulation, that, I'm sure). There is a feeling just beneath my skin. A prickling sensation.

Just a set of chimes.

I return to the counter, tell Angela, I mean Constable Johnson, that I'll be right back. Then I go into the back. Down the set of stairs, grey concrete, low ceilings. Along the narrow corridor, dark walls and blue doors with a couple of cells behind them. At the end, the only wooden door, the one leading to the archives.

Takes me a while to dig out her file. It's still on paper. I can't believe I haven't looked at it in so long. The prickling turns stronger.

I have sharp instincts, I do. I wonder if it's coincidence. I wonder if she knows.

That Teoman is back as well.

LINN

I know it's silly to have gone to the detective. To Graham. I couldn't believe it at first, when I saw it was him standing behind that counter. Not because of how much, but of how little he seemed to have changed. Sure, he looked different, but he still talks, moves, listens exactly like he did all those years ago.

I try to relax my hands around the handle of the suitcase. Graham was kind enough to take note of my complaint, and the lock *was* very old. It may have come undone, simply, like the chimes. It gets fairly windy here, even down in the hollow in the woods. We've arranged for a new one to be put in. The locksmith will be by later today.

Now I am standing in the hall of the house, clutching my bags. The house I have not been in for nineteen years. Slowly, I put down the bags and push open the first door on the left. It leads to the mud room. Cloakroom, my mum called it, a euphemism if ever I heard one. There is the low wooden

36

bench we threw all of our coats on, and the rack for the shoes and the wellies, and the shelf for the gardening tools that Mum said she needed at hand, not all the way out in the shed in the garden. All of it is covered under white sheets. The Kenzies must have done this after the funeral. I pull off the sheets, one by one, dropping them onto the floor. The tools are still up on the shelf, some of them rusty, some of them still shining bright, bought only recently, never to be used.

I put my coat down on the bench and toe off my shoes. A pair of trainers sits on the rack still. They were my father's.

I go back out into the hall, the kitchen the first door on my right, the staircase to the first floor right ahead. I go into the kitchen first, pulling away sheet after sheet, uncovering birch wood and local pottery, the blue heavy plates and mugs from my childhood. The sitting room next, windows and the back door leading out into the garden, framed by high bookshelves. Looking out, I can see the shed behind the house by the tree line, blue paint flaking away.

And then I climb the wooden staircase, the carpet soft under my feet. The stairs still creak in all the right places as I ascend to the first floor, to the two bedrooms and the bathroom. Here, the furniture under the sheets is all of dark wood. It was my grandma's, and so are the doors. The house still looks so much like it did back then. It even smells like back then, because everywhere, on every available surface, sit Mum's dried flowers.

Stopping at the top of the stairs, one hand on the bannister, my yellow socks on the blue carpet, I stand and stare. At the door leading to my parents' bedroom. The room where it happened. I stand and stare and breathe.

Involuntarily, I turn back around. I have to go into town. I need to get some more groceries before the locksmith comes over. Besides, I should also begin investigating. Find out who is still here. Find out where to start.

I collect the sheets I dropped and leave them in the mud room, before I check the cupboards in the kitchen, making a quick shopping list. Then I grab my coat from the mud room and rush back outside. With the grey, bright light in my eyes, I drive back to the main road, allowing it to take me back into the village. The fog has lifted, and I find the short-stay parking lot up on the High Street without any trouble.

I kill the engine, looking through the windshield at the village where I used to play. The narrow stone bridge across the brook is right in front of me. Even sitting inside the car, I can hear the sound of the water rushing down across the stones and into the valley. It used to be our favourite place, this bridge and the brook. It is surrounded by cottages and houses with names, RIVER VIEW and BLYTHE'S COTTAGE and THE OLD DAIRY.

And on the High Street goes, across the bridge up to Cobblestone Snicket, which looks like a house but really is only a façade leading to an old, narrow snicket, an alley with a cute café and an antique shop. Its façade's been repainted, blue and red now instead of green and yellow. Other than that, it hasn't changed. Not even the High Street seems to have changed, the small houses of grey stones or white plaster turning grey, the shops and the pub and red parasols packed up for the cold season, sitting amidst gnarled alder trees and bare rowans. I remember my father made jelly from the rowan berries in our garden and put it on the table when we ate game, its taste bitter and tangy.

I realise I missed that taste. I missed the alder trees and the rowans and bright red parasols.

Sitting in the car, I have trouble tearing myself away from the view. Now that I am here, where do I start? Originally, my plan had been to return to the house first, get my bearings, unpack my bags. Go into the bedroom I haven't entered in nineteen years, see if it would help me remember anything like the nightshade did. But the village is as good a place to start.

Determined, I take a notebook out of the glovebox, a pretty one from Paperchase, and dig into my old handbag, the red leather faded to a pale pink, in search of a pen. I chance upon the USB key in the shape of an astronaut that I bought seven years ago, as well as two dangerously dry chrysanthemums I nicked from the neighbour's balcony, and an old bright-red lipstick, before I finally find a pen at the very bottom of the bag. Crouching over, I prop the notebook up against the steering wheel and think.

This is where I grew up. This is where I rang the doorbells playing knock, knock, ginger, all up and down the High Street. Everybody knew. Everybody could have done it.

But not everybody was at the crime scene that night. When I came back to my parents' house, I was not alone. The police were already there, Detective Inspector Walker. He had been called in by my best friends, Anna Bohacz and Teoman Dündar, who had found me. And I have a blurry memory of Jacob Mason's face, my ex-boyfriend. Quickly, I jot down their names:

Detective Inspector Walker
Anna Bohacz
Teoman Dündar
Jacob Mason

I hesitate as I write Jacob's name. What was he doing there? We had been friends as children and dated as teenagers, but we had not been on speaking terms for a while at that point.

Tapping the pen against the steering wheel, I keep thinking. Of course, there is also Miss Luca – the school therapist. She wasn't at the scene, but we went to see her afterwards. We all did, separately of course. Anna, Teo, Jay and me.

I add her name to the list. Then I stare at the pen, the red plastic, a freebie from the London Planetarium. Wasn't there someone else? There is a shadow at the back of my mind, but whenever I reach for it, it recedes, like a whisper just loud enough that you can hear it, but too quiet to understand what is being said.

Graham would know; I should ask him. There are places I could try visiting, too, retracing my steps of that night: the party at Jacob's house; the way home from the village through the woods; my parents' bedroom.

I shiver as I think of the bedroom. As I remember the searing pain, the scent of lavender, of sweat and blood. My parents' sheets, damp under my bare skin. My dress, torn all the way up to my breastbone.

I can feel my skin go clammy. Quickly, I add a list of places to the piece of paper, my hand shaking so badly I nearly scrawl the letters all over the page.

Detective Inspector Walker
Anna Bohacz
Teoman Dündar
Jacob Mason
Miss Luca, school therapist
Jacob's house (party)
way home (woods?)
bedroom

I'm shaky as I get out of the car. I will have to speak with them. With whoever's still here. And if there is one person who'll know, it is Kaitlin Parker.

I walk out of the parking lot, across the bridge and up the High Street, listening to the rush of the water as I hope that Kaitlin's copy shop's still there, the one where I interned when we had to get some work experience. Kaitlin was our village gossip. She used to know about all comings and goings in this place. She always wanted to get out of here, but she wouldn't be the first not to make it.

As I walk, I realise I had forgotten how many flowers there are in the village. They grow in everyone's front garden, in every window box, even just on the side of the road: roses climbing up the walls of shops and cottages, bushes of marsh orchids growing in front of the Old Dairy, yellow hay rattle and white bogbean peppering the riverbank. Someone must be nursing them, otherwise they would not be in bloom still so late in the year.

I have just passed the bank where I opened my first account when I see it: the copy shop. As I approach, I realise that they have a new sign, bit more modern, but it is still Kaitlin behind the counter – Kaitlin and Anvi.

For a moment, I stop and watch them through the window. It comes as a shock. Kaitlin has grown so fat. Her face is still the same, but it seems distorted, like it has been pushed out into all directions, like dough that's been rolled out.

Then I see my own self reflected at me in the window and hurry inside.

'Ey up,' Kaitlin calls out the moment I walk in. Recognition shoots through me at the familiar greeting, the phrase I have not heard in years. 'What can I do for you to—'

She doesn't finish the sentence. I see her small eyes widen as she takes me in. Within moments, her expression turns from naturally friendly to flabbergasted. 'Hellfire, is that ... Linn?'

'Hello, Kaitlin,' I say, a little embarrassed. A grin spreads out over her face.

'Is it really you?' she says as she comes around the counter. She wears felt. Her brown hair has thinned out. She still blinks far too often, looking at me with her bright-green eyes. 'Is it really? I can't believe it. I really can't. Think I gotta sit down.' Instead, she grips the counter, staring me up and down unabashedly. 'Wow! Sorry, I just ... Never thought we'd see you again! Now that your parents, God rest their souls ...'

'Yes,' I say hastily, mouth twitching before I shape it into a grin. 'It is good to see you. Good to be back. Hello, Anvi.'

'Ey up, Caroline,' Anvi says. She always used my full name. Said it was a sign of respect. She is as slim as ever. It's the first time that I've seen her wear a sari, though. It looks pretty, all orange and purple. She is much more collected than Kaitlin, who is still gripping the edge of the counter, looking a lot like she could use a drink. At least Kaitlin's grinning, though. Anvi, on the other hand, is watching me with what can only be called hostile suspicion. 'How have you been?' she asks.

'Good,' I say, corner of my mouth twitching into another smile. 'Very good. And you two?'

'Great,' Kaitlin says. 'Just peachy.' She has taken out her phone. 'Sorry, luv, I just got to let Mum know, she won't believe it when I tell her ...'

See? Village gossip.

Anvi is still watching me. 'Everything is fine. A lot has changed, of course. Not that you would know. But at least the shop is doing well.'

She is dropping the 'g's at the end of her words just like Kaitlin. I have missed the way people talk up here. No 'g's at the end, no 'h' in the front, that dialect that instantly feels like home. Suddenly self-conscious, I wonder if I sound like a Londoner to them. 'I'm glad to hear it.'

We fall silent. It turns awkward as we look at each other, looking for the traces the last nineteen years have left.

Wondering if we look as tired, as old, as the person we see standing across from us. Wondering who these strangers are that use the voices, the tics, the gestures of people we once knew. Abruptly, I remember being sixteen and helping print T-shirts for hen dos. An exciting night out in Leeds, in Blackpool. Remember worrying about my braces. Remember how Kaitlin and Anvi were only a few years older than me, really, always fighting behind the curtain in the back of the shop, trying to make ends meet.

This isn't exactly a boom town. When the weaving loom went out of fashion, everyone who had legs to walk on left the Dales, and that was in the eighteenth century. There's only 18,000 of us left now. If there is any reason for people to have heard of us, it will be because of *Emmerdale*. Highly arguable if that's an honour.

And I left too, didn't I? Even though I loved it here. The memory comes back to me as unexpectedly, as painfully as the nightshade: the way it felt to live here and *love it*. Even this copy shop, these two wide-eyed young women, trusting that their community would have need for their business. I remember that Anvi wore trousers even though her father didn't want her to and how Kaitlin could make amazing cinnamon rolls. I remember the wildflowers in the Dales and how they made me want to be a florist: the small blooms of pink bell heather and the beautiful golden globe-flowers. I remember Mum showing them to me, all the way at the back of our garden, where Dad had cut the first line of trees.

She showed me the deadly nightshade too, the dried

flowers in her bedroom and the fresh ones in the woods. 'Kings and queens used them to assassinate their enemies,' she told me, speaking conspiratorially, as if she was telling me a secret. 'Ten berries can kill a grown man. And two are enough for a cat or a small dog.' Their taste is sweet, so sweet you won't be able to tell, really, if they've been mixed into a heavy red wine. I should know. 'They are called *Atropa belladonna*,' she explained to me as she showed me the exact shape and colour of the plant, taught me to tell it apart from the bitter nightshade. 'That's from Atropos, one of the Three Fates, the Greek goddess who cuts the thread of every-body's life. And *belladonna* means pretty lady; they were used for makeup once upon a time, that's why. Only this pretty lady is here to kill you,' she said, and pressed me close to her, both arms around my shoulders. 'But don't worry,' she whispered into my curly hair. 'Mummy and Daddy will protect you.'

The memory almost makes me choke. Dragging myself back to the present, I pull out the USB key I brought. I did not only spend last night packing: I also updated my CV. I have a little money saved up, but I'll be needing a job soon. 'I would like to print something, actually,' I say, before the silence in the copy shop can turn even more awkward.

'Aye,' Kaitlin says, taking the little astronaut off me with her free hand. She is still gaping at me whenever she glances up from what is quickly turning into texting the entire village. 'Seriously, I can't believe it! How have you been? How is Oliver?' Her fingers are sweaty. I flinch. Her eyes widen again. 'Sorry! Have I put my foot in it? Here I am, just assuming ...

Last time I talked to your parents, they mentioned that you two ... It's just we don't get any news of him any more since his parents moved away, I mean with their divorce and all that ...'

I laugh it off. *To have and to hold, till death do us part.* 'No, it's fine. We live in Leyton now. I trained as a florist. Oliver went into nursing, he's a health manager now, he ... We have this lovely flat in London, no balcony, but still, I mean, can you imagine finding a flat in London at all – it's insane.'

'I bet,' Kaitlin says as she walks to the computer. Still holding her phone, continuing to type with one hand. 'Must be down south. Just wait till I've told Mum, she won't believe it, she really won't, it's ...'

'So you have come back with him?' Anvi asks. Her eyes are narrowed. She hasn't let me out of her sight once.

'Oh no,' I say lightly. 'No, not at all.'

'Where's Oliver, then?' Kaitlin asks. 'Hellfire, haven't seen him in nineteen years either, have we?'

I knew they would ask. 'At a conference,' I say and can't help but think of him. What he's had for breakfast. If the pillows in the hotel are soft enough for him. The blinds dark enough. He will be so busy with his presentation. I wish I could have helped him more, supported him.

I know Oliver won't realise what's happened till he comes back. He will be texting me from the conference, trying to call, too, but he knows how I get sometimes, especially when he's gone: not answering the phone, not texting back. He knows I bury myself sometimes. He's learned not to push.

'He is not with you, then?' Anvi is watching me. Why is she watching me like that?

'No,' I say, the moment that Kaitlin makes a pleased sound. Actually, she almost squeals.

'Oh, CVs? You want to apply for jobs here? It would be so good to have you back, luv! People don't come back often, you know how it is. Not a lot of jobs. I mean, they do some-times come back, but usually for Christmas or funerals ...' She peters out. Keeps glancing at her phone. It pings. And pings and pings. 'See, they won't believe me! Maybe we could take a photo, for proof.'

'Yes, definitely looking for a bit of work,' I say. Trying to sound as casual as I can, even though the words alone are scaring me. I haven't worked in years, not since 2008, you know? Not a lot of demand for florists since then.

But my training still counts, doesn't it? They need people, don't they? That's what they've been saying in the papers, at least, and on TV. Well, in the health sector mostly, not exactly in floristry. Because of Brexit. Anyway, I need to get these CVs sent out. Maybe a florist in Northallerton, or Leeds, or even further north. Maybe in Scotland.

But that's not what I came here for. 'So,' I ask, trying to sound casual as I think of my list. 'Who else is still around?'

'Oh, quite some people,' Kaitlin goes on, obviously in her element. 'The two of us, of course, we never left, did we, Anvi? Even though we always said we would.'

'Evidently,' Anvi says drily.

'What about the Masons?' I ask carefully. 'What about Jacob?'

'Yes,' Anvi says, putting as much distaste into the one syllable as she can. 'He is still here.'

'Oh, don't be like that,' Kaitlin says as the printer starts up. 'Yes, the Masons still live here, in the same house, too. Though it's only Jacob now.' She leans over the counter conspiratorially, motioning for me to come closer. 'It's outrageous. He sent his mother to a nursing home a couple of months ago. Barely seventy and already in a nursing home, can you believe it?'

Anvi lets out an angry snort. 'Instead of caring for his mother at home, where she has lived all her life. It is a disgrace.'

Kaitlin just seems gleeful. 'Isn't it just?' she says, sounding rather thrilled about it. Then her eyes widen. 'You went out with Jacob for a while, didn't you?'

'And Miss Luca?' I ask, avoiding her question. Anvi is narrowing her eyes at me again. As if she is seeing right through me. 'I'm just so curious,' I offer. 'After so many years.'

''Course you are,' Kaitlin says happily. 'Antonia Luca's still around, too. Has her own practice now. She lives on the outskirts of the village, on the corner of Meadowside and Foster Lane. Nice house, that. Number 32.'

As the printer whirrs away, I try to memorise what they're telling me. I hope I can still find the Masons' house, hope they haven't changed it too much. Kaitlin is still fiddling with her phone, in all likelihood preparing to take a photo. They are both so shocked still. Kaitlin's even shaking a little with excitement; Anvi's all tense. As if I was a robber.

Or worse. 'Why didn't Oliver come?' she asks. 'How is he doing?'

I will myself not to think about him. 'Like I said. He is at a conference. Do you still have envelopes, too? Could I get, oh, I don't know, ten, maybe?'

Anvi hands them to me, then collects my money. 'It is just such a coincidence, isn't it? That you and he would both come back to town?'

'Oliver won't be in town,' I say, trying not to let my impatience seep through. I haven't come here to talk about my husband. My – about Oliver.

'I do not mean Oliver,' Anvi says, her voice hard, even as Kaitlin's camera clicks. 'You know perfectly well who I am talking about.'

'I am afraid I don't,' I say as I take the CVs that Kaitlin hands me. I feel the little hairs on the back of my neck rise. On my arms. As if a cold draft has come in through the door. From behind the counter.

You know perfectly well who I am talking about. Suddenly, I can't wait to get out of there. 'Well, it was lovely seeing you two.'

'So chuffed that we got to see you, luv!' Kaitlin says, walking me to the door, obviously happy to see me even if she still doesn't quite believe it. 'In a bit!'

Without turning back, I walk out the door. If I walk a little more quickly, nobody has to know. I might be in a hurry. Hurrying to get to the post office before it closes. When do post offices close in a place this size these days? If there's a post office left at all. I think of where it used to be, by the car park, the back lot where we smoked in secret, and I decide that I might get the groceries tomorrow – there is enough left for a few meals, I'm sure. Anything not to think about him.

He cannot be back.

Teoman swore he would never come back.

THE NEIGHBOUR

The car returns at noon. I am upstairs in the corridor, both arms buried elbow-deep in the second wardrobe, ready to bring out the winter clothes. My summer clothes sit next to me in a pile on the floor, all freshly washed as I listen to the sound of the engine coming up the road.

It is her.

I know it is her.

LINN

The house smells like baking. It is a smell that makes me feel all loose-limbed. All happy, like it hasn't in years. The locksmith has been by and put a new lock in. And I sent out ten applications. Surely, one of them will work out. I'm a trained florist, did some gardening work as well. Something just has to work out.

Getting ready for bed, on my first night in this house that I was so scared of, I am in the bathroom, a plate of shortbread precariously balancing on the edge of the sink next to me. No cinnamon rolls. I have earned shortbread. As I remove my makeup, I don't think of silly Anvi and her silly allusions, but of the businesses, their sleek websites. I will have clients. Colleagues. After-work drinks. There might be promotions. There will be money.

I need to reopen my bank account. Put in the money my parents left me, the money that will tide me over in the mean-time.

Once the makeup has come off, I bend over the sink and have a drink straight from the tap. The water tastes wonderful up here, clean and fresh, very different from London. I collect it in both hands, then splash it onto my face. Drying my skin off on my parents' plush towels, I look into the mirror once more. For a moment, it doesn't even scare me, the prospect of work, of a new job, a new life. That I will have to leave the house every day. That I will be in a place I don't know, that I can't navigate. That it might be loud and dirty and confusing and there will be buses with a silly numbering system. Like when Oliver and I moved to London for the first time. It was our second flat; we'd never lived on such a busy street ... It was lovely though. Oliver had found it by marching straight into a local pub, getting drunk and then asking everyone in the vicinity if they knew of somewhere that was available. It got us a two-bedroom flat. Not bad. Only one set of keys, the heating working intermittently at best, and a leaky tap, but still not bad.

Now, it does not scare me, the prospect of a new place. No, it actually ... it gives me a thrill. Like seeing the shock on Anvi's and Kaitlin's faces when I walked into their shop today. Like I couldn't be overlooked. Like I was really there.

I haven't felt a thrill like that in years.

It is what bolsters me as I take one last look into the mirror. Take up the plate. Straighten my shoulders.

Then I go into my parents' bedroom.

The floorboards creak as I cross the threshold. The bed in the centre of the room is still the same, its frame of dark wood, its tall headboard, the small nightstands. The bed almost disappears under all the pillows and blankets. The wallpaper has changed, midnight blue on one wall, a wooden texture on the others. To the right of the bed is a door to the en suite I did not use – it feels too much like my parents' bathroom still – and on its left a window overlooking the hollow, right above the roof of the front porch.

Carefully, I put the plate of shortbread onto the nightstand on the right. My nerves are fluttering. Have been ever since I decided to sleep up here tonight.

To see if it will trigger a memory.

I stare at the bed. At the spot at its foot, the wooden floorboards in front of it.

That is where I woke up.

Slowly, I pad over there. My dressing gown billows up around me as I lie down. My bare skin touches cold wood, my thighs, the sides of my legs, my panties. I put my cheek to the floor, feeling the cold seep through me, and close my eyes. Ready to remember.

The floorboards creak. Outside, the wind sneaks through the hollow, through the treetops, shaking their leaves, whispering at the edges of the old window frames. The room smells dusty. There is a hint of another scent, but they are both overshadowed by the shortbread, still warm, sitting on my nightstand.

It smells really good, that shortbread.

I sit back up.

Well, this isn't working.

I let out a breath I didn't know I'd been holding. Then, out of nowhere, I feel something rise in my throat. A giggle. It comes out before I have even realised what is happening. Goodness, look at me. Crouching on the floor, hoping for some kind of revelation.

I stand up, dust off my nightgown, draw the curtains and return to the hallway to take out fresh sheets. On the way, I fetch my begonias as well, and once I'm back inside the bedroom I put them on the nightstand next to the shortbread. Then I take the nightshade from the pocket of my dressing gown and stow it in the drawer of the nightstand. Making up the bed with the fresh sheets, I realise that I do not recognise them: black flowers climbing across dark blue fabric, a silken touch to them. They must be new. They feel soft on my skin.

Taking up a piece of shortbread, I sink into the bed. Gently, I stroke the purple petals of the begonias sitting on my nightstand as the warm dough fills my mouth. They have raised their heads a little. I feel the earth in their pot, just to make sure they have had enough to drink. Then I smile at them, swallowing the shortbread. 'Goodnight, my darlings.'

Snuggling down into the covers, I breathe in their familiar smell. Still the same detergent. It feels as if I'd never left. As if Mum and Dad were merely away on a holiday, a hiking weekend in the Highlands. And the dried flowers, too, spreading their scent all through the house. Mum had such a passion for them. People brought dried flowers to her funeral, hers and Dad's. Heaps of them. There were piles of dried roses, of rosemary and thyme and laurel, even some bell heather and globeflowers. The Kenzies sent me pictures. They were dropped onto the coffins, they surrounded the funeral wreaths gifted by those who didn't really know my parents.

One of those wreaths was mine.

I know what you must be thinking. I wish I could make you understand what it's like to hear that the two people who've always been there, as long as you can remember, are gone, and not feel anything. Your mum, who used to be your idol, with her white hair and incredible bravery, and your dad, who would hug you like it meant everything just to hold you. To look at your husband as he takes you into his arms, trying to give you comfort, and swallowing down the truth, which is that you're feeling nothing. That he might as well have told you about the death of a badger he had hit on the way home, or a wasp he had squished outside the pub with his beermat.

Maybe that was when it became unbearable, actually. When I decided something needed to change. That I needed the truth. Maybe it wasn't the Kenzies' parcel and the deadly nightshade. Maybe that was just the last straw.

We had a ceremony in London, of course, Sweet-O and me. That's how I said goodbye to my parents.

I turn on my back, staring at the white ceiling. And here I am. Lying in their bed. Finally back in their house. Our house.

The deadly nightshade is back too, sitting inside the nightstand drawer, on top of one of Mum's old Chilcott catalogues: one of those mail-order companies where you could get homely pillows and handmade blankets and scent diffusers. Every single one of their products came with a pouch of British lavender. I wonder if they still exist.

Above the bed hangs a spray of lavender. When my parents still lived here, it always smelled so much like lavender in this room, like there wasn't any other smell in the world. Only once or twice a year would my mother go for rosemary and thyme instead, usually in winter and spring. She would never have both out at the same time; it was either lavender or rosemary and thyme. Now the scent is so subtle it barely registers with the shortbread right next to me. It's comforting. The pillow feels soft beneath my head. I feel like I am floating. It may be a little frightening, but it's also exhilarating. To be so light. I did the right thing.

I will have the truth.

Before I turn off the light, I have another piece of shortbread. I feel like I can have as much shortbread as I like now. Don't know what to call this feeling. Maybe it's the shortbread feeling. The-world-is-your-shortbread.

Involuntarily, I giggle again as I close my eyes. The pillows smell like home and the crumbs taste delicious and the night is deep and dark.

It is still dark when I wake up.

The room smells like lavender. Just like that night. The odour of the old, dry flowers feels heavy in the air. Like it is pushing down on the blanket. Like it is wrapping itself around me.

My legs are sweaty. So are my armpits. It smells.

Slowly, I breathe in and out. It's cold. Why do I feel trails of perspiration on my body when it is so cold? Like light cuts on my skin.

I turn onto my other side, keeping my eyes closed. *Go back to sleep,* I tell myself.

Why is it cold?

Why does sweat run across my skin like clammy fingers?

I open my eyes. The curtains are too thick. It is dark.

I close my eyes again. Maybe I'm running a fever. That's why I might feel cold and hot at the same time. That's it.

Wrapping the blankets more tightly around my body, I tell myself to go back to sleep and close my eyes again.

I am already dozing off when I think:

Why did I wake up?

The doorbell rings.

I turn onto my other side, mumbling into the pillow. The drunks from the pub. They'll go away eventually. It smells like lavender.

It takes me a moment to realise.

I am not in Leyton. I am not in my flat with Oliver.

I open my eyes. It is dark.

That is what has woken me.

Someone is standing in the hollow. Someone is standing in front of my door.

Someone is ringing the doorbell.

THE NEIGHBOUR

Her house is dark in the night.

THE DETECTIVE INSPECTOR

The one case I couldn't close.

THE NEIGHBOUR

I am not obsessed.

LINN

I cannot breathe.

Those aren't the drunks from the pub.

I lie as still as I can. There is no pub. There are no neighbours, nothing but the Kenzies' old place. This is a back road, a dead end, dwindling down to a path through the woods. Dead trees on all sides, rising like thin fingers through the thick fog.

The sheets rustle beneath my shaking hands. I ball them into fists. It might be nothing. They might need help. Maybe their car broke down.

On a dead-end country road.

I feel the sweat collect beneath my armpits. Between my thighs. There is no sound. Only the stale smell of dead flowers and perspiration. There is someone standing down on the porch. In front of a large, dark house. The door isn't sturdy. They could come in if they put their mind to it.

Maybe they already have.

Maybe they are already inside, walking through the hallway, towards the stairs leading up to my bedroom. The carpets, grey and silent, swallowing the sound of their steps. More than one person. Or just one man. One man and his silent steps on the stairs to my bedroom. The closed door coming into view. His hands are gloved. His breath is going quickly. His pupils dilated. His heart beating with excitement.

I almost choke on my own breath.

Stop. A car's broken down, that's it.

Should I check? What if they need help?

They would ring again then, wouldn't they?

Wouldn't you ring again?

I pull the blanket up to my nose. There are no sounds at all. I didn't hear a car. You hear cars from miles off on this road.

As the minutes pass by, I start wondering. Did I only imagine it?

My teachers always said I had an overactive imagination.

Slowly, I sit up. Rise, carefully. Tiptoe across the carpet. To the window. I don't dare draw back the curtain. Only lift it, not even by an inch. Through the narrow gap, I peek out.

It takes my eyes a while to get used to the darkness. When they have, I look out across the hollow.

There isn't a single soul. Not a car, not a bike, nothing. Only the long shadows of the bare birches, a little darker even than the night, like fingers stretched out towards the house.

I drop the curtains again and move back under the blanket.

I only imagined it.

The sweat dries. It leaves sticky patches in the dip between my collarbones, on top of my breasts, beneath my arms and at the seam of my panties. Slowly, I close my eyes. I listen for sounds. A breeze strokes through the naked boughs of the trees. Wood creaks. It's not the stairs. It's no one coming up the stairs. It is just the trees. Just the trees and their long shadows.

The sweat is cooling on my skin. It prickles.

Chapter 2

*I*t is a summer day in the year 1988. Three children are running up the High Street, out of breath. They are giggling as they turn into Cobblestone Snicket to hide, two girls and a boy. The heat lurks in the narrow alley, the air oppressive. A thunderstorm may be coming. Everyone is wearing shorts, skirts and crop tops, humming 'I Should Be So Lucky'.

The kids all try to peek back around the corner at the same time. 'Move, Linn,' the boy hisses, 'I can't see!'

'Shhh,' Linn, the girl in front, says to the boy, her dark eyes wide and curious. 'Shh, Anna!' to the other girl.

The other girl's blonde hair is falling down onto her shoulders and she's whispering, 'Don't let them catch us, please don't …'

Five houses down, a front door is thrown open. A woman in her forties, she seems ancient to these kids, steps out. Her son is watching from the window. He is their best friend, Jay is, but he has been grounded. His mother is wearing a brown cardigan and frameless glasses, sweating in the heatwave. 'I know you are there!' the woman calls out. Her name is Mrs Mason. She is their teacher in kindergarten, teaches them colours and songs and the clock, which is really hard. Now her doorbell had rung *just like the stupid fake clock she brings into kindergarten with her to bully them. Ding, ding, ding, three short chimes. Linn giggles.*

Mrs Mason steps out of her doorway. Anna's murmuring turns louder. 'Please, God, help us, make her not see us, make her not see us …'

'Come out!' Mrs Mason calls again. Anna slinks back further into the alley, praying in another language now, one Linn doesn't understand. Teo is clutching Linn's shoulders. 'What do we do?' he whispers. 'She's coming right at us!'

His brown eyes widen as he sees how close Mrs Mason is already, her flat shoes making funny sounds on the pavement. 'Come on, Linn!'

Teo takes her hand and pulls her with him, following Anna, who's already well ahead. They run down the narrow alley, pushing through the stifling heat, emerging on the other side into the parking lot of the supermarket. It is new and shiny, and they run up to it and inside and pretend to be looking at the sweets machine. The sweat prickles as it dries on their skin. Anna is looking so hard at the sweets, Linn is afraid her eyes will pop out like the chewing gums pop out of the machine. Teo keeps clutching her sleeve and Anna's, and then Anna takes Linn's hand. 'Girls Just Wanna Have Fun' is playing over the speakers.

Finally, Anna glances up and grins, in her pretty floral dress and her pretty ponytails. 'Ding, ding, ding,' she whispers, and the three kids start giggling until they are out of breath all over again. 'Ding, ding, ding.'

LINN

When I wake up in the morning, I'm sticky all over. It takes my eyes a while to focus on the ceiling. And for my brain to remember what happened last night.

What I imagined, anyway. I lie in the damp sheets, breathing more heavily than I should. I did not expect the first night to be easy, but I will deal with the nightmares. I've dealt with them before. They are a price I am willing to pay. And the begonias look bright and purple in the daylight, and the deadly nightshade is buried deep in the nightstand drawer.

'Good morning,' I say to the begonias, determinedly cheerful, taking them to the bathroom to make sure they get their breakfast. Then I go down to put on the washing machine for the sweaty sheets. There is only a little detergent left. As I stand bent over my parents' old machine, in that basement, naked light bulbs casting dark shadows into the corners, I tell myself that I cannot feel fingers of sweat on my body. On my eyelids.

Hurrying back upstairs and into the bathroom, I tell myself I can still try and find a hotel in the area, should the nightmares get worse. Although that would be too expensive, I fear. And there are no friends I could bother.

There were only ever the three of them, really, weren't there? Anna, Jacob, Teoman.

One of whom has come back, too.

Teo.

Standing naked in the bathroom, waiting for the water to turn hot, I watch the frost flowers on the windows while I remember them. Teoman and Anna and Jay. My best friends for as long as I could remember.

Teo. The only one the police ever arrested.

Involuntarily, I shiver. The Detective Inspector let him go the next day and said all the evidence pointed to a stranger. Maybe the DNA sample could have helped, but it was contaminated. Got mixed up in the lab. Human error. All too human.

I never asked Graham what made him take Teo in. What made him let him go.

I didn't want to know.

Besides, it didn't matter, did it? We thought it was a stranger. Now, things look a little different.

Every muscle in my body cramps up. As I step into the shower, I resolve to speak to Graham as soon as I can. Find out what he thought about it, about them: Anna, Jacob, Teo. And we all went to see Miss Luca, too, afterwards, so she's someone to speak to.

After the shower, I make some porridge with the blueberries I brought from London, listening to my favourite Dresden Dolls song, 'Girl Anachronism'. Some of the blueberries are already mouldy. Today, groceries, no matter what. When I've breakfasted, I put on a pair of wellies, grab the car keys from the mud room and go out.

The cold folds around my body like the clammy sheets in the night. Lifting my shoulders, I wrap my coat more closely around me. It's a city coat. Useless. But at least the fog has lifted. I can see the hollow lying before me, the front porch surrounded by dead grass covered in hoar frost, and the brown circular driveway up to the top. The wood of the porch creaks under my shoes, the soles loosening thin splinters of wood.

My hands are still cramping as I get into the car, no matter how forcefully I rub my palms. I start up the engine, go up the drive and onto the main road. It's Sunday, so Graham won't be at the station. Where did Kaitlin say Miss Luca lived? Corner of Meadowside and Foster Lane, wasn't it? Maybe it's time to pay her a visit.

I thought of her as old back then, but she can't have been much older than thirty. She wrote me a letter, after Oliver and I had moved, recommending a few therapists close to his university, but I never phoned them up. I know what you must think, but I was already struggling to feed our fish. Even though the aquarium had been my idea. As I sit in the car, the corner of my mouth twitches upwards as I remember. I'd wanted something to care for, some company, too. We had one fish we'd called Buttercup, a big yellow one, our favourite.

When I found Buttercup swimming upside down three months after we'd moved in, Oliver suggested I get rid of the aquarium and try with a cactus first. He grinned as he said it, but his eyes were worried, and I knew what he was thinking: I wasn't even capable of taking care of a fish. How would I take care of myself?

I turn into Meadowside and make my way past the kindergarten. There is a kindergarten not far from our flat in Leyton. I remember how Oliver would stop at the playground to watch the children. He had worked at a children's hospital for a few years, bringing home drawings all the time, of small stick people with blond and black hair holding the hand of a stick person with no hair at all, laughing at his own baldness.

On the corner of Foster Lane, I kill the engine, peek out of the windshield. That must be Miss Luca's house. Kaitlin was right: it's very nice. All white, three storeys, a slate shingle roof. Green hedges growing all around it, a metal gate in front of the white gravel driveway.

Go on, ring her doorbell.

But all I do is keep sitting in the car. My limbs are heavy.

Come on. Get up. She might be able to tell you something.

I try and move my legs, but they won't budge.

Move. Raise your arm.

Slowly, I raise my eyes. Look into the rear mirror and focus on the tip of my nose. Then I breathe.

I am raising my hand to open the door. I am raising my hand to open the door. I am raising my hand to open the door …

My hand is moving, inching towards the door handle. I use the momentum to go all the way and push the door open. Mrs Dündar taught me that trick, Teo's mum, when I was a child. Teo called it magic. That made her laugh. We all thought it was magic when we were kids.

I get out of the car. Autosuggestion it's called, I know that now. An easy trick. That's how I managed to open the door to the delivery man the night the Kenzies' parcel was delivered. That's how I manage most of my life. Oliver thinks it is stupid. Says I don't need hocus-pocus like that. I think it reminds him too much of how far gone I am sometimes.

Slowly I make my way towards Miss Luca's house. The gate isn't locked, opening almost silently. The gravel crunches under my feet as I walk up to her door. Check the name on the bell. LUCA. I'm in the right place then.

Nervously, I lift my hand. Ring the bell.

Then I wait. I can hear nothing moving inside. Maybe she's out in the garden. It's Sunday, but really a little cold to be out. I ring again.

When nobody opens up, I return to the car to tear a piece of paper out of my notebook. Before I can change my mind, I scrawl my name on it, tell her I'm back at the house and ask her to get in touch if she wants to. I almost leave her my phone number, but then remember that there is no reception at our house. Never has been. I remember getting my first phone and how I always had to go into the village to do anything with it. Reception is fine in Northallerton and Kendal, and even here on the High Street my phone works well enough, and on the tarmac road into town. Maybe it's the hollow. Maybe that gives them trouble. The Dales are difficult to tame, Mrs Mason always used to say.

God, how long I haven't thought about Mrs Mason. About Jacob. Jay was what we called him. How long I haven't thought about the peaks, Bolton Castle after dark, Cobblestone Snicket and how we say snicket instead of alley and flayed instead of scared.

I still haven't thought about where it was that my parents fell.

I drop the note into her postbox, watching it slot in place next to an issue of *Psychology Today*. Then I get back into the car. When I sit down in the driver's seat, I feel like I've run five miles. But I'm also proud. I made a start.

Turning the car around, I glance at my list. Jacob Mason is next.

On my way to his house I stop at the supermarket. Considering that the shop still looks the very same on the outside, it comes as a surprise that they've changed practically everything on the inside. It's impossible to find anything. The products are different, too. Did they sell avocados back then? I don't remember. All I remember is going shopping with Mum, and how large I thought the trolleys were, and meeting Mr Dündar in aisle 7, bent down very low to pick up the raisins he was looking for. 'These are the good ones,' he used to say, and give me a few straight from the package, right in the aisle. Mum was scandalised. The cashiers never minded, I don't think. I don't know. Mum always pulled me on after the barest bit of small talk. Whenever I turned back to look at Mr

Dündar as a child, I saw him watch us leave, his expression inexplicably sad.

After a few confused rounds through the aisles, I finally manage to get a sense of the place. In aisle 6, I run into Mr Wargrave, who was already old when I was born and now uses a walking frame but seems all right otherwise. Only when he greets me with a friendly 'Hullo, Martha dearest,' do I realise he might not be holding up as well as I thought.

'Hello, Mr Wargrave,' I say. 'How are you?'

'All right, aye. Getting a paper. The obituaries,' he says, pointing shakily at the local newspaper sitting on his walking frame. His nails have turned yellow. They are splintering at the edges. Then he grins at me. He's got new teeth, I think. 'It's always good to see you're outliving all them bastards, isn't it?'

I smile, not sure what to say to that. 'Mason,' he goes on. 'She's still going strong. Nursing home now. Good for her, though, with that son of hers.'

I furrow my brow. 'What do you mean?' I ask him. Jay adored his mother.

But Mr Wargrave only waggles his eyebrows, grown far too long, just like the hairs sprouting out of his nose. 'I'm not in a home yet. All alone at my place. Neighbours are gone, too. No one to listen in on us. You remember that, Martha.'

Well, that was a disturbing experience. As quickly as possible, I go to one of the self-checkouts, grabbing a prepaid SIM card as I pass. I will be needing it. I don't think I'll be able to bear seeing all of Oliver's messages and not respond.

For the first time, I'm almost grateful there isn't any signal down in the hollow.

Once all the groceries are in the boot, I steer the car towards the High Street and put the Dresden Dolls back on. 'Coin-Operated Boy'. Sing, under my breath, watching the houses I drive past, looking for the Masons'. There's an uneasy sensation at the bottom of my stomach. *He is just a toy, but I turn him on and he comes to life, automatic joy …*

What did Mr Wargrave mean when he talked about Jacob like that? I remember the way Anvi and Kaitlin talked about him, too. The tone of their voices, far too disapproving for the boy I remember: Bright eyes, well-spoken, well-mannered. Entitled, maybe, but good at heart. He'd wanted to be an artist, or a graphic designer at least. While we went out, and when we were friends, too, he would make me little drawings and pass them to me in class. Of flowers, instead of giving me bouquets. Of chocolates, to tease me. Of myself, when he was feeling particularly brave. I was the only one he showed his sketchbook to.

The uncomfortable feeling at the pit of my stomach intensifies as I get closer to where his house should be. He was my friend. The first person I fell in love with. You don't forget your first crush. I haven't seen him in nineteen years, and even at seventeen, we'd been split up for a while. Goodness, we'd been so young when we got together, we didn't even have sex. Even though we did do all sorts of other things. He wasn't exactly shy about what he wanted, and neither was I. We weren't in a healthy place, so we thought the more bruising it involved the better. I still remember how he'd sneered at me when I broke up with him, sneered and insulted me to hide how hurt he was, a teenager about to lose everything but unable to stop it.

Driving down the High Street has memories batting into me on every corner. About the first time that Anna, Teo, Jay and I tricked the goody machine, spilling sweets into our laps like a miniature version of Willy Wonka's chocolate factory. The first time the three us scratched our names into a bench, Anna and Teo and I, in the small park by the graveyard. The first place I rode a bicycle, in the parking lot just behind the town sign, with Jay teaching me, already carrying around his box of crayons wherever he went, painting broad colourful patterns onto the pavement along the High Street and into their front garden.

I follow the road past the red parasols. Just behind the bend, that's where it should be.

And then it comes into view.

It looks just the same. The door is still painted red, the stone still grey, the front garden filled with sad shrubbery and grey stone tiles, the front room hidden behind large artificial flowers. I don't think they've even changed the curtains. They look like they're straight from the Eighties.

After parking the car on the side of the road, I walk up to his house and ring the doorbell.

Something moves in the front room. I think the telly is running. Footsteps approach. Then the door is thrown open.

I don't recognise the person I'm looking at. 'Sorry,' I say, instinctively smiling at the strange man. 'I must have got the wrong door.'

The man looks at me, dark hair and bright eyes in a sunken face. He is wearing a sweaty Burberry shirt, and is still in the motion of throwing on a Barbour jacket, dark green with orange lining. I can tell it used to be fine once. A bad stain sits right on his lapels. His hair is too long for him, and the colour of his skin is paler even than his eyes. He looks like someone who worked out for a while but then gave up on it again, fat and muscles creating a threatening bulk. Even as he straightens his tie, hastily put together, his eyes are slightly unfocused.

'I was just looking for an old friend, but he must have moved after all,' I continue. 'You wouldn't happen to know where ...'

His eyes narrow. Then they widen very suddenly. 'It's you! Caroline Wilson, as I fucking live and breathe!'

He's grinning. I stare at him. Right into those bright, pale eyes. Right at that wide grin. The crooked incisor at the bottom on the right.

No.

This cannot be Jay. He cannot have changed so much. But he's grinning, and I recognise that grin, as if this old, tired man has stolen it and put it on, stolen it from the young man who drew me flowers on pieces of paper he'd torn out of his books, who took me to a fine art museum on our first date, who'd laugh just as easily as he'd sneer. 'You're back! Bloody fucking hell,' Jacob says and takes a

76

step towards me. His voice sounds scratchy. There's a smell coming off him.

'Jacob,' I say, suddenly out of breath. 'Hi.'

His eyes are running all over my body. Like I am something he can hold on to. The first friendly face in years. 'You are looking good, Linny.'

I wish there was any way that I could be saying that back. 'I just wanted to see how you were,' I say. My brain still cannot compute that this man could be Jay. 'I've only got a minute, I got somewhere to be, but I thought we ... we might ... that you could ...'

He watches me stammer. He is still smiling, but it is morphing into something smaller. Something bitter. 'Somewhere to be?'

I don't know what to say to that.

He steps closer. That must be whisky on his breath. 'Do you want to come in, Linny?'

'Listen,' I say, still completely shocked. The mere thought of going into that house with that man to ask him questions, feeling that door close behind us with a final click, makes my stomach quiver. A public place would be better. A much more public place. 'I would love to, but I can't just now. I just wanted to let you know I was back, and that we should catch up some ...'

'Everybody knows already, Linny,' he says, swaying on his feet, reaching for the doorframe to steady himself. It seems to be a practised gesture.

The moment he realises he's done it, he straightens as quickly as if someone slapped him, letting go of the doorframe.

Trying to stand on his own two feet. He tries for a smile. It is supposed to look harmless, I think. 'Kait's texted the whole village. It was a wild night at the pub last night, let me tell you.'

For a moment, I see his eyes clear, see a shrewdness return to his features. He takes another step towards me. 'The Detective Inspector was all over the place. You should have seen him. Didn't even have time to stick his hand down some poor young thing's pants in front of the ladies'.'

My throat is dry. He's too close. His breath smells sharp. My mouth twitches. I hope he doesn't realise. 'Listen, Jacob, I am sorry I made you get up. I really do have to run now, but we should definitely catch up. Maybe in a couple of weeks? Definitely coffee ...'

His hand shoots out before I can stop him. His fingers wrap around my wrist. 'You don't have to lie, Linn.'

I try to shake off his hand. My throat is closing up. 'Let me go.'

His gaze goes right through me. His voice drops to a whisper. 'Is it so bad? Do I really look so bad, Caroline?'

'Jacob, let me go,' I say.

He puts on another smile. It tries for jovial but ends up desperate. With a jolt, I remember that expression. That is what he looked like when he had been hurt. When he was about to lash out in return. 'You are looking lovely, Linn, you really are,' he says. 'I hope you don't swing the other way any more?'

I grit my teeth. 'What on earth do you mean?'

'Remember what a good party we had. At mine. That night,

before it … you know. Happened.' His fingers are wrapped so tightly around my skin that his knuckles are turning white. His eyes are going in and out of focus. 'What a comfort to finally find out why you had broken up with me, wasn't it, when I saw you with your tongue down Anna Bohacz's throat for the better part of the night.'

All the air is punched from my lungs. 'Fuck off,' I say, pulling my arm away in earnest now.

It doesn't even seem to register with him. He is still stronger than me. 'Just checking. Gave me a right shock. And the big O, too, you know. Oliver Dawson. He had even let you pick his perfume, remember? He smelled like something out of Mum's Chilcott catalogue that night. I think he thought he would marry you one day.'

'We are married. Let me go!' Finally, I manage to tear my arm out of his grip. With shaking hands, I turn on my heels and rush to the car. I force myself not to look back even once, my nerves taut as rabbit wire, trying to get out of there as fast as possible. My legs are trembling as I push down the clutch.

When I drive past the house, Jacob is still standing in the doorway. Staring at me. All the will to hurt has vanished from his expression. He looks at the ground, hugging his jacket to his body against the cold.

Do I really look so bad?

My feet won't stop shaking even as I speed across the bridge and out of the village. My stomach is filled with dread now, heavy, sticky dread. It is a relief to turn onto the dirt road leading up to the hollow, far away from that man who stole

Jay's name, his voice, even his eyes. The voice that used to tell me about paintings we saw in Manchester, paintings and sculptures and weird things that I didn't think of as art. The eyes that would shine when he painted rainbows onto the concrete of the parking lot, or brim with tears that he wouldn't let spill as I walked away from him.

I shiver. Driving past the Kenzies', I glance down their drive. The upper curtains are drawn. I keep driving, stretching my prickling hands. And what was he talking about, anyway? I'd kissed Anna once. Twice, maybe. We'd been stupid. Fooling around. That was all. I run a hand over my mouth.

I know I will have to go back to see Jay once more to ask him about that night. But definitely in a public place. Much more public than his front door, at least. I do not think he would have seriously hurt me, but what do I know about Jacob Mason? I haven't seen him in nineteen years.

Maybe Oliver would know. They used to be mates, Oliver and Jay, both of them on the swimming team. After it'd no longer been the four of us. Best mates even, I think.

But I cannot ask Oliver. I can't ask him anything ever again.

The thought makes me choke up.

Turning into the hollow and driving down towards the house, I try to calm down, breathing as regularly as possible. Nobody in sight, not even a cat. It would have been nice to have a cat. Our neighbours, on the second flat where Oliver and I lived, they had one. She used to stop by at ours a lot, that beautiful cat, black body and white paws. We moved out shortly after she died.

Unloading the bags from the boot, mouth twitching, I think about the cat and how she used to love the treats I'd bake specifically for her. I was the only one who could feed her straight from the palm of my hand. I do my best to think of the cat and not of Oliver. About how he could help me if he was here. About how we would be playing karaoke tonight, if it was a regular Sunday. About the karaoke machine he had organised for our wedding. It came as such a surprise to me, *me*, who had dedicated almost a year to planning this wedding, sitting on the couch in the evenings as we watched TV and making our own confetti.

It was a fairly small affair, in that comfy pub in Shoreditch. It was one of my good phases, where I felt relatively stable. Relatively alive. And we didn't need a crowd. All we needed was to sing 'One Way or Another' and 'Every Breath You Take' together and dance like silly people having a stroke. Or 'Build Me Up Buttercup'. There were buttercups in the decorations and in my bouquet. Like our fish. The one I accidentally killed.

I lick my lips, shifting the grocery bags around. The wood creaks under my feet as I walk up the stairs to the porch. A bird is rustling through the bushes somewhere, or a rabbit. The chimes are singing in the gentle breeze.

I freeze.

Then I turn to the side.

There they are. Moving gently in the cold wind, three silver pipes on worn strings.

The chimes are back.

And even as I listen to their sounds, standing rooted to the cold white ground, I hear another sound: the engine of a car.

It's coming towards me.

THE NEIGHBOUR

This time, when I hear her car passing along the road, I get up. When it comes into sight, I am already at the sitting-room window, peeking out through the white curtains, my desk and work abandoned.

As she drives past, I stand there, biting my lip. I know I must finish this translation by tomorrow. It is tiring, translating a government document, but it pays well. And they want their deadlines kept. It is too lucrative keeping them happy not to. At least until I hear back from the ESA.

So I turn back to the desk with a sigh. The concert is still playing over the stereo (I still use a stereo; why not? It works. Who has time to put all their CDs onto their computer, anyway?), the Swedish Radio Choir performing the Verdi *Requiem*. It calms me, and I try and sing along and wonder whether I could still sing properly, if I joined another choir. If I could remember the lullaby my grandmother sang to me the few times I saw her, not nearly often enough to understand

83

why she was so gentle when she sang yet so brutal when she spoke.

I have just sat down again when I hear it:

Another car. As if following the first. As if following her.

Immediately, I am back at the window. Furrowing my brow, I stare outside. There. Up the hill it comes, a dark-green Jeep, the tyres all muddy. It almost disappears between the trees, between the evergreen of the pines and the slim trunks of the birches.

They might have turned down this road by accident. They might reverse once they have realised their mistake.

I open the window and listen to the Jeep's engine. It continues along the road. I hear it slow down. Brake.

But it does not stop. It does not turn back. Even as the engine quietens, I hear the gravel churn. Hear it turn into her driveway.

Glancing back at my computer, I hesitate. Then I slink into the hallway. Put on my boots, pull my jacket on top of my threadbare dress and reach for the rifle by the coat rack.

Then I am out of the door.

LINN

It is a muddy Jeep coming down my driveway. I'm alone on the steps of the front porch. The handles of the shopping bags are cutting into my skin. The chimes are singing. For a moment, I think about running.

Somebody returned the chimes. Were they already here when I left for the supermarket in the morning? It's hard to remember. Maybe I overlooked them. I could have.

The Jeep comes to a stop on the side of the driveway. The soles of my feet are curling in on themselves, pain shooting up my calves.

I see the door open. Two legs swing out. They are thin, well dressed in a pair of Paul Smith trousers and shiny riding boots. A body emerges from the car. It's a woman in a fine suit, wearing pearl earrings and a tasteful necklace, hair freshly cut, large sunglasses sitting on top of her head. She looks incredibly put together. Like a first lady. Like a prime minister. Only her face seems very thin.

That's how I recognise her. 'Miss Luca?' I say.

Her voice is exactly as I remember it, full of professional concern even when exchanging the most casual of greetings as she walks up to me. 'Ey up, Ms Wilson!'

Her lipstick is bright in the hollow. I remember clearly that she never used to wear makeup. Even as a teenager, I admired that about her. Now, her face is perfectly painted. The tone of her lipstick. Her foundation, clearly expensive, so carefully applied. My last name is Dawson now, but I don't correct her. 'So it is you! When Kaitlin told me you were in town, I simply could not believe it.'

She comes to a halt in front of me. Her eyes are running all over my body, just like Kaitlin's and Anvi's. She is much better at hiding her shock, but it is obvious that she is just as surprised as the two of them to see me standing in front of her. When she looks at me like that, it feels like my body is taking up more space than it should.

'I hope you don't mind my dropping by unannounced like this. I found your note when I came home, and I was just on my way to go for a walk in the woods anyway,' she explains. 'So I thought: why don't you stop by her house and see for yourself, Antonia. See about this note. See if what Kaitlin says is actually true. To be fair, though, I have never diagnosed her with mythomania.'

We both laugh at her joke, awkwardly. 'It is me,' I say, shifting the grocery bags around. 'In the flesh.'

'So it is,' she says, still staring at my face. 'I could not quite believe it, you know. It really is so unexpected. And your note, too.'

I guess I should have been prepared for this. They cannot have expected ever to see me again. 'I hope you don't mind.'

'Not at all,' Miss Luca hurries to say. 'I come by here a lot, to go out with the dog, you know.' She points at the Jeep. I don't see a dog. 'Your parents were always so friendly. We had tea together sometimes, when I came back from my walks. I am so sorry for your loss. We all miss them very greatly. We were sad not to see you at the funeral.'

She is looking at me with that smile and that probing expression of hers. Making me as speechless as I was all those years ago, when I went to see her after that night, just for a few sessions. There wasn't any time for more: Oliver and I moved away almost instantly. I had to get out of here, and he already had a place at university to train as a nurse.

Miss Luca's eyes are still just as sharp as back then. As if her mind is going a hundred miles a minute behind the disbelieving expression she is trying to hide under a friendly smile. 'How have you been, then?' she prompts. 'I cannot believe you are back, really, Ms Wilson. It is such a pleasure to see you again!'

I can't believe how old she's grown. If Kaitlin's got fat, Miss Luca has turned into paper. You cannot see it in her face, because of all the makeup. But there are the wrinkles on her throat, on the backs of her hands, her skin like blotting paper. It feels like all you'd need to do is run a finger along her throat to take off the skin. But she still looks so collected. Nothing could unsettle her, not Miss Luca.

For a moment, I wonder what I must look like to her. Would she have recognised me if she had not known I was back? The person I am now cannot have anything to do with the young woman she knew. If you'd told that young woman her story would turn into mine, she'd have laughed at you. *It's up to me what my story is,* she'd have said, then grinned and hopped onto her bike without a helmet to pick up her two best friends. That is how people must remember me here: a young woman, strong-willed, stars in her eyes, dreamer and troublemaker. Her and her two friends, the three inseparables: Anna and Teo and me.

One of whom the police suspected.

It is that thought which helps take me back to the present. It is a godsend that Miss Luca came straight by. I have so many questions, all warring in my head, not knowing where to start. Perhaps that is why the first I blurt out is: 'Did you see the chimes?'

Her brow furrows for a split second. 'Pardon?'

I take a deep breath. The chimes suddenly returned. As if someone's watching me. 'Just, on your walks through the woods, recently, I wondered whether ...' This is silly. I fiddle once more with the grocery bags. They are growing heavy. 'Oh, never mind. I'm glad you came by! How have you been?'

'Oh,' she says with a laugh. 'You know us. Life moves slowly out here. Nothing much new, I suppose. Even after such a long time, really! Gosh, let me think ... Well, you're back, for one. And Teo Dündar, of course.'

I am about to ask her about that, about him, when something flashes in the corner of my eye. My head shoots around.

Miss Luca's brow furrows again. She takes a step towards me. 'Ms Wilson? Are you all right?'

I look for the movement but can't spot anything. 'Yes. Sorry. You were saying ...'

She takes another step closer. 'I was surprised to hear that you were back. Happy, though. Did you ever approach any of my colleagues in London?'

There is something very urgent to her question. Like finding an old book in the attic, one you loved as a child, as badly as you loved your cat and your parents and the stars, and suddenly realising you never finished it. 'Yes,' I lie. My eyes are still searching the trees. The corner of my mouth twitches upwards. 'Thank you so much for your recommendations.'

A leash is dangling from her right hand, but still no sign of a dog. 'Not to worry. Just because I never heard from you again. Professional interest, you see. It is hard to contain.'

She laughs again, but it still sounds urgent.

'I trained as a florist,' I say, on my way to working up the nerve to ask, *I know it's a little out of the blue, but did you know it wasn't a stranger at all who attacked me nineteen years ago? Oh, and who's the alcoholic who lives on the High Street and stole Jacob Mason's name, eyes and grin? And what about Teoman Dündar? Since when has he been back?* 'All the wildflowers here, that's what made me think it would be good. I wanted to care for something.'

'How lovely,' she answers. 'Mark and Sue mentioned it, actually.'

Again I open my mouth to ask her at least one of those questions. I could start with Jacob.

A cracking sound. It came from the woods to our left, the trees separating our grounds from the Kenzies'.

'Kaitlin mentioned you were looking for work?'

I take a step down the stairs. The chimes are singing in the wind. The bags are turning to lead in my hands. Miss Luca does not seem to have heard the noise, the noise in the woods. She is looking only at my face. 'You know, I would love to invite you over for tea before you leave again, Ms Wilson. Kaitlin said you might not be here to stay? I'm so curious about how you have been, and we were all so sad to see you go, back then, you know. Sad that we didn't get to see you again.'

'Yes!' I say, perhaps a little too quickly. 'Yes, I'd love that. I'd love to talk to you. You know. About things. About things that happened. Here.'

She is observing me closely as I try to tear my eyes away from the woods. 'Right.'

'Just because being here,' I say, struggling to get the words out, 'it ... it brings things back.'

She nods, slowly. Looking down. It gives me pause. It's as if she can't look me in the eye for a moment.

'I am so happy to hear you have chosen to come back to this house,' Miss Luca says. 'It looked sad with nobody living in it. Besides, it means that you must have come a long way. Being able to live here. After everything.'

There. I see it again. The flash of a movement. A silhouette, making its way through the forest, moving from trunk to trunk.

The chimes are singing, right next to my face.

It is the white silhouette. From the top window.

'Wait!' I shout. 'Stop!'

Even as Miss Luca flinches, the silhouette stops.

Then it turns around and runs.

Without thinking twice, I drop the grocery bags where I stand and run after it. Miss Luca calls my name, shocked, but I pay her no heed. All I can think about is the chimes, and the doorbell that rang in the night, and how I woke up with traces of sweat like fingers on my skin.

Twigs crack beneath my feet as I dash towards the tree line. Even before I've reached the first row of trunks, I'm out of breath. I don't work out. I keep running. The silhouette isn't so far off that I can't still see it, white like a ghost in the frosted woods. 'Stop!' I call again. Why would a person run if they were only here on a walk? Why would anyone run from a stranger calling for them? And if it isn't a stranger, then …

I speed up. My lungs are burning. I know I used to be faster than this. I remember I could run from this porch all the way to the Kenzies', all the way through the forest, all the way without any trouble whatsoever. I remember only last year, I could run from our flat to the river and back, I could …

That was three years ago, actually. Maybe it would have been better not to make fun of Kaitlin and Miss Luca.

The silhouette seems to be getting away. With every ounce of willpower I possess, I try and speed up even more. Frost crunches under my soles. Branches break. I'm getting closer. It feels like I'm getting closer. There it is, a white shadow, a ghost, a ghost in the shape of …

My legs give out. I stumble. The burn in my lungs has grown so bad I can't go on. My hands and knees hit the ground as the silhouette takes off. I didn't come close enough to recognise the person. But I did come close enough to see that they were holding something. It looked thin and long and black against the frost, like a club. Or a rifle.

Behind me, I hear hurried steps. Miss Luca has followed me. I wouldn't have thought she'd have it in her. Not wearing shoes like that. 'Ms Wilson, gosh, are you okay?'

Slowly, I rise, grateful for her hand on my elbow, supporting me. Blood is pumping through my legs, my arms, my entire skin prickling. My body feels hot and pulsing, my breaths coming in short bursts. I've completely forgotten what it felt like to exert oneself. To run further than the bus stop when you spotted the driver pulling up a few yards ahead. Further than to the jammed front door. I thought if I always took the stairs, I'd be fine. Bloody lie, that.

'Ms Wilson, what happened?' Miss Luca says. 'Tell me what happened. Take your time.'

I remember her voice. Her inquisitive voice, not making demands, just asking questions. But never looking at me when we talked about it. Not once.

I remember, very suddenly, that I liked her.

'The chimes,' I tell her. 'Somebody's come back with my chimes.'

THE DETECTIVE INSPECTOR

Sexual violence? No. No, no, no. And if we did, believe me I'd make sure to get the bastard myself. We haven't had anything like it in ... nineteen years?

And even back then, it was an anomaly. I still think it was someone from outside, you know? Outside the community. No one would have done a thing like that, no one who lived here. Everybody knows each other, you know? You wouldn't have got away with it.

No, whoever did that to poor Little Linny, he must have got in and out within the same night. I mean, the motorway is only twenty minutes away. What would stop you from coming here, finding that abandoned road, that lass alone in her house ...? And then taking off again? Two hours, and you could be in Manchester; hell, you could be in Turkey in four if you made straight for the airport.

Don't know what made me think of Turkey. Well. I do, don't I? But I couldn't prove anything, back then. It was the one case of my career, the one that mattered, anyway, that I couldn't close. I couldn't give her justice. Some stranger's come to our town one way or the other and did that to her and I couldn't even give her justice. Still makes me mad. That's why she didn't come back, I know that. That's why Mark and Sue never got to see their daughter unless they went to her. That's why we lost her to the South. God, can it already have been nineteen years? I mean, *nineteen*? How old does that make me?

Anyway, it's no surprise she's all mixed up now. Being back at that house, it would make you skittish, wouldn't it? Her chimes are back now, she says. And there was someone in the woods, a white figure, like a ghost.

Antonia Luca is with her. I respect that woman. I respect her a lot. Doing so much for our community. Taking care of those kids, the difficult ones especially. Makes sure they don't end up downstairs in our basement when their own mothers don't take care of them.

Linn and Antonia Luca are talking to the PSV. The Police Support Volunteer. Good lass, that. Blonde. I can hear that she's doing it by the book, just as she should. She only comes in four hours a week, but she's already learnt a lot, and at such a young age, too.

'Nothing was stolen, then, Ma'am?'

'No,' Linny says. 'But don't you think it's odd?'

'No one was hurt, Ma'am?'

'No,' she says again.

'Then I am afraid I do not know what I can do for you, Ma'am.'

'Don't you think it's odd?'

'Was anything taken? Were you hurt in any way?'

'No, I ... Look,' Linn says, her voice rising once more. 'Look, doesn't that mean somebody was at my house? Somebody who stole them before? The thief returning to the scene of the crime?'

'But they are back now, are they not? Your ...' the PSV consults the sheet I filled out '... chimes?'

'Yes.'

'So nothing else was taken?'

'No, I, listen ...'

'Nobody was hurt?'

'You have to listen to me ...'

'Was anybody hurt? Has anything been taken?'

Linn falls silent. I can watch them from the break room, the door a little ajar. She looks at our PSV; I keep forgetting her name, it's embarrassing really. Anyway, Linn is looking at her with an expression I do not think I have ever seen on her face before. She doesn't look like Little Linny all of the sudden, not any more. Instead, she seems ... angry. 'No.'

'Then I am afraid I cannot help you, Ma'am. Everything seems to be in order, Ma'am. I will file this away, Ma'am, now that your chimes have returned.'

I don't like seeing that expression on Little Linny's face, so I step out of the break room. 'Here, sweetie, let me,' I say. 'Thanks for handling this so well. What was that about somebody in the woods?'

That's when Antonia Luca says she didn't see anyone. She speaks in a calm, quiet voice. She's good at that voice. Used it on me a few times. Not that I ever went to see her in a professional capacity. You know the force has staff for all that now, specially trained staff. For those who need it. I don't need it. It's for them London folks, probably.

Anyway, Antonia Luca says she did not see anyone when I press her, and then asks if Linn's really ever been to see anyone about the incident at the house. Linn says no. 'Then you lied to me, before,' Antonia Luca says.

'Yes,' Linn says. It's a bit unnerving, the way she looks at us.

She must be all in a jumble, Antonia Luca says. Maybe if she wants to get a hotel? But Linn says no. Good, that. That's good. She asks me about the chimes. 'Good thing they're back,' I tell her. 'Maybe it was some teenagers after all, some of the mischief-makers from Priston Lane, who stole it when the house was abandoned and brought it back now that you've returned. I can file that away at least,' I say and laugh, trying to lighten the mood. I know she's not in any danger, don't I? Besides, that's what we called them when they were kids, her and her friends: mischief-makers. 'Remember that, Linny? Maybe it's mischief-makers like you were?'

'I would encourage you to consider checking into a hotel,' Antonia Luca repeats. 'Just for a few days, until you have figured out something else.'

'Listen here, Linny,' I say, a little mithered because Antonia Luca is starting to get on my nerves with her nagging. 'I'll come back to the house with you. Have a look at the chimes. See if we can spot anything unusual in the woods. It's your house. Nobody will chase you from your own house, if I have anything to say about it.'

I put a hand to the small of her back. Sometimes, all a woman needs is a bit of reassurance. The kind of reassurance only a man can give her. No psychological hocus-pocus. Not that I don't appreciate what Antonia Luca does for the kids, mind you. It's very helpful. It's just not the same as having a man with a gun by your side, is it?

LINN

Graham comes back with me to the house. He inspects the chimes closely. He even asks me if he should take them back with him to the station, to have them checked out if he can.

'I'm happy to do that for you, Linny,' he says. 'You see, there's nothing else I can do, because nobody's come to any harm, and nothing's been taken. But I could take it back and ask someone for a favour. Maybe just have a closer look in proper light. What do you say, Linny?'

His hand is on the small of my back again. Laughing awkwardly, I slink away from his hand, pretending my movement is involuntary. I do not tell him who I thought I saw in the woods. It's obvious that he doesn't believe I saw anyone at all.

Antonia Luca gave me her calling card, though. Told me get in touch with her. I nodded at her, gratefully.

Graham doesn't seem very enthusiastic about her. 'Don't

get me wrong, I really appreciate what Antonia Luca does for the community,' he says before he gets back into his car. 'But I don't want anyone to chase you from your home into a hotel, Linny. This is yours. It belonged to your parents and now it's yours and that's exactly how it should be.'

'Thanks, Graham,' I say, and decide to make the most of this unexpected opportunity to be speaking to him in private. 'Listen, I went to see Jacob Mason today.'

Graham makes an unhappy sound. 'Ah. Yep.'

'He's ...' I don't know how to put it '... changed.'

'You know,' Graham says, 'some people manage, others ...' He heaves a sad sigh. 'He's not been well, Jacob. You used to be friends, didn't you? I remember that incident at Bolton Castle ... It's such a shame. You know I coached him when he was a teenager. Both him and Oliver, they were our golden boys. Really promising. But Jacob decided swimming wasn't for him, he wanted to earn proper money, and I can't blame him, can I? Anyway, he lost his job a while back, recession and all that, and hasn't found anything new since. He's been walking by the train tracks an awful lot lately. And then his mum came to see us last week. Was shaking like a leaf, poor old lady. She claimed she fell, and with a woman that age, you don't know, do you? Possible. But I think he'd hit her. She was good on her feet, she was. Anyway, she's in a nursing home now. Detective Sergeant Zwambe arranged it; it was very good of her ...'

Graham peters out. I take a deep breath. 'He said he saw you at the pub last night. That you were ... that everybody was all over the place.'

Graham narrows his eyes. 'And he'd remember, pissed as he was? What I'm trying to say is, Linny, best stay away from Jacob Mason. He's got enough to deal with.'

Even after Graham has driven off, I remain standing in the hollow, barely even feeling the cold. Jay Mason, hitting his mum?

I know how that makes him sound, but he had an alibi for the night it happened. He'd been with Oliver at his party when it happened. They'd accidentally locked themselves into the master bathroom, Jay arguing with Oliver about Oliver's scent or something stupid like that. Oliver had finally succeeded in breaking them out a couple of hours later. He'd broken his watch as he did, that's how he knew what time it'd been. It had already happened by then. I just hadn't regained consciousness yet.

I return to the woods. There are no traces left of my chase through it, the frost gone entirely. I stand silently between the sycamores and the rowan trees. There is no one here but me and the crows in the trees.

Is it possible that there wasn't anyone in the woods at all?

I close my eyes as the cold embraces me. If only I didn't think that I might have recognised the silhouette.

It looked like Anna.

Maybe Graham's right. Maybe I'm a bit messed up today. Seeing Jay like that, and then from my dream last night, too. Miss Luca didn't even see the person in the woods. Maybe there was nobody there.

It takes me a while to realise that my muscles are so tense my entire body is hurting. Stretching them, I return to the house. It seems damp. The heating is only working intermittently. I go down into the basement to check on the boiler but I can't find anything wrong with it. I'll have to call someone about it. But I've got to be careful with my funds.

I shiver. I put on the kettle, bring down the begonias and take out the fertiliser. 'You'll be all right,' I promise them and work while the waiter boils. 'It'll be all right now.' I haven't heard from any of the businesses I sent applications to. It's only been a day, I remind myself.

Once the pot has boiled, and the begonias are taken care of, I take the tea into the sitting room. Burying myself under an IKEA blanket, I fiddle with the cup, with my phone. I should do something to calm me down. The shelves are still filled to the brim with my parents' books. Still stretching my palms, I get back up and take out a really slim book, one that'll be easy to get through. It's a play. A play we did in school, in the drama club. It's called *The Trojan Women*.

Suddenly, I remember that it was really good. It was about the women of Troy, what the Greek captors did to them once the city had fallen to their army. I remember that Anna wanted to be in it, but she wasn't allowed, because of her accent. It was the first time I realised she had one. Before, I didn't even notice.

I was so sure it was Anna in the woods. My heart rate picks up. So sure. My hands are cramping now, my arms, my throat, my whole body. It's an attack. I can feel it coming.

I cannot just sit here. I have to do something about this.

With all the willpower I can muster, I go get my new SIM card and change it without turning on the phone; after I've set it up, I take out Miss Luca's card and type in her number. I hit CALL and wait.

Nothing. There's no signal in the hollow, none at all. I hang up, put on my coat and walk up to the road to call again.

She picks up after the fifth ring. Tells me this isn't a good time, that she will call me back in a little bit.

Of course, I hear myself say, no problem. Waiting for Miss Luca to return my call, I stand in the dirt road, surrounded by trees, pale in the dusk, and stare at my hands. There are red marks where Jay held on to me this morning. The man who pretends to be him, anyway. It's like Jacob Mason is gone.

Oliver's gone, too. He doesn't know it yet, but when my husband comes back, next Saturday, he'll find my note. There will have to be divorce papers. Our flat, it's gone. My life, the dishes and the washing and the groceries, *can't you see, you belong with me.* The soles of my feet have gone back to cramping; my legs, even my lungs.

Maybe we could have adopted. Oliver was already looking at houses. Outside London, somewhere the children could play, maybe even in our own garden. The commute? 'No bother.' If he lost his job? 'I'll find something else.' How to afford it all? 'Linnsweet, we will make it work. Isn't that what makes life worth living? Isn't that what we're put on this planet for?' I remember how excited he sounded, even if his voice stayed as quiet as always.

Carefully, I trace the veins on the back of my hand with my eyes as I shiver in the cold wind. They are sharper than I remember them, the skin already turned thinner. The cephalic and basilic veins. It surprises me that I still remember the words. A book comes back to me, a book I bought when I still thought I would go to uni. Become a nurse or a doctor, if not a botanist.

Oliver did. Become a nurse, that is. I remember how we studied for his exams, remember running my fingers over the parts of my body I was trying to memorise. Remember Oliver running his hands over the same body parts.

Another shiver runs through me. Quickly, I look away from my hands, back into the woods. Half expecting to see her. The flash of white. That way of running, using all of her body, as if her life depended on it.

Holding a rifle.

I must have imagined it. Anna couldn't hurt a fly.

Can I have imagined it? And if I did, wouldn't that mean I was going mad?

I press my hand to my cold mouth, warming the skin with my breath. Dusk is settling over the road as I wait. The days are short already. The trees' shadows turn longer, their trunks darker. The wind is picking back up. It blows leaves my way, grey in the light, grey like the gravel I am standing on.

I should have gone back inside.

Just as I am about to turn back, my phone rings. I pick it up without speaking, suddenly afraid it may be Oliver. That he may have got this number. That it may have all been in vain.

'Ey up,' Miss Luca says. 'Excuse me, this is Antonia Luca. Am I speaking to Caroline Wilson?'

Again, I don't correct her. 'Yes, this is her.'

'Hullo?' Miss Luca says. 'Hullo, Ms Wilson?'

I start walking further up the road, towards the Kenzies'. 'Sorry, there's almost no signal at the house. Can you hear me, Miss Luca?'

'Yes,' Miss Luca says. 'Sorry, you are breaking up sometimes. I am so glad you've called, though.'

I stand in the middle of the road, watching the shadows of the trees reach for me. For my feet. For the house down in the dip. For my body, calming back down. 'I thought it was Anna.'

Miss Luca doesn't say anything, not right away. She's putting her voice back on, the voice she uses on her patients. 'The person you thought you saw today?'

'I know the way she runs.'

'When did you last see her, Ms Wilson?' Miss Luca asks gently.

I swallow. 'Nineteen years. It was ... the night after it had happened. She and Teo, they came to our house. Teo was ... upset. He was shouting my name, at the top of his lungs, demanding to see me. He attacked my dad and Oliver, trying to get in, and Anna was right behind him.' I swallow. That's when Teo had shouted it: that he would never come back to this *fucking shithole*. That was when I first saw him like that, wild, no longer able to control himself. My best friend. 'Dad and Oliver barely managed to fight them off. Teo left at some point, I remember. But I think Anna, she ... she stayed out on the porch all night.'

'Tell me about her,' Miss Luca says, voice still gentle.

Inside my wellies, my socks are sticking to my feet. I am sweating. In spite of the cold. 'You knew her. We were friends.'

'And now?'

I stand very still. 'I think of her.'

She says nothing.

'Do you believe I'm imagining it?' I ask, my voice suddenly desperate. I don't want to be thinking of Anna. Even less than of Teo. I want her to leave me alone. She's been in my dreams for nineteen years; she cannot come back into my days.

'Do you think it is possible I imagined it?' I ask her. Even I can hear that I sound like I'm begging. 'Coming back here, it may have messed with my head, right? It is a possibility?'

Still she says nothing. I remember her doing that, too. So I plough on. If I'm going mad, at least I want to know about it. 'I dreamt somebody rang my doorbell last night.'

Her breath hitches. Has she been wondering? These past nineteen years, have they all been wondering? Have they really not forgotten, not moved on?

They are still telling my story. They are still wondering what really happened. Who did it.

'Returning to the house for the first time, alone, would put great strain on your mind,' Miss Luca says. 'Exposing oneself to such a trauma, even after a long time, may indeed lead to symptoms such as you describe. It does not reflect on your mental faculties, Ms Wilson.'

I let out a relieved breath. The moment she hears it, she rushes to add: 'Of course, it is impossible to tell from a distance. Ms Wilson, why don't you stop by the practice tomorrow? I will be happy to see you after our opening hours.'

'Yes, that sounds good. Perfect, actually. What time would be good? I'm available any time,' I say eagerly.

'At three-thirty?'

We hang up, and I return to the house, stepping over ever-longer shadows. The setting sun is hidden behind a wall of clouds, the light growing dark and grey. Down in the hollow, I look around myself. Look at the abandoned flower beds surrounding the house, the trees that need cutting, the spot where Dad used to grow veggies.

I raise my hand to the bark of the sycamore in the centre of the hollow, and run my palm down its stem. 'Don't worry,' I say quietly. 'You are still beautiful to me.'

The dying leaves whisper in the wind, few remaining now that winter is crawling ever closer. The wood creaks. There is no answer. 'Don't worry,' I say, a little more forcefully. 'There is nothing to worry about.'

I grab my phone and walk back up the road again, to do a search for Jacob Mason. See what pops up. Seems like he worked for a bank out in Halifax some time before he got made redundant. The picture I'm looking at shows a man in his early thirties, smartly dressed, smoking, laughing with colleagues, wearing a sparkling party hat and antlers, possibly at a Christmas party. That's the Jacob I recognise. He's kissing a woman on the cheek who is trying to laugh while she wriggles away from him. The photo isn't that old, actually. Only a few years, it seems. I thought Graham had said something about the recession.

My fingers hover over the screen. I could type in Anna's name.

Instead, I send a few e-mails to some people, offering to volunteer. I mean, I've been to the Homeless Shelter in Kendal, the Women's Aid in Lancaster. Not feeling too much is a great advantage in these places. I also e-mail a garden festival coming up in Northallerton. All the places that are usually so under-funded they'd be desperate enough to take anyone. Anything will be better than sitting around the house, hallucinating old friends into the woods.

Back at the house, I eat a fruit salad, looking at my list. I put down *public place – pub? / phone?* next to Jay's name. Behind Antonia Luca's name, I have added, *Tomorrow 3.30 PM!* And *back* sits next to Teo's name now, as well as a *?* next to Anna's.

A memory flashes through me as I take a bite of pineapple. Balancing a ring of pineapple on my nose, making Oliver laugh, just after we'd moved out. We used to buy only canned fruit back then. I shudder to think of it. And proud to say that that wasn't my fault – no, ma'am. It was Oliver who was scared of fresh fruit until someone invented a label that said organic.

After I have eaten, I look back at the list, this time at the places I put down. I could go for a run, check out at least the surroundings of the house, see if I can retrace my steps of that night, how I made my way home from Jacob's party. I can't remember it, but I must have come back on foot. Nobody would have been able to drive me. Everybody had been drinking excessively, except Jay, who'd been locked in the bathroom.

Glancing outside, I see that it is already dark. A tremor runs through my palms.

But I straighten my shoulders. Just up the drive and through the woods to the main road and back. *You can do this. You want this. You want the truth.*

I go into the mud room to get Dad's trainers. Sitting down on the bench, I caress the material for a moment. I have this sensation, like I am outside my body, like it is someone else looking at their dad's old trainers, holding them a little too hard. As a result, all I do is clutch them even more closely to my chest.

Taking the old headlamp, I make my way outside. It is already dark. Leaving the porch lights on, I put on the shoes then jog up the drive.

Once I've left the hollow behind, it turns pitch-black. The lamp sprinkles patches of light onto the forest ground. My breathing is laboured. I keep looking to both sides. Listen to my heavy breathing, resounding through the night. It is all I can hear, my breath. It is all I can see, my hands, white in the darkness.

I don't even make it to the main road. Nowhere close. By the time I'm a few hundred yards into the woods, it feels like fingers are scratching at my lungs. I slow down, but it is too late. Another hundred yards and I feel like the fingers are tearing out the alveoli. Taking another three stumbling steps, I come to a stop, bend over, supporting myself with a hand against a wych elm. Its bark is cold.

All I do is breathe, staring at the patch of ground lit up by my lamp. The soil looks black not brown, a large root sticking out of the ground like a gnarly finger. Dad's shoes. Breathe.

Just breathe.

I look up. To the right. The left. Then up ahead.

A flash of white.

My hand slips down the bark. It cuts my palm. I curse, instinctively turning to my hand, the blood running down skin. It looks grey in the night.

Then I look back up ahead. But there is nothing.

Only the dark woods. So very dark, the trunks of trees like black fingers, their limbs reaching for me.

My heart is pounding. Don't let anyone chase you from your own home, Graham said. The blood runs down my palm, thick and slow.

Turning around, I start jogging back, not waiting till I've caught my breath, not looking left and right any more. It didn't bring anything back. There's no one in the woods. There's nothing out here except me and the blood dropping from my palm onto the ground.

Once I am back at the house, I reach for the list, put *retrace your steps* in brackets, bring the begonias into the sitting room and drop down onto the couch, a bit calmer already. My feet have stopped cramping, at least.

A frame sits on the table next to the flowers, the picture of Mum and Dad, the one the Kenzies sent me. Their last holiday before the accident, hiking in Spain. They look old, even in the sun. I see Dad's hand resting on the small of Mum's back.

My eyes burn. I turn on the telly and sink back into the couch. As I rub my eyes, I realise how heavy my lids are. I should go upstairs and shower, but I'm too tired. It took quite a bit out of me, the cramps, the fear, sprinting down the drive into the hollow, towards the light on the front porch. Someone's on the telly, a man in a suit, must be saying something important. '... without access to the single market, the defence sector will decline,' he says while I try to fiddle off one trainer with my other foot.

'Are you sure?' another man asks back. 'It's interesting to hear you say that, that you think our defence sector will decline if it's not closely aligned with Europe.'

My eyelids are drooping. Got to go upstairs for a shower. Or to bed. Put a plaster on my palm, too. I'll get blood on the couch.

I curl my hand into a fist. It burns. Just this one bit, I tell myself. I'll just watch this one bit.

Focusing my tired eyes on the telly, I make it a point not to glance at the windows.

There's nothing out there.

THE DETECTIVE INSPECTOR

Don't let anyone chase you from your own home, I told her. That was a good thing to say.

THE NEIGHBOUR

Nights are the worst. Unless I go out into the woods. Where it is so cold that you simply must stop thinking.

THE DETECTIVE INSPECTOR

A very good thing to say.

LINN

When I start awake, I'm still on the couch. Must have fallen asleep in front of the telly. It is pitch-black outside. Disoriented, I sit up. Supporting myself against the backrest, I hiss in sudden pain. Right, my hand.

I get up, walk into the kitchen, put on the kettle once more and finally find a plaster. As I am about to apply it to the cut, my eyes catch on the stove. The gas flame, blue and hot. I glance at my hand, suspended in the air. Then back at the flame.

Don't do it. I bite my lips. Stare at the flame. *Don't.*

Hurriedly, I slap the plaster onto my skin, breathing heavily as I rush out of the kitchen. The shirt, trousers and socks are sticking to my skin. Dried sweat is freezing my body from the outside in, cold seeping through into my veins, my blood. Like a large, perspiring body is pulling me into its arms. I want to tear them off. I want to put both hands into the flame, feeling the pain turn hot and real.

The moment I've thought it, I recoil from my own mind. Thoughts like that have become rarer, but they still occur. And especially in the first few years, I could barely shake them. I would step into a London street without even looking, claiming I hadn't done it on purpose, tears running down my cheeks I didn't even notice. Or Oliver would come home to find me obsessively cleaning the bedroom, the sheets grey from their third washing that day; or I would go from periods of total silence to uncontrollable tearless sobbing I couldn't feel within a matter of moments.

An hour later, I would always feel stupid and childish and ashamed, apologising profusely, but the moment it happened, I was convinced that feeling *anything* would be better than this unbearable emptiness. Even a car tearing straight through my flesh would be better than this grey, bland numbness, spreading through my veins like dried, dead climbing vines. Oliver let it show occasionally, when he thought I wasn't looking: that taking care of me was just too much work sometimes. And I get it.

Shaking, I turn on the radio in the bathroom, then the shower. The deadly nightshade flashes through my mind, the memories I've pushed away. Hands on my body, in my mouth, fist on my tongue. On the other side of this wall, in my parents' bedroom.

While I take off my clothes, I try to push them away again. I need to stay focused. For a while, all I do is let the hot water pour over my body, waiting for it to warm me up. Taking up the old-fashioned washcloth, I lather it in the shower foam.

Rubbing myself until my skin is hot and red, I take off

all the sweat and the bit of blood and dirt from the elm. I've got to check up on my tetanus shot. Don't want to end up as one of the *Daily Mail*'s Latest Headlines: UNEMPLOYED FLORIST TOO STUPID TO UPDATE HER SHOTS, DIES AGED 36 OF A DISEASE ERADICATED 100 YEARS AGO. Oliver used to pull them up when he wanted to cheer me up. He would scroll through them until he found a particularly funny one, then he'd read it out loud, and then another, until I couldn't help but laugh. This one would be right next to a picture of Kate Middleton in some dress or another, looking fabulous while pregnant (newsflash: You don't get the job if you don't).

What would it have felt like, I wonder. What would it have felt like to have a baby inside me?

Something changes on the radio, I think. It might be a jingle, to announce the news. What time is it? Two in the morning? I didn't check my watch before coming upstairs. Hoping to hear the radio host say something about the time, I open the shower enclosure, water still running. It's not the news after all, though, I realise. Somebody's still going on about the economy. Must have misheard.

I return under the spray for a little while longer.

Again that jingle. Turning off the water, I step out of the shower. This time, I can't miss the news.

Drops of water are running down my body, dripping onto the floor. They're like feathery touches all over my skin. I can hardly see, the steam's so thick. Half blind, I feel my way to the window and pull it open. The cold night air makes me shiver, the water turning cold on my skin immediately.

'... you have to admit that. Housing prices are at an all-time high, and society is increasingly feeling the pressure ...'

I furrow my brow. That isn't the news.

Again, I hear the jingle.

Only it's not on the radio.

I stand naked in the bathroom. The wind drives icy fingers across my skin, impossibly thin fingers. Outside, the chimes are singing.

And the doorbell is ringing.

I know that rhythm.

Ding, ding, ding.

Chapter 3

*I*t is an autumn night in the year 1996. Four teenagers are running up the High Street. They are drunk. Which is why they are stumbling rather than running, trying to get away from the house where they just rang the doorbell. They are giggling like little kids, thinking about the Detective Inspector having to drag himself out of bed at this hour.

They are fourteen, so they did not even get their beers semi-legally. Linn is taller now than Teoman, who doesn't like it. Right then, though, he doesn't mind. Too drunk to. Same is true for Jay, with his rakish hair and the pencil tucked behind his ear wherever he goes, always the right one, a cigarette behind his left if he's got any. Only Anna has not touched a drop of alcohol. She keeps looking at Linn, then looking away. Linn does her utmost not to glance at her at all. At her blonde hair, worn in a fish tail, like that actress.

Linn is wearing her own hair like Spike: really spiky. She likes her. They watch Degrassi together, Teo and Anna and Jay and her. Teo and Linn shout at the screen, Jay laughs at them until he cries, and Anna is so invested she cannot look away, not even for a second.

Hiding behind the dumpsters in the short-stay parking lot, they huddle around Anna, who takes out their cigarettes. They're sharing a pack she pulled from her mother. Then they decide which Spice Girl they are. Jay is really easy. He's Posh Spice, no matter how much he protests. Teo would be Sporty Spice. His voice has turned really dark already, and it's got a few girls after him, even older ones like Kaitlin.

Nobody's much interested in Linn. She thought Jay was, but apparently he's more into Anna. Right that moment, though, his bright eyes are focused on the ground, the pattern he's drawing into the cigarette ash. It might be the way Linn dresses. Or like … her tits. She's got no tits. And she looks like a boy sometimes, her mum says. That feels horrible, it does. If anything, she is Scary Spice.

But she's made out with a few boys. Liked it well enough. Especially when they leave a bruise on her neck or bite her lip or make her cower back against the wall. The boys gossip, say that she's weird, but they don't mind when they're doing it. She just hopes Teo and Jay haven't heard, or Anna. Who's definitely Baby Spice, by the way.

'You think Mister Detective Inspector will find out it was us?' Linn says, trying to sound condescending. They all laugh, even though they are a little bit scared.

'Not likely,' Teo says, tapping Linn's hand with his finger. Ding, ding, ding.

Linn's heart skips a beat. Then she raises her free hand. Her forefinger. Touches the back of Anna's hand. 'Ding, ding, ding,' she whispers.

Anna looks at them both. She smiles. Turns her hand around to reciprocate. Jay taps his finger against Linn's cheek, laughing. 'Ding, ding, ding,' they all whisper together.

They do not know that the Detective Inspector has seen them and is on his way across the street.

LINN

It keeps ringing. Ding, ding, ding. I stand in the bathroom, entirely naked. My eyes dart from the open window to the door, laid with glass, to the feeble key.

I don't know what time it is. I don't know who it might be. But I know that rhythm.

Ding. Ding. Ding.

I choke. Turn the key. My eyes dart back to the window, which is wide open, showing only the dark night and darker trees. The bathroom is out to the back. There'll be nothing to see.

Unless it's two of them. Unless one of them is ringing the bell to distract me while the other is sneaking around the house, looking for a way in ...

I choke again. This time, it's audible. I press my hands to my mouth, press it shut. Can they hear the radio?

My feet are turning to ice on the bathroom floor. The water freezes on my bare body, drops of water on my lips, my hipbones, between my legs. Washed and prepared. All they have to do is come in. Kick in the door. Climb up through the window, open wide. They'd find me here.

They might already be on their way. They might have seen the open window. Found the ladder behind the shed. They might already be putting it up against the wall. Wrapping their fingers around each rung with relish. Looking forward to wrapping their fingers around my wrists as they push me onto the floor, their knees on my thighs to hold me down. Pushing me down, onto my stomach. They'll tie my hands to the towel rack, watch my back arch. They'll put their hands to my breasts, pinching them to make me shout. And when I do, they'll hit me. With their flat palms at first, so that my cold pale skin turns hot for them. Then they will hit me in the face. When I kick out, they will hit me harder. Till I bleed and the pain becomes too much and I whimper and stop.

Only I wouldn't kick out in the first place. Only I wouldn't shout. I would whimper into their hands, holding my mouth shut, tasting the fabric of their gloves, black leather, afraid of what they would do if I fight back. They would take their time because they know they've got nothing to fear from someone like me. They'd leave me tied up where I was once they were finished, sweat and blood and semen drying on my skin.

They'd have enjoyed it.

I flinch. The doorbell hasn't rung for a few seconds. More than a few. It might be a minute now. I don't know. Slowly, I inch towards the window, breathing as shallowly as I can. Close it. Whatever you do, get it shut.

I tiptoe closer. Expecting to see a hand wrap around the windowsill. Five gloved fingers, and then another hand. A body, pulling itself up, its silhouette large and stark against the white tiles.

Closer still. Only a couple of feet now. I reach out with my arm. My fingers, blue from the cold, grip the handle.

Pushing forward, my hand, my arm, my entire body, I close the window. My naked body hits the glass for a moment. It drives ice through me. I let out a noise as I fasten the lock, then step back as quickly as possible.

Then all I do is breathe.

Nothing. Only the murmur from the radio. Only the cold water drying on my skin. Like thin fingers.

Slowly, I creep back up to the window. To peek outside. To make sure that there is nobody there.

When I have reached the window, I look outside. The meadow, the sky, the woods are black. Everything is black.

Then I see something move.

It hits the window. I stumble backwards, slide on the floor, almost fall. The tiles of the bathtub dig into my knees and shins, so cold. I slide down against it, wrapping my arms around my knees.

It rings again.

Ding, ding, ding. I press my hands to my ears.

Then, nothing.

Nothing until the news comes on. It is three in the morning. The news passes, and there is nothing. Another half hour of a music programme, calm and classical, and still nothing.

But I know that rhythm. I know it like I know this house,

this hollow, the woods surrounding it. Better than the flat in Leyton, better than my own body.

That is how we rang the doorbells. Playing knock, knock, ginger on the High Street, Anna and Teoman and Jay and I.

I can't move. Not an inch. It wasn't a stranger.

Everybody knows.

I'm back.

And so are they.

THE NEIGHBOUR

In the morning, I see my therapist.

I always have my appointments in the mornings. This way, I have the entire day ahead of me to get work done afterwards. It usually helps me with my work, afterwards, I have noticed.

'You are bleary-eyed,' my therapist says. We have a rapport, she and I, where she is allowed to say such things. 'Did you not sleep well?'

I would rather not talk about that. 'I am translating something rather difficult at the moment.'

She raises her eyebrows. Her pearl earrings are very shiny today. 'You are translating something rather difficult? Difficult in which way?'

'It is not the words. It is the content,' I say, smoothing down my shirt.

'And that is what's troubling you.'

She does not sound incredulous. She would never sound incredulous.

'How responsible are we, you think,' I ask, 'when I help a government translate something that is full of lies, how responsible am I for those lies?'

'What do you think?'

Does anybody like it when they do that? Ask a counter question? 'I feel responsible.'

This used to be so much easier. It used to be easy, to take work from governments. Everybody used to agree, roughly, on the same things.

'So it's your translations that are worrying you.'

I hate that she phrases questions as statements and still expects me to answer. 'I am just wondering. How long are you responsible for something you have done wrong?'

She takes off her rimless glasses. 'Psychologically speaking? As long as you feel responsible.'

I swallow.

As I pack up my things, the phone on her desk rings. 'Detective Inspector?' she asks, obviously surprised. 'What can I help you with? Just a moment.' She presses the phone to her chest and smiles at me. 'I'll see you next month.'

I leave but stay outside the door once it is closed, pretending to be searching for something in my bag. Through the door, I can hear her speak.

By the time I leave, I have heard more than I should have.

Back at home, I sit at my desk and translate, but I cannot focus. The Polish government wants a TV commercial on German Death Camps; I stop at 'today, we are still on the side of truth' and switch back to the Westminster project; the government needs someone to turn the website of the Department for Exiting the European Union into Polish. Between them, they are keeping me employed.

> YOU WILL NEED TO:
> PROVIDE AN IDENTITY DOCUMENT AND A RECENT PHOTOGRAPH TO CONFIRM YOUR IDENTITY
> CONFIRM YOU STILL LIVE IN THE UK
> DECLARE ANY CRIMINAL CONVICTIONS

Declare any criminal convictions.

Not a good time for her to have come back, then.

For years I wondered. Whether it would have lifted some of the burden off my shoulders if someone had convicted me. I suppose I can consider myself lucky now that it did not come to that.

It still must not come to that. Where would I go? To Poland, where the government is so much on the side of truth that they need to make YouTube ads about it? To Turkey?

I lean back in my chair and a groan escapes me as I stretch my neck. I am thirty-eight and my back is already doing its utmost to permanently curl in on itself. Like my hair, intent on turning white before I am even forty. The same thing happened to my mother, and my grandmother before her. Grandmother used to say that her hair had turned by the time the war had ended. That is what I told my mother last week when I went to see her. I said, it is final, *Mamusia*: I am growing old.

That is not what I am thinking about, though. Not my

back, and not my hair. Not even the truth, nor the lies I am telling.

I am thinking about what I overheard.

I am thinking about her.

LINN

'Has anything been taken? Was anybody hurt?'
I'm at the station, leaning across the counter. The walls are white, the shelves are white – everything is white except Graham's uniform. 'They threw something at the window,' I say forcefully. Even though I couldn't find it this morning, whatever it had been, and I searched the entire lawn.

'Are you sure?'

I stare at him. He looks back, seeming really sorry. He doesn't believe me.

'Listen now, Linny, if we said it'd broken the window, there'd be something I could do, but this way ...'

'They rang my doorbell in the middle of the night.'

'I can't charge anyone with ringing doorbells, Linny. If I could, you'd have a criminal record from here to Leeds.'

'I didn't imagine it.'

Did I?

Suddenly, it comes back to me: what it was like, coming

back to that night and not remembering anything. Who did it. How it happened. What it was like lying in the hospital, remembering nothing. Mum and Dad were there. Dad took me into his arms, stroked my hair, shushed me, and I felt tears on my cheeks, tears that robbed me of my voice, the voice I needed to tell them everything. If only I knew what everything was. I couldn't remember who'd done it. I burrowed into his arms instead, Mum's hand stroking my back, her voice in my ear, singing something. I felt Mum's hand shaking. On my own body, trembling. Crying didn't help, not one bit.

'They didn't do anything. It may've been some kids. Why didn't you call us right away? We could have got them.'

'There's no signal at the house,' I say.

'None at all?' Graham asks. 'Why don't you have a landline? Get a landline, Linny.'

'Listen,' I say, looking over my shoulder, then leaning in. Dropping my voice, I tell him about the rhythm they used. The reason I decided to come here.

Ding, ding, ding.

The expression on his face changes, turning even more apologetic. 'Linny.'

'I heard it.'

'Listen,' he says. 'You got to get some rest. It's muddling you all up, being back here.'

'I'm not ...'

'You're safe here, Linny,' he says, looking at me intently. 'Let me promise you that. You're safe here.'

'Listen, Graham.' My lips are dry from the cold air, from where I have been biting them. I'm dressed in Mum's old winter

131

clothes. They used to be Granny's. Mum's my size. I'm in her lambskin coat and in Dad's boots and looking at Graham and feeling like an impostor, but I cannot let this go. Not again. 'You know I don't remember most of what happened that night. The night it happened, I mean. I remember being at Jay Mason's party, and then I remember being home, and waking up in my parents' bedroom ... well. After it'd happened. But I think it wasn't a stranger, I think we —'

Graham won't let me finish. He puts both hands on my shoulders. 'Listen, Linn.' His left hand wanders from my shoulder up my neck to the side of my face. 'You are upset, I know, but you've got nothing to worry about. Not on my turf, all right? Just get in touch with me next time anything scares you. Don't call the station, just get in touch with me. Get a landline, okay? They'll install it pretty quickly if you go to the local shop.'

I swallow, resisting the sudden urge to take a step back. He always used to touch me like that. Like we were related. Like he was my uncle. I remember what Jay said to me. I can't believe that Graham would still be going after women half his age. It had been an open secret back then, but this was twenty years ago. 'You've heard he's back, haven't you?'

'That who's back?' he asks, pretending to be clueless.

I look at him. 'Teo. Teoman Dündar.'

Graham lets me go to sink his hands into his pockets. Pushing out his chest, his shoulders. 'Ah, yes. Yes, I have.'

'I just always wondered,' I say. 'Why you took him in for questioning back then. Teo, I mean.'

132

'Well.' Graham looks at his feet, shuffling them, then back at me. 'Look, if you found a testosterone-filled young man at a sexual assault crime scene, you'd also take him in. And ... well, he did always follow you around, didn't he?'

'We were friends,' I say forcefully.

'I don't know, Linny,' Graham says. 'I mean, when you were children, maybe, but then you grew up, didn't you? That boy had needs, anyway; that much was obvious. And he was jealous all right. Remember when he got into that fight with Jacob Mason after you and Jacob had split up? Teoman had a nasty streak. I mean, just think of the night he came to your parents' house, the day after it'd happened. How he attacked your father, demanding to be let in. He's lucky your dad didn't wanna press charges.'

I try to laugh. 'Jealous? Don't you know every boy in our form was crushing on Anna at the time?'

He looks at me. Very sincerely. 'Not every boy.'

It's true. I'd just started going out with Oliver back then. Quickly, I lift my cup of coffee, take another sip, hiding my face. It's good coffee, but I've always preferred tea. I remember how much tea Oliver used to make for us, after we'd just moved out, never coffee; coffee would make me nervous, skittish. We always had three boxes of Yorkshire Tea in the flat, no matter what.

'Anyway, it's pretty standard procedure,' Graham says. 'Or was, at least. With a crime like that, when you have a man at the crime scene, you take him in. Just to be on the safe side. And he was the only man.'

'What about Jay?'

133

'Mason?' Graham furrows his brow, removing his hands. 'Mason wasn't there.'

I stare at him. 'Yes, he was,' I say.

He looks at me carefully. 'No, Linn. He wasn't. He was with Oliver Dawson. At the party Jacob was throwing. Still locked in that bathroom. Took Oliver two hours to break them out, drunk as they were. That would have been about the time the call got in that you'd been found. When I got to the crime scene, it was you and Teoman Dündar and that Anna lass. Ah, and Miss Luca, of course.'

'Miss Luca?' I ask. My voice sounds high. That's not how I remember it. I knew Jay couldn't have been there at the time it had actually happened, but by the time I woke back up, I could swear I remember him being there ... And I don't remember anything about Miss Luca being in the hollow. 'Antonia Luca was there?'

'Yeah, the lass phoned her up after they'd rung the police. They wanted somebody to speak to. She got there before I did.'

He can tell I don't believe him. 'It's all in the file,' he adds. 'Don't tell me you don't remember this?'

I look away. Try to remember, the silhouette in my memory, the person I tried reaching for but who would always escape my grasp. Was it Miss Luca? I look at the nameplates on the counter. DETECTIVE INSPECTOR GRAHAM WALKER, DETECTIVE SERGEANT MARY ZWAMBE, DETECTIVE CONSTABLE ANGELA JOHNSON. Angela is also behind the desk, looking at me from the side. She's pretty young, but already looks very determined. Like she is going to get somewhere in life. She has short brown hair – too short, Oliver would have said – and her hands are large. She remembers me, I think. A moment ago, I thought she was studying the pages of a small book, but now all she does is look at me. Maybe she thinks I'm going insane, too.

'You remember Linny, don't you, Angela?' Graham says, obviously to ease the tension. 'Linn delivered the flowers for your grandpa's funeral – isn't that right, Angela? You worked for the florist, didn't you, Linny, at the same time as Mary – Detective Sergeant Zwambe, I mean.'

I only nod. So does Angela. She doesn't resemble the girl she used to be, with the long ponytail, playing tennis because her friends did. Now we are both grown up and this is the third day I have been in here. She must think I'm hysterical.

Maybe I am.

At least I am not still holding a flowerpot. With Graham's private number in the pocket of my jeans, I step outside, pressing my clenching palm against my chest. Fiddling with the nightshade with my other hand, back in my pocket, staring at the grey pavement.

Is it possible? Was it not a memory at all, that I saw Jacob when I woke up? Maybe he was there, but left before Graham arrived?

But that would mean he'd been there *before* it had happened. That's impossible, isn't it? He was in that bathroom with Oliver.

Did I just imagine it, then?

As I walk up the High Street, I realise just how much I look like the teenager I used to be, dressed in baggy clothes, hair a mess, the strong wind pulling it into all directions.

None of the boys would look at me in school. I was a bit too old by the time Avril Lavigne became popular. And even then, I didn't have her straight hair. Mine's always been curly when it wasn't short, unruly even, so that growing it out didn't help one little bit. I thought it would make me more feminine. More attractive. Lovely, the hairdresser said. It'll make you look lovely.

Only Oliver. He wanted me.

He never wanted Anna. He was the only one in the form, I think. Most of them expected that she'd be up for a night of fun. Being from Eastern Europe and all that. Most weren't that interested in talking to her, in any case.

I loved talking to her.

I stop by the Vodafone branch. I must stay safe. When I enquire about a landline, they look at me like it's Christmas. The salesperson gets incredibly enthusiastic. Actually, it's a former classmate of mine. Takes me a moment to recognise him. Nick Parker. 'Anything, Caroline. I mean, right, to call your loved ones, you'd want a landline.'

I do everything I can not to think of Oliver. Vodafone says to call the number they're giving me, and that it will probably take a week or two to have it all put in.

A week.

I stand outside the shop, in my parents' old clothing, and stare down the grey street. *Teoman had a nasty streak.*

Did he?

I never spoke to him again. To them. I couldn't. The fear was too great. That taking one look at his face, up close and proper, would bring something back to me that would kill me if I remembered. I didn't speak to Anna again, either. Much better to believe it was a stranger. Much easier.

I square my shoulders. Then I walk into the copy shop. Kaitlin opens her mouth to greet me, but I make straight for Anvi. 'Where is he?' I ask.

Anvi raises her brows. 'Who?'

She knows exactly who. 'You said he was back,' I reply, my heart in my throat. 'Where is he?'

I will go see Teoman.

THE DETECTIVE INSPECTOR

Look here now.

Am I concerned? No, I'm not.

Because, you see, I know my town. I know everything that is going on. So when I tell Little Linny there's nothing to worry about, there isn't.

I only wish she'd believe me. She didn't look good when she came in, her hair all in disarray, that pretty body of hers buried under that horrible coat. When her mother wore it, sure, that was different. I mean, Sue had her age, didn't she, God rest her soul. But not Linn. Not that body of hers. Not that lovely hair. I like that she keeps it long. It suits her. I hate to see her turn in on herself again. It's not right. That coat, those boots, her hair. She wasn't wearing any makeup either. It looks wrong on Lovely Linny.

Not that it's up to me to decide what she wears. That's all

up to her. But you know, if even the Muslim women wear tight clothes under their hijabs, you'd think you knew something was wrong with a lass like Linn if she hid her body like that. I worry for her.

I decide to call Antonia Luca. Just give her a bit of a ring. Let her know. Just a bit of a chat.

While it rings, I take out the book I'm reading. It's an old one, *Retribution*, it's called. I like the beginning. It's so good at the beginning.

I mean, poor Little Linny. Why didn't she call me? I know signal's poor down there, but she might have tried to send a text or something? Or come over in her car? She's got that car of hers, doesn't she?

It occurs to me she might have been drunk.

That was the problem the last time, you see. Nineteen years ago, I didn't catch the bastard because of Linny. She couldn't say anything about her attacker. Couldn't remember a thing, she was so pissed when we found her.

Well. When *they* found her.

Not Jacob Mason, no, what made her think that? Anna Bohacz and Teoman Dündar.

Not that I want to say anything against them. Benefit of the doubt. I still think it was a stranger who did it. One way or another, he didn't belong.

Just saying, though. Teoman Dündar was there. He was jealous. I mean, his hatred for Oliver Dawson was practically pouring off him. Plus, he'd been the first at the scene. And he had the background to match. You see what's on the news, don't you? Grooming young girls, all that. In Turkey, they're not allowed to smile now, I've heard. Women, I mean.

I mean, not that he was like that. Not Teoman Dündar. Not that we know.

LINN

Teo's got a flat just beyond the church. Above the Indian place, opposite the pub.

I look at the cute cobblestone house. It is only noon. Broad daylight. Kait gave me his address. All I have to do is ring the doorbell.

Instead, all I do is stand on the pavement. He might not even be home. He might be at work. His parents always told him how important it was to work. They did nothing but work, Ms and Mr Dündar. And give us coins to put in the goodie machine and let us use their balcony to drink, secretly, just a little bit of beer, just one bottle. They thought it was better to keep an eye on us, I think, than if we did it alone in the woods.

Not that we didn't also do it alone in the woods.

He won't be at home, I think. There is no point in ringing the doorbell.

I feel cold.

He was jealous. He had a nasty streak.

Slowly, I lift my finger to ring the doorbell. I hesitate. Then I turn on my heels and go straight to the pub. I need a drink before I do this.

It's good to be out of the wind. I've only just ordered when my phone rings. I don't recognise the number. Panic surges. I search for it online. Relieved to see it's Antonia Luca's practice, I pick up. As I do, I realise I forgot to come by today. Fuck.

She doesn't sound angry. I'm angry with myself instead. 'I am so sorry,' I say.

'Not to worry; tomorrow at nine instead?' she answers.

Grateful agreement before we hang up. It's only when I've cut the call that I realise I didn't ask her about being at the crime scene. I'll do it tomorrow.

I add it to the list, then I eat and drink a pint. And then another. The barman strikes up a conversation, and the waitress as well. It is so easy around here to do that, to just sit and start chatting to a perfect stranger. So different from London. It's all coming back to me.

Once I've got a moment to myself, I check my e-mails while I have signal, the new address I set up, my fingers stroking the nightshade in my pocket. No one's got back to me yet. None of the florists, none of the garden businesses. Oh, there's a message from the garden festival. They say thank you for my generous offer. How thrilled they are to have received it. Unfortunately, seeing how long I have been out of work, and without any credentials I could present or any past volunteer work, they cannot put so much responsibility on my shoulders. That would not be fair to the plants, the visitors or to me. Surely I understand. They invite me along, though. Maybe bring my family, if I want. Say hello, get to know them. Maybe next time.

I feel so nauseous that I go to the bathrooms. Bent over the toilet pan, I retch, but nothing will come out. My throat burns. It feels hot.

I sit there another while, guiltily relishing the pain. When somebody knocks on the door, I flinch. Groaning, I hoist myself back up, clean up as much as I can and return to the table.

Then I have another beer. Who knows? Jay might come in, right? And still be reasonably sober as well. And this is as public a place as can be.

Some people come in for dinner. Tea, as we used to call it up here. Dinner was what we said for lunch. I move to a table at the very back. The crowd turns louder. They're laughing. And yelling. Rugby's on. I've always liked rugby.

Angela comes in at some point. I huddle up, slinking deeper into the corner. She never liked me when we were young. And I hated her guts. Even setting the age difference aside, she was one of the shining tennis girls while all the trophies I had to show for myself were bruises and teeth marks.

I could swear her eyes catch on my table as they skim the room; ready to jump to my feet and leave, I watch her, but all she does is sit down at a table of her own and take out a small book. It looks like a book of poetry. She sits with her back to the TV and starts reading, silently mouthing the words.

I wonder why she decided to stay up here. In this village of all places.

After my third beer, I finally rise, using the back exit. I've put it off long enough. It is late on a weekday, the street lying completely abandoned. Everyone else is still inside the pub, clamouring for their pints. There might still be some customers at the Indian place, although restaurants stop serving quite early around here, and I am the only one outside. It must have started raining a while ago. The wind is still tearing at my clothes, my hair. The lamp posts are lighting up patches of the wet concrete, casting the rest of the street in even darker shadows. Between the cones of light, it is impossible to see anything.

Moving through the darkness, I come to stand in front of his door. Breathing. Listening to the sound of the rain hitting the concrete. The water touches the skin of my face like the stream from the showerhead, only a little more gently. On the doorbell, it says DÜNDAR, handwritten, next to another name, this one printed. All I have to do is lift a finger. Push it three times.

Like we used to. As kids. As teenagers.

My fingers are cold, hanging frozen in mid-air. My throat no longer burns.

That was how the doorbell rang that night. That is how it rang last night. Ding, ding, ding.

He had a nasty streak.

My palm cramps. My feet. My heart. It rushes through me. All my muscles tensing, relaxing, tensing up again. I feel like my organs are growing roots, digging into my veins, drying them of all blood.

Not another attack. Not now.

I turn around. Rush down the street, towards my car, shoulders hunched, collar put up as far as it will go against the wind and the rain. Glancing furtively into people's flats and houses, their homes, as I make my way down the High Street. My insides are twisting. Flowers on the windowsill, orchids that are not in bloom, spurred violets that look like they've gone thirsty for too long.

In the car, I put my head between my knees, trying to breathe normally. Just breathe. Don't think about it. Don't think about him. Don't think about how afraid you are that seeing him might make you remember something you'd rather forget.

Instead, I think of Oliver. Wonder how his keynote went. Wish I could call him. My knees pressing up against my temples, I think of him singing. At our wedding, the best part of it all, after dinner, when he made his speech. When he started singing for me, without the karaoke machine to back him up. Hearing his voice break on *Oh can't you see, you belong to me* and seeing the tear run down his cheek ... My heart rate still picks up when I remember it. By the time he got from 'Every Breath You Take' to 'One Way or Another', practically everybody in the room was in tears.

We had it in a beautiful pub in Shoreditch. Had a barbecue, right there in the backyard of the pub, surrounded by wild peonies swimming in pools of water. There were potted palm trees and a beautiful canopy of artificial flowers. Oliver standing at the barbecue, his soft face shining with childish delight as he grilled burgers and steaks and sausages, talking to Matt, his colleague with the glasses that kept slipping, and his cousin Anthony, who was well into his fifth pint (we found him a couple of hours later, curled up behind one of the flower bowls, lip-synching a scene from what we thought was *Notting Hill*). And that amazing thyme sauce, and then the little salmon entrées his mum had made, his mum of all people, doing something nice for us. I remember how much that gesture meant to me, exhausted from eleven months of planning as I was.

Finally, I can feel my breathing calm down, my muscles relax. When I feel like I wouldn't be a danger to anyone, I lift my head and start the engine. Mindful of the wet roads, I leave the village, looking at the houses on the High Street, thinking of a flat in Leyton, of dying flowers and white ghosts in the woods.

And then, when I can no longer avoid it, I think of Teo. How clever he always was. How he used to look at me, when we were crouching behind the dumpsters in the parking lot, Anna sharing her mum's cigarettes with us, listening to music sometimes. He was strong, too, once he started working out.

Why did Teo come back? He did well for himself, I know he did. Looked at his social media profiles occasionally, once he got them. He works in film, went to uni, ate and travelled and shared videos of documentaries he'd made or late-night-show hosts delivering hilarious political punches.

As I turn back onto the dirt road, I feel for Graham's number in my pocket, then for the nightshade in the other. Checking my phone, I see there is still signal on the road, but the further I drive towards the house, the fewer bars do I see on the screen.

Maybe I should get a hotel.

Slowing down, I tap my fingers against the steering wheel. There's no hotel in the village, but there are a few very secluded B&Bs down the A684, a little further along than Hawes. Nobody would even know I was there.

But my money supply is finite. And when it's used up, I've got nowhere to go but back to Leyton. Or the food bank. I shiver as I think of the food bank. I've seen it in a film, how it works. Oliver and I went to see it together last year. *I, Daniel Blake*, it was called. He stole my popcorn throughout the film, made me laugh in all the inappropriate places. He can be hilarious, Oliver. It's only rarely that he gets upset. When I've done something stupid, mostly. Like when Oliver and I were standing by the playground that one time last year in autumn, and a couple of kids came up to us, a girl with tight curls and a boy with red hair. Shyly, they gave us two chestnut people they'd made. Oliver crouched down and oh'ed and aw'ed and made all the right noises, grinning at them. Once we got back home, he put the chestnut people on the windowsill.

When I threw them away in the spring, he got angry. Oliver doesn't slam doors or throw a fit. He just turns very silent. Still, it was an exhausting weekend with a passive-aggressive grown man in a two-bedroom flat.

He locked me in accidentally on the third day when he went back to work. We were still waiting for a second set of keys to be made. I've never seen anyone so apologetic when he came back from work that night. A week later, he was already making self-deprecating jokes about it. Don't you dare clean up anything, Linny, or I'll have to lock you in the flat again. Bad girl, trying to clean up, really. An outrage.

Lost in memories, I haven't been paying attention to the road. That's why it catches me off guard.

A sound, like a dull shot. I look up. In front of me, a person, in the middle of the road, right where I'm driving.

I hit the brakes so hard the ABS lights up. The car swerves on the wet gravel. I steer against it, trying desperately to keep the car clear of the ditch as it slides to the side. Adrenalin is pumping through my body. Once the car has stopped, I stare at my hands for a moment, breathing heavily. The adrenalin feels good.

Did I stop paying attention to the road on purpose?

Please, no, I can't have.

Body cramping all over, I look up. I haven't hit the person, thank God. They're still standing in the middle of the road. A tall man, face in the shadow of his hunter's cap. He must have shouted, that must have been that sound. I put down the window, about to apologise profusely.

That's when I recognise him.

Jay.

This time, his Barbour coat is clean, his silk tie carefully tied. He looks at me, eyes bright, jaws working. His gaze clear. The same way he looked at me right before we split up. Right before I walked out on him. As if he knew that something horrible was about to happen, but he had no way of stopping it. Only now there is no hurt in his face. Only resignation.

'Jay,' I say, the way I used to call him, intuitively.

148

He flinches as I say his name the way I used to. Then he turns around and rushes off.

I call after him, but he won't even slow down. Staring at his retreating back, I realise my breath is coming far too quickly again.

What was he doing here in the middle of the night?

I put the window back up, protecting myself from the rain, and drive on to the house, muscles still spasming every once in a while. I will phone him up first thing tomorrow. Down the dip I go, determined not to be frightened of the night. Of Jacob. Of Teoman. It is just a doorbell. It's been nineteen years.

Maybe it's my imagination that's driving me crazy.

My headlights cut through the darkness. Lighting up the dead grass, the gnarled trees, the front porch, the chimes that were returned.

And the white figure, sitting on the stairs beneath them.

I stop the car halfway down the drive. There's no doubt. No doubt at all. I recognised her in the forest, running from me at a speed I couldn't keep up with. I will be damned if I don't recognise her in glaring headlights, sitting still on wet wood, in an old leather jacket and a worn dress, her hair golden.

It's Anna.

She's not holding a rifle. She's not holding anything. Except a hand to the battered chimes, gently making them sing. Her blue eyes are looking right at me as she stands, fingers still tangled in the chimes. Cornflower blue.

I can't tell their colour from this distance. I just know.

I can't breathe.

Anna takes a step towards me. She still moves just like she did back then. Deliberate. With a certain poise, a certain caution. Something tugs at my chest, my lungs, pressing them together. My heart is pumping blood through my body, oxygen into my brain, but I can't feel it. Only hear it. In my ears, so loudly. The beat of my own heart.

It's been nineteen years.

Finally, I drive all the way down, stop the car and get out. I didn't imagine it, then. It was her in the woods. For a moment, I don't know if my limbs will unfold from the seat. Looking into the rear mirror, I focus on the bridge of my nose. *It's been nineteen years. She can't touch you. She cannot touch you.*

When I can, I climb out. My boots make squelching sounds on the wet ground. She is wearing wellies as well. When I step closer, I see she has changed. Her hair especially, turning white and grey at the temples, at the front. There are wrinkles around her eyes and mouth. Somehow, if anything, she looks even more radiant than she did back then. Less frightened.

All the more frightening.

Just fooling around.

Neither of us says anything. The pattern of her dress is flowers, blue flowers, fine like snowflakes.

What is she doing here?

'Hello,' she finally says. Her voice hasn't changed a bit. That voice. Suddenly, I feel all warm inside. Like an old cat waking up to you, stretching its limbs. Like our neighbour's cat, scratching gently at our back door, curling up in my lap once I let her in.

'Hello,' I say back. Rain is falling onto my coat. My face. I force myself not to go up to her. Not to hug her. Against every impulse. *You don't know this woman,* I remind myself. *You don't know her any more. You never wanted to see her again.*

And yet, I remember everything about her. The way she tilts her head. The way she speaks. The way she blinks.

'I am sorry,' she says. Only her accent seems a little thicker than I remember. A shiver runs down my back. 'I only wanted you to know. That it was me. In the forest.'

Anna smiles. The cat pushes closer, elegant and soft and purring, as she adds: 'I did not want you to feel like you were going out of your mind.'

The corners of my mouths are curling upwards of their own volition. I clamp down on it. I don't want to feel this. There's a grin on her face. I remember that grin: standing in front of the goody machine, nicking her mum's fags, tapping ding ding ding on the back of my hand. 'I am sorry I ran away from you,' she says. 'I just realised it might look odd. Me, all bedraggled, coming out of the woods holding a rifle. It was not my intention to scare anyone.'

The cat is purring. I still haven't said anything. Seeing her reminds me. It reminds me of the nightshade and its berries and their sweet, heavy taste in my mouth, scent in my nose, juice on my lips.

But it also reminds me of something else:

How happy I used to be.

For a moment, I think the memory is going to make me

double over. It's too painful, being reminded of that. Of feeling that warmth vibrate inside you, your veins, your blood, against your beating heart. All I can do is stand there and stare as Anna puts her hands into the pockets of her jacket, awkwardly shuffling her feet. A grown woman of thirty-eight years. 'What was that?' she continues as I don't speak. 'You are saying I should consider not running through dark forests with a rifle then? Good point. I might consider it.'

Involuntarily, I laugh. Even before I've realised. I have no time to stop myself.

Anna joins in.

It's too late.

'It might help, yeah,' I say, feeling like I haven't felt in years. Like singing 'Quit Playing Games with My Heart' in a pub in Leeds, standing on a table that's about to collapse. Like lying in a hammock together, my first-ever mobile phone in my lap, taking turns playing Snake, staring wide-eyed. Like ditching the end-of-school dance to go climb to the top of Bolton Castle after nightfall. Not even shortbread comes close.

So that's how happy I used to be. So that's what life used to feel like.

There's no way I can't ask her in. She makes straight for the mud room, to take off her shoes, then for the kitchen, and we make tea. Of course she knows where everything is. Nobody knows this house better than her, not even Jay, except me. And Teo, of course.

I watch her as she sits at the kitchen table. She looks no less luminous inside. I feel like my entire body is humming.

Singing. I'm surprised how quickly it happened. How very little it took. It makes me feel heady. Drunk. Already we're both laughing again. Already it's like we were never separated.

'I mean, you would not believe what the Kenzies kept in that house,' Anna says, her fingers wrapped around the mug she always used when we were teenagers, the blue one. I gave it to her because it matches her eyes. She's leaning across the table. 'Who would own an entire set of cardboard cut-outs of the *Coronation Street* cast?'

I spill some hot water when I pour it into our cups, trying and failing not to laugh. 'You're not serious.'

'I wish I could make this up.'

'Why didn't they get rid of it before they moved?'

'Maybe they were under the misguided impression that they were doing me a favour?'

I snort as she pours us milk. I put in two spoons of sugar for her, one for me. Her grip around the cup turns tense for a fraction of a second. By the time I notice, she's already eased up. 'Well, I suppose they also left you a rifle,' I say.

'Don't forget about the fully functional mantrap in the attic,' she adds drily.

'It's a trade-off,' I deadpan as I sit.

'Trood point,' she replies with a grin. My heart beats frantically for a moment when I hear her use that expression. When we were twelve, Teo and her and Jay and I, one afternoon sitting on Teo's couch, playing SNES, she said that, garbling *true* and *good point*. I still remember Mrs Dündar coming in at some point and telling us to get off that video game console, we'd been playing for hours. We went to Teo's room and played on our Game Boys instead.

'Trood point,' I say, warmth spreading through me like a blanket around my shoulders. 'Have you used it already?' I say, making a vague gesture.

'The rifle?' She takes the first sip of tea. 'Hellfire, no. Well, yes. Once. The old cat, when it was time to go. But other than that, no. I would never. Mum would murder me.'

'How is your mum?' I ask, shivering with pleasure at hearing her say *hellfire*. That's what we used to say up here instead of *God* or *Goodness me*.

Anna puts down her mug. 'Good, mostly. Retired. She was thinking about moving.'

'Somewhere sunny?' I ask, grinning when I remember her mum's incessant trips to the tanning shop in Kendal.

'No,' Anna says evenly. 'Gdańsk. But since the last election, she has changed her mind. She feels a bit lost with everything that is going on, I think. She does not feel safe, neither here nor there.'

I look at the table. 'The referendum?'

'It was a bit of a shock to her,' she says, still calm.

'And you?' I ask, looking back up.

'It was a bit of a shock to me, too.' Anna stares right back at me. 'Did you go vote?'

'Of course I did,' I say. I would like to sound more outraged, but I almost didn't. I was sick on the day and Oliver didn't want me to go out. I made it, last minute. 'I dragged myself out of the flat so that I could. Oliver said he'd never seen me paler than that day.'

She looks up so suddenly that I flinch. 'Oliver?'

I look down, at her bare hands. Her chipped nails. 'We got a flat in Leyton.'

I can't tell her. Not her. That I've left him.

We were just fooling around, her and I. It wasn't anything serious. She lets out a breath. Still staring at me. 'Where is he?'

'Not here,' I say evasively. 'I've come up to look for work.'

'You only arrived this week,' she says.

I mock-furrow my brow, grinning. 'Do you keep tabs on me?'

Anna does not reply. Her stare is unnerving me. 'Linn,' she says. Her voice is so beautiful it hurts.

Does she still think of our kiss? I suddenly wonder.

What am I thinking? It was just a joke. We knew it was wrong. I can feel the muscles in my fingers contract. That's how the attacks always start, just in my fingers. Desperately, I ball my hands into fists to shut them down. Not now. When all I want is to appear like a normal person. Like someone who isn't broken.

Anna stays silent. Then she smiles again. She looks exhausted. We finish our tea speaking of other things, of movies, we always loved movies, and of books, she says there is this excellent poetry collection by Ella Wheeler Wilcox that Angela Johnson recommended to her, and then that sci-fi show on Netflix. When we were really small, we wanted to be astronauts. Really, seriously wanted to. We even phoned NASA once. Apparently, Anna's looking to get work with ESA now.

She doesn't rise until we've finished an entire pot of tea. I accompany her back outside. She looks radiant in the light of the front porch. I look at her face as if I can't look away.

'How did you know? That I was worried about having seen you?' I ask.

She tilts her head that way. 'You know how it is. A small town. And the Detective Inspector phoned Miss Luca while I was with her. He told her you'd been to visit. I may have overheard.'

'You are seeing her?' I ask. For some reason, my throat has gone dry. There was this rumour about Miss Luca, you know. Back then. That there was a reason she wasn't married.

She's still not married, you know. I wonder why. If the makeup is any indication, it's not for lack of trying. Or lack of presentation. I remember how I used makeup at seventeen, right after it had happened: I would put on so much foundation that you could hardly see I had a face, the mascara as thick as it would go, the lips the same bright colour as my eye shadow. Anything that would hold me together. It took Oliver years of telling me I was beautiful to make me tone it down a little.

'Are you?' Anna asks back.

'No,' I say hastily.

'No,' she repeats. That feeling is back: like fingers pulling at my lungs, my cardiac valves. Her eyes are large. Still brilliant and piercing and large.

'So you bought the Kenzies' place,' I say hastily.

'Yes,' she says, her voice soft. It takes every bit of willpower

I have not to reach for her. 'They put it up for a very good price.'

'Good. That's good, with the housing market what it is.'

She doesn't answer and just looks at me.

'I mean, prices are crazy,' I say. 'When Oliver and I were looking to rent in London, it was ...'

'Yes,' she says as I peter out. 'I bet it was.'

I look away. 'Let me drive you home.'

Anna's head is still tilted. I see it from the corner of my eyes. 'No, you go to sleep,' she says. 'It's so close.'

'It's no bother,' I repeat. 'It's late. And dark.'

When I catch myself almost telling her a cautionary tale, I fall silent. That's the last thing I want.

'Goodnight,' she says gently. Slowly, she steps down the stairs, backwards, facing me. She won't look away. Neither will I.

'Goodnight,' I say. Anna does not reply. Only keeps looking at me. She brushes the chimes as she makes to turn around.

'They went missing,' I say impulsively. I don't want her to go yet. I still have to ask her. There's so much I need to ask her. About that night. About Jay. About everything.

If I can bear the answers.

She is back to looking at me. 'I know,' she answers.

'Small town?' I ask, even smiling. An answer about the chimes, that shouldn't be too hard to bear, right?

She smiles, too. It looks twisted. 'Not quite.'

'Then what?'

She stands still, staring at me with that expression of hers. 'I know because it was me who took them.'

THE DETECTIVE INSPECTOR

That Anna girl? Well, yeah. She was a bit of an odd one, wasn't she? Very pretty, of course. You'd have had to be blind not to find her attractive, even at fifteen. Especially at fifteen, maybe.

Only, you couldn't quite shake the feeling that there was something a little off about her, could you? She did not know how things were done here in the beginning. Neither did her mother. And that's fine. Takes a while to adjust, doesn't it?

Only you got the impression they didn't *want* to adjust. That they were even proud of some of the things they did, or the way they did them. Excellent cook, her mother, can say that for her at least. Went to church a lot. Had to drive to Leeds to find a church she liked. Don't think the girl ever went.

Did we bring her in? Of course we did. Took her statement myself.

What do you mean, what did she say? You flatter me, really,

but for the life of me I can't remember. Getting older, we all are, aren't we?

Well, yeah, of course it's in the file.

Sorry, what?

You want to see the file?

LINN

It was Anna who took the chimes.

Borrowed, she said. *I put them back when I saw you had returned. No one was expecting you to come back, you know.*

I'm in bed, but I cannot sleep. The list is sitting on my nightstand. Behind Anna's name, it now says *back.* I've crossed out *public place* behind Jay's name, underlined *phone.* And I've underlined Teo's name, too. Put *GO* behind it in capital letters. I've also put down the next date for Miss Luca and me.

But all I'm thinking of is Anna. Coming to the house. Replacing the chimes.

That's the explanation for their disappearance then. She said she didn't want them to go rusty outside, with no one living at the house and the Kenzies no longer there to take care of it all. How she remembered how much they had meant to my parents, those chimes, how they'd often been out on the porch, my mum desperately trying to grow some red dahlias while my dad played with the chimes, staring off into the distance. That she returned them the moment she realised somebody had moved back in.

That means she came to the house and I never noticed. Of course, all she has to do is walk through the woods. I wouldn't even hear a car drive by.

Did I hear a car? The past two nights? Did I hear a car when the chimes were tossed against my window?

I can't remember. I might not have.

All I know is how insanely good it felt to talk to her. I still can't believe how we talked, just like that, as if no time had passed at all. One smile. One joke. That was all it took to make me feel like I was seventeen again.

And that's why I did not want to see her.

Because she would remind me of what I'd had.

That I'd been happy once.

Because she would remind me of why I left this place as soon as I could. Remind me of the night I regained consciousness, my legs spasming, my lower abdomen hurting like someone had clawed the womb from my body. Tracks of perspiration were cooling all over my skin, freezing my blood, like the scratch marks of excited fingers. There was saliva drying on my back. I was lying prone, on my stomach. I was surrounded by my own vomit. My best friends rushed me to the hospital. The next night, they came back to my house. I watched them from the window. And then I realised what that expression on their faces was.

C. K. Williams

You want to know?
Of course. Everybody wants to know.
But I'm not telling.
I can't tell you.

THE DETECTIVE INSPECTOR

Okay, fine. You want to know? You want all the gory details? You want the photos, the statements?

Shouldn't have to show you, of course. Shouldn't even look at them myself. But sometimes I do. I mean, those bruises on her thighs and her right butt cheek, swollen blue. How she bled, between her legs. Do you know what dried blood looks like on skin that pale? And then that dress of hers, that ridiculously short dress, torn all the way up to her breasts.

It was an anomaly, let me tell you. This doesn't happen here.

I mean, we still don't know, do we? She was so drunk, you wouldn't believe a woman could drink that much. It may very well have been consensual.

You want to know what happened to her? Want to see the bruises and the blood and where the saliva was drying in her hair? It's all there in the file. Right here.

Go for it.

C. K. Williams

POLICE REPORT

CASE NO: ▮▮▮▮▮▮▮▮   DATE: ▮▮▮▮▮▮▮▮
REPORTING OFFICER: DETECTIVE INSPECTOR GRAHAM WALKER
PREPARED BY: ▮▮▮▮▮▮▮▮
INCIDENT: SUSPICION OF SEXUAL ASSAULT AT ▮▮▮▮▮▮▮▮
▮▮▮▮

VICTIM: CAROLINE WILSON, 17 YEARS, BORN ▮▮▮▮▮▮▮,
LIVING ▮▮▮▮▮▮▮▮

At approximately 0130 hours last night, an emergency call
was received, stating that a female victim had been found at
her parents' home unconscious and injured. The police force
found the female victim (Caroline Wilson, 17) as well as two
witnesses, male (Teoman Dündar, 17) and female (Anna
Bohacz, 19), at the given address in a bedroom on the first
floor. Miss Bohacz had phoned 999. Likewise on scene was
Antonia Luca, MSc, psychologist at ▮▮▮▮▮▮ High School.
She claimed to also have been contacted by Miss Bohacz. The
first member of the force on the scene was Detective Inspector
Graham Walker.

The emergency doctor reported that Miss Wilson's injuries
seemed to be due to painful sexual intercourse that had
taken place approximately forty-five minutes to three hours
previously. Miss Wilson was heavily intoxicated (0.1). Shards
of an empty bottle of a so-called alcopop (Bacardi Breezer)
were found next to her body. Mr Dündar and Miss Bohacz
reported that Miss Wilson claimed she had been raped, but
at the time she was taken to hospital, no coherent statement

164

could be taken from Miss Wilson due to her degree of intoxication.

Afterwards, she claimed not to remember the act itself. She was found surrounded by vomit; her own. Dried saliva was found in her hair as well as scratch marks between her legs – as if somebody had mimicked penetration between the soft skin of her upper thighs – and inside her genitals. The inner skin of her genital area was bleeding, presumably from the force of the penetration. Large bruises (> 5 inches in diameter) were found on her pelvis, the inside of her legs, her knees, and her buttocks. Smaller bruising (< 5 inches in diameter) was found on the backs of her legs and around her anus. Preliminarily, the doctor on scene could find no physical indication of attempted defence, such as skin under the victim's fingernails. Both witnesses were taken to and their statements recorded at the local police station. Detective Inspector Walker has detained Mr Dündar for questioning.

LINN

No. I said I wanted the truth, so I'd better be honest myself. I will tell you.

Because do you know what's most unbearable? Even worse than not remembering?

I've never told anyone, but it's what made me reach for the nightshade. You see, the doctors only kept me in the hospital for one night, letting me go home the next day. Oliver was waiting for me when I came home with my parents, a bunch of freshly picked flowers in his arms. And in the evening, Teoman and Anna came to see me.

My parents wouldn't let them in, but they didn't need to. I could see the expressions on their faces from the window as Teoman shouted, as Anna stood there, completely silent.

They looked guilty.

I took one look at their faces. Turned on my heels. Walked

up the staircase to my parents' bedroom and took out my mum's deadly nightshade. The chimes were singing, and the doorbell was ringing.

I swallowed the plant in one go.

Chapter 4

It is a winter night in the year 1999. A teenager is lying on her mattress, on top of a blanket that's really too childish for her now, with Sailor Moon and all that, but she likes it. It's late. Her parents are out to see a show in Manchester.

Downstairs, the doorbell rings. Ding, ding, ding. She jumps to her feet, hastily throwing a woollen blanket over her bed, then races downstairs.

It's Anna. 'Where's Teo?' Linn asks as they go upstairs, to her room. Anna's wearing red, lots of red, a red scarf and red mittens and a red sweater. Her mum says it's a phase. Linn likes this phase.

'Teo is sick,' Anna says. 'He tried to come up here, but then he puked into his helmet.'

Linn laughs, even though she doesn't know what to do now that Teo isn't gonna come. She had this planned. Had it all figured out. They would have watched Titanic *or MTV and smoked some weed and then she could have finally made that move on him. Everybody said it, didn't they? That her and Teo – it made sense. That it was why he was still hanging around them, her and Anna. That that's why he got into a fight with Jay after*

C. K. Williams

their break-up. Her throat still constricts when she thinks about that, how Jay isn't there any more. Not even as their friend.

They throw themselves down on her bed, crumpling up the blanket, putting the movie on anyway. 'The smell must've been horrible,' Linn says, grinning.

They share the spliff. And then a bit of wine, anyway, 'cause who needs Teo to have a good time? They decide Titanic *is boring and put on* Thelma & Louise *instead. Linn looks at Anna's hair spilling over the pillow. It's so blonde. Linn's tried bleaching her hair; everyone's been bleaching their hair. Apparently, no one wants to go into the new millennium without massive amounts of hydrogen peroxide on their skull.*

'You really think all computers will shut down?' Anna asks, looking at her nail polish. One nail is still green. She has trouble focusing on it. The booze is working.

Linn shrugs. Their shoulders are pressed up against each other. Linn's tapping the back of Anna's hand with a finger. Tap, tap, tap. 'I don't know. Does it matter?'

'Aye,' Anna says, furrowing her brow. She turns her hand around so that she can tap Linn's palm, too. She's humming something. 'Hit Me Baby One More Time', it sounds like. 'I think everything might break down.'

'Does that matter?' Linn asks.

Anna turns her head to look at her, tilting it in that way of hers. Their faces are very close. Linn's heart is beating like crazy all of a sudden. She can feel Anna's breath on her lips as she speaks. 'Of course that matters. You don't want to go into the new millennium without computers, do you?'

She looks so serious.

Linn wants to kiss her.

Just a peck on the lips. She's seen older girls do it, Anvi and Kaitlin. It's no big deal.

So she does. Anna's lips are warm against hers. She tastes like wine, like the woods. Her skin smells like paper.

When Linn separates, Anna's expression is still serious. 'What did you do that for?'

Linn doesn't know what to say. The blood's still pounding in her ears. 'I could do it again.'

Anna nods.

This time, it's not just a peck on the lips.

LINN

I start awake. Pale light is filtering in through the window. My body is warm under the blanket, the sheets underneath me dry. The smell of fresh dew is stronger than that of lavender.

It's morning.

The doorbell did not ring last night.

I sit up, look outside, blinking into the daylight. Check for the nightshade, back in the nightstand. Quickly, I make my way to the window, bare feet on the cool wood. Pulling back the curtains, I stare at the drive, the front porch. No tyre marks. No footprints. No nothing. Not even bad dreams.

I did dream, though. Of that night when I was seventeen. I knew I would. Seeing Anna again, I knew it would bring it all back. The nightshade only gave me glimpses. Seeing Anna again pushed me onto the tracks, my memories barrelling into me like a high-speed train. The warmth of happiness. Her guilty expression. The nightshade in my mouth.

The truth is: when Graham announced it had been a

stranger, he saved my life. If I had kept believing my best friends had anything to do with it, I would have gone through with killing myself.

Rubbing my clenching palms, I get dressed, thinking as I do, glancing at my list. I am glad to be going to see Miss Luca this morning. And at least the Detective Inspector has begun sharing some things with me. Among them, his suspicions of Teo.

Whom I still haven't been to see.

Today, I promise myself against the pounding of my heart. *No more excuses.*

Downstairs, I check the postbox. Not a single letter. Trying not to feel disappointed as I stand with my hand on the box, looking into its dark emptiness, I remind myself the businesses may have e-mailed as well. I won't be able to check my new inbox until I get into town. I won't check my old address, don't want to see if Oliver has written.

That is when I see it.

I look at the postbox, leaning in closer. There is something after all. A small item stuck in the slit. Like someone dropped it off in such a rush that they didn't wait for it to go all the way in.

Carefully, I take it out. It takes a little fiddling. Paper. Cheap, thin paper.

It's a note.

I don't recognise the handwriting. Quickly, I unfold it.

My place. Wednesday, 8 p.m.

– J

At the bottom of the note, someone has drawn a flower and stick figure, looking intently at a picture frame in their hands. It is a heartbreakingly childish sketch, done by a hand desperately trying to hold still against its shaking.

I stare at it.

It must be from Jay.

I trace the letters with my finger, the handwriting I didn't even recognise. Was that why Jay was here last night? To put this into my postbox?

I go on to trace the flower, the stick figure. The shaky lines break my heart. Why would he want to see me tomorrow? And at such a time? Should I go? It is not a public place, but I need to talk to him ...

I can't tear my eyes away from the drawing. Looking back, it's easy to say that what we had was no more than a crush. A teenage rush of hormones that went away as quickly as it had come. But at the time, he made me so giddy. I couldn't wait to see him, in school, at his mum's house, at mine, in the woods, on the benches in the park, the parking lot, wherever. Didn't matter. And he loved me like he loved his art: with abandon. Jay didn't compromise, and he taught me to do the same. *Loving you takes my breath away,* he said one night, both of us leant back against the old stones of Bolton Castle, giggling from climbing the fence, from all the rules we'd just broken. *I can see it in the air, feel it, taste it, like flower pollen.*

A sudden gust of wind startles me out of my reverie. Pulling my cardigan more tightly around myself, I check my watch. I'm meeting Miss Luca at nine, and if I don't want to miss it again, I'd better hurry. Putting Jay's note into my pocket, I pass by the sitting room on my way to the kitchen, taking up my begonias. 'How are you this morning, my darlings?' I ask them quietly as we go to the sink to get them some water. I have some tea and oatmeal while they drink. Afterwards I put on the coat and boots and head outside, the note sitting heavily in my pocket.

The drive still lies abandoned, although some rays of sunshine are trying to break through the cloud cover. Seems like they're failing. The hollow looks gloomy. I'm sure my hardy begonias would love the flower bed in front of the porch, lying idle at the moment, covered in dead foliage and sturdy weeds. They would dig in their roots and grow as tall as the porch roof, large bushes of flowers every season. And then I could also plant some wildflowers, out on the meadow closer to the trees. There could even be a hammock, a honey farm and a small pond, right over there where the ground is wet with dew, shining silver.

Burying my hands in my pockets, making Jay's note rustle, I walk down the front porch.

Only to step on something.

Glass cracks under my soles. Instinctively, I curse, flinching backwards, and look at the doormat.

There lies the rest of what must have been a glass bottle before. Not just any glass bottle, though.

It looks like a bottle of Bacardi Breezer.

The weeds shoot into my lungs, the climbing plants creeping through my body underneath my skin. Slowly, I look to the right. To the left. Then back at the bottle. I circle the

175

house, inspect the meadow, the line of trees. I even check the shed and the windows and the entire front porch, but there is nothing. I can see nothing, hear nothing.

Only the song of the chimes.

The chimes I heard singing that night. The bottle of Breezer on the floor, in shards, next to my naked body. How Anna looked at me, lavender so heavy in my nose, lying in my own vomit.

I stand in front of the doormat, staring at the shards again, still listening to the chimes. How she touched them last night. Her fingers on the metal, playing with them, gently.

How I didn't drive her home after our cup of tea.

She might have come back. Jay might have, too.

Bending down, I inspect the shards more closely. I realise that there is no label. It might not be a Breezer bottle at all. Some gins come in bottles like that, don't they? Everybody's drinking gin these days.

Hellfire. I straighten back up, throw the shards in the bin and leave. It's almost nine, and Miss Luca is waiting for me.

Her practice sits on the other end of the village than her house, down by what we call the river. It's really only a beck, dribbling along between two meadows, the all-inclusive picturesque package of ancient low stone walls and grazing sheep. You'd think Visit Britain had put this up.

I get out of my car, painfully aware of how long it's been since I've really walked anywhere. You don't walk places in London unless you're a tourist, very poor or a homeless person. Somebody set a homeless man on fire, not far from our flat in Leyton, just after we'd moved in. Oliver had been on another conference, his first one abroad, in Lille. It was horrible. I read about it online the next day.

I run a hand along my dry lips as I get out of the car. They twitch under my fingers. It would be too far from the hollow to come here on foot, anyway. It was such a bother, growing up here, that you couldn't get anywhere without your parents driving you till you got a bike. Once I'd bought my bike, we used it to go everywhere, Teo and Anna and me, into the village and to Catterick Garrison Cinema and Bolton Castle at night.

It was really fun, though. Wind in your hair, roaring laughter in your ears, Teo's arms round your waist and Anna's hands brushing your back.

Miss Luca's practice is in an old house, pretty red brick, a well-kept garden, even a cute chimney. I used to resent that everything here looked so picture-perfect. It made me curious, too, though. What was she hiding behind those lovely brick walls, under the quaint chimney and pretty roof?

Today, I recognise the handwriting of a woman with taste and money. Subtle, yet unapologetic. Inside, the interior is strikingly modern, crème walls and clean lines, white curtains. The waiting room is filled with women, most of them a decade or so older than me, maybe even two decades. They're reading *Psychology Today* and *Happinez*, which are all the magazines provided on the large glass table. Oh, and *Farmers Weekly*. Apparently, there has been a FLURRY OF SHEEP THEFTS REPORTED IN NORTH YORKSHIRE. Stifling a chuckle, I walk up to the reception. 'Caroline Wilson,' I say, giving my maiden name without hesitation. It slots back into place as if it was always meant to be there. They never tell you how weird it is, suddenly having a new name. A name that never used to belong to you, and all of a sudden it's supposed to be you. Not looking up when people address you. Feeling like you're beginning to disappear. 'I'm here to see Miss Luca.'

'Hello, ma'am,' the receptionist, a well-dressed woman with fashionable glasses, says smoothly. 'Do you have an appointment?'

'No.' I say. 'It's a private visit. She said 9 a.m. She said nine in the morning.'

The receptionist watches me stutter with an expression of slight condescension. Then she smiles, takes up the telephone. 'One moment, please, ma'am.'

While she phones Miss Luca, I look at the paintings on the wall. Patients' watercolours, mostly flowers, some landscapes. From around here, of course. There's one of a large grey barn, looming tall and dark in a stormy night.

'Miss Luca's office is through there,' the receptionist says once she has hung back up. I hurry to follow her outstretched hand to a nondescript door and walk straight in.

The office looks just like the rest of the practice, except that the pattern on the curtains consists of large golden triangles. Miss Luca rises from behind her desk, a large slab of glass, very fashionable, very impressive, and walks towards me, hand outstretched. She is still wearing those oversized sunglasses on top of her head, as well as the jewellery. This could very well be a first lady's office. Does the first lady have an office? I wonder. 'Ms Wilson, how very good to see you. Please sit.'

'Thanks,' I say and sit on the chair she's indicated, not so different from the one in her school office, actually. Memories bat into me once more. I remember sitting in her room at school and telling her what I kept telling everyone: *I don't remember. I don't know how much I'd had. Yes, I'd been drinking, or how do you think I got to 0.1?* And then the nightshade. *It was an accident,* I kept repeating to anyone who'd listen, lying and lying. *I thought they were blueberries.* 'Sorry about yesterday,' I say.

She raises her hands good-naturedly as she returns to the chair behind the desk. 'Not to worry, not one little bit. I am so glad you could make it today.'

Sitting down, she folds her hands under her chin. Her pearl earrings glisten in the tentative sunlight. She was popular back when I was at school, Miss Luca. With men I mean, and not just the faculty. Lithe, young, caring ... She always had one bouquet or another sitting on her desk when you came in, with a card, usually from an anonymous admirer. She said it didn't matter to her, that she wasn't flattered, but then why did she keep them? I wondered.

Now, her desk is empty of any gifts. When I lean in to adjust my chair, I see how she hastily pushes a brochure under a stack of papers. *OurTime.co.uk. Dating for men & women over 50.* It looks well worn, as if she has turned it over in her hands a thousand times already. I look back into her face. She's wondering if I've seen. Something passes across her expression, something that almost looks like fear.

Then Miss Luca catches herself, leans back, asks me how I've been. I tell her a little while the receptionist brings in a pot of tea, waiting till she has left again.

'Oh, by the way,' I say, trying to sound casual, determined not to invite in another attack. 'It was Anna whom we saw in the woods.'

To Miss Luca's credit, she does not even hesitate, continuing to pour us a cup of tea. 'It was?'

'She came by the house last night.' I keep up the conversational tone as well as I can. 'To tell me. Said she didn't want me to think I was going bonkers.' I laugh.

Miss Luca smiles. 'Did you enjoy her visit?'

Suddenly, it's much more difficult to uphold the casual tone. 'Yes.'

Miss Luca looks at me with her piercing dark eyes. 'Remind me again, how long since you last saw each other?'

'Nineteen years,' I say.

She raises her brows. 'So you didn't keep in touch at all?'

'No. You know how it is.'

'Actually,' Miss Luca objects, gently, 'some people keep in touch, don't they? Especially such good friends as yourselves. The mischief-makers.'

'Well,' I say.

Miss Luca does not budge. 'You didn't want to?'

For a moment, I sit absolutely still. Should I tell her?

I used to trust her. Once.

'Miss Luca,' I say haltingly. 'The Detective Inspector told me that you were there ... the night I was found.'

She lets out a breath. 'Yes. Yes, I was, Miss Wilson. I was

called in to provide psychological assistance. Unfortunately, I wasn't able to do much for you. You were barely conscious.'

'Who else was there?' I ask, holding my breath.

'Teoman Dündar and Anna Bohacz. And the Detective Inspector, of course.'

I wait. She looks at me expectantly. 'No one else?' I prompt. I seem to be making her uncomfortable. 'What do you mean, Miss Wilson?'

'Jay Mason,' I say. 'I thought he was there. I remembered it.'

'Jacob Mason?' she asks. 'No. No, let me assure you, he was not there when I arrived.'

'Then why did you start treating him?' I ask. I remember this. I *know* it. 'He became one of your patients, didn't he? We all did.' She nods. Relief surges through me. At least I wasn't wrong about that. 'Why did he come to you if he wasn't even there?'

'You know that I cannot divulge anything he said during our time together,' Miss Luca says, hesitating. Deliberating. 'But I am sure it did not escape your notice at the time that he was deeply shocked by the events, as we all were. It brought up many issues for him, issues he had not worked through. Your separation had been especially painful for him. It is often like this with teenagers: They cope well with break-ups until their former partner finds someone new. Only then do they snap.'

'Snap?'

'Well. Process it. There were violent fantasies, of course. He was heartbroken.'

I look at her, a shiver running down my back as I remember Jay in the middle of the road last night. She seems to sense my discomfort, because she hastily adds: 'Listen, this was a very long time ago. Fantasies are one thing, action quite another. And Mr Mason certainly has very different problems now.'

'Graham says he's suicidal.'

Miss Luca flinches. 'I would not like to comment on that,' she says primly. 'But we are trying very hard to make progress.'

I think about the note in my pocket. 'It's so odd. I could just swear I remembered that he'd been there.'

Miss Luca draws a hand along her chin. 'He drove you home.'

'What?' I say.

'That's how you got home that night. He drove you.'

I shake my head. 'I can't remember that.'

Something flashes across her face. It's that expression again, from when I spotted her brochure. 'Then maybe I'm mistaken.'

'What made you say it?'

'I must have made a mistake.'

'What made you say that, Miss Luca?' I ask her, urgently.

She hesitates. 'I would be betraying a patient's confidence if I kept talking, Miss Wilson.'

I swallow. My mind is racing. Someone must have said something to her back then. Maybe even Jay himself. He could have told her. In confidence.

But if he drove me home, he couldn't have been in the bathroom with Oliver.

There were violent fantasies, of course.

'Was he suicidal back then?' I ask, carefully. 'Was he ... desperate?'

'I assumed you knew,' Miss Luca says. 'Mr Dündar and Miss Bohacz certainly did. They expressed concern over his state of mind.'

I stare at her. 'They knew?'

'Evidently. The four of you used to be friends, did you not, before you broke up with him? I remember him covering for the other two when you were caught breaking into Bolton Castle. Weren't they afraid they were going to be deported if they were prosecuted?'

That is true. Graham threatened them with deportation when he caught us trespassing at Bolton Castle. He couldn't threaten Jay or me, which is why we covered for them.

'Of course, it turned out that the Detective Inspector was perhaps exaggerating a bit,' Miss Luca goes on, trying for a smile. 'Nobody could have been deported for a bit of trespassing, but that is not what the Detective Inspector made you think, if I remember correctly. He meant to scare you off doing it again. Understandable, if you think what could have happened to four children in that dark castle, climbing wherever they wanted. But Jay didn't see it like that back then. Sometimes, he would get very angry.'

So, that is why I remembered his face. Jay was the last one to see me before it happened.

It doesn't make sense, though; Oliver wouldn't have lied, not about this. Not about being in the bathroom with Jay.

Maybe he didn't lie. Maybe he thought he was telling the

truth. We'd all been drinking. His watch might have stopped at a later point, some time during the party, and he didn't realise until later, thinking it had happened when he'd forced the door.

I remember Jay's hands around my wrist on his front step, not two days ago.

'I just can't explain it to myself,' I say, a fissure in my voice. 'Why would anyone do something like that?'

Miss Luca looks away. Uncrosses her hands. Her nails are manicured. For a moment, she seems helpless. 'There are many different reasons, Ms Wilson. Sometimes it is simply a matter of opportunity. Most of the time, however, it is someone close to the victim. They use it to exert control over a person that they cannot control any longer by other means.'

Your separation had been especially painful for him.

'You are absolutely sure, Miss Luca? That is was him who drove me home?' I ask her.

She won't look at me as she answers. 'That is what I believe to be true, yes.'

She lifts her cup when I don't say anything. Swallows heavily. Puts it back down. 'It does not define you,' she says. 'That is important to understand.' For a moment, her fingers tighten around the porcelain cup. 'How have you been, Ms Wilson? I mean, really been?'

I don't say anything. She waits, patiently. As if I knew what to tell her. Should I tell her about the way Oliver's colleagues teased him about how quickly his hair had turned grey before he shaved it all off, especially the women? About the drawing of the stick people he brought home and the way he smiled at them? About the tears in the Kenzies' voice and none on my face? About Google searches on bridges in London? That I know it wasn't a stranger who came for me that night, but someone I knew? Someone I trusted?

That burn at the back of my eyes. It burns and burns and suddenly I don't know where to look. 'There's so much to say,' I end up answering as honestly as I can. 'I wouldn't know where to start.'

She takes a sip of tea as I look down. When I say no more for a very long while, she finally asks: 'How is Oliver Dawson?'

Again, I don't know what to say. I don't know how he is. I ask a question in turn, desperate to get away from the burning at the back of my eyes that will not turn into tears, my lungs cramping, my throat, my feet: 'What has changed here, in the village?'

Miss Luca must realise I'm changing the subject, but thankfully she lets me get away with it. 'The supermarket will be done up next year. They will even close it down for a couple months.'

'No!'

'Yes. And the primary school moved last year. They are in a new building now.'

I sit up. 'They are?'

'Aye. Down on Glastonbury Road. Oh, and Teoman Dündar is rumoured to be reopening his father's shop.' She is watching me closely. 'Have you been to see him, too?'

'No,' I say.

'Curious,' Miss Luca says. 'That you two would come back almost at the same time.'

My lungs feel like all air is being sucked from them.

'A good opportunity, perhaps?' she adds.

I stare at her.

We were best friends. They made me feel that life was worth living. That I could do anything. Be anyone. Even though I looked like a boy. Even though I was too loud, too brazen, too bossy.

We are all back, and my doorbell is ringing again.

Jay was at the crime scene. Jay drove me home. That is what is important right now. I need to stay focused. 'Does Graham know about this?' I ask. 'Does he know that Jacob Mason drove me home?'

ANNA

I cannot work. I cannot focus. Cannot think.

The woods surround me on all sides. I like them. Trees are benevolent. They are not like people. When people surround you, you'd better run as fast as you can.

That is what my grandmother used to say. She lived in Gdynia, a port town 30 kilometres outside Gdańsk, during the Winter Offensive of 1945.

The ground is covered in frost. The bark of the birches shimmers silver in the cold air. I have not talked to Teo in years. Or to Jacob. Nineteen years. How could I have? After what we did?

My grandmother never talked about what happened to her that winter. Left me her letters instead. The ones she wrote, like all the women, in Polish or Yiddish or German, no matter, to tell their friends, aunts, cousins, daughters, to stay inside. For if they were to go out into the streets, they would be taken. The commanders claimed that their men deserved this. That

187

they were entitled to it after risking their lives to fight for Poland's freedom.

Standing quite still, I close my eyes, attempting to soak up the way the wood is quiet. The rustling of birds and the wind in the boughs and the distant, beautifully distant sounds of the road. It used to make me feel at home, this forest. This wayward, wonderful landscape. When I was a little girl, and still at nineteen. Last year, even.

Now all it is, is a quantity of sounds, strung together to form a random sequence of noises. I do not feel at home any more. I do not feel safe any more. Except when I sat in her kitchen, my hands wrapped around that blue mug. That felt like home.

I remain standing still. Her house stands only a mile up ahead. Mine only a mile back. And only a few miles down that road and into the village sits Teo's flat at the back of the pub.

It used to be us. Even with Jacob long gone, the three of us stuck together. It was always us.

I turn back. I need to get the bike out of the shed.

LINN

Graham is in the break room. He's the only one. Inviting me to sit down, he puts the kettle on. While he makes us tea, I tell him about the bottle I found in the drive this morning. Feeling like a right lunatic, but I tell him anyway because my throat is too dry to ask him what I just found out about. *Did you know Jay drove me home that night?*

'Now, listen, Linny ...' he starts, sitting down across from me.

'No, I know it's nothing,' I say. 'It just made me think of ... You know. That night. When you found the bottle next to the bed, all in shards.'

He scrunches up his face. He could use a shave, the grey and white stubble on his face not as flattering as he thinks. Then again, it gives him a bit of a Harrison Ford look. God, when did he get so old, Harrison Ford? But still. Graham's clearly uncomfortable. 'Aye, that. I mean ...'

'We never talked about it, back then,' I say. 'I mean, you

189

and me. I never worked up the nerve to ask you at the time. You were the Detective Inspector, you know.'

That puts a satisfied smile on his face, just like I thought it would. 'You can ask me anything, Linny.'

I sit in my chair, fiddling with my mug, rubbing a hand over my dry lips. 'Actually, there is one thing ...'

'I do feel bad, you know,' he says, putting down his mug, not letting me finish. It seems to have been a promotional gift. Funny that he should subscribe to *Psychology Today*. 'I am sorry we never caught him, Linny. I am sorry that we didn't get that bastard. I really am. Didn't do right by you.'

I hold on to my mug, looking at him carefully. 'Jacob Mason left a note at mine last night.'

Graham furrows his brow. 'A note? What did it say?'

'Just to meet him tomorrow at eight,' I say.

'I wouldn't go on a date with that man,' Graham advises me sagely.

'I don't think this is about a date.'

'Then what do you think it's about?'

When I don't answer, his expression turns sour. 'Linny, you can't seriously believe that this man has anything useful to tell you. He can barely remember his mum's birthday, let alone anything that happened twenty years ago. He *beats* his mum, for fuck's sake.'

I wet my lips. Swallow heavily. Work up all my courage. And then I go for it, finally, just go for it. 'Listen, Graham, he drove me home that night,' I say. 'Did you kno—'

I'm surprised when I don't even get to finish. 'No, he didn't,' Graham interrupts.

190

My expression turns incredulous. 'How do you—'

Again he won't let me finish, cutting me off so sharply that I flinch. 'I know because it was me who broke the two of them out of that bathroom.'

That makes me go quiet. 'Jay remembers it differently,' I say, treading carefully. At least Miss Luca does.

'Jacob's a bloody alcoholic!'

Graham obviously has trouble reining in his temper. His voice has risen, making me flinch. *Don't back down now. Don't back down.* 'You never said anything about breaking them out.'

'They were my boys for the Olympics!' he hisses. Closes his eyes, takes a few deep breaths. 'They were on drugs. Might have counted as doping. I'd have had to kick them right off the team if I'd told anyone. So I told Oliver Dawson to stick with the story about his watch instead. It wasn't untrue, anyway. He'd really broken it trying to get them out. Besides, it's all in the report. I just didn't want the entire village to know.'

I stare at him. Did Jay lie to Miss Luca, then? But why would he lie about such a thing? Why put himself at the scene of the crime?

Graham's trying to calm himself back down. 'Listen, I really appreciate that you're back, Linny. But it's messing with your head. Stirring up this old business. It's been twenty years, Linn. Most people don't remember what they had for breakfast when you ask them at dinner. They'll simply make something up. And it'll feel true to them, too, but it's not. Nothing any of us says they remember about that night would hold up as evidence in a court of law. It's been too long.'

I look down. The kettle has boiled, but neither of us goes to get it. He rubs a hand over his tired face, looking at the floor as well. 'I'm really sorry,' he says.

'And what about Teo?' I ask.

'What about him?'

'He was at the house that night?'

Graham's expression darkens. 'Oh, believe me. He was definitely there.'

I nod around the lump in my throat. My windpipe. Then I rise. 'Thanks for the tea. In a bit, Graham.'

For a moment, he seems to want to say something else. We look each other in the eye. He opens his mouth.

But then he just bends back over the file on the table, and I walk out.

THE DETECTIVE INSPECTOR

It's good she still comes to talk to me, even though she knows full well there's nothing I can do. What would I do about a bottle on her doormat? Some mischief-maker could have come down to the house to drink. They wouldn't have to know somebody was living there again. They might have seen the car, but you know what kids are like these days. All this binge drinking, though it's got a little better. But when they don't binge drink, they binge watch TV. Netflix. Something. As long as it's on a screen the size of a stamp, it seems to be good enough for them.

I still think Sue and Mark shouldn't have left her alone, God rest their souls. You can't leave a girl alone at night. It's sad, but that's how the world is. That's what I think when I see one of those slut walks, you know, there were quite a few of them for some time, not so much any more. Or when I hear of that MeToo thing (that also seems to be mainly happening on stamp-sized screens). It's not that I don't approve of what they're doing. It's great they're expressing themselves and all that, but that's not the real world, is it? In the real world, if you leave a lass like Lovely Linny alone in a house for a night, she gets assaulted.

Or, well. She was so drunk. She might not have said no. She might have liked it, even. She was in that school play once, something about Troy, and you can't tell me she didn't enjoy some of the things that happened to her up there on that stage. And if you knew what the boys were saying about her in the locker rooms ...

Don't get me wrong. I don't blame her. I'm just saying something wasn't quite right with Little Linny. Something's never been quite right with her.

LINN

His doorbell looks just the same as it did last night, only now it's light out.

Again I stand in front of Teo's flat, absolutely still. The smell of mint and cardamom and coriander is wafting out from the restaurant, where they must be preparing for lunch hour.

Nothing any of us says they remember would hold up as evidence in a court of law. It's been too long.

Graham's words are haunting me. He's right, isn't he? Memories are famously unreliable.

But there was somebody at my house. Last night.

And the inconsistencies, I'm not making those up. Graham claiming he broke Jay and Oliver out, Miss Luca saying she knows Jay drove me home.

Maybe he simply remembered it wrong.

Or maybe it's me who's remembering it wrong?

I'm standing in front of Teoman's door, my doubts eating

195

me alive, gnawing through my insides like cobra lilies. I came here because I thought the nightshade made me remember something. If I can't trust myself, then who can I trust?

Staring at Teo's doorbell, I know I have to ring it. He's the last one I haven't seen. The last chance that something might be brought back to me. Something that will convince Graham, Miss Luca, myself, that I'm not going insane.

If only I could bring myself to lift my finger. Closing my eyes, I remember what Ms Dündar taught me. Think of the nightshade in my pocket and how it sent me on this mad quest for a memory I may have only imagined after all. I take out the pocket mirror I never use for anything but this, look into it and focus on the bridge of my nose. *Your arm is lifting. Your arm is lifting. Your arm is lifting.*

I feel my arm lift of its own accord. Once more, I use the propulsion to go all the way. Without giving myself a chance to think, I ring the doorbell. And then I am glad I am frozen to the spot. If I weren't, I'd already be running.

Staring at nothing but the dark brown wood of the door, at the old-fashioned milky glass, I wait.

Just wait.

The smell of yoghurt, of fresh fruit, of spices, intensifies. I can hear a stove being fired up.

Nothing happens.

Inside the restaurant, voices are murmuring. Behind me, cars are coming up and down the road. Inside my head, I can hear my heart pounding.

Still nothing.

All right. I tried. Nobody can say I didn't try.

Maybe Graham was right.

I turn around, feeling both lighter and heavier. Nobody can say I didn't try.

'Linn.'

I recognise that voice. I would recognise it anywhere.

There he is. Standing right behind me. Staring at me, an expression of utter disbelief on his face. Holding two plastic bags in his hands, filled to the brim with groceries. I wasn't prepared to see him. Not in this tailored navy pinstripe suit, black shirt and black tie, his large hands clutching the plastic bags. His stubble. I wasn't prepared to see that he too has grown older, even taller, broad-shouldered as ever, but temples greying, eyes serious.

Most of all, I wasn't prepared for his grin. That mischievous grin, as unchanged as the trees in the woods and the stones of Cobblestone Snicket. 'Linn!'

He drops his bags where he stands, strides towards me and pulls me into a hug.

My entire body convulses. And then it relaxes. Before I know it, I am hugging him back, pressing his body so close to mine that I can feel his chest push into mine every time he breathes. 'Fuck me,' Teo says when he separates, beaming like a madman as he looks at me. 'Fuck me, you're here. I never thought I'd see you again. I ... Fuck, this is incredible!'

I never thought I'd see him again, either.

Judging from his expression, he is similarly overwhelmed, rambling like a person in shock. 'Sorry I wasn't in, I was just getting some ...' He motions to his abandoned groceries. Then turns red as he quickly reclaims then, taking them out of an elderly woman's path to escape her glare. 'Captain Obvious, aren't I? Would you like a cuppa? Come in, come up. Please, no, I insist. I got this excellent Assam, it's literally from New Zealand, I didn't even know they grew tea ...'

My heart jumps as we climb the stairs to the second floor and he unlocks the door of his flat, trying to balance his keys and the bags while putting away his earbuds at the same time. 'Sorry, I didn't have time to tidy up.'

He wouldn't have needed to say so. The flat we enter is meticulous. We step right into the open-plan living area, sofa and armchairs in the centre, a sizeable kitchen at the far end of the room, as well as a couple of doors, presumably leading to the bathroom and the bedroom. The interior design is flawless, looks like it's straight out of a magazine, state-of-the-art kitchen appliances, polished hardwood floors and modern art up on the walls. Only the sofa, where he motions for me to sit, looks a little worse for wear.

I remember it with a twist to the gut as I sink into it. It used to be his parents'.

He is still talking as he leaves the groceries on the kitchen counter and switches the kettle on, a fashionable thing, Italian design, it looks like. He puts the radio on as he works; it seems to be an instinctive gesture. 'Since when have you been back? I can't believe that you're here. I really can't. And then again, it feels so natural. So right, to see you standing there, you know what I mean?'

I stare at him, his words shaking me to the core. He is looking at me like he means it. 'Are you back? Or just visiting?' he goes on. 'I am so sorry to hear about your parents. I was shocked when Mum called to tell me ... Came up for the funeral, but you weren't ... You know, I thought, but then you ... Anyway. Why did you raid their closet?'

'I ... What?' I manage to squeeze out. I think I might be staring at him like a simpleton. He does not seem to mind, still grinning at me as he takes out his New Zealand tea, glancing at Mum's jacket and Dad's boots as he bustles through his kitchen. My lips form a grin of their own accord. My body is tingling. It is like sitting in his parents' living room, playing Karaoke Studio on his sister's NES, her first video game console, both of us shouting Japanese pop songs into the same microphone. It is like sitting across from him at my parents' kitchen table, building towers out of tea mugs, snorting with laughter. Like lying next to each other on my bed, talking about our favourite superheroes and why my mum's sad so much and his can't work here, even though she has a psychotherapy diploma.

'How are your parents, then?' I ask. Something lurches inside me when I remember them. Mrs Dündar's open heart and sharp eyes, looking right through you, and Mr Dündar's way of staring at his veggies, as gently as anyone could look at anything.

'Excellent. They have this amazing place in Blackpool now,' he says, the water already boiling. 'Right on the seafront. Makes me jealous. They're coming to visit next week. I don't steal their clothes, though.'

'I don't steal my parents' clothes,' I protest, my mouth twitching into a smile as I watch him pour the water, his fingers wrapped around the kettle, as elegant as the thing itself. He has always had that about him, Teo. That elegance. My voice sounds giddy even to my own ears. There's a rush in my belly, in my chest.

He laughs as he joins me on the sofa, carrying two steaming cups and a kitchen timer. It's counting down from two minutes thirty seconds, two twenty-nine, two twenty-eight ... 'Forgive me for demasking you, but I'd recognise that coat anywhere, Caroline.'

'Oh, would you, Teoman?' I say, falling into our pattern as if it was only yesterday that we last saw each other. I thought about him so much, and tried not to think about him at all, but none of that seems to matter now. It's like I'm operating on muscle memory.

'Aye,' he says, putting on a solemn expression. Such fondness spreads through me at that word. Hearing it from him. 'You don't forget the coat that was wrapped around your shoulders every goddamn time you threw up in your best friend's parents' bathroom.'

I snort out a laugh. 'Oh, my God, yeah,' I say. 'Mum was a bit pushy, wasn't she?'

'She cared,' he says, adopting a philosophical tone. 'As your dad said the first time I threw up at your place: "We've all been there."'

'God, Dad said that?'

'While he was patting my back, too.'

The laughter keeps bubbling up. It rushes through me like blood, warm and quick. 'Where had I got off to?' I ask just as the timer rings. He takes out the tea leaves, then hands me a mug. Mine is from MYKONOS, GREECE. His was bought at a museum in Paris. 'You were with Anna, I guess? Sorry, I didn't have the resources at the time to worry too much about the two of you.'

Looking at him, I raise the mug to my lips. He is staring intently at me with his dark eyes, like volcanic ash. At least that's what Rachel Simmons said about them in fifth form (she'd been to Hawaii in the summer, we'd all been very jealous). For a moment, I don't know why he is looking at me like that. Then I take the first sip.

The texture is smooth, soft, like liquid chocolate. The taste is rich like cream. I can feel my eyes fall close. 'My God, that is bloody amazing tea.'

'Did I promise too much?' he says, looking positively gleeful. He does not seem to feel awkward. Then again, a man like him probably never feels awkward. He even looks like he finds the time to work out.

Actually, he looks exactly the way you want to look when you are approaching forty. Fit. Successful. Having a place in life. Not like a character from a Lily Allen song. 'What have you been doing with yourself?' I ask, pretending I didn't stalk him on social media.

'This and that,' he says, waving it away, not taking his eyes off me, as if I will suddenly disappear if he dares to look away even for a second. He always was sheepish about his success. Even his good grades: his parents and us would be the only ones he told about them. 'Went to uni. I'm a producer, TV and some things online. Advertising at first, then feature films and documentaries. Founded my own company. Advertising is bringing in the revenue, documentaries are what I love. Feature film is almost impossible to break into, it's insane ... We shot a few things, though, and it's great to be on location. Though pretty stressful.' He furrows his brow. Then grins. 'No, to be honest, I hate being on location. But it sure makes for good shots. And people go crazy when you post pictures on Twitter from location shoots, you wouldn't believe it.' He laughs, embarrassed, looking away then, if only for a moment. 'That's all boring, though. What about you?'

'Oh, no,' I say, my heart plummeting as he looks back at me. 'You don't get to do that. Tease me with film stars and location shoots and shitstorms and then change the subject.'

I don't want to talk about myself. Now that I have seen them again, I remember it all: everything we talked about when we were teenagers, everything we wanted to do, everything we dreamed of. Teo had always wanted to be someone. He'd watched his parents batting down stones to carve out a place for themselves here, he'd watched them being put down and humiliated and smiling through it all, building a life for their family. He wanted to show everyone that this place was theirs, was his. It made sense he would go into film, into something that people would see.

And Anna, she'd always wanted to be a translator if she couldn't be a singer. It just made sense to her. She who didn't speak a word of English, her first day of school. Who was put into a form with people two years younger, feeling humiliated every time she walked into the classroom. It made sense.

I dreamt of things. And it wasn't going to the supermarket and baking three-tiered cakes and going to a film première in London every once in a while, waving at the stars when I was in a particularly adventurous mood. I dreamt of NASA, of the Moon, Mars even, being a doctor, a programmer or, best of all, a botanist in space. That's what I'd wanted to be. A botanist on the Moon.

'It's really not as exciting as it sounds,' he says, his voice darker now, calmer. The smile is still on his face, but it is heavier, somehow. Like it's been fought for. Like there are some things he would rather not talk about. 'To be honest, it's a very quick, superficial business. Even if you do a good thing, everyone's forgotten the next day. And you forget, too. Nothing stays.'

He looks me in the eyes. I look back. 'I'm sorry,' I say.

'Don't be,' he says. His eyes are running over my face. 'It has upsides, too. Money. Recognition. I go to dinner with MPs. Plus, I'm trying to do different things. Some of those documentaries, you should see them. We did something on the situation in Calais – it was un-fucking-believable. Or that protest in Turkey, you know, the men in skirts? I wore a skirt, too, spent weeks in Istanbul, it was ...' His thumb is gliding along the rim of his mug. 'I mean, my job is mainly to get these things funded, but that's the world we live in. Unless we want to talk about capitalism, and I'd rather talk about you. What about you?'

I look at his hands. Can't keep looking him in the eyes but can't look away from him either. His veins are stark as well, but it suits him. They don't look like mine. 'God, I mean, what do you say about nineteen years?' I try to laugh. I feel the sudden urge not to disappoint him. To tell him not a single bit of the depressing truth. Not like I told Anna. My mind is racing, searching for something to say. Anything. 'I'm feeling good,' I finally say, glancing at his face. I wonder when the last time was that I said that and didn't lie.

I'm happy. Since Anna sat down in my kitchen, that's what I've been feeling. All the tension bleeds from my shoulders. So maybe Graham's right. Maybe what the nightshade made me remember never happened. Maybe my two best friends didn't look guilty that night at all.

Maybe I took this away from me, this feeling, this friendship, for no reason at all.

Teo smiles at me, openly, honestly. 'I'm very glad.'

Maybe that means that I can finally have it back. This feeling.

His fingers are tapping the rim of his mug now. Tap, tap, tap.

'And,' I say, rushing out the words. 'You? Are you alone here? I mean ... you ... I wouldn't have ...'

I stop myself. He laughs kindly, but it seems even harder won than the smile I saw. 'Aw, ta, Linn. That's flattering. I'm on my own, though. Got this place for something we're shooting. Some location scouting, you know. It's just a temporary thing.'

I look at him, surprised. 'Somebody said you were reopening your dad's greengrocery?'

Teo laughs. 'Who said that?'

And then I am laughing too. 'Somebody. Anybody. Doesn't matter.'

I'm fucking happy.

'God, I'd forgotten what it's like in such a small village,' he says. 'It was Kaitlin, wasn't it? Anyway, this is a friend's flat. She's abroad for a month. I'm watering her flowers and feeding her cat. She was nice enough to put my name on the bell so that I could get my mail sent somewhere while I was out here scouting for the shoot. She's a dear. My parents gave her this sofa when they moved to Blackpool.'

He's scooted closer. I think. Our legs are almost brushing. 'And you?' he asks.

'Me what?' I say. The smile won't leave my face. All these years, I've made myself go without it. Because of something I thought I remembered. Because I was convinced they'd lied to me.

'You out here all alone?'

His finger is still tapping the rhythm.

'Yes,' I say, though I almost add, *not any more*.

He grins.

It is at that moment that his doorbell rings.

Ding, ding, ding.

I blanch.

Teo rises to open the door. I can't breathe. Hurried steps resound in the stairwell.

It's Anna who appears in the doorframe.

I hear Teo's sharp intake of breath. 'Anna,' he says. Turns back to look at me. She spots me before he has even finished speaking.

There they are. Both of them looking at me. Their faces flash in front of my vision, mingling, at seven, at twelve, at fifteen, at seventeen. The feeling rushes through me. Warmth spreads all through my body, rushes from the top of my head to the tips of my toes, making my skin tingle, my eyes water. It's like I'm flying. Like I weigh nothing at all.

That's why I didn't want to see them. Not because it would be horrible. But because it would be brilliant. Because it would make me remember what it felt like: racing to Bolton Castle on the same bike, wind in your hair, arms and hands holding your body. Telling each other about your stupid dreams, once you'd finally got out of this place, even though it was scary to think about the future, though not so scary when they were with you. How they made you believe that you could be a botanist in space if that's what you wanted. That you could be anything.

And then waking up, bloody, and your best friends being taken to the police station. Your best friends being questioned.

Your best friends – and the police think it may have been them. I know what Graham truly thinks. No matter how often he says it was a stranger. He thinks it was Teo. That Anna kept quiet, gave him an alibi. He always thought it was Teo.

'I knew it was you,' Teo is saying to Anna.

She looks at him. 'Of course you did.'

But maybe I was wrong. Maybe it's *me* who remembers the story all wrong. Who tells it all wrong. My windpipe constricts. It feels like climbing vines are wrapping themselves around it, growing stronger by the second, pulling faster, choking me from the inside. I can't breathe. My hands shoot up to my throat, but there's nothing I can do. The climbing vines press and throttle and choke me. I rise. 'Thanks for the tea,' I try to say, but I don't know if it comes out garbled. I can't stay here. It's too much. The pain, the warmth, the vines.

'Stay,' Teo says quickly. Something passes over his face, something almost like desperation.

'No,' I answer. My blood is pulsing in my ears. My knees are shaking so hard I can barely stand. 'Sorry.' If it wasn't them who lied, maybe it was me. All these years.

'Dinner, then,' he says, taking a step towards me, carefree expression back on his face. 'The Indian downstairs is excellent. Tomorrow?'

'Sure,' I say, choking the words out past the climbing plants' deathly grip. I think of the first drawing Jay gave to me, of Oliver singing to me at our wedding, of Teo pulling me close and Anna kissing me in my bed, and climbing to the top of Bolton Castle together to get as close to the Moon as we could.

'Good,' he says, moving towards me for a hug. Anna's hand brushes mine as I slide past her. I breathe in her scent, paper and forests and the cold fresh air. Of course she would ring the doorbell like that. It was how we rang the bell for each other, always did. It doesn't mean she comes to my house at night to terrorise me.

Maybe there's no one coming to my house at all.

I am practically running down the staircase, out the door and to the car. I wish I could calm myself down, but seeing the two of them together, the three of us, like it was ... like nothing had changed and my life had gone according to plan. What if that night had never happened? What if we'd grown up, if we'd all gone to uni, I'd never become a stranger to my own parents, the place I used to call home; if I'd never thought: *Was it you?*

Was it you who did this to me?

I could have been happy.

When I arrive back at the house, no one's waiting for me on the front porch. The chimes are right where they are supposed to be.

My knees still weak, I put the kettle on in the kitchen, then rub my palms against each other to warm them up again. It does not seem to be working. When I laugh, it sounds hysterical. I look at my distorted reflection in the kettle on the stove where it's heating up. When I lift the kettle to pour water, my hand clenches, like a seizure taking hold of my body, twisting all my limbs. The water comes splashing all over my hand.

A shout is torn from my throat as the scalding water hits my skin. With a deafening clatter, I drop the kettle back onto the stove. That's what happens when I allow myself to feel. That's why I turned myself numb, inside and out. Pain shoots through me as my skin burns, my mind revelling in the ability to feel, relishing it. Warmth, lightness, the rush.

The moment I realise what is happening, I shrink from myself, shrink so suddenly that I stumble backwards. A cooling pack, quick, a cooling pack.

My palms still cramping, my legs trembling, I go sit on the sofa, pressing the pack to my hand. Distraction, I need a distraction. I turn on the telly and sit and stare. It's difficult to keep track of time passing as I watch people cook and bake things, my hand burning. It's not enough, though. I get up hastily, return to the kitchen, pull out all the ingredients I need for cinnamon rolls. Turning on the radio, I get to work. Distraction.

By the time the cinnamon rolls are in the oven, I feel a little more like I am back in my own body. Like I'm in control. On the radio, the news comes on. It's midnight. God. My eyes wander over the mess I've made, the kitchen counter covered in flour, the dirty dishes piling up in the sink under the window, the burnt skin on my hand. My face heats as I stare at my hand. Shame. I remember that feeling, too. I'm only lucky the burn isn't too bad.

With joy comes pain. Everybody knows that. You can't feel the joy without the pain, the peace without the fury, isn't that what they say?

If only my fury wasn't so prone to turn on myself.

Stepping up to the sink, I put in the plug to let the dishes soak for a bit. While I wait for the water to fill the sink, still cooling my hand, feeling the heat of embarrassment all over my body, I look outside. The window faces the drive, but I cannot see any of it, because it is pitch-black outside. Not the gravel, not the front porch or the steep climb and the trees.

As I stare out of the window, I realise that I am still expecting my parents to come home. Returning from a day's hike, or a show in Manchester, or work, like they used to, arm in arm, giggling sometimes, exhausted other times, but always holding each other up.

The sadness pulls me down. Pulls at every limb of my body, an inescapable black mass, like the black hole at the centre of the Milky Way. I cannot give in to it. If I give in to it, I'll ... I've got to push it away.

I still cannot believe they are dead.

I cannot believe there is nothing but my reflection in the dark glass, staring back at me. That burn on my hand and the liquid on my cheeks, dripping off the tip of my chin.

As I keep staring, it takes me a moment to realise that I am perfectly visible from out there.

Somebody could be standing on the other side of the glass, only six feet away from me, and I wouldn't even know. Right now. Staring right at me.

I shiver and turn away. Stop it.

For a moment, I reconsider the hotel. I even think of Anna, a mile down the road.

I could go to her. I could trust them. Could go and see her, with fresh rolls even.

It's past midnight, Caroline. I draw the lace curtains and return to the living room with a new cooling pack, back to the telly. Keeping my hand as still as I can, I consume twenty minutes of nonsense TV until the kitchen timer rings. I take out the rolls and spread them on a cooling rack on the counter. I'm surprisingly tired. But the dishes first.

I pack the dishwasher, then fill up the sink once more with fresh water, for the bowls that wouldn't fit into the machine. While it fills, I try very hard not to look out of the window. What would be the first thing I saw, I wonder, if somebody was standing on the other side? Their silhouette? A movement?

Don't be ridiculous. Nobody's out there. Once the water is ready, I wash up the bowls. My skin is prickling. I make it a point not to look at the window. Like as a teenager, when I made it a point not to look under the bed any more, to check for monsters. Monsters don't exist.

My hands are dripping with water and dishwashing liquid by the time I finish, and I feel pins and needles under my burnt skin. I pull out the plug, then shake off the wet drops from my fingers before I dry them on the kitchen towel. There is a tight feeling in my chest. I am staring at my feet now. The hairs at the back of my neck are standing up. Fear uncoils inside my stomach, irrationally, rising through my body, from my belly through my ribcage, clogging up my throat.

Fear is what comes with feeling. Sadness. Desperation. Panic. There is nothing there. I will prove it to myself.

Jerking my head upwards, I finally look at the window.

All I see are the lace curtains, and my reflection in the gaps. My drawn face, older than I think it should look. My forehead furrowed like my mum's the last time I saw her. My eyes, blinking too quickly. There is no silhouette, no movement.

See?

I stare at my reflection. Remember Anna sitting in this kitchen, laughing about the rifle; remember Teo's leg against mine. Feel the smile tug at my mouth.

I watch my lips curl upwards. That's better. I watch closely. Wait.

Just where my mouth is, I see something. Not a movement. Not a silhouette.

The window fogs up.

Just a small circle on the glass. As large as the exhalation of a breath.

I'm too far away for it to be my breath.

I stumble backwards. The window fogs up again. As if someone is breathing against it. Horror freezes my lungs, my lips, my vocal cords. Its long fingers wrap around my throat and press. I choke. Letters appear on the window. One after the other.

D

I

N

G

Panic surges.

I run. Blindly, I stumble backwards into the living room. Crashing into the sofa, I fall over, fall down. The edge of the couch table catches the side of my head. It cuts my skin. Pain pounds through me. I drag myself back up, turn around, run up the stairs. Ding, ding, ding. The doorbell rings. The wood creaks under my stomping feet. Downstairs, the rusty lock of the front door groans. I run. Run to the bedroom door. I throw it shut behind me. Turn the key. Ding, ding, ding. That ridiculous key. As if it could stop anyone. I walk backwards until the backs of my knees hit the bed. I don't fall over. I don't want to lie in this bed. If they come up, I don't want to be lying in a bed.

It rings again. Rings again. Again. I'm seventeen all over again. Every time it rings, I feel it: stumbling down the stairs as a teenager, the wood hard under my bare feet. The tracks of sweaty fingers on my skin. The hand in my hair, gripping so tightly I thought the scalp would come off. The taste of sweet, deadly berries in my mouth.

It was a night just like this. I was all alone.

I sink down onto the floor. Turn myself numb. Turn myself hollow. I am hollow. This isn't my body. I'm nothing.

It rings. Rings. Rings.

I could look out. The window, showing the drive. I could see them. Go. Go and look!

But I can't move. I can't move.

I am moving. I am moving. I stare at the dresser. At nothing but the dresser. *I'm moving.*

The ringing stops. For a moment. Ten seconds. Twenty. Staring at the dried lavender below the ceiling, I squeeze my eyes shut. *I'm turning my head. I'm turning my head. I'm turning my head.*

Slowly, my head starts turning. Towards the window. *Look out. It's dark in here. They can't see you. You might see them.*

I open my eyes and look out. Thirty seconds. Forty.

There is nothing to see except the night sky. Except the tops and trunks of the trees. Moonlight is scratching their shadows into the ground, their fingers, creeping towards the house.

Then I hear something downstairs. A creaking sound.

Was that the front door?

Chapter 5

*I*t is the first day of the new millennium. Three seconds in. A group of teenagers is celebrating in a forest. All the underage drinkers of the surrounding villages, sixty, seventy, maybe even a hundred.

Three seconds in and Linn is looking around her. All night, all everybody has been worrying about is who their New Year's Eve kiss is going to be. Linn is looking around even while she cheers and hoots and whistles for the year 2000. Teo and Anna are on her arms, Anna on her right, Teo on her left; they're jumping up and down, all three of them.

Before midnight, all she wanted was to kiss Teo. She's been planning it for ages, right? But now that they're jumping, and she's looking around, Linn's eyes get caught on Anna's face. And Anna is gazing at her. They're both smiling. And it feels natural, drunk as she is, to throw both of her arms around Anna and kiss her on the mouth.

Teo hoots and claps. Anna smiles under the kiss. Linn puts her hands to Anna's cheeks. They're warm.

'Wow, that's hot,' someone calls out.

When they separate, Linn sees who it was. It's Jay. Jay, who's stopped drawing in class, just staring at his stupid fingerless gloves, jaw working, hair falling into his face. Oliver Dawson is standing next to him, his new best friend apparently. He's smiling shyly. Unlike Jay, who whistles. 'Now, who's up for a New Year's Eve kiss?' he asks, his grin only pretending at jovial.

Linn laughs, uncomfortable. 'We just had one.'

'A girl can't be your New Year's Eve kiss. That's cheating.' Jay pushes Oliver towards them. 'You go, mate.'

Linn feels Anna go rigid next to her. She's gone rigid herself. 'Shut up, Jay,' Linn says. Oliver mumbles something. Linn can't understand what it is. He's very quiet. And really good at swimming. There might be a scholarship in it for him. Linn likes Oliver. He never makes her feel awkward. And his arms have become really well defined with all that swimming, his frame broadening. It's hot.

But she didn't think Jay would do something like that. She even thought that they might be friends again one day soon, Jay and Anna and Teo and her. He's just trying to get back at her, isn't he?

Anna's already turned around, turned to Teo. Before he can say anything, she's pressed her mouth to his.

Linn sees it. She bites her lips, then she takes the two steps towards Oliver, grasps his jacket and kisses him. Longer than Anna.

Jay laughs but he seems pissed off. Or not pissed off. More like he's about to cry. His eyes are glistening.

But Oliver's lips feel nice. He's had vodka to drink, Linn thinks, and no orange juice either. He doesn't pull at her like other boys do, or do stupid things with his hands in her hair. He just seems to enjoy it. When she separates from him, he is smiling, a little dazed. Linn grins, then returns to Teo and Anna. She's confused. She's dizzy. It's a new millennium.

'Linn,' Anna says, reaching for her hand. 'Linn, Linn.' And then she says it again, pulling her deeper into the wood, leaving the others standing in the clearing. 'Linn, Linn, Linn.'

LINN

Is that the sound the front door makes when it opens?

Finally, I remember I have Graham's number. Yanking the piece of paper out of my pocket, I tear it. I take out my phone, but there isn't any signal. Not even a single bar. No mobile data, nothing.

I lift the hand holding the phone. No change. Then I slink into my parents' en suite. Still nothing. 'Come on,' I hiss, staring at the screen. 'Come on, come on, come on!'

It doesn't help.

That means all I can do is listen. There is something moving in the roof space, creaking wood. It could be the wind. It could be mice in the attic. Tap, tap, tap. It could be the pipes.

Or someone's climbed onto the roof. Somebody's hiding in the attic. Someone's coming up the stairs.

Coming up to the bedroom.

*

I don't even know when it was that I fell asleep. All I know is that I start awake to the sun in my eyes and the bathtub against my back. It takes me another thirty minutes to creep out of my parents' en suite and go downstairs. The first thing I do is try the front door.

It is still locked. Nobody came in last night, then. I stare at the door, clearly locked. I look at the kitchen window, cleared of all fog.

I'm not losing my mind.

Far too erratic to make any breakfast, to get dressed even, I make sure the begonias have everything they need before I drive into town in yesterday's clothes. It's Wednesday. Jay's note's still in my pocket, asking me to come see him tonight at eight. My first trip is to the Vodafone branch. 'Can we speed it up? The landline,' I ask. 'I called the number, but a couple of weeks is a little long.'

Nick looks at me. His joy has turned into vexation. 'I am really sorry, Caroline.'

'There's no signal where I live.' I try to make him see how urgent this is. I know I sound like I'm begging, but I don't care. I'm ready to beg. 'I need a phone. What if something happens? What if there's an emergency?'

His face shuts down the moment I say it. 'Vodafone cannot be held accountable for anything that happens in your home, ma'am.'

'Of course not, Nick,' I say, 'I was just wondering if ...'

'There is a procedure for such things,' Nick says. 'We make it our mission here at Vodafone to deliver only products of the highest quality. You can call the number again, maybe they can speed things up. But if you want the quality we can provide, this cannot be rushed.'

'That's ... I ... And there is no way ...'

'We make it our mission here at Vodafone to deliver only products of the highest quality. That is our foremost priority, ma'am.'

'But what if something goes wrong and I need to phone someone?'

He smiles affably. 'You want only the highest quality, don't you?'

'What I want is a landline,' I say.

'Of high quality,' he adds.

'Why are you calling me ma'am, Nick?' I ask, at a complete loss for what to say.

'Do you want to complain?' he asks immediately. 'If you wish to complain about a service provided to you, we have a form right here. You may take down my full name and send it to the branch in Leeds. You can also complain online. Do you wish to complain?'

'No, I don't want to complain, I want a landline.'

'You can also file a complaint online, ma'am,' he says. 'The address is right here on the form.'

'I don't want a complaint form, Nick!' I say, my voice rising. My hands are balling into fists.

'Is there a problem?' A woman comes over. She is wearing a smile and a suit. Her hair is very carefully put up. 'Is there a problem here, ma'am?'

I open my mouth. 'This lady isn't happy with our services,' Nick says.

'It's not that,' I say.

The lady is looking at me intently. She's wearing lip gloss, very subtly. 'I see Nick has handed you a complaint form. Has he pointed out to you that you may also complain online?'

'Yeah, but that's not what—' I say, speaking more loudly to interrupt her.

'Ma'am,' the woman says, not letting me finish, speaking even louder. 'If you get aggressive, I will have to ask you to leave the store.'

'I'm not aggressive!'

'You are, ma'am,' the lady says. The manager, it must be. 'I would ask you to leave now. We don't tolerate aggression at Vodafone. If you would like to complain, please fill out the form.'

I turn on my heels and leave.

Outside, I stand on the pavement, not moving at all. I never really smoked, not seriously, but now I yearn for a cigarette. It would make me forget about the burning pain at the backs of my eyes, the doubt devouring me from the inside out, the dried flowers at my parents' funeral. Fuck, everybody was smoking back then, weren't they? None of this holier-than-thou shit.

I'm still standing on the pavement, fantasising about throttling either Nick or that manager, when someone calls my name. 'Caroline!'

Teo is jogging up to me. He is smiling widely, but his face falls a little when he sees my expression. 'Teoman,' I say.

'What's wrong?' he asks, coming to stand in front of me. He does not pull me into a hug this time. I wish he would.

I can smell his aftershave. There are no grocery bags this time, but he's holding a Mars bar. He's always loved Mars bars. It's like a punch in the gut that everything about him still feels as good as it used to. He's equipped with sunglasses and a camera today, wearing another suit, this one charcoal grey.

'Vodafone isn't exactly customer-friendly,' I say, my voice beleaguered. 'Did you know Nick works for them now?'

'Nick?' he asks, forehead creasing. 'Nick What's-his-name? The bloke who fell into the river that Guy Fawkes Night?'

'Yep.'

'How unnerving,' he says.

'What is?'

'For a moment, I'd completely forgotten Nick Parker ever existed,' he says, then offers his arm to me. 'You want to come with me? I'm going location scouting.'

I stare at his arm. Already the warmth is coming back. The lightness. Maybe this is worth the pain.

'On foot?' I ask.

'Are you kidding?' he says. 'This is the entertainment industry. *Nothing* happens on foot.'

I laugh. The moment I put my arm through his, the moment we start walking, the warmth spreads through every last inch of my body. We fall back into step, the familiar pace of his legs. We used to do this a lot, the three of us. I always took the middle spot. My right arm feels strangely empty. 'What sort of location are you looking for?' I ask as we make for the short-stay parking lot by the bank and the police station.

Teo pulls a face. 'Just give a shout whenever you see sheep.'

'I'll be very busy then.'

It makes me giddy to hear him laugh. We walk down the High Street while he explains his project.

'What did you want with Vodafone, then?' Teo asks once he's finished. 'Still no reception in the dip?'

I shake my head. 'There's not even any Internet any more. Landline's gone, too.'

'No Internet?' he asks, pretending at outrage. 'How do you survive?'

I see he is watching me closely. Worried I'll run out on him again, maybe, like last night. He's back to smiling, but there are bags under his eyes. The way he looked yesterday comes back to me, that expression of desperation. I wonder how it fits into the life of a successful producer who dines with MPs. 'I remember when your parents got their modem,' is what I say. 'I mean, do you remember that?'

'Don't remind me,' he says, face set in a painful expression. 'Prehistoric. That sound it made when it tried to go online. Do you remember you had to actually *go online*? And they charged you for … I don't know. Every minute? Every second?'

'Must have seriously limited your porn consumption,' I say. For a moment, I wonder if I've overstepped.

'And yours,' he says nonchalantly. I stifle a giggle as we walk past the police station. Through the glass front, I can see Graham at the counter. He looks up, smiling at first. It occurs to me that I could ask him to come with me tonight. To see Jay. Then I wouldn't have to go alone.

Nothing any of us says they remember would hold up as evidence in a court of law.

223

Graham raises his hand. I wave back at him as we move on.

'Who are you waving to?' Teo asks, slowing down.

'Just Graham,' I say.

'Lovely,' Teo says, still smiling, but it looks a bit forced. I look back at Graham.

He isn't smiling any more, either.

'Let's get going,' Teo says, setting us back into motion. He's still holding his Mars bar.

'Glad to see that some things don't change,' I say.

'Huh?' He glances at me. Pointedly, I look at the Mars bar. Embarrassed, he laughs. It is a welcome sound. 'Well, yeah. "Don't say that, Wendy, we'll never grow up" and all that.'

Something lurches inside me. 'That was the saddest book ever.'

'I know. Still makes me cry.' He falls silent for a moment before he shakes his head. 'Come on, let's get to the car. There's a radio play on BBC4 that I don't want to miss.'

'You know your radio schedule,' I joke. He grins, but it doesn't reach his eyes.

We're turning into the parking lot when I hear it: 'Linny! Wait up!'

I turn around, untucking my arm from Teo's. It's Graham, coming towards us with measured strides, sucking in his belly as he does, puffing up his chest. 'Ey up, Graham,' I say. I could tell him about last night. But then what would he say? What would he say but *Was there anything taken? Was anybody hurt?*

'I saw you going past, couldn't help but come out,' he says.

He isn't looking at me, though. Instead, he's fixated on Teo. 'Hello, Teoman. Long time no see.'

'Detective Inspector,' Teo says smoothly, but his expression has changed entirely. A professional mask has settled over his features. 'It's good to see you.'

'You back for long?' Graham asks conversationally.

'Just scouting for a shoot,' Teo answers. 'I'm in film now.'

'Oh, wow,' Graham says, his voice dripping with irony. Then he turns back to me: 'Linny, say, d'you wanna come in for a bit? I wanted to ask you something about … your situation.'

Teo furrows his brow but doesn't ask. 'I'll be by later,' I say, feeling the warmth drain away and clinging to it.

Teo is already turning to his car, but Graham speaks up: 'Because I was thinking. Maybe it *was* time we looked into it again.'

Slowly, Teo turns back around. 'Look into what again?'

'I'll be by later, Graham, all right?' I say sharply.

Graham raises his eyebrows but then just pulls me into a hug to say goodbye. Pressing his entire body up against mine, as if he doesn't want to let me go. It doesn't feel comfortable, but I don't want to make a scene. 'In a bit, Linny.'

Teo's car is, to my surprise, a Toyota Prius. I'd have thought you had to drive something more pretentious when you were in film. When I tell him this, he laughs, but his heart clearly isn't in it. I'm glad he doesn't ask what Graham was talking about. Especially because the honest answer might have to be *nothing*.

As soon as the engine starts, so does the radio. He is right:

a radio play has just started, an adaptation of *The Talented Mister Ripley*. I tune out the voices and focus on the land-scape.

By the time we've done five miles, I've shouted 'sheep' approximately twenty times. I have forgotten how much I missed this place. The Dales, bare hills and old walls and the peaks that look like you're going straight to Mordor, the biggest adventure of your life. And what I haven't missed. The smell of dung, for example. I'm pretty sure it's too late in the year to be fertilising.

After an hour of driving around familiar back roads – roads that we sped along on bikes, not caring whether there was someone coming towards us, honking carelessly before taking the next sharp bend – we take a break. 'Aren't you famished?' Teo asks, and that's when I remember that's what we'd say, never hungry, always famished, and how hungry I actually am.

Flayed instead of scared. That's another thing we say. Flayed and famished.

Teo stops at the Black Rabbit, a great pub we never made it to when we were teenagers because it was so far out of the way. We sit by the windows, warm light falling in to touch our neck and shoulders, a view of the pond outside, glittering in the sunlight, ducks gliding past on the water. A couple of tourists from the Peak District are finishing up their drinks at the table next to us. They ask us about the sights, what to see, what to do. We chat until they are off, falling into an easy silence. Teo waits until we've both got our food until he says: 'Don't you think it's funny the copper'd call you Linny?'

I shrug, feeling my insides twist. 'It's just what he's used to, I guess.'

Teo drops it.

We spend all day driving around the Dales. By the time we get back into town, the police station is already closed. It occurs to me Teo might have done this on purpose. There doesn't seem to be any love lost between him and Graham.

'Dinner,' he says when we get out. 'You said we would.'

I look at him. The sun's setting already. I'm famished again. Dusk draws long shadows onto the High Street. Only a couple more hours till I've got to go see Jay.

Maybe I won't have to go alone.

'I didn't go to see Graham,' I say.

Teo is looking at me intently. 'It's too late now,' he says. 'He's gone home for the night.'

The police station is dark.

'Dinner it is then,' I say.

Maybe I can trust him.

THE DETECTIVE INSPECTOR

Fine, you know what? I'll be honest. I don't like him. Teoman Dündar. Never have.

Or it's not that I don't like him. Don't know him, do I? Not really. It's that he has always behaved strangely.

It's been nineteen years, you say? Move on, is what you think?

Okay, sure. But look at what he's doing now. Look at what he's doing to Little Linny. He knows she's married, doesn't he? He knows she belongs to someone else. Still he takes her on a drive around the country, all day. 'Location scouting.' Right. It's a credit to Linny that she wouldn't see through that, that she wouldn't suspect anything, that she'd see the best in people. But it's pretty naïve, too. No offence. That's just what men are like.

And I get it, you know. I get why she would go with him. Anything that would make her feel safer, I guess. That's understandable, isn't it?

Though of course you could say she wouldn't have needed to put herself in this position in the first place, couldn't you? I mean, no one made her, did they? No one made her stay in an old house all by herself in the middle of the woods. You've got to have some common sense.

And him too, Teoman, I get him. I mean, look at her. For a woman her age, she's stayed in shape, somewhat.

Oh, you can't say a thing like that any more, can you? Well, I just did, so deal with it. She looks great, our Little Linny, for a woman her age. It's not her fault she's growing old, is it? I mean, she could lose a pound or two maybe, but who am I to judge, really?

So, Teoman, mate, I get you. I do, really. Who wouldn't want to have a go if they had the chance?

The thing is, you don't do this kind of thing. If you know she's taken, you don't do that. It's just not decent. And I don't want him to give her any ideas. I mean, it's painfully obvious that he's out of her league. That he's just in it for a bit of fun.

Besides.

Doesn't she think, not once …?

I mean, she told me how her doorbell rings at night. What she thinks is happening at night, anyway. Just like they used to ring the doorbell when they played knock, knock, ginger when they were kids. Doesn't she think about that at all?

I'm just saying.

I mean, does she know he's been to prison? I called up a few colleagues down south when he came back, just to make sure. Arson, they said. It's not on his record because he was sentenced under juvenile law, but still. Looks like young Teo used to think burning places down was just his sort of evening entertainment.

And, I mean, you know what the Turks did to the Armenian women and children, don't you, back then? It's not the same thing, of course. I'm just saying. If she needs someone to protect her, why would she pick him? Wouldn't it make much more sense to ask me? Or Oliver Dawson?

What? Oh, yeah. Yeah, see, I have been thinking about getting in touch with him. Oliver, I mean. Ever since she came in that first day, actually, looking so scared and confused. I tried looking him up, but he isn't listed, and I don't have his contact details any more. The last phone number I have was from when he was a student. A landline. Dead end. I'd ask his parents, but they moved away after the divorce. This was years ago. Pretty much the same time that he did, actually. His mum went back to where she'd grown up, some place in the South, a village close to Brighton, I think.

His dad, though. He didn't move quite as far, Peter Dawson didn't. He's in Sheffield. Actually, I might still have his number somewhere. I couldn't find it a couple of nights ago, but maybe in one of the boxes in the attic, with the papers I couldn't squeeze into the study any more. I'll have to have a proper look on the weekend.

And until then, I'm just supposed to sit here and watch this happen?

Tell you what: I won't just sit here. No, I won't.

I'll do something.

LINN

The Indian place is packed. Teo is raving about their lassis as we sit at the last empty table. Everyone and their mum seem to have come here tonight, and there's no corner to hide in. Teo doesn't even seem to notice that we are being watched. 'I haven't been coming here enough,' he says as a waiter hands us the menus. 'It's insane how crazy I am about this place. I had to go without Indian food for a while, it was ... I mean, can you imagine? What would the world be without garlic naan?'

Looking at the menu, all I think is that I won't be able to hold up this lifestyle for very long. Lunch at the pub was expensive enough. I've got a bit of money on the side, of course, but maybe I shouldn't spend it on Spotted Dick or naan bread.

Come to think of it, no matter how much money you have, you should never spend it on spotted dicks.

Involuntarily, I snort. Teo raises his eyebrows at me above the menu. 'Caroline?'

'Teoman?' I ask as innocently as possible.

'What were you laughing at?'

'Nothing.' I manage to hold out for approximately seven seconds. Then, keeping an absolutely straight face, I add: 'Spotted Dick.'

Teo bursts into laughter. 'You know,' I say, still trying to hold it together, affecting a haughty tone, 'there is nothing whatsoever funny about that term. Spotted Dick is a very traditional, very tasty English dessert.'

Taking up his napkin, Teo presses it to his face. 'Stop, Linn,' he says, 'please!' but I am on a roll. I sit up primly, like Mrs Mason would have, and look at him sternly: 'I do not see what you should find so amusing about it. This country has given you refuge. It would be very ungrateful of you to laugh at its puddings, wouldn't it?'

'Poor Anna,' Teo manages to wheeze out between breathless laughter. 'God, do you remember that? How old were we, like six? I didn't even know what "dick" meant at the time.'

'Neither did Mrs Mason, apparently,' I say, finally laughing myself. I remember Anna, as small and angelic as you please, asking Teo and me under her breath in the canteen whether it was normal to have a spotted penis for pudding.

The waiter arrives to take our orders. I haven't even decided. I was so busy thinking about Anna and looking at Teo. It's hard to do one thing without the other. I don't know whom I can trust any more. But I know whom I want to trust, and he's sitting right across from me. All that's missing is Anna by our side.

I end up ordering what I always have when we go to an Indian place, a veggie Garam Masala. There was one close to our first flat, which was good, made it easier to get something nice for Oliver every once in a while. Teo picks something vegetarian himself, hands over the menu, then puts his fingers on the table, drawing absent-minded patterns on the white cloth. I'm careful not to watch his face when I say, once the waiter has left: 'I didn't know you and Anna were still in touch.'

Looking down as I am, I see his fingers clench around the knife for a moment. Then he relaxes them again. 'We weren't. Not ... Well. We weren't. But we chatted for quite a while last night. Catching up.'

'How is she doing?' I ask, trying to keep my voice matter-of-fact.

His fingers still on the white tablecloth.

I can feel him looking at me. He has a way of looking at you, Teo. 'She came to talk about you, you know.'

My heart stutters. Stops. 'What's there to talk about?' I ask, mouth twitching.

'Linn.' He's using his serious voice as he watches me scrub a hand across my face. I remember that voice of his like I remember my nan's Irish stew, Oliver's eyes, my dad's favourite lullaby, the smell of lavender in my nose that night. Like a thing that's been scratched into your skin.

I don't let him continue. Instead, I reach with my hand for his. So suddenly it's no surprise it shuts him up utterly. He hesitates. His hand twitches under mine.

But he doesn't pull back. 'Linn, Anna told me what you said to her. About you and Oliver and your flat in London.'

'It's insane, right? That we found anything that we could afford at all, and even at the end of a tube line,' I say, not moving my hand. That's all I want. Sit here with our hands touching. Nothing more.

'Absolutely,' he says, his voice tense. 'Don't ask me how long it took me to find a decent place. But as eager as I am for your real estate secrets, it was just ...' His knuckles push into mine. His thumb runs along the side of my forefinger. 'I was surprised to hear. That you and Oliver were together.'

My breath is coming in curiously short bursts. People are watching, I remind myself. God, this was the most normal thing. When we were teenagers, we always used to sit like this, Teo and Anna and me. 'We're not,' I say quietly.

'Sorry?' Teo asks.

'We're not together any more.'

'He's not here then? He's not coming?'

'No,' I say, one word caught between relief and hysteria. So much for *till death do us part.*

'Good.'

His voice is so intense. I can't help but look up. Teo's looking at me as if he wants to look straight into my soul. If you could do a thing like that. I know you can't. You can't tell from the outside what people really are and think and do.

Then a smile spreads out across his features, a big, wide smile, like the ones I remember. 'That's good,' he says, and turns his palm upwards. This is how we sat, as teenagers, as friends, just like that. The waiter brings the drinks, but we don't separate. Automatically, our fingers start tapping. Tap, tap, tap.

And I remember what the Detective Inspector said. If there was somebody there with me. At the house.

Maybe I don't have to face this on my own. Maybe I can ask him for help.

Maybe I can trust them.

'Anna was glad to see you,' Teo says.

'Me too,' I say. 'It was ... She's ... There is no one like her.'

Maybe that is the solution. 'Do you know she offered to marry me?' he says suddenly, his face scrunching up with laughter.

I don't look too closely at why that hurts. 'I wouldn't have thought she would fall for your charms.'

'Fat chance,' he says. His skin feels soft in mine. Tap, tap, tap. Softer than mine, too. He must have been taking care of himself. Using lotion and all that. 'It was when we were teenagers and Dad was between jobs, and it looked like he wouldn't find anything until our residency expired.'

'What would you have done?' I ask, remembering how worried I used to be about this, how we constantly worried about it. Them being kicked out. How they never even did drugs, worried that the smallest offence would get them deported. How we never went back to Bolton Castle after we'd been caught once, Jay taking all the blame to protect them.

Is he worrying about that again? Is Anna? 'Would you have gone back to Turkey?'

'For a holiday? Sure,' he says. 'I'd have married Anna, of course. Too bad that we were both approximately thirteen at the time.'

235

'I'm glad you didn't have to,' I say, leaning in. Think of Anna, sitting at my kitchen table. My throat constricts.

He leans in a little as well. I can smell his aftershave again, light and elegant. I think of Anna, sitting at my kitchen table, smelling like trees and a really nice perfume and paper. 'Why?'

I open my mouth to reply. Before I can do so, a voice interrupts us: 'There you are then, Linny.'

I see Teo's expression cloud over for a moment. Just a moment. Then he turns to Graham with a smile. So do I.

Graham's still dressed for work. He is wearing this long trench coat, too, like something out of American TV. He is standing by our table, his collar put up, and smiles. It looks a bit forced. 'Sorry,' I say. 'The station was closed by the time we came back.'

'You still have my number, don't you, though? Can call me any time, you know that, don't you? Mind if I sit for a moment?'

'Actually,' Teo says smoothly, 'I do.'

Graham simply takes one of the empty chairs, turns the backrest towards the table and sits down on it. It looks like it is taking him a little effort to move so fluently. Like he's tense. 'Why, Teoman?'

'Mr Dündar,' Teo says. I glance at him.

'Why, Mr Dündar?' Graham asks conversationally. 'Don't have anything to hide, do you?'

Teo clenches his teeth. 'Detective Inspector, if you have anything that you wish to discuss in an official—'

'Easy, tiger,' Graham interrupts. 'Just sitting down to have a little chat with two kids who've grown up.' He shifts, dropping his arms over the backrest, looking at Teo intently. 'Just sitting here and wondering what would bring someone like you back. And at such a time, too.'

Teo's eyes narrow. 'Graham, please,' I start, but the Detective Inspector won't let me finish.

'Haven't told him about it then, have you, Linny? About the Doorman at your house? Only came to me, didn't you? That's good. That's very good. Wouldn't do to trust just anybody.'

'Trust them with what?' Teo asks. He seems angry. Or worried. He is turned towards me, not even looking at Graham.

Graham doesn't like being ignored. 'And you, Teoman? You trusted her with what you've been up to? Spot of arson here and there, I've heard?'

My eyes widen. When Teo speaks again, he sounds like he is hissing. I glance up to see desperation flicker across his face. 'How do you know? It's not on my record.' He takes a deep breath, trying to compose himself. 'It was stupid. It was unforgivable. But it was a long time ago. I've changed.'

Graham barely manages not to snort. 'Listen, Teoman,' he says, legs spread wide, voice a low drawl. 'Whatever you're back here for, know this: you've come to the wrong place. This one's under my protection.'

The way he's speaking, I feel like I am not even there. Except Teo is still looking at me. 'Protection from what?' he asks.

'Nothing,' I say. Graham's ruining this. Pretending he believes me to get back at Teo, that's what he's doing. And it's working already. I want to ask about the arson. Want to know why he did it. When. Where. Why.

At the same time, it shocks me to realise how willing I am to believe him. *I've changed.* In this suit, with such a grin, his old weakness for chocolate bars.

How desperate I am to believe him. To have him back. Have them back.

'It's nothing,' I repeat, mouth twisting. 'Everything's fine.'

'Linny,' Graham says.

The Detective Inspector is looking at me, looking me up and down. He's not the only one. Anvi is sitting three tables down with Kait, clutching shopping bags from a trip to what must have been Leeds, and I think that's the manager from the Vodafone shop by the door, and there's a man I only know from the supermarket checkouts at the very back of the restaurant. They are all looking me up and down, then glancing at Teo. Have been ever since we've come in together.

And suddenly I get what that expression on their faces is.

At first, I thought it was incredulity. I thought they were thinking, *Doesn't she ever think …? Wasn't he the only one the police ever took into custody? Is she truly willing to take that risk?*

But that isn't it. Not it at all.

It's pity.

Here I am, a woman closer to forty than thirty, who hasn't run a mile in five years, can't remember the last time she's used lotion or talked about something more profound than whatever's been on *Great British Bake Off*; there he is, a man who's someone, who's made it. Who regularly visits his parents in Blackpool, who always knows what's on BBC 4, who has his own company and dinner with important people. *Fuck, look at her,* they are thinking and pitying me. *Even if it was him, even if he did it, he'd certainly not want to do it again.*

It doesn't matter that I don't want him like that. Doesn't matter to them.

Graham leaves us when the food arrives. Teo does not even touch his cutlery, his gaze focused entirely on me. 'What was he talking about, Linn?'

'It's nothing.'

'Bullshit!'

I am taken aback by the urgency in his tone. 'Sorry,' he says, but he doesn't sound very apologetic. He sounds as if he is barely reining in his temper. 'What was that about a Doorman?'

I stare right back.

Can I trust him?

He does not look away. Suddenly I become hyper aware that I am still in yesterday's clothes. That I didn't even shower. If there ever was makeup on my face, it's no longer where it should be.

I take a deep breath. 'Later,' I say.

'No, listen, Linn—' he starts, but I interrupt him.

'Dinner's getting cold. Please. Just ... let me just enjoy this.'

Teo presses his lips together. Looks down at his plate. But apparently I can still rely on his kindness. He does not ask another question.

He doesn't say anything else, though. When the silence becomes too oppressive, I steal away to the bathroom, trying to exert some damage control, but all I see when I look into the mirror is a tired woman who looks desperate when she smiles.

When I get back to the table, I order a glass of wine. Should have done that ages ago. The wine makes me talkative. Brings the conversation back to life. Eases the frown off his forehead. I talk of everything I can think of, everything but Graham, arson, the Doorman. I'm babbling, and eight o'clock is fast approaching.

He could come with me.

When dinner's through, I get up. 'Let's get out of here,' I say, slurring my words a little. It's already a few minutes past eight.

Outside the door, Teo digs his hands into his pockets, rocking back and forth on his heels. He seems to want to say something. I cut in for fear that it's *goodnight* or *goodbye*: 'Teo, there's somewhere I need to be. Do you want to come with me?'

He is still looking at me. *Me.* Like I matter. 'Is it *later*, then? Can we talk about this now?'

I take out Jay's note. 'It's from Jay,' I say.

Teo's brow furrows as he reads it. 'Jacob Mason? Why would Jay want to see you?'

'Are you coming or not?' I ask, the challenge obvious. I'm drunk and it makes me brave. I'm not afraid. I'm no longer running away.

I am going to trust him.

He seems to consider the question for a moment. Then a smile spreads across his features. 'Lay on, Macduff!'

It's not far. Only around the corner and then down the street. That's good. It's already a quarter past eight by the time we turn onto the High Street.

The moment we turn the corner, I spot the blue lights.

There's a police car in front of Jay's house.

An invisible fist closes around my lungs. It could be nothing, I tell myself. Absolutely nothing. But I don't feel like it's nothing. I speed up. Start running. Running ahead of Teo.

Jay's front door is wide open. Already, some bystanders have gathered around the police tape. I'm glad Kait's still in the restaurant, not storming the tape yet. Blue and white tape. Crime-scene tape.

I suck in a breath. No. Please. Not the teenager I remember, with his bright pale eyes, shining when he'd managed to make me laugh with another one of his drawings.

Graham is standing by the front door. He's lost his coat and is sucking on a cigarette like nicotine's his lifeblood. It's barely been forty-five minutes and he looks completely transformed. Grey in the face. Exhausted. Desperate.

'Graham!' I call out, forgetting all my suspicions. He's here, and he can help. 'What's going on?'

When he spots me, his fingers clench around his fag. Then he puts it out and comes to meet me by the tape. Lifting it up, he motions for me to cross over to his side. 'We're too late, Linny.'

The bystanders protest when Graham lets me in, but I ignore them. Out of breath, I follow Graham into the house.

'Now, listen, I can't let you contaminate anything, but you should have a look. I guess he wanted you to find him ... Good thing I got here early.'

Our steps are muffled by the thick carpet in the hall. There's a chaotic coat rack on our left, buried under a mass of jackets, most of them his mother's. Shoes are strewn all over the floor. Up ahead I can sneak a glance at the old-fashioned kitchen; to our right is the front room. The door's wide open. It's as chaotic as the hallway, clothes everywhere, most of them dirty, plates of food gone bad weeks ago. On the old sofa, heaps of Chilcott pillows and blankets, carefully stacked, folded, handled with care. Their lavender pouches are emanating a sweet, heavy scent mixing with the rotten food, the dirty clothes. Next to the pillows, a stack of framed drawings. His art. The telly is running. The volume is deafening.

'Didn't want anybody to hear what was happening, I guess,' Graham says, while all I can do is stare at the centre of the room. The chair kicked over. The rope, fastened to Mrs Mason's chandelier, her pride and joy.

They're only taking down the body now.

Nausea rises inside me. I turn around, rush back into the hallway. Almost stumble. Graham follows me. He looks as pale as I feel. It can't be true. 'When did it happen?' I ask Graham, feeling incredibly weak.

'Too soon to tell, but the neighbours said he'd only turned up the volume once *Emmerdale* had finished, so around seven-thirty. As far as we can tell at this point, he sat down to watch the episode and then got everything ready. It's ...'

Graham peters out. It obviously takes effort for him to

speak up again. 'Linn, you can't stay here. I just wanted you ... Because of the note he left for you. But this isn't a good place for you.'

'There was no letter?' I asked. 'No message? Nothing? He just wanted me to find him?'

'Looks like it, yeah. You would have got here at exactly the right time to find his body,' Graham says. 'No letter that we've been able to uncover, not yet, anyway. I'll let you know if we do, but even if we did, it'd be for his mum to look at. Hellfire, his mum ...'

Graham scrubs a hand over his face. I wish there was anything I could do to help. 'But ... on the sofa, we ...' Graham hesitates. 'It has your name on it.'

He returns to the front room. I watch him bend over the drawings. Only then do I realise that they have been labelled with Post-it Notes.

Graham returns to me with one of the frames. *Caroline Wilson*, the yellow Post-it Note reads in Jay's shaky hand-writing. Carefully, he hands it over. 'I'm sorry, Linny, you cannot it take it with you just yet, but I wanted you to see it at least. To know that he ... he thought of you, you know? In his last moments.'

My hands are cold when I close them around the frame. 'Thank you,' I mumble. He just nods, says to take all the time I need. I sink down onto the bench in front of the coat rack, on top of all those jackets and coats and scarves and hats that make up a lifetime of living in the Yorkshire Dales. The shock is turning me numb. He can't be gone. Not Jay.

I stare at the drawing. It's charcoal, Bolton Castle at night.

A full moon sits high in the sky. Four figures are leaning against one of the walls, barely visible in the shadows of the old stones.

I can't believe Jay would have come all the way out to my house just so that it'd be me who'd find him. We hadn't seen each other in nineteen years. We hadn't been in touch.

Maybe he thought it was better if it was me than his mum? Is that why he made her move out? So she wouldn't be the one to find him?

That's like I remember him. He loved his mum. He cared for people. I fight the nausea as I keep looking at the drawing. At the four small figures. There seems to be something above their heads. Like ...

My eyes narrow.

Aren't those letters?

I lift the frame, bring it closer to my face.

Open me.

I stare at the words.

Then I glance around. Graham's back in the sitting room. Nobody's watching me.

Quickly, I turn the frame around. Loosen the clips, remove the back.

A piece of paper falls out. Another note.

I'm hot all over. This is it. This is it, I think as I reach for it.

For a moment, I think about shoving it in my pocket and getting out of here as quickly as possible. But I have to know.

I unfold the note.

For a moment, I'm expecting a confession. I'm almost sure.

Then my eyes finally manage to focus on the words he has written.

They are all lying to you.

Every part of me is turning ice-cold. The climbing plants are back in my body, cobra lilies sprouting through my veins quicker than my blood flows. They thrust into my lungs, shoot upwards to burst my windpipe. The words blur in front of my eyes for a moment, the words written below. But I catch sight of a single letter, an *ü*.

There's only one name we both know that's spelled with that letter.

Before I have time to clear my vision, to read on, the note is torn from my hands. Graham is saying something, his voice loud. I protest, but he's furious. 'Tampering with the evidence' and 'For his mother' and 'Have you no decency?'

'It's for me,' I say, almost dazed. My vision won't clear. The alcohol, maybe. The vomit fighting its way up my gullet.

'If there's anything in here for you, we'll make sure it finds its way to you. This is a crime scene, and if you don't want me to take you in for tampering with evidence, you get the hell out of here *right now*!' Graham says fiercely.

I barely make it outside, barely manage to bend over the bare shrubbery before I throw up. The bile burns my throat, the Indian food coming back out, barely digested. A rancid smell fills the air, sour and sweet in a sickening way, decay and bodily fluids mixing with strong spices and the scent of lavender.

I throw up again.

The crowd in front of the tape has grown larger, some of

them making shocked noises. Angela's there to fend them off. Kaitlin's on the other side of the tape with Anvi, and so many of the people we saw in the restaurant.

And Teoman's still standing there, too. Right there, waiting for me.

All I can see is his face. Anna's face.

And myself, almost falling for it again.

They are all lying to you.

I stumble down the stairs. Everybody's staring. 'Linn,' Teo says, sounding worried. 'You shouldn't be driving. Let me drive you.'

He's not driving me. I can drive fine.

'Linn!'

Someone's following me as I stumble towards my car.

It's Kaitlin. 'Linn, luv, you don't look so good. Let me give you a lift.'

Anvi's with her. I almost insult her. All she wants to know is what happened. She'll ask me, in a second. 'We've had such a shock,' Kaitlin says. 'Hellfire, what happened in there?'

'You'd like to know, wouldn't you?' I snap, speeding up, barely managing to swallow all the profanities on the tip of my tongue. I don't want to talk to her. To anyone. My vision is spinning. Teo's face, Anna's, Jay's body, dangling from the ceiling. The note I should have pocketed.

'What are you implying, Caroline?' Anvi asks sharply.

I whirl around to face them. They're in their good coats. Kaitlin's wearing far too much makeup. 'Just leave me alone! Leave him alone! Why can't you leave anyone alone?'

Anvi straightens. 'It's you who came back, isn't it?' she hisses.

'Look at you, marching back here as if the place belonged to you, raking up all that old business again. And now Jacob Mason has hanged himself, and Tony is once again a regular guest at the Detective Inspector's, Antonia Luca, I mean, picking up their disgusting affair ...'

I don't even want to hear this. 'What the fuck are you talking about?'

The words break out of Kaitlin, eager to share whatever she's seen, even now. 'Started twenty years ago, didn't it? When he came to your house that night, you know; when it happened, she'd been staying over at his. Saw her leave, didn't I? Right across from the copy shop, his place is. Why else would she leave his house at midnight after he'd just driven off? And she was back at his last night, saw her myself.'

I stare at them. Even now they'd be gossiping. Even with Jay's body not yet turned cold. I turn around. Shake them off. I'm running to the car.

The road is dark in front of my eyes. I don't have trouble driving. Just sometimes, when I skid over into the opposite lane. When I can't make myself go back into the right one. But there's nobody on the road. Nothing except a rabbit. I make it back all right. Absolutely all right.

Except I'm not all right at all, am I?

They are all lying to you.

I was right all along. They were all lying to me.

I don't know how I end up in the hollow, but suddenly, here I am. Once I've parked the car, I stumble into the house, then pour myself a gin and tonic. A nightcap. Mum always

C. K. Williams

had nightcaps. Mostly port, when I was younger. It helped her sleep. I take a sleeping pill too, which I find in the bathroom. Take the box down with me. Feel the begonias' soil, picking up the petals they have dropped. Useless. Can't even help them.

There is no mail. Of course there's no mail. What was I thinking? That anybody was waiting for me? Waiting for my CV, trained as a florist, work experience approximately twelve months in total? Fucking lucky they don't want headshots any more with applications. No one's benefiting as much as I am, ugly cow that I am. *That's what you wanted, isn't it?* I ask myself. *You wanted all these feelings. Wanted to face them. Well, here you go. Have them. Thought you could deal with them, didn't you?*

Or did you know they would be what pushed you off the bridge? Finally off that fucking bridge, you fucking coward. Was that why you came?

The first G&T's really good. I want another one.

It's good, this gin and tonic. I'm glad it's so much in fashion right now. You can drink it and almost not taste the alcohol at all.

It's really good.

The couch is soft, in the living room, it's really comfy, and there's something on the telly, it doesn't much matter what, does it? I believe that there's a blanket lying on top of me. Must have spread it out. My fingers are greasy. There's a bowl of crisps sitting on the living-room table. And crumbs in my mouth. My mouth tastes like gin and tonic and shortbread and crisps. There should be a drink with that flavour. Shortbread-

248

crisps-G&T. Maybe you could put crisps in gin and tonic. Like cucumbers. Only crisps. Giving the world a new drink before I go. A legacy. Something to remember me by.

I'm not making any sense.

Look at me. Covered in grease and crisps and crumbs, and that's alcohol sloshed down my shirt, isn't it? Those stains?

Is that what my nightly visitor wants to see? What did Graham call them? The Doorman. Is that what they are looking for? A chubby woman turning forty, skin and clothing stained with food and booze?

That didn't stop them last time. Last time, you were lying in your own vomit.

They are all lying to you.

I shiver. It's cold suddenly. There's something else entirely on the telly now. That's what Jay wanted to tell me. That's what he used his last breath for. Dead men don't lie. They have no reason to any more.

I reach for the box of pills and push another one out.

Remember the last time.

Another one.

The thing is, it wouldn't happen like last time.

Because this time I wouldn't be so useless; because that was bloody useless of me, wasn't it? Just opening the door like that. Trusting it would be a friend. Trusting anyone.

That won't happen to me again.

Suddenly, I become aware of how drunk I am. What time is it?

I become aware of what could happen at any point. The doorbell.

Shaking, I try to stand. Just put your feet onto the floor. Just sit up. It wasn't that much alcohol, was it? It wasn't so many pills. Come on. Stand up.

The thing is, I can't.

I can't even stand.

I couldn't run to save my life.

Like last time.

ANNA

Leave it to me, Teoman said.
Only why should I?

THE DETECTIVE INSPECTOR

I did my best. Our very best we did, you hear me?

LINN

Maybe they're not even coming. Maybe I'm just imagining this.

Maybe ...

Ding, ding, ding.

THE DETECTIVE INSPECTOR

You hear me?

LINN

The telly is still on. At least I didn't turn the lights on. At least there's nothing but the telly and the bright, bright moonlight, falling in through the windows, through the back door at the far end of the living room, leading out into the garden. It's a glass door, that one, milky glass from the middle up.

The doorbell rings.

Don't move. Just don't move, I keep telling myself. Lying on the couch, on my back. Just don't move.

I didn't hear a car. Didn't hear anything.

God, I was too drunk to hear anything.

Now I hear them.

The Doorman.

Steps. Slow, creaking steps. My vision is spinning slowly. As slowly as they are making their way along the house wall. Across the porch. There is a light scratching sound. As if somebody was dragging something across the wooden wall. A key. A fingernail. A shard of glass.

I do not dare to breathe. The scratching is light. Like a caress. It is coming closer. They are moving around the house.

They are coming along the outer wall of the living room. To the back door.

Bile rises in my throat. I listen to their steps, the smell of Mum's dried flowers in my nose. Dusty, tangy. Past the curtains, I hear them walk. Hear the scratching. So light.

They are coming.

Again, I try to stand. Again, the nausea pushes me back into the cushions. My vision tilts before my eyes. I can't move. All I can do is stare at the back door. At the pale, milky glass.

The steps halt.

I breathe.

A light sound. Shoes on grass. I'm not imagining this.

Then I hear creaking wood. Someone is climbing the three steps leading up to the back door.

One.

I stare at the door. The smell of the flowers turns even stronger. The stale, dead petals, shrivelled up. Silent and still, like my heart. My breath. I try not to breathe.

Two.

There is a shape in the window. There is someone coming up to the back door. A dark silhouette.

Three.

I press my mouth closed. The nausea is overwhelming. Stare at the silhouette. The telly is on. They can see that the telly is on.

They know I am here.

The silhouette does not move.

Until it does. I see how they raise their arm. Slowly. Very slowly.

The glass shakes when the hand comes down against it. The Doorman knocks. Once. Twice. Three times. Knock, knock, knock. Again and again. Stronger and stronger. The window trembles. The bile shoots into my mouth. My eyes roll into the back of my head. I press my hand to my mouth again. They are knocking. The old glass groans.

It takes me a moment to realise.

The Doorman is not knocking. The Doorman is trying to shatter the glass.

I slide off the couch. Cower on the floor, crawl underneath the table. The nausea pushes up. I can't stop myself. I feel the bile rise. Saliva mixes with vomit with the heavy tangy air. I throw up. On the edge of consciousness. Not again. Not again. Stay awake. Run. You have to run. This can't be happening again. I'll kill myself before it happens again.

I think of the deadly nightshade, up in the drawer.

I'll kill myself.

Just like Jay. He knew when it was time to go. When there wasn't anything to hold on to any more.

A loud crash. I pull all my limbs into myself. It's happening again. That was the glass. The window broke. The window *broke*. I am in delirium. The nightshade. I'm going. I'm gone. I'll kill myself. Everything's dark and black. Everything's disappearing.

The window broke.

Chapter 6

It is the first Saturday in the year 2000. Computers haven't crashed, the world didn't end, Linn's entire house still smells like her mum's dried rosemary. At least it's a change from that goddamn lavender. The house is also still down in a godforsaken hollow where you don't get a modem or signal for your Nokia 8210.

Linn is walking through the woods. The snow crunches under her shoes, so do the first daisies, early this year. They're Anna's favourite flowers. Linn is making her way down to the road, hunting for signal. She tries to play Snake while she walks, but it's hard because she has to try not to fall and she's wearing shit shoes for the forest and she should've put on her wellies or just stayed the hell inside.

The thing is, she's waiting to hear from Anna.

Linn's texted her. She'd been agonising all night over what would be the right thing to say. After that kiss. And then she just texted Anna what she thought was true.

I think I love you.

Now she's cursing herself. Anna didn't text back. Not for the entire trip to the supermarket with her parents. On the way

259

back to the dip, Linn kept watching the screen, watching the bars disappear.

'What are you doing?' her dad asked her.

'Nothing,' she said.

'Nothing,' he repeated, laughing under his breath. Linn didn't know what there was to laugh at. Why did she text something stupid like that? What if Anna thinks she's weird? What if Anna pretends not to think she's weird but really does? God, what if she's totally mixing this up? She and Jay have been split up for a while, maybe her body's getting desperate. Maybe that's all it was.

Linn breathes in the sharp air as she keeps marching through the woods. What if it wasn't, though? What if she really loves Anna? It'd be perfect. They could go away to uni together. Linn could be a botanist. In space. They actually need botanists there, did you know that? And Teo wants to go to uni too. They could all go to the same uni or see each other on the weekends. And after uni, Linn would get a job with the ESA, or somewhere else. And then she might have a proper house, not in a hollow, but on a real tarmac *road. Anna would be a famous singer. She'd get them tickets for all the good shows, the best tickets for the three of them!*

If only Anna texted back.

Maybe she already has. *Bloody signal!*

Linn starts running. She's completely out of breath when she finally reaches a stretch of wood close to the main road where finally *a bar appears on her screen.*

Her heart skips a beat when her phone rings. Three times. Ding, ding, ding. She takes out her phone. Two missed calls.

One new message. *She almost drops her phone when she hits* OPEN.

It's not from Anna.

It's from Oliver.

Do you want to go to the cinema tonight?

Linn swallows. Her throat has constricted. She stares at the ground in front of her, at the daisies caving under the snow. Three are still visible, their green stems and drooping heads.

She keeps standing in the woods until her fingers turn blue, but there is no message from Anna.

LINN

There is vomit on my tongue. Vomit and the taste of cheap gin and the dusty floor. Over the stench, it is difficult for anything else to register. Anything but the smell of dried flowers.

Involuntarily, I dry-heave, but there is nothing else that could come out of me. I'm scared to feel. If I did, I might feel it again: the pain between my legs, dried blood on my thighs. Saliva sticking to my hair, wet on my skin. Sweat, like famished fingers, all over my naked body. My hand on the dried petals of deadly nightshade, one day later, standing in my parents' bedroom, wondering if the flower could finish me off, betrayed by the only people I ever trusted.

It is light out, the world bright even behind my closed lids. Slowly, I open them. Slowly, I heave my body out from under the table. My head hurts, my stomach, my insides twisting.

But there is something else I feel, too. My legs. They feel fine. As I sit up, back up against the couch, I realise I am still fully dressed. Unchecked relief surges through me. It didn't happen again. The jeans, spoilt as they are, sit firm and warm on my skin, buttons all fastened, zipper done all the way up. I can feel them against my belly, around my legs, my hips ...

Wait.

When I lower my hands to my trousers, they are trembling. I fiddle with the buttons, trying not to panic.

When I've opened my jeans, I see that it's true.

I'm not wearing panties any more.

My head is spinning. I crawl away from the sofa, trying to throw up once more. I'm fine, I tell myself, I'm fine. They didn't do anything. But they must have come in. They must have undressed me. I am retching, but nothing is coming out. I try and pull myself up. Use the table to support my cramping body, to sink down onto the couch. Tears are burning at the backs of my eyes. There is vomit around my feet. The stench is sharp in my nose, in my eyes.

They took my underwear.

I start crying then. And I can feel it. All of it. I can't push it away any more – it's all there, right here, the doorbell, the chimes, the hands spreading my legs. The pills, the vomit, the empty bottle of gin. The flower I held in my hands, nineteen years ago, on the day after it had happened, standing in my parents' bedroom. How I swallowed it whole, leaves and berries and petals. How Mum found me. Mum's and Dad's graves. Jay's notes. Jay's body.

The tears are starting to shake my entire body. I look up, my lashes wet and sticky. At the door, the broken glass.

They came in. They pulled down my trousers, took my underwear.

They are real.

I've got to get out of here. An ambulance. I have … I have to pack. I have to go back to London.

Shakily, I pull myself to my feet. Surveying the living room, I feel like I'm suffocating. On the table, the empty bottle of gin and empty blister of pills. Did I take so many? Did I … Do I …

I almost ended it there and then. Almost ended it myself. I wanted to end it.

My stiff body, purple and pale, lying next to the dead begonias, shrivelled like their petals, their leaves. That would be the end of my story. Finally, an ending.

Just like Jay. I can't stay here. If I stay here, I'll end it.

There isn't much to pack. It's all upstairs, everything except the begonias and my parents' picture and my coat. I throw everything I brought into my bag, not worrying about anything else, the sheets on the bed, the food in the kitchen. All I want is to get out of here.

Clutching my bag in one hand and the begonias in the other, I walk out the front door and onto the porch. The air is fresh and sharp. It smells like wet leaves and frost. For one last time, I look at the brown hollow. Listen to the chimes singing in the wind, a sound that fills me with terror when it used to give me joy.

I furrow my brow as something draws my attention towards a tree. The large sycamore, in the middle of the hollow, halfway towards the drive up to the road.

Something has been scratched into its bark.

I put down my bag and the begonias on the porch and slowly approach the trunk.

Two words, stark and clear, have been scratched into the trunk:

GO HOME.

I stare at them.

So this is what they want.

They want me to go. To scare me away.

They don't want the truth to come out.

At my sides, my hands ball into fists. My skin is prickling, my nerve endings firing. I can hear the blood pounding in my ears. Nineteen bloody years, I accepted that the police could not help me, could not protect me, accepted what Graham had said. A stranger, in, out, there was nothing we could have done. That became my story.

Even though I knew it wasn't the truth.

They lied to me. I was right. I did *not* remember it wrong.

My body turns hot. Hot and white and strong. And I can feel it. This isn't happening to anybody else. I can feel every ounce of rage boiling inside me, of fear morphing into bloody fury. They took everything from me, but they will not take the truth.

If I go back now, I will never know who did this. And I will stay no more than a bogeyman, a story used to scare others, to silence them.

But I do not want to be a cautionary tale. I will write my own story.

It feels like there is electricity running through all of my body as I turn away from the sycamore and march back to the front porch. Taking up my bag and the begonias, I go back inside. In the kitchen, I swallow an aspirin and put on the kettle. My knees are no longer shaking.

Instead, I bring out the list again and sit down at the kitchen table. I draw a gentle line across Jay's name. Then I write down, in capital letters on the very top of the list: *THEY ARE ALL LYING TO YOU.*

Looking at the names, at two in particular, I press the red pen to my lips. I remember the night that Anna and Teo came to my door, Teo just released from prison, shouting, demanding to be let in. I remember the expression on both of their faces. Guilt. It's what I remember. Whatever Graham says, it's the truth. For nineteen years, it's been the truth. There was something they weren't telling me. I had loved them. I had loved her. I loved her, I trusted her, and all she had for me was lies.

I'm lucky Oliver was there. He already had his place at uni, a programme for nursing, on a swimming scholarship. I could take all the time I needed, he said. He would be there for me. He would take care of me. I could come with him.

And I looked out of the kitchen window as my parents and Oliver opened the door for Teoman and Anna. How Teo didn't even hesitate. How he lunged at them. My father had to shove him off. Teo looked wild. Later, Oliver told me Teo had attacked him; had come to his house and attacked him. I couldn't believe it.

The water boils. I get up and fetch a cup, then I sit back down. Taking the pen again, I write another sentence under *They are all lying to you*, between the heading and the list:

Who is the Doorman?

They think they can come to my door and terrorise me? They think taking nineteen years from me is not enough?

They won't get to take my life, too. I won't let the Doorman come near me again. I have to think of some way to keep them away.

No. Even better. I have to think of a way to trap them.

Letting my gaze wander, I look out of the kitchen window. Look at the hollow and the sycamore, the carving in the bark.

Involuntarily, I feel my lips spread into a smile.

Do you know what that carving means?

It means they came past the sycamore. That means they must have come down the drive. That means I know where they walk when they come here.

The next time they ring the doorbell, I will be prepared.

ANNA

I hear her drive up the road. It is morning, milky light seeping in through the windows. They could do with a wash, I think, sitting at my desk in a white linen dress that is far too light for this weather. I left my woollen sweater in the cloakroom. A shiver runs down my back and I wrap my hands around the warm mug of tea sitting next to my computer on the desk.

It would be a lie to say I am actually working. Who could be working? After what happened with Jay?

What happened. That is one way of putting it. One way not to ask any questions about responsibility.

When she has made it to the crest of the hill, I hear her slow down. My brow furrows. This is unusual. There is nothing up there. Nothing except ...

I rise. As I make for the window, I keep telling myself: I am not obsessed.

Even though I would have good reason to be.

Pulling back the sitting-room curtains, I peek outside. Her car is sitting on the road, right at the top of the Kenzies' driveway. My driveway. The engine is running.

She seems to be waiting for something.

Glancing to both sides, I shift from one foot to the other. Move closer to the window. Brown leaves swirl past in a gush of wind. It is freshening up. The milky light seems to flicker, dark clouds on the horizon. There might be a thunderstorm. I stare right up the drive, right there at the windshield. That is where her face should be.

Can she see me?

Standing here in the large sitting-room window, a white silhouette, blurry behind the glass.

I hear the noise of the engine increase. Slowly. Before my eyes, the car moves off. It reminds me of something. So deliberate. Like the police cars when I was a child. They used to be all over Gdańsk, prowling through its narrow, decrepit streets, houses grey and brown that used to be patrician jewels of red and green.

Just as she is almost around the bend, just as I have turned away, I hear the noise.

She honks.

One. Twice. Thrice.

She is watching me.

LINN

It is a bit of a drive to my first destination, back along the A684, towards the motorway. Putting the Dresden Dolls on, I sink back into the seat, revelling in the way the music pumps through my body. My heart is still pounding when I think of what I just did. How I sat at the entrance to her drive, squarely in the middle of that dirt road, and looked down at the Kenzies' house.

How I saw the curtains move. How I let her know I was watching her, too.

Gave me a right kick, sounding my horn like that. All the way up to the A684, my hands were shaking almost imperceptibly, and I was too excited to even really look at the road. I'd forgotten what it felt like, being excited. Being in control. How it makes your body tingle. How it makes you want to sing.

Jay gave me one last gift. I'm not going to waste it.

Now it's the music and me and my old Toyota Corolla, so

used when I bought it that they weren't even being produced any more. It was the first generation to be equipped with ABS, I think. The seats smell like something rotten, but they're practically moulded to my body shape.

I check on my phone to make sure the garden centre is still where I think it is. Thirty minutes later, I take the exit towards the Garden Warehouse.

It takes me a good half hour to find everything I need. Last are the spades. There is an insanely large selection. I simply reach for a model that looks like the one my parents used to have. It's heavy, good to grip. At the checkout, after a quick chat with the pregnant young woman in line behind me, who is holding a particularly large hammer, I inspect the flowers I selected, the autumn and winter blooms as well as some saplings for spring, like rhododendrons. Dahlias and winter aconites sit happily in their beds of earth, stretching their necks into the stale warehouse air. Their petals are orange and pink or bright yellow, a proper dash of colour. And red. For Mum.

They will brighten up the hollow all right. It is a dent in my funds, but nothing to the raised middle finger that they'll be. *Not going anywhere.*

On my way back, I take the route through town. As I drive past Teo's flat, I make sure to let him know I'm there, honking three times. Then I leave the car in the short-stay parking lot and go looking for Graham.

He's back in the break room at the station. I catch a glimpse of him before someone bars my way. Detective Constable Angela Johnson is at the front. She's watching me closely.

'Maybe there is something I can help you with?' she says, her voice low. She is not wearing any makeup. I wonder if she has a boyfriend. She seems so … fierce. Again, I wonder what made her stay up here.

'Thank you, but I'm here to speak to Graham,' I say, raising my voice so that he will hear me. I won't be sent away again.

'I would be happy to help,' Angela says, voice lowered once more. I almost snort. It's too late for the police to help now. Her Northern accent is soft, but still audible if you know what to look for. She leans across the counter. That is when I realise her nails are polished black. 'If there's anything …'

'Linny?'

Graham's head is peeking out of the break room. He must have heard my voice. Smiling tiredly, he waves for me to join him.

'Ey up, Linny,' he says once he's pulled the door firmly shut behind him. 'Looks like a bit of storm's coming, doesn't it?'

'It does,' I answer, sitting down at the table, nodding yes when he offers me tea. He pours me a cuppa in silence. I watch him. Think about how best to go about this. How to find out what I've come here for.

I know Graham won't show me Jay's note. He's lying to me, too. Got something to hide, the Detective Inspector. But it's all right.

I will catch them in the act.

'Here you go,' he says, putting the mug down in front of me. Apparently, I'm subscribed to the *Psychology Today* one now. I appreciate the irony. He's already put in milk and sugar for me. 'How are you, Linny? You look a little tired.'

I think of the spade in the back of my car. That's nothing to how tired I will be once I've got to work. 'I didn't sleep well. It happened again last night.'

He leans back in his chair. 'It did, did it?'

'Aye,' I say, leaning in. It's the first time I've used it in a long time, *aye*, and it feels like coming home. 'What about the note I found at Jay's?'

'It's still with forensics.'

'You see, it—'

I don't get to finish. I wasn't expecting him to let me. In fact, I was hoping he was going to try and distract me with his favourite topic.

'Don't you think it's odd at all, Linn?' he asks me, his eyes sharp. 'I saw him standing there, you know. Don't you think it's strange?'

'What is?'

He stretches his neck, like a boxer about to step into the ring. 'That this would happen. Just when he's back, too.'

'You still think it's Teoman.'

He raises his hands defensively. 'Now, look, Linny, I told you what I thought. A stranger. In, out. Nothing we could have done.'

'Yesterday you said it might be time to look into it again,' I say. 'And then you came to see us at dinner. That's just what made me think about it.'

'I'm just saying,' he answers slowly, looking at me intently. 'Don't you think it's strange?'

I lean back in my chair now too, picking up my mug, glancing into the dark liquid. The bag's still swimming in it, covered in crystalline sugar. Then I look back at him, unrelenting. 'What did he tell you? When you took him into custody back then?'

'It's been years, Linny.'

'I know.'

'I just didn't like seeing him with you,' he says, shifting in his seat. 'Made me nervous. He makes me nervous. Colleague of mine told me he'd gone to prison because he'd burned down a couple of buildings in London. All abandoned, mind you, but who knows what he'd have got up to if they hadn't caught him when they did? And look at how defensive he got the minute I joined you. Why would he if he had nothing to hide?'

'What did he tell you? What made you think it could have been him?' I ask.

'Well, I don't know, do I?' Graham asks. His hair is almost white. He doesn't dye it. His eyes are narrowed all the way. 'I just thought it was odd. When I took him here all those years ago, do you know what he did?'

I shake my head. A frisson runs down my spine.

Graham scratches his chin. Then looks at me. The hairs on my arms are standing up. 'He didn't even deny it. Didn't even defend himself. He just said nothing. Sat there and said nothing at all.'

The frisson turns into a shiver. 'Nothing?'

'No. He didn't want an attorney, either. We got him one, of course, he was underage, barely, mind you, like yourself, but he just sat there. And stared at me with this ... murderous expression. Did you ever see the photos we took of him back then?'

I shake my head. My blood is roaring in my ears. 'We took photos of everyone who was there, we did,' Graham says as he rises. 'Everyone we brought in. I could ...'

Again he looks at me, his expression doubtful. 'I could show you,' he finishes.

'That would be great,' I say as calmly as I can.

'Look, Linny,' he begins, but then stops himself again.

'I know you could get into trouble,' I say, but I am not letting him off the hook this time.

He is still staring at me. 'Well,' he says. 'That's true.'

Then he turns around and leaves the break room. I count my breaths while I wait, just count them, trying to calm my pulse. It's the first time I'll see those photos. It's the first time I'll see the file. Time for the true story.

When the door opens again, it's Angela. Slowly, she walks to the kitchenette and pours herself a cup of tea. Every move of hers is precise, even when she pours herself a cuppa. Then she turns back around, eyes on me. She seems about so say something when her phone starts vibrating. Hastily, she pulls it out to look at the screen. Her entire face softens. Then she glances at me, and something akin to embarrassment passes across her expression. Quickly, she makes for the door, answering in such a low voice that I cannot catch anything she says except the softest 'ey up'. A few minutes later, I hear her hang up. And then steps in the stairwell. Graham coming back up from the archive.

She stops him. Starts talking. Whispering, more like. Don't talk him out of it. Don't let her talk you out of it, Graham.

I get up but before I can make it outside, the door opens again. Graham comes back in, a dusty old file in his hand. He spreads it out on the shaky plastic table as I lean in.

It is a simple brown folder, a little worn with age. Someone must have thumbed it time and again, the corners are all thinned out. Out of the folder, he pulls a few sheets of paper, long protocols, and a set of faded photographs. This was the year 2000. Photos were still developed. The original film is stowed safely in a pocket of the folder. I catch a glimpse of four negatives.

'Here you go,' he says quietly, glancing at the door as if to make sure that nobody is listening in. 'I mean, just have a look at this.'

I bend over the table, squinting at the photo. It is Teo, and something pulls at my heartstrings for a second. Teo at seventeen, as handsome and young as I remember him.

Just. There's something wrong with his face. He's not smiling. It was hard not to see him smiling when you looked at him back then. Instead, he has the same expression on his face as that night on the porch when he'd been released from custody. Of someone to be frightened of. Someone who was no longer in control of themselves. I'd never seen him like that.

'It was just an instinct,' Graham says, taking me back to the present. 'Just an instinct, but I knew something was wrong with him. I mean, you can't take someone to court for looking like a madman, you just can't. But look at this. And then he's still aggressive today. He was aggressive when I came up to him yesterday, wasn't he?'

He was. Unlike Anna, a slim figure on the front porch in the cold and the dark. 'Have you got a picture of her?' I ask. 'Of Anna?'

He takes out the other photos: next to Teo, he puts down Anna, and then Miss Luca. Anna seems like she can hardly bear looking into the camera. No one surprises me like Miss Luca, though.

Her professional expression, her calm veneer, is gone. Entirely gone. She's crying in the picture, crying as if it was her who'd been assaulted. She's evidently trying to hold it together but failing miserably.

I didn't realise how shocked Miss Luca had been. She never seemed to let it get to her, her patients' fate. Never. Not once when I was with her, either.

'Are there more photos?' I ask. Didn't I see four negatives?

Graham reaches into the folder, taking out quite a few more. He hesitates before spreading them out. 'Are you sure, Linny? I mean, are you sure you wanna see this? It's the crime scene, you know. It's pretty ... Truth be told, it's pretty bad.'

I nod. A second slip of negatives sits behind the second, much longer. I don't have enough time to count them before he has spread out all the photos on the table in front of us.

Graham was right. The crime scene is humiliating. I feel like somebody has pushed me onto my knees, holding me down, hand in my hair, pulling it back to bare my throat.

It's like a movie, only worse. Worse because you don't just see it, you can also feel it. The pictures are jogging my memory, even after all this time. Of waking up, the smell of lavender and sweat and blood, the pain of each and every wound on my body. There's a photo of my nails as well. They're clean. As if I didn't fight it.

Graham shifts uncomfortably in his seat as I keep going through them. The police photographer was diligent. He photographed every inch of my parents' bedroom, every shard of the broken Bacardi Breezer bottle and bit of vomit, every trace on the old stairs worn down by the feet of generations.

It's the first time I see what it really looked like. They wouldn't show me these when I was underage; they said it would be too much of a shock and serve no purpose. My parents' large bed. The dark imprint of sweat my body left on their blanket, my belly and face pressed firmly into the fabric. The places where I'd torn the sheets, probably with my nails, maybe with my teeth. Pain sears through me, suddenly, without warning, even while I sit at that cheap plastic table in the dull break room, a cup of tea going cold in front of me. The vomit on the floor, the impression of my knees and my shins in that degrading puddle.

And there's something else.

My breath hitches as I lean in a little closer. There's something in that pool of vomit. Two things, actually. One a small rectangle, the other a long, thin object.

'What was that?' I ask, pointing at it. Graham keeps glancing at the door even as he leans in. He seems anxious.

'Wait,' he says, fumbling for another sheet of paper. A list of everything found at the crime scene. 'A box of matches,' he says, looking at his meticulous record. 'See, we even put down where it came from: it was the FilmBox, the place where you worked. Your parents confirmed that.'

I nod. That's true, it's where I worked. 'What else did you find?' I ask, stealing a glance at the list.

Graham keeps looking over his shoulder as he pushes it towards me. 'Not much that your parents couldn't place. The matches, the broken bottle of course.' He hesitates, pretending to casually rest his hand on the sheet, but I see that he is trying to cover up an item. 'Other than that, it was all the usual: your mum's flowers, mostly.'

The flowers are all at the very bottom, six items on the list. Roses, deadly nightshade, the caspias Mum brought back from our holiday in the Canaries, daisies, rosemary and thyme.

Something's wrong with that list. I furrow my brow. Glance back at Graham's hand, trying to catch a glimpse of the item he is covering up when we hear footsteps approach. Graham clears his throat and hastily shuffles the documents back into his file. As he does, he has to lift his hand. Before he lets the sheet disappear in the folder, I have seen what item he was trying to hide.

tall candle (used on the victim / penetration)

He throws the file onto the table and his jacket on top, shielding it from curious eyes. By the time Angela swings open the door, I've already reached for my mug again, looking as calm as I can even though my insides are spasming.

'Detective Inspector?' Angela asks, black nails resting on her black baton. 'Would you mind coming out here for a second?'

She's still staring at us. None of the softness is left.

He nods hastily as he rises, speaking very loudly. 'Of course, my lass. Thanks for stopping by, Linny. It was nice seeing you!'

When they have left, I finish my tea and put the mug into the sink. I try not to think about what I've just read. I reach for a pile of Post-it Notes and a pen, and leave him a note, telling him about the broken window in my sitting room, if only to establish a paper trail, then make my way out through the back door. It locks automatically behind me.

Emerging into the parking lot, it only takes me a few steps to get back to the car. The spade is lying across the back seat, its metal glinting silver in the grey light. Even though it's only noon, the sun seems already to be setting, the sky turning orange, the clouds black. We are due for some dirty weather.

As I drive, I think of the candle. *Used on the victim.* My thighs clench involuntarily. I push my legs firmly together. Try to suppress the cramps. No more cramps. Heat shoots through me. Shame, fury, rage. They are making my blood boil. No surprise Graham wanted to spare me. He thought seeing it would be horrible for me, humiliating.

All it does is make me furious.

I want the fucking truth. I want the world to remember.

All of it. Even the bloody candle. It's nothing I've got to be ashamed of. I didn't put it there, did I? I think of the candle, the nightshade, the other flowers, the matches. I want to remember it all. All that I've made myself forget. All that Graham doesn't want me to know. Where was he, anyway, that night? If he didn't break out Jay and Oliver, where was he?

I want the world to remember. The candle, the matches. How much it hurt when I spread my legs, for weeks afterwards. How I had to quit my job at the FilmBox, the job I loved. Cinema seemed to be so exciting at the time, and the FilmBox was a lovely old thing. We didn't have too many customers, but we had great snacks from the local bakery and free matches and did a raffle every Saturday and Wednesday where you could win free tickets for a film recommended specifically by the owner, Ms Roberts, a lady in her seventies who addressed everyone as *luv*. Sarah, she said I should call her.

It suddenly occurs to me she might be dead.

Sarah can't be dead. I would have wanted to see her off at least, be at the funeral. She was everything I wanted to be, a retired biology professor putting her passion for film to good use. Never wore any makeup and still looked so stunning. I would have wanted to be there. She'd have deserved that.

Like my parents.

I want to go see them. I haven't seen them in so long. As I think it, I feel the tears burn at the backs of my eyes again.

Only this time, they really fall.

And I let them. Allow myself to remember them, for the first time: Dad and his way of wanting to but never knowing how to be there for me, all hesitant touches and awkward conversation openers and warm hugs. Mum, always smelling like earth or cigarettes or her flowers, a pragmatic, who would have done anything for me, but what she never managed to say was 'I love you.' And neither did I.

Not once.

Now that I am back here, back at our house, now that I see our things, our life, once I have let the tears fall, I cannot seem to stop them. Cannot stop thinking about Mum's flowers, her lavender, her herbs, her roses. Mum loved them like she loved us. She would have loved her own funeral, the heaps of dried flowers, and Dad would have smiled and pressed her hand so gently, both of them in their best clothes, the worn black suit and long black dress, sitting in the back, crying freely.

Sobs are racking my body. Stopping the car at the top of the drive, I rest my head against the steering wheel. I wish I'd said goodbye. I wish I'd been here. I wish I'd told them I loved them, and that it wasn't their fault. I wish I'd cried before. The tears feel hot and the sobs ring loudly in my ears and shivers shake my body as I remember what it is like to feel. Remember that life wasn't always this bland, grey thing, a thing that you didn't get rid of only because that would have meant caring enough to bother.

I cry until no more tears will come. For another while, I sit with my eyes closed, just feeling my body, the blood in my ears, the pulse of my heart. Remembering my mum's way of showing me things, patient, strong; my dad's long hugs and his rare grin. Feeling the overwhelming guilt that I made them suffer, that I couldn't be what they needed, that I locked them out. Knowing they'd forgive me. They'd already forgiven me. Otherwise, Mum wouldn't have given away the nightshade. She wouldn't have.

When I put the car back in gear and head down the drive, I feel warm. Clean. Like you feel after a long hot shower after a whole day at work in the garden, washing out the sweat and soil from under your nails and out of every line of your skin.

My parents didn't remember me as a cautionary tale. They weren't perfect, hellfire, no, sometimes awkward and sometimes too quiet and sometimes too loud, but they remembered me as their daughter, not as a victim.

It's time I proved them right.

Fortunately, it has not started raining when I park the car in front of the house. Not too close this time. After all, I will need the space.

I know I'm not particularly clever. Never finished my A-levels, did I? Never learned anything proper. Oliver even called me his silly-billy sometimes, in an affectionate way of course.

But I'm a florist. We did gardens, too, in training. That means I know how to dig a hole. They're really useful, holes. At least this one will be.

A hole that you won't see in the dark when you come down the drive and up to the door. A hole you won't see until it's too late.

ANNA

She has been past his place, too. I went to see Teo, and he told me.

He told me other things, too, as I sat on his couch and he made tea for us with trembling fingers. Told me about Jay. About the arson offences. He looked so upset. I had forgotten, just a little, what Teoman looked like when he was upset. Like a blunt knife suddenly sharpened, it came back to me. It turns him into a wild thing.

They promised it would not go on my record! he said, pacing in his flat, clenching his fists. The radio was on. He rushed to the counter, stabbed the off button, a tight ball of frustration. *They said I had a clean slate! A chance at a life.*

I sat on his parents' worn cushions, bare feet tucked under my body. I wonder now whether I should have been afraid, provided I were not physically incapable of being afraid of him.

Teo was shouting, about the Detective Inspector. *That*

bastard didn't even listen! Every day, I go through life making sure I don't look like a threat, performing the good brown guy for the sake of arseholes like him, and he won't even listen!

They never listen, I said.

Nobody listened to Jay either, so that is how he made himself heard, Teo went on. His eyes were red. *You have to make yourself heard,* he finally said.

Not by setting buildings on fire, I said.

Why not?

The moment he had said it, his eyes widened. He sat down. He apologised. His hands were shaking. *You know what it's like,* he said.

I looked at him. *Don't apologise,* I said.

Now I am home, putting a CD into the stereo. One he gave me, The Cranberries, No Need to Argue. That was what we did, Teoman and I: music. He played the guitar, the piano. I sang.

He still plays. Took it up again after his time in prison. That's why he knows the radio schedule so well: the only connection to the outside world he had in his cell, and the only source of music. *All I had,* he said, *was a radio and time to think. It was all I needed. Except a guitar. I missed my guitar so fucking much, Anna.*

I am so glad to have him back.

It is dark out. I look out of the sitting-room window, out at the road. Into the woods. They are dark. Teo was still upset when I left.

My hands are shaking when I put the CD in.

You know what it is like.

LINN

When night falls, everything is prepared.

I am inside the house, still sweating like a pig. I mean, have you ever tried digging a hole in your garden? Putting in a new flower bed? When the last time you worked out was in the previous decade? The spade kept slipping through my slick hands. It took me an hour to remember what work gloves were for and another twenty minutes to find them in my parents' shed. They always used to be in the cupboard under the sink. I almost gave up halfway through, but then remembered my mum and dad didn't. JFDI, as she used to say.

I thought about the case file while I worked, the photos and that list of flowers. Something is wrong with it. It must be the daisies. You know that you can't dry daisies, right? And Mum only ever kept dry flowers in the house.

I look around. Blink as perspiration drops into my eyes. It burns. I blink again, but my vision will not clear.

Impatiently, I rub my sleeve across my eyes, my face. Dusk is settling over the hollow now, the woods, the dirt road. The shadows of the trees have already grown long, sneaking over the front porch, my body, my face where I am standing in the dark kitchen. Dirt and dust are shimmering in the oppressive air where I worked, thrown up by my spade. I feel the little hairs on the back of my neck stand up, feel the sweat drying on my skin.

The trees outside are tall, black sticks in the fading light. There's nothing to hear over the hum in the air, over the pressure in my ears. Things seem to whisper. Seem to move. Leaves, rustling. Birds, curiously silent until they take off with a sudden flap of their wings. Beetles and worms, crawling through the undergrowth.

Slowly, I glance into the darkness, where the hole should be. It is too dark to see now. I dug up the flower beds as well, put in the winter aconites, the dahlias. *All the red dahlias you want, Mum.* Pretended I was digging holes for plants, not people. But there it is, a hole in front of the porch. It's not as deep as I'd like it to be, but it's there. A gap in the ground, as wide as the steps leading up the porch and the front door, four feet deep I should say. If you step into it without knowing it's there, you'll sprain your ankle at the very least.

The spade felt heavy in my hands as I put it away, as heavy as two loads of washing. As heavy as the pink slip in the midst of an economic crisis – 2008 was the last time I'd had work. But how good it feels to look at them now: the flowers, right there in my garden. In front of my porch. My house. A distraction from the hole I dug for my nightly visitor.

My begonias are sitting in the kitchen with me. Together, we settle in for the wait. The hole might not stop the Doorman, but it'll slow them down enough for me to catch a glimpse of them. It'll give me a warning when they shout. It'll let them know that I'm not willing to take it lying down.

And it might make them angry.

What would the Doorman do? If they were angry?

The last time, they came in and took my panties. Would they leave it at that when they were mad with pain and wounded pride?

They wouldn't. They would come in. They would tear off my trousers, stained or not. They would press their hand to my mouth so that I couldn't scream. *You stupid whore.* They would whisper so closely to my ear that I could feel their saliva spraying against my skin. And then they would pull off my panties. Push their legs between my knees. If I fought back, they would thrash me. Push their fist into my mouth till I choked while they penetrated me.

I start, choke. Stare outside. Feel the sweat dry on my skin in the night air. Glance at my car, where it should be. I know it's parked a little out of the way, sitting in the drive, even though I can't see it in the darkness. The air is still heavy, a thunderstorm lurking.

I am not going back.

With a determined straightening of my shoulders, I march to the mud room and grab the spade, stowing it by the front door. Not a bad weapon. Then I climb up the stairs to the bathroom. I won't run. There's been enough running. So much that I didn't even say goodbye to my parents when I ought to. But I will. First thing tomorrow, we'll make a trip to the graveyard, me and the most beautiful flowers I can find.

Plus some dried ones.

Once in the bathroom, I undress, feeling the rivulets of sweat on my skin, under my armpits, between my thighs where the fat rubs together when I walk, when I stand. It makes me think of the photo from the file, the imprint of sweat I left on my parents' bed, the shape of my body clearly visible. My slim waist, the round curve of my breasts, the length of my face.

It makes me think of what they found on the crime scene; that box of matches. Mum's dried flowers. Roses, nightshade, caspias, rosemary, thyme. The daisies. And the candle.

That bloody candle.

And those matches. I'm still thinking about them, too. The candle, the matches, the daisies. Like I was getting ready for a date.

Daisies were Anna's favourite flowers, weren't they?

Once in the shower, the warm water calms me down a little. I make it quick though. I don't want to run the risk of missing any sounds from outside. Drying off hastily, I put on some more of my mum's clothes – her jeans, her jacket – Dad's thick boots. It feels good to be in their clothes. Proper. Like I'm back where I belong. Then I sit down at the kitchen table, turn the lights off and wait.

Sitting in the dark is a strange thing. It makes you think.

Anna used to love daisies. They grew all around the house, still do, actually, I think. People would come pick them in the forest all the time. If I'd wanted to make it nice for her, I would have picked some daisies for her for sure.

I realise my pulse is going too quickly. Just from thinking about it.

Her.

The truth is, we weren't just fooling around.

Listen, it was different back then. Maybe in London you could go for it, maybe even in Manchester, but out here, it just wasn't done. And after that night, I couldn't bear the thought of anybody touching me – man or woman, it really didn't matter. Only Oliver felt safe.

Still.

It's come back to me a few times. In my dreams. Kissing her. And other things.

I told you she'd been in my dreams the past nineteen years, remember? Bet you didn't think it was quite in that way.

I shift. Think of the candle. Think of Anna and me, both of us alone in our dark, lonely houses. I know Graham believes it's stupid of me to be here. Even back then, he didn't make a secret out of it, that he thought my parents shouldn't have left me alone.

What would he make of my little theory, I wonder?

Not that he's trustworthy. And even if he was, not that I could ask him. *He*'s sitting alone in his house, isn't he? He goes wherever he pleases, or doesn't go, for that matter. I thought he might react to the note I left him. Maybe even stop by, finally take a statement now that something had finally broken. No sign of him though.

I shift in the darkness, glancing outside. The hollow is dark.

Pitch-black.

And I keep sitting here, thinking of Graham in his home. Jay's body in his front room. Teoman in his flat. And of Anna, only a few miles up the road. How she didn't text me back all those years ago after New Year's Eve. How I went to the cinema for a first date with Oliver when she wouldn't answer, not telling him how I felt about her. Oliver and I went to the FilmBox and laughed till we cried; he told me he wanted to help people for a living; he kissed me, this good-looking young man kissed me, and it felt good, it really did. At the end of the night he and I said we'd meet again; how great it had been. He thought we were going somewhere, didn't he?

It is absurd to remember it, a time when I didn't know Oliver inside out; when I didn't know the way he slept, always on his side, always curled up like a foetus; the way he breathes more heavily when he is upset, the only sign you'll get; the way he lit up when he first looked at his shaven head, worries about his receding hairline and grey hairs finally a thing of the past.

Because we ended up going somewhere, didn't we, after that night had happened. We became husband and wife. After I had looked into Anna's guilty face and realised she was a liar, after I had almost killed myself with a flower, I went with the man who made me laugh. Never went to study nursing myself, or medicine, or botany. I couldn't deal with any bodies – not with my own, not with strange ones. I couldn't even deal with going outside. How would I have gone to uni? Oliver had trouble getting me out of the flat to go to the cinema with him once a week.

He must be glad he's finally free of me, I think, not entirely fairly.

There's always the Open University. It's not the first time I think about it. Over the years, it popped back into my mind again and again. But Oliver always said, *Look, I earn enough for the two of us, don't I? Why put yourself through that?*

Time to put myself through a few things.

I know Oliver only wanted to protect me. My mouth twitches. But I wish he would have encouraged me. Not that it would have helped, I suppose. I'm not blaming him for my fuck-ups.

After an hour of waiting, I realise it's probably far too early for the Doorman to come by. They usually don't come until it is well into the night, I think, past midnight. It's only half nine. I get up to put the kettle on. With a steaming mug of tea in my hand, I retreat to the sitting room. The list is lying on the couch table. I've added *candle and daisies – date? What's missing?* If I check the clock regularly, I can return to the kitchen in an hour or so. Till then, I leave the television off, nothing that could betray my presence, and stare at the list.

Unfortunately, looking at it won't help. I put it down after a very unproductive few minutes and reach for my ancient copy of *Get into UK Nursing School for Dummies* instead.

While I wait, I look at the anatomy charts. The thing is, I realise, pictures like this, they actually help: looking at the body in this clinical way. Seeing that the parts of me that have been used have names. Proper names, like ectocervix. That I can finally tell where it hurt, not just that it did. That I can begin to put into words what has happened to me. They are just parts of my anatomy, parts of everybody's anatomy. Well, or 50 per cent of everybody's. The ectocervix can't define me. It's only a part of me, a tiny part ...

I sit up suddenly. Didn't realise how deep in thought I'd been. Was there a noise? Anything I couldn't place? Anything I'd missed? Hands still on the old pages, I look about myself. Check the clock up on the wall. It's barely ten. Too early still.

My tea's gone cold. I put down the book and turn off the reading light just to be on the safe side, plunging the house into complete darkness. Carefully, I pick my way through the sitting room towards the kitchen, suddenly blind. When my hand wraps around the door handle, I hesitate. The last time I was in there late at night, they were already standing in front of the window. Watching me.

But now it's dark in the kitchen, and there's no light in the sitting room, either. They couldn't see me. My eyes are slowly getting accustomed to the dark, slowly. I can see the outline of the doorknob now.

Besides, I'm done being afraid.

With a deep breath, I push open the door.

The kitchen lies dark before me. There's almost no light filtering in through the windows. The sky hasn't cleared. I steal into the room, making sure not to stand in front of the window. It is far too early, I remind myself.

I put the kettle on again, lean back against the stove and wait for the water to boil. While I do, I push my fingers into my body parts. The fat at my thighs. Subcutaneous fat, I remember. It feels good using my head again. Recalling things. I try to remember more, moving along my body with my fingers: stroking over my forehead to feel the cranium, down between my breasts for the scapula, for the sternum. I have the impression I can feel my brain rewiring while I try to recall the terms, the words, from the back of my mind. Ulna and radius, the two bones of the lower arm. It reminds me of being in school. How long I haven't been in school. When was the last time I really thought? Sat down and thought, instead of rushing from one chore to another, managing life, even the very small life that I had, which sometimes meant nothing but managing to get up and to the washing machine, to the supermarket and back to the couch to watch TV at night and make sure I kept going long enough not to go look for deadly nightshade berries.

In London of all places. Good luck with that, anyway.

Not that I didn't like TV. Except for the medical procedurals, there used to be so many I couldn't stand to watch, just because none of it made any sense, even to someone like myself, with no more than a layman's interest. I liked *Scrubs* though. That one was good. Really good.

Involuntarily, I smile as I think of that young doctor in the show, the main one, and how the janitor always accused him of jamming a door with a penny on his first day. Then I remember the musical episode. Catch myself giggling. God, that was funny, wasn't it? So much fun. I laugh, alone in my kitchen.

Would my parents still have the DVDs?

I return to the sitting room with a fresh cuppa and pull the first season out of the cupboard. The player still seems to be working. It's even still hooked up to the TV. They had this amazing intro song. It begins playing the moment the menu comes up. 'Superman'. Can't remember the band now. I hum along as I settle on the couch, glancing at the clock once more. Fifteen minutes. I can afford fifteen minutes. Just till half ten. Then I'll turn all the lights back off.

The intro starts playing. I can't help singing along. 'I can't do this all on my own, oh, I know, I'm no superman ...' Wow, they look so young, these actors. Why did I never realise how young they looked? Or, rather: why does it only occur to me now that they must look so much older now? Still recognisable, still themselves, just more wrinkles, more body fat.

That's when I hit PAUSE to go for a pack of crisps in the kitchen; nothing like thinking about body fat while digging deep into a plastic bag of salt and vinegar crisps with your greasy fingers. Making sure to turn all lights off again before I enter the kitchen, I make my way towards the cupboard where my parents kept their stock of snack foods.

It's then. When I open the cupboard, the old wood creaking, I hear it.

A scream.

My blood freezes. My head shoots up, towards the window. It is coming from the front of the house.

I know that voice.

THE DETECTIVE INSPECTOR

God, have I made a mistake?

Chapter 7

It is the first Sunday of the new millennium. A young woman is parking her bike in front of the local cinema, the FilmBox. A young man is waiting for her. He has already bought two tickets. 'You shouldn't have,' she says. He answers with a shrug. His eyes are blue. Oliver Dawson knows how to behave. His father taught him well.

They go inside together. Once in the cosy lobby, he makes for the loo. While he is gone, she buys two apple turnovers, still warm, and two Cokes. He looks at her oddly when he comes back.

They are surprised and excited to find out that they both love the film, love it so much, still laughing when the credits roll. Still laughing when they go for a walk afterwards, rehashing the very best bits. The FilmBox is always a bit late; it was Austin Powers: The Spy Who Shagged Me. *Much more fun than* The World Is Not Enough, *they both agree. She acts out her favourite parts and he laughs in that quiet, pleased way of his, that way she really likes.*

They sit down by the river to look at the stars and listen to the sound of the water. He tells her he wants to be a nurse. He wants to help people. So do I, she says, enthusiastic. Unless I can be a botanist on Mars. That'd be even better. They compare what they know about body parts already, poking each other, playfully, a live anatomy competition. When she puts a hand to his cheekbone and says zygomatic bone, he smiles. He really wants to kiss her. He tells her his parents are getting a divorce. She puts a comforting hand on his arm and feels him shiver. She likes his arms, the feel of his muscles shifting under her palm. But she likes him even more.

She tells him about her uni plans. Going to Edinburgh or Nottingham with Anna and Teo, becoming a doctor or a biologist. He is strangely silent while she does, Linn notices.

When they're back at her bike, he asks whether they should meet up again. She says yes. He says he's going downtown tomorrow, he needs a few things. Clothes, a new fragrance, maybe even a watch; his father gave him some money for Christmas. For the party on Friday. She'll be there, won't she?

Aye, she says. I'll be there. My parents will be out in Leeds! Oliver smiles, but it looks sad.

'Why do you look so sad?' Linn asks.

He seems too embarrassed to say it. Then he straightens his shoulders. Breathes in, breathes out. 'It's just so sad. That we've only gone out for the first time now, and soon, you'll be off to uni and we'll never see each other again.'

'Of course we will,' she says.

'No,' he says. 'You'll forget me. Once you're out there, a doctor and all, you will. Like Mum forgot about Dad.'

Linn laughs. 'Don't be so gloomy!' She is glad to hear him laugh in response. 'I'll see you tomorrow at school.'

Flowers for the Dead

Then she takes off. While she drives, all she can think about is that Anna still hasn't got back to her. That Anna's still all Linn can think about the minute she's no longer distracted. About her lips and her singing and her smell. About how it will be all awkward now. That she has fucked this up. That she needs to speak with them.

Aye, she thinks, she'll go speak with them. With Teo, at least. Linn turns her bike around and makes for the Dündars' apartment. She rings the doorbell like they do. Ding, ding, ding. Teo's voice rings out through the intercom. 'Come up, Caroline.'

'Ta, Teoman,' she says. And then rings the bell again, just for fun. Ding, ding, ding.

LINN

I turn on the outside lights in the hallway, throw open the front door and rush outside.

It's Graham. Graham's caught his leg in the hole. He's cursing like a mad homeless man on the bus in London. His face twisted in pain, he pulls his leg out of the hole and looks up at me. 'What's going on here, Linn?'

I stare at him. He got caught in my trap. The Detective Inspector.

What did Kaitlin say? When did he leave the house that night to come to my place? Midnight?

Wasn't that far too early?

The spade's still leaning by the doorframe. I take a step back.

'Why is there a hole in front of your ...' He peters out as he spots the outline of the spade behind me. His expression changes. 'Linny?'

I take another step back, just a small step. He watches me. 'You serious, Linn? That was your plan?'

I still haven't said anything.

They are all lying to you.

He tries to put some weight on his foot, gingerly, but judging from the expression on his face, it hurts too much. 'I found your note,' he calls out, fishing around in his pocket, then pulling it out. Raising it up. 'I thought I'd come by to check on your window. Wanted to call you, but then I remembered you still haven't got any reception.'

Again I retreat as he limps a little closer. Move closer to the spade. My mind is racing. 'At this time?'

'Couldn't have Mary know, now could I?' he asks. 'I mean, Detective Sergeant Zwambe. And Angela. About how we looked at the file. Had to wait till she'd left. She's been watching us, you know? Good lass, but suspicious. It's in her nature, I think. Not a bad lass, not at all, Mary Zwambe. Just a little over the top sometimes. Bit hysterical. She found your file down in the archive. I'd got it back out after you'd arrived here. She's been on my case lately, I don't know.'

I relax infinitesimally, glancing at my watch. Still early.

I cannot trust him. But there's something I'd like to ask him.

Reaching for his arm to support him, I help him up, his face still twisted as he hobbles up the steps and into the kitchen. 'Tea?' I ask while handing him an ice pack, but he shakes his head.

'No, thanks,' he says. 'It's just you really got to take care of yourself, Linny. I don't mean like this. Don't like this one little bit. A man like that ... Don't want to provoke him.'

I remember what Anna's mum used to say. *If you shouted, at least you'd used your voice.* Think of the item he didn't want

301

C. K. Williams

me to see. *A man like that.* The thing they found on the scene of the crime.

The candle.

It makes me think of the picture of Miss Luca and the rumours about her. The rumours that just wouldn't go away. How she used to look at me from across her desk, then look down quickly once I caught her staring, how she'd play down the flowers. Her affair with Graham.

And again and again, my thoughts return to the candle.

'Teo was the only one you took into custody, wasn't he?' I ask. 'The night it happened?'

He looks up sharply. 'Why're you asking? Why would you ask that?'

He sounds upset. Is he thinking the same thing as I am?

All these years, were we looking for a man? Because that's what you expect, don't you, when something like this happens?

'What about Miss Luca? And Anna?'

'They were brought in for questioning of course.' Graham looks at me, still unfavourably unshaven, his stubble looking like dirt, the bags under his eyes surprisingly large. Already he sounds calmer. But he hasn't put the ice on his ankle yet. 'What are you getting at?'

'They didn't say anything? You didn't question them about ... You treated them as witnesses?'

Graham's brow furrows. I can see how the penny drops.

Then he bursts into laughter.

'God, sorry,' he says, wiping his eyes as he finally presses the ice to his leg. 'I'm so sorry, Linny, really. I just ... For a moment I thought you were being serious. That you'd actually seen something that'd been overlooked all these years. God, I really ... Sorry.'

I have never seen him laugh like that. His entire body is shaking with relief. I turn away, reach for the begonias, to water them in the sink. They need to be repotted, I realise. That is why they have been struggling so much. It is time for them to go outside, into a bed, or a larger pot. I look back out of the window, out towards the porch. But all I see is Anna's face. Miss Luca's photo, in tears, as upset as I'd ever seen her. Graham, leaving his house too early. Leaving her alone. 'She never got upset. No matter what happened.'

'Linny,' Graham says while I keep watching the hollow in the window, blending with our reflections. 'You can't take someone into custody for getting upset at a crime scene, you really can't.' He's calmed down a little, looking more serious now. 'Look, statistics are on my side here. The great majority of violent crimes are committed by men. Simple fact. You're just way ahead of us there, women, I mean. I mean, it's good to have a man by your side in a tight spot, right, but there's downsides to everything.'

I turn back to him. 'You didn't want me to know about the candle, though.'

He flinches. Looks down. 'Hellfire, Linn.'

I stare back relentlessly. 'You covered up the list today.'

'God, Linn, really.'

'It's possible,' I insist.

He puts up his hands. 'Trust me. This wasn't a woman.'

'Like it wasn't somebody we knew?'

He presses his lips together. Then he rises, still careful not to put pressure on his foot. 'Want me to have a look at that back door of yours?'

I nod, my brain going one hundred miles an hour. All these years, I didn't know about the candle. Matches, flowers, a candle. Like a date.

What did Jay say? That Anna and I spent the entirety of his party kissing?

I go ahead into the sitting room, where *Scrubs* is still on pause, and stuff the list into my pocket before Graham can spot it. He picks his way through to the back door, takes one look at it and says someone definitely tried to come in. Asks me to come to the station with him. We should file a charge. Establish a paper trail. Every little helps.

Before we leave, he helps me board up the broken window. I make sure all doors are locked, then step out onto the porch. His car sits up at the far end of the drive. I didn't hear him drive up, not with the TV running. 'You better fill this hole back up, Linny,' he says as we walk to our cars. 'It's a danger to everyone. Including yourself.'

Nodding, I turn off the outside lights. He's right. I already have a better idea for the bloody Doorman. Doorwoman.

A happy ending for this story.

As Graham unlocks his car, I lock the front door.

That's when I see it. From the corner of my eye.

A figure slipping away. Into the garden. Into the woods.

And if the figure wasn't holding a rifle, I don't know what else it was.

THE DETECTIVE INSPECTOR

That's just stupid. I mean, seriously. A woman?

Don't wanna complain though. I'm just relieved. I really thought that she'd seen something that had been overlooked. I really thought, that candle ...

But it's all good now, isn't it? I mean, she can dig all the holes she wants. Not bad, anyway, that initiative. Haven't been giving her enough credit, apparently. And it would make sense for her to think up all these theories, wouldn't it? Now that she's back here. I shouldn't have shown her the file.

Then again, it was the only thing I could do, wasn't it?

Because the thing is ... You see, I take my job seriously. Always have. That's why Jay Mason came as such a shock to me. Believe it or not, he's the first one I knew, really knew who ... went and did it. I always thought it was my job to protect my people. The people of this town, especially the children, the teenagers. They're still learning, aren't they, what's right and what's wrong. Sure, they make mistakes, but should one mistake really be allowed to ruin your entire life? They belong here, and here is where we need to protect them.

What if it costs a lie to do so?

What's one lie?

We're all of us liars. It's how we get by. You can't spend all your life with the same couple of hundred people and always tell the truth. It'd collapse, all of it. Because deep down, we all make mistakes and don't want to admit to it.

It's just for the kids. It's for them that we keep pretending we don't make mistakes.

We are all liars. Linn, too. I know what she looks like when she's lying. She does something with her face, a twitch of her mouth, always has, even as a child. Still as a teenager, when I caught her and her strange friends in the parking lot in the middle of the night, where she brazenly claimed they'd never rung my doorbell at all. Ding, ding, ding.

Don't you realise she's lying to me? Don't you realise she's lying to you?

LINN

The next morning, I use some of the soil to repot my begonias. They look good in one of my parents' large pots, sitting bright and chuffed on my porch, like a dare. 'You look bloody amazing, my darlings,' I tell them, and draw my hands along the chimes as I leave on foot, humming along to their song.

My legs are burning, but in a good way. I went for a run right after I got up. The ache is setting in already, pulling at the muscles in my thighs and lower legs, even the soles of my feet. But it's a good ache. I can tell you exactly where it hurts: the quadriceps. The hamstrings. I know why it hurts and how it happened. They are a part of me, my muscles, the quads, the tendon behind my knee. They belong to me. I use them and nobody else.

Now I'm using them to stride through the woods. I know exactly where I'm going. The air is still heavy. That storm might still be coming.

When the Kenzies' house comes into view, I slow down. There's a bike sitting in the drive. I settle in for a wait.

Before noon, I see her emerge from the door. She's wearing another white dress, no print this time. Her helmet's blue, dark blue like the faux leather of her jacket. Once she's put it on, she mounts the bike, kicks it to life and takes off.

I wait another five minutes. Then I move. Back to the house, to get my car. I park it in her drive, get out and sneak around the house and to the back.

The Kenzies never locked the door to their basement. I know for a fact it didn't even have a lock.

Looks like Anna hasn't upgraded. I pull the hatch open, shut it behind me and climb down the stairs.

Where did she say the Kenzies kept that mantrap?

The basement looks much like it used to. Only when I climb up to the ground floor do I realise how much Anna's presence has changed the place. The moment I step into the hallway, I catch a whiff of her. The way she smells. Not just her perfume. No, the way she smells when you put your nose to her neck, pressing your bodies against each other as you hug. Paper and perfume and pine trees.

Not that she's redecorated much. It's her jackets up on the coat rack, her shoes under the bench by the front door, her laptop on the desk in the sitting room, but other than that, I recognise it all. It seems like she hasn't moved in to stay. As if she's still waiting for something.

Quickly, I climb the stairs to the first floor, then the second. There's only one room up here, the Kenzies' old bedroom. A large space, walls already slanting. The wood creaks under my feet as I enter. The bed is pristine, the white sheets and blue pillows. I wonder if they smell like her. There sits a vase on the nightstand as well as a few books and an old alarm clock. The vase is azure porcelain. The curtains fall light and white from the ceiling to the floor, translucent fabric, beautiful things.

That's where I saw her standing, by the bedroom window, the day I arrived here. Where I saw the silhouette.

That is also where the trapdoor is, leading up to the attic.

Dust crawls into my lungs the moment I open it and start climbing the ladder. By the time I make it all the way to the top, I am coughing so strongly my eyes are tearing up. It's dark up here, the air stale. With my fingers, I feel around for a light switch, trying to remember where it was. To my left, wasn't it? Low on the slanted wall.

I reach through cobwebs, sticky and soft against my fingers. Feel something small and hard, like mice droppings. When I finally touch the wooden wall, I feel splinters. They sting my skin. I curse as I hit a nail poking out at the wrong angle, drawing blood. It burns.

Then I hit the plastic of the light switch and flip it. A single light bulb flickers to life. Its light is dull and yellow, the glass frosted. I don't think they even make these any more. There was this EU law everybody complained about, wasn't there?

Squinting, I look around the attic. It's crammed with stuff, boxes, shelves, such a chaos of things you don't need but don't want to get rid of. I know for a fact that my parents' attic doesn't look any different. The boxes and shelves throw long shadows everywhere, blocking the bulb, making it hard to see.

The thing is, a mantrap is hard to miss.

I knew the Kenzies had one. They showed it to my parents once, a curious heirloom from Mr Kenzie's grandpa, who'd apparently been a landowner in the South in the late nine-teenth century. The type of landowner who thought mantraps were a good idea, especially covered with leaves outside the house, to keep poachers off their hunting grounds.

Seems I'm one of them now.

They said it's a leg trap. When you step onto a metal plate in the centre, it snaps shut. It doesn't kill, only immobilises your leg. Only you might not be using the limb any more afterwards. I look at the heavy steel and the sharp spikes, waiting to drill into your flesh.

I remember Mum saying they'd been illegal since the 1800s. Not inside your house between sunset and sunrise, Mr Kenzie corrected her. He showed us how the trap works, too.

It sits between a couple of boxes towards the back. The boxes aren't hard to move; the trap is. It's so heavy I'm not sure I can carry it, much less without setting it off.

Biting my lip, tasting sweat and dust, I lug it across the attic towards the trapdoor. Fortunately, the ladder has wide steps, allowing me to pull it down one step at a time. When I've made it back to the bedroom, I return to the car for the hand trolley I brought. It helps me get the trap down two floors and into the back of the car.

While I'm still by the car, hoisting the hand trolley into it, I hear the roar of an engine. A bike, coming up the dirt road.

Flowers for the Dead

Hastily, I reach for the old blanket in the back and spread it out on top of the trap. I close the boot, jump into the car, start the engine.

I've already reversed and turned back towards the road when I stop.

Anna's scent is still in my nose. So uniquely hers.

I kill the engine. The candle. The matches. The daisies.

My mother only ever kept dried flowers in the house. Always either rosemary and thyme *or* lavender in the bedroom, never both, and *never* fresh flowers.

It must have been a date. There is only one person who wasn't Oliver who would have come for a date to my house nineteen years ago. And she is driving towards me.

I won't run. Not any more.

The bike comes into sight between the tall trunks of the trees. I sit behind the steering wheel and wait. Anna hesitates the moment she spots me. Slows down until she can put her feet to the ground. Stands up. Watches me. I can't see her face through her helmet, but I could swear she's watching me.

Then she kicks the gears and comes down the drive, practised, not minding the loose gravel. She stops right next to my window. Takes off the helmet. Her blonde strands are in a terrible disarray.

She only looks at me until I finally put down the window. 'Hello, Linn,' she says.

'Hello, Anna.'

Her voice sounds perfectly calm. Everything about her seems poised. Her perfume is light in the heavy air. 'What are you doing here?'

I don't say anything. *Why were you at the house, last night?*

It's time to find out if she was serious about me. If she really loved me. If she could have been so jealous of Oliver that she ...

'Do you want to come inside?' she asks.

'I shouldn't,' I say, mouth twitching, even though what I think is *yes*. My mind's still working on muscle memory. My gut is telling me to go with this woman. *It's what you want. It's what you've always wanted.*

You want to know.

'Not even for one cup of tea?' Anna asks. She tilts her head.

We go inside. She makes tea in the Kenzies' uncannily modern kitchen, then we move into the sitting room. While she takes the armchair, I sit down on the sofa, a fine thing, also left by the Kenzies. Look at us. Living off the generation before us, who could still afford property and furniture and nice things.

Anna has wrapped both hands around her mug. She's still watching me. I'm watching her, too. The lines on her face and the white in her hair and her long, strong fingers. Imagine them wrapped around a candle. Wax instead of porcelain.

Ding, ding, ding. I never would have suspected anything evil.

You see, I never actually found out whether she wanted me. Graham always suspected Teo because he was convinced that he was in love with me, upset that I'd gone to the cinema with Oliver, upset that he couldn't have me. Graham didn't even think about Anna. Neither did I. After she hadn't replied to my text, I couldn't even fathom she might have any interest in me. That's why I went on that first date with Oliver.

My parents were relieved, I think. They'd never been sure about Anna and Teo. They'd always thought they were a little strange, that boy who was much too friendly and the girl who never said anything when they were in the same room. They didn't show it to them, of course. And I never explained it to them, not properly. I know Mum would have understood, the moment she'd seen how Teo talked about his future, the way she had always talked about my own, as something filled with possibilities. The future was never scary to my mother. And so would Dad, just as soon as he'd seen how Anna ran, like someone who had everything to lose. He would have hugged her like he hugged me, trying to protect us with his arms and his silence.

But if Jay was right, if Anna and I kissed again at his party, all night even, does it not stand to reason that we might also have gone on a date? That same night? That she might have come to my house and rung my doorbell?

'Why are you looking at me like that?' Anna asks. She's not moving. Just tilting her head.

The trouble is, I don't even know if Anna really wanted me. Still don't know if she didn't just kiss me for a lark. New Year's, or at Jay's party. I tried to play it casual, as teenagers do, after that stupid text. Didn't want it to ruin everything.

It just wasn't talked about so much back then. *Queer As Folk* had only just aired, caused outrage, and that was about men mostly, not women. It wasn't like today. Out here and back then, you would've made damn sure nobody suspected that there was anything about you that wasn't perfectly normal. Just think of Miss Luca. And no one would have believed Anna, anyway, even if she had said anything of the kind. Not a woman like her. Not someone who was blonde and had a fine face and was from Poland too. It wasn't possible, not with that neckline.

Time to find out.

'I think I love you,' I say.

She draws in a sharp breath. Then she puts down her mug. I expect her to say something. My heart is hammering, suddenly. I watch her rise. Watch her sit next to me on the sofa. Our legs brush up against each other. My skin is tingling where they touch. 'Is this all right?' she asks quietly. The fabric of her dress is thin, worn. I can almost feel the heat of her skin.

And just like that, this turns into something different altogether.

I lean in to kiss her. She doesn't turn away. We kiss like teenagers, sitting next to each other, no parts of our bodies touching but our lips and the sides of our legs. When she separates us, just by a few inches, I chase her, involuntarily. We kiss again, making my legs go giddy, before she looks at me and I at her. 'Is that all right?'

I nod. I don't know why there are tears burning at the backs of my eyes. Because nobody's ever asked, I think. Not even Oliver.

She seems to hesitate. It is a sight I'm so used to it almost hurts. Then she angles her body towards me. And smiles. 'Then how about we do it properly?'

When I lean back in to kiss her, it is not like teenagers any more. My skin flushes, heat spreading out from my lap. I'd forgotten it could feel like that. I have forgotten you could be so entirely in your own body.

I'd forgotten how much I'd been in love with her.

Made myself forget.

And it almost makes me forget what I came for. 'So,' I say, breathless, when we separate again. Just for a moment. 'You wanted this? Even back then? You were in love with me?'

Anna looks back at me. There is no guilt, no lie, no prevarication in her expression. Only a smile. 'Yes. I was.'

ANNA

That she would have to ask.

What is incredible is not how I feel about her. It is that she might feel the same way about *me*. Linn had pretended that it had all been a huge joke, when we saw each other again at the party at Jacob's, the Friday after New Year's Eve, kissing me again but claiming it was just a bit of fun.

And aren't we all a little too old for this? These silly doubts. This back and forth. This believing that you would not be good enough for somebody. Believing that you could still be happy. As I feel her cheek under my palm, her lips against mine, her knee shaking against my hip, I realise that believing you are not good enough for somebody is still very much a thing I am capable of.

Besides.

This is Linn we are talking about.

My therapist thought it was an obsession. I did not dare

to tell her the truth: that I was not obsessed. I could have let Linn go. I *did* let her go. I never went looking for her. I never tried to contact her.

I merely never stopped loving her.

I was never obsessed. I was always in love.

That is why it was so unbearable. What I did.

What I did not do.

How I did not text her back, being a frightened teenager from a Catholic Polish family in a country where everybody laughs at your accent and expects nothing much of you except silent hard work and gratuitous sex.

But I shouldn't blame my circumstances. Maybe the simple truth of the matter is that I am a coward.

I never told her the truth.

Is she telling it to me?

It surprises me how much effort it takes for me to separate us. My heart is beating so swiftly, my skin is so warm, my pulse so loud in my own ears. Already I have scooted as close to her as I can, already I have spread my legs, already my hand is travelling down her jaw, her throat, her clavicle. What surprises me even more is the tremor I do not manage to keep out of my voice. 'Why did you come here?'

Her expression shifts. Have I ever told you about her face? How beautiful it is? Even though it looks nothing out of the ordinary. It is her expressions that make it special. I have had relationships in my time. At least one of them, I even thought it would work out. But none of the others I loved could compare to the expressiveness of Linn's face. All the ways that

317

she can laugh, and grin, and smile. There is the smile that was reserved for Teo and me, when we were teenagers. There is the quiet giggle that runs through you like a pleasant shiver. And the loud laughter you could not help but feel shaking you to your core.

As she starts speaking, I do not let her get past the first word: 'Don't lie.'

Her mouth falls shut. I lean back a little. So does she. Fuck, no.

We watch each other in silence. Then she speaks up: 'Do you know what they found at the crime scene?'

My body is tingling. *Finally*. After all these years.

'A candle,' she says, her eyes boring into mine.

I hold my breath: 'And?'

'And?' she asks, her brow furrowing. I want to smooth it over with my thumb. With all the willpower I possess, I refrain. It would not do to touch her unprompted.

'What else did they find?'

She is staring at me. To see the familiar impatience flicker across her face, it almost makes me weep. 'What're you getting at, Anna? Mum's flowers?'

Maybe she does not remember. Not the way I do.

'Dried flowers?' I prompt.

Linn's expression turns from confused to serious back to confused. She looks down. Shifts. I know she feels awkward in her body. I do not see why. Carefully, I reach for her hand. And start tapping.

She looks at our fingers. Then up at me. 'Daisies,' is what she says. 'You loved daisies.'

The surge of adrenalin is so sudden that I start shaking. 'Daisies, and ...?' I ask.

Linn is still looking at me, eyebrows still drawn. 'And the candle,' she says. 'That candle.'

Her voice breaks. *And?* I want to ask again, but keep quiet. Because I see she has not finished yet. Because I do not want to talk over her. Because I am afraid to scare her away.

Afraid she might find out, and that it would make me lose her again.

I cannot lose her again.

I lick my lips. See her eyes follow the movement of my tongue. Then she looks down. 'You were disappointed. When I ... brushed you off that night. At the party,' she says, voice wavering between statement and question. 'When I pretended it was nothing serious. After my date with Oliver.'

'No,' I say.

She looks up, surprised.

'I was not disappointed. I was heartbroken.'

The truth, I remind myself. Tell the truth for once. Taking a deep breath, I go on: 'And I was furious with you.'

LINN

I'm glad she said it. *I was furious with you.*

It is what gives me the power to leave. To put down her hand, to extricate myself from her embrace. To say, *Thank you for the tea* and not to turn around when she calls my name as I leave. Like she has more to say. As if there was anything more to say.

Yes. I was.

I was right then. She wanted me for real, back then, and she knew about Oliver. She thought the worst, after I'd pretended our kiss didn't mean anything.

At least that is something that could have shocked Miss Luca: to see a girl, a young woman, commit such a horrendous crime.

And it would have given Teo a reason to lie. If Anna had been convicted of a crime, she could have been made to leave the country. Just like him.

Downtown, I sit by the beck. Research Open University classes. Stare into the water.

There was something else Anna said, though, that won't leave me be. 'Daisies, and ...?'

And what?

For all I know, she might be distracting me. From what I really came to her for. The trap, aye, but really, the candle. Why she looked at me so guiltily and never told me why.

That kiss.

I can still feel her body against mine. And the heat pooling between my legs. Feel the pull in my fingers, all my limbs, pulling me her towards me. Pull her flush up against me. I haven't felt this way in ...

Nineteen years.

But still, there is something that's nagging at me. Why can't I put my finger on it?

Determinedly, I sit up, dust off Mum's trousers, then walk up the short stretch of green till I reach the house of red brick. Miss Luca's practice. The receptionist doesn't want to let me through. I tell her to give Miss Luca a message. That I found out about the candle.

The receptionist takes up the phone to let Miss Luca know. She barely has time to hang up before the door to Miss Luca's office is thrown open. 'Miss Wilson,' she says, standing in the doorframe, the sunglasses shaking on top of her hair. 'How lovely of you to stop by. Please, come in.'

She sits down behind her large glass desk. I don't sit. Looking up at me, she seems to realise that this puts me at an advantage. To her credit, she doesn't get back up. Her mascara is thick. As thick as mine used to be.

'What can I help you with, Miss Wilson?' she asks. 'I believe you said something about that night when you were assaulted in your parents' home.'

'I saw your photo,' I say without preamble. I'm done with prevarication. 'The one they took at the police station.'

She puts her elbows onto the table, settling her face back into the professional expression I know so well. 'I hardly remember.'

'You were very upset.'

'It was a horrible crime, Miss Wilson.'

'What was most horrible? Was it the candle?'

She takes a deep breath. Reaches for her handbag. Pulls out a pocket mirror first, then her lipstick. Refreshes it. The mascara as well. Looks at herself in the small mirror. Then she puts it all away again. Her jewellery clinks as she straightens. 'Won't you sit, Miss Wilson?'

I do, then. Once I have, Miss Luca continues: 'We agreed that it would be best not to tell you.'

'Who's we?'

'The Detective Inspector and myself.'

'Some pillow talk,' I say, cuttingly.

Miss Luca's eyes widen. 'Excuse me?'

'You had an affair, didn't you? At the time? You were with him the night that it happened.'

'I ...' She stutters. 'Listen, Miss Wilson, I do not know where you get your information, but I assure you, this has nothing to do ...'

'Like the candle has nothing to do with it?' I ask mercilessly. 'Why didn't you tell me, if it had nothing to do with it?'

'Isn't that obvious?' Miss Luca has paled considerably. 'Wasn't it kinder to spare you such humiliating knowledge? When you were blessed enough not to remember?'

We're sitting across from each other. The light outside is blinding me a little as I look at her. Her lipstick has smeared around the corners of her mouth. 'You didn't think that changed the picture?'

'How, Miss Wilson?' she asks.

'A woman could have done it,' I say, not mincing my words.

She flinches. 'Ms Wilson, I realise that it is only natural for you to enquire into ... these events, and that returning here has come as quite a shock to your psyche. If you were to permit me to help you, there are strategies we could practise together, how to deal with panic attacks, with the memories – you do not fight it, you see, you watch it ... But as things stand, the trauma has never been resolved, and you are facing it now all at once. But let me assure you that the presence of the candle was never considered relevant to the investigation. It was just a candle.'

I swallow. Why is it that everybody relaxes when I speak about the bloody candle? Can they really not fathom it? Not even begin to think it?

Or ...

I mean, isn't it nagging at you, too?

I take a deep breath. I need to get my hands back on that file. That list in the file.

She leans across the desk. 'Ms Wilson,' she says. There is a fissure in her voice. Something isn't right. 'Everybody believed they were acting in your best interest.'

'When they kept my file from me?'

'It does not define you,' Miss Luca repeats.

'When they lied to me?' I raise my voice. 'Why did you never tell me you had been with the Detective Inspector? Why did you never show me my file?' Keep raising my voice. 'Didn't you want anybody to know about your aff—'

'Miss Wilson, please!' Miss Luca looks seriously distressed at the prospect of me finishing that sentence at the level that I am speaking. I barely manage to suppress the smile. 'I see now that it may have been a mistake, underage or not, to keep any information from you. I assure you that your parents were kept in the loop the entire time.' She stops. Looks at me. 'And if you would like to see your file, I am sure it could be arranged. All of it. To assure you that everything was done properly.'

I look at her. 'I don't think Graham would be up for it.'

She makes a quick motion with her hand. 'I will arrange it with the Detective Inspector. Leaving it at the glimpse you have had would not be beneficial for you. It will not help you deal with the trauma. All you will do is start seeing ghosts. Tomorrow? Shall we say nine?'

I look outside, then down, to hide my grin. The days are getting shorter. If I still want to set my trap, I will have to get going. Then it'll only remain to be seen if I'll still be needing to see the file tomorrow morning.

'Good.'

She accompanies me back out of the building. In front

of the door, I turn back to her. There's one more thing I need to know. 'I'm so grateful, Miss Luca. It's just, when I'm in that house, in my parents' bedroom, I always remember. The candle, and that smell ... Do you remember the smell?'

I peter out. Her fingers are cold. 'Believe me, Ms Wilson,' she says so very earnestly, looking into my eyes. 'It was just a candle. Your average Tesco candle. I was upset in the police photo because ...' She lowers her eyes. Staring off into the distance. 'You remember, obviously. The stench. Ms Wilson, it was unbearable. The blood and the sweat and the vomit, and all of that mixed with this heavy smell of ... of rosemary, of thyme, but especially of lavender. It was so ... sweet. Like decay.'

Yes. It was.

Miss Luca lets me go. She doesn't go back in until I have driven off. I watch her in the rear mirror. While I drive, the mantrap still in the back, I remember it. That smell of lavender, as if it was sticking to me, all of me, as if it had made my sweat, my skin purple and pungent.

Lavender. Rosemary and thyme.

Doesn't it make you think?

When the Doorman comes back tonight, I will finally know.

There's something else in the back. Something I took from Anna's house before she got in. Its outline is long and thin under the old blanket.

Back in the hollow, I take the old rake from the shed and start sweeping leaves. Spreading them out in front of the house, in front of the porch. I fill the hole back up, though not completely, leaving a foot or so. This is where I set up the trap, then spread leaves over it. In the dark, it should be near impossible to spot if you don't know what to look for. Especially if you don't have a light. And I know the Doorman does not bring a light.

Once I am done with my handiwork, I go into the garden and see if I can figure out how to use a rifle. Not a bad way to pass the time till night falls.

The moment it is dark, I return to the house. The sky is still clouded over, the thunderstorm waiting to break. The hollow is pitch-black.

I hope it makes them angry. I hope it hurts. I hope it will teach them what it means to lose control. Can't move when you've got steel teeth dug into your leg, can you?

This time, I stick to my plan. Don't put on the TV. Don't retreat into the sitting room. Instead, I sit in the kitchen and wait.

It's ten o'clock when the first raindrops start falling.

It's eleven when the storm breaks.

Sitting in the dark kitchen, I pull a chair up to the window. Thick raindrops are slamming against it, so loudly that it is impossible to hear anything else, hail hammering against the roof and the walls and the windows. It quietens down again after fifteen minutes, hail turning back to heavy rain. That is when the first lightning strikes.

I see it stretch out across the sky, a flash of light branching out over the clouds and the horizon to hit the ground running. For an instant, it throws the hollow and the woods into sharp light, the silhouette of the trees long and stark. I bite my lip. Pray the Doorman will not spot my trap during a stroke of lightning. The thunder that follows moments later sounds loud through the wooden walls.

Around midnight, the thunder is following directly after the lightning. I can't even tell if they're not one and the same thing any more. Every single one sounds as if it will bat the walls down. And still I sit and wait and watch. I can tell a scream apart from thunder. And I want to hear that scream. I would do anything to hear it. It's all I can think about. I've been lied to. By everyone. Everybody's lying. Punishment. Revenge. It's all I think of.

I don't even care any more if I find out. All I care about is that they get hurt.

As I'm hurting.

Because when you control someone's pain, you control them. Believe me, I know.

By one in the morning, I get up to make a pot of coffee. I need to stay awake. Sober and awake. No touching the gin today. Only coffee.

By three, I feel nausea rise through my body. Too much coffee on an empty stomach. Still I refuse to move.

By five, my lids are drooping. I've gone to fetch the gin.

Maybe this is one of the nights where they don't come. Maybe they won't be coming.

They'd better be coming.

THE DETECTIVE INSPECTOR

The thing is, you can't trust Little Linny. That's why I did what I did back then.

ANNA

My rifle. My rifle is gone.
She does not know how to use it.

THE DETECTIVE INSPECTOR

And it's too late now, isn't it?

LINN

By six in the morning, I cave. It's still dark out, but they have never been this late. I stretch, rise and rub my bleary eyes. I only had one gin and tonic, not enough to seriously knock me out. It's the tiredness. That's why I feel like an old cat, limping along the road just before she gets run over by an even older Toyota. I can't even fathom having another cup of tea or more coffee; the heartburn's bad enough as it is. Heartburn. One more joy of your thirties. That's why I decide to go out, hoping the fresh air will revive me a little. A glimpse of my flowers, too. My loyal begonias out on the porch.

I use the back door, not keen to step into my own trap. That would be unpleasant. The meadow lies fresh before me, glistening in the dark, once more covered in dew. The storm's gone, and with it the oppressive autumn air. It's cold again. Winter is coming.

Snorting at myself, I step out onto the grass, listening to the crunching noise my shoes make. The sky has cleared. The

331

moon's out. It's almost full, lighting up the hollow, chasing away the pitch-black darkness of the night in the storm.

It feels good to stretch my legs as I walk around the house. There are corners of this garden I haven't been to in such a long time. While I approach the front porch, I keep rubbing my burning lids. No sleep is no good.

A flash of colour catches my eye as I turn the corner and step onto the front porch.

My begonias.

They're still there, still in their pot. But the pot isn't where it's supposed to be.

Instead, I see the trap has sprung.

I run towards it. Someone has sprung it, but not by stepping on it.

They've thrown my begonias into it. The flowers and pot lie shattered all over my doormat. Their petals torn off, the ceramics blown apart. But that isn't all, I realise as I turn towards the drive.

In front of the sycamore, someone's spread out my dahlias, my winter aconites. They shine bright and yellow in the dark, arranged in one neat row. Stepping towards them, my body goes cold.

There they are, laid out like bodies. I step closer.

Each head has been cut off the stem.

And then I realise their stems have also been dealt with. From the middle down runs a precise vertical cut. At the bottom, the two new ends are spread apart, like legs. The ground between them has been violently hacked.

It's impossible not to feel it again. The sweat on my body,

the lavender in my nose. The fingers on my skin, my butt, my inner thighs, spreading them apart with such force a scream is ripped from my throat.

The message is clear. I wouldn't have had to look up and see the new carvings in the bark of the sycamore, right under GO HOME.

THIS IS THE LAST WARNING.

Chapter 8

It is a very rainy day in the first week of the new millennium and two teenagers are bravely wandering the streets of the closest town, trying to shop. They'd have needed to go to Leeds, really, but they didn't. The closest stations are Garsdale and Darlington, and they didn't feel like a thirty-minute bike ride only to go on an hour and a half's train journey.

It's okay, though, because they really like each other. Oliver's quiet and generous and enjoys fart jokes as much as she does. And he looks at her like he wants her. That's a very nice change from Anna. Linn went to see Teo last night, and didn't ask about her, but Teo seemed to know. He kept looking at her like that, anyway. Oddly. Weirdly. Linn knew everything would be weird now. Fuck, why did she ever send that message?

Why can't Anna just love her back?

They're at the local chemist's now so that Oliver can pick out his new fragrance. For the party on Friday. They're both nervous about that party. Linn knows why she is: 'cause she'll see Anna again. Oliver seems to be nervous when it comes to people in general. It's so great he still wants to go into nursing, she thinks. 'I might not go,' he says when they get in line, clutching his new perfume. It's a woman's brand, but Linn doesn't mind. Smells like something out of Jay's mum's Chilcott catalogue, but as long as he likes it.

'Why not?' she asks.

'I dunno,' he says. Then he looks at her. 'You'll be there?'

'Knock on wood,' she says.

He looks around for wood, but there isn't any. So he smiles. 'Knock, knock, knock,' he says.

She gives him a thumbs-up.

LINN

The moment I've dressed and washed, I drive into town. The police station can't open quickly enough. While I wait, I pace in front of their closed door.

The Doorman spotted the trap. During the thunderstorm, they must have seen it. And then they decided to send a message.

The Doorman is angry.

In order for me to be doing anything other than fiddling with my thumbs, I take out my phone. The registration form for the Open University is still opened. Biology, BSc. I fill it out while I wait. They ask me to choose a module straightaway. An excited tingle spreads through me. Only afterwards do they ask for payment.

Payment. Right.

I put the phone away. Look around myself, at the quiet street, the abandoned police station, the dark lamp posts, this village where everything's all right and it'd better be because if it's not, the closest 999 operator will have to send someone in from Kendal.

At least the air is clear and the street's slowly turning grey with milky morning light, falling onto the houses and Cobblestone Snicket and the concrete parking lot at my back.

I think of my begonias, shattered on the porch. Torn to pieces. My hands are balled into fists of rage. I flex them, take my phone back out. Consider.

GO HOME.

My old e-mail account.

Oliver must be back by now. He must have found my note.

My fingers hover over the screen. Then I type in the URL of my former e-mail account. I type in my username, my password, and wait.

It's churlish. It's unfair. My lips twitch. But I want to see what he's written.

As soon as the inbox turns up, I see that there are more new messages than I've had in a lifetime.

They're all from Oliver.

At first, they are sweet messages from Cornwall, enquiries whether I am all right, but not pushy. He knows the way I get.

But now he's back in Leyton. He's found my note. Breathlessly, I read his message. I can hear him say it, in my head. His quiet voice, but no less urgent for it. *I found your note, and you have to hear what I have to say: I don't care. Do you hear me? I do not care about any of it.* I can practically hear him speak. *All I care about is you. Us. I was serious when I married you: till death do us part. In good times and bad.* His soft, beautiful voice. *I love you. I can't do this without you. Go on without you. Let me know where you are. I will come pick you up. No matter where.*

His voice. As soft as his face. *Sweet-O-nly for you, for ever.*
Even as I am still reading, a new e-mail comes in.
<Oliver.Dawson@hotmail.com>
Please. Come home.

'Ms Wilson!'
Hastily, I put my phone away, the message unopened, and look up. It's Miss Luca coming up the road. The Detective Inspector is walking next to her, both dressed for a day of work, not half starved and with bloodshot eyes.

I rise to meet them. 'Linny,' Graham begins as they get closer. 'God, you look awful, doesn't she look awful?'

Miss Luca presses her lips into a thin line. She has forgotten her blusher this morning. She looks pale. I even manage to feel a little sorry for her. 'How are you, Ms Wilson? Ready to see your file, and properly this time?'

Aye. I am ready.

Graham unlocks the front door and ushers us inside. He seems very nervous, constantly checking over his shoulder. As if he's afraid someone might be watching. That Angela should flay him like that ...

Though I suppose it makes sense *now*, doesn't it?

This time, we go into the basement to look at the file after Graham has locked the front door again, making sure nobody can come in. It's cold down in the archive, colder even than outside. There's a constant draft, drawing goosebumps up my skin, whispering in my ear, caressing the hairs on the back of my neck.

'Paper,' Graham says. 'It needs to be kept in good shape, doesn't it, if it's supposed to last.' His hands are shaking when he hands me the file.

I spread it out on a small metal table as all of us bend over to inspect it. Graham fusses, makes a point of pushing the negatives deep into the pocket; 'They mustn't catch any light,' he says, while I take out the photos of the crime scene once more, as well as the list of items found in the room, a neat list of bullet points.

The photos have lost nothing of their horror. My parents' bed, the one I slept in when I had nightmares as a child. The outline of my sweaty young body on their blanket, my breasts pressed into the mattress, my face.

It does not define you, Miss Luca had said. *It was half an hour of your life. It does not define you.*

Sure. I suppose if I'd done something else with my life, it wouldn't have defined me. If I hadn't seen Teo's and Anna's faces, if I'd not started believing it might have been one of my best friends, the only people I'd trusted, loved, I might have come out of it.

I keep looking at the photos. Looking for it. It's not the pool of vomit I am lying in. All that makes me remember is the taste of leather on my tongue where somebody had forced my mouth shut by pressing a gloved fist between my lips, pushing their fingers in and out and down my throat until I puked, again and again.

They liked that.

It's like the photos are taking me back there. Now I wish I was feeling that this was happening to someone else. Instead, I keep looking more closely, at the bed from all different angles, at the floor, the walls and ceiling.

There are so many photos. One of them shows the entire room, lit up brightly with a flash. The bed, sheets rumpled and torn, the window, open, the dried roses and caspias on the nightstand, the rosemary and thyme up on the ceiling, hanging over the bed.

I look at the photo, searching. Then I pull the list of items towards me, check them over. *Rosemary (dried), Thyme (dried), Roses (dried), Caspias (dried), Deadly Nightshade (dried), Daisies (fresh).*

I sort through every single photo. Find the candle, blue and long, from Tesco. The daisies and the matches, like this had been a date. But I don't find what I'm looking for.

Miss Luca said it too. And I remember it so clearly.

Truth be told, though, I was afraid it wasn't going to be there.

And it isn't.

Don't you see?

That is the reason why all I can think of is revenge.

ANNA

Have you ever heard the story of Cassandra of Troy?

Cassandra was the Seer of Troy. She was called witch, mad, a proud woman with dark curls and dark eyes, her skin as brown as Teo's, her mind as sharp as a hunting knife. She foresaw the fall of her city, but no one would believe her. For, you see, Apollo had cursed her after she had refused to have sex with him, and he had declared that none of her prophecies would ever be believed. She was murdered in Greece, far away from home, everybody calling her a liar.

LINN

I didn't tell Graham about the flowers. I didn't tell him anything.

Instead, I went to the bank and had them send all that money to the Open University. Now I'm making my way to the graveyard. Between the stones, I look for the headstone I should have gone to see the moment I arrived.

It's not hard to find. My grandparents are buried under the same stone. I remember their names up there on that limestone from Tadcaster, handpicked by my nan.

Now, there are two more names.

When I arrive at the stone, I see the plot has fallen into some disarray. The Kenzies must have been the last ones to properly visit. Some old candles sit between wild weeds, interspersed with single stems of dried flowers. And there they are. My parents' names.

'Ey up, Mum,' I say. 'Ey up, Dad.'

I don't feel silly.

'Look what I brought,' I say and put down the flowerpots. Fresh herbs on one side, new winter aconites and red dahlias on the other. I pull out the weeds, replace the candles. Scratch some moss off the headstone. 'Don't worry,' I say as I do. 'I'll come back to do this properly. There's just something I have to do first.'

Stupid bitch. Stupid fucking bitch.

Myself, I mean.

You see, I always thought I was good at lying. Turns out the only one I really lied to is myself.

Taking out my phone, I type in a familiar number. The Kenzies' landline, never changed. I let it ring three times.

Then I walk to Teo's flat. I ring the doorbell.

Three times.

Ding, ding, ding.

The Doorman is here.

THE DETECTIVE INSPECTOR

I don't like it. Don't like any of it. Women not being safe. Not being where they're supposed to be. Huh? No, still haven't found Peter Dawson's number, but there's a couple of boxes I haven't been able to check yet. It's got to be somewhere.

You know, it's ... You know, I thought she was lying back then. I really did. Or, well. Not telling the whole truth. That's what I told her parents, too. *Listen, Mark, Sue,* I said. *Listen. We've no proof it wasn't consensual. There are no signs she fought back. You really want to put her through that? You really want everybody to think your Linny likes it rough when she's shit-faced, then throws up and accuses innocents of rape? That's what you want them to say in the papers about your own daughter?*

She wouldn't even have needed to be lying. Just, maybe, changed her mind. You know, in hindsight or something. The thing is, I couldn't help but imagine it. And it felt right, you know? It seemed plausible. That someone like Linn, with a pale thin body like hers, with breasts so round and small, with such a big mouth, would beg for it. That she'd want it hard. There were rumours like that about her, too, you know. The boys at school, they said stuff like that. It's stupid to believe that sort of gossip, but you can't help but overhear, can you? When the swimmers talk in the locker room. Besides, I remember what it was like: being that age, being a scrawny boy whom none of the lasses looked at. I get it. I get it makes you mad. Makes you angry. You deserve to be looked at just like the next man, don't you?

It made me angry, I know it did. Didn't change till I went to join the Force. Suddenly, they deigned to look at me. When I stopped them for speeding or putting bloody mantraps on their land, suddenly I had their attention. When they can get something out of you, they're chuffed to oblige, aren't they?

Don't get me wrong. I don't condone any of what's done to them. Of course I don't, I'm a bloody police officer. I'm just saying, when a kid in the States shoots down forty people in his high school because no girl will go with him to the prom, you might think it would have saved a lot of lives if one of them had danced one dance with him. What's one dance? One kiss? One night? C'mon. We're all here to save lives.

And all these years, Linn was happy with the explanation I gave her, wasn't she? She didn't push it at all. Just went with Oliver and moved out and it was fine, wasn't it? Didn't complain to Antonia Luca, either.

And that's the thing about what's happening today; that's

what's bugging me so much. You know, these women, they could have come forward years ago, and suddenly now they decide is the right time? That's when they decide it wasn't okay what happened to them? What if they liked it at the time? What if they wanted it? Like the women who would ask me to get them out of a tight spot with those smiles and those lipstick mouths of theirs?

Now, don't get me wrong. I don't want you to misunderstand me. We did all we could. We did the best we could for Linny.

It was the best for everybody. Besides, she got something out of it, didn't she? That man. A good man. Oliver could have done better for himself, couldn't he, but he really loved her.

Listen, I did the best I could. You need to protect these kids the best you can, don't you? And I protected them. All of them.

Because what if it'd come out? What if it had all come out? What would have happened to those kids? All of them?

What will happen now?

LINN

I'm back at the house.

It is all carefully planned out. This time, I know what I'm doing. This time, I won't be in the house, but in the car.

I know what was missing now. Graham confirmed that they never found any of it.

Do you? Or have you already known for much longer than me? And never said a word. Never a single word.

It's all right, though. It's all right. The end is coming now. It's here.

I sit in the car and wait. The rifle is lying on the back seat. I'm in fresh clothes, bought them today, clothes like Angela would wear, maybe, someone who is comfortable in their body. Things that fit. Things that ... you didn't buy because you thought they made you look sexy, but just because you liked them. Things like that.

I've got a bottle of water and a blanket and the rifle and I'm ready. Watching.

Watching as the shadows of the trees grow longer and longer, once more creeping towards the house, the porch, the front door. Even through the car doors, I can hear the chimes sing gently in the evening breeze. Remember Anna's fingers on the metal, glinting in the dark.

The Doorman will be back. It was their last warning. I feel for the dried nightshade in my pocket. A reminder.

This won't be my story.

An hour later, the moon rises, throwing its silvery light through the trees. The higher it moves, the more light falls into the hollow. It lights up the sycamore, carved up, the flowers, beheaded, their stems spread like thin legs.

When I look in the rear mirror, I see the drive, the road. I also realise I haven't had to use autosuggestion in a few days. Looking into the mirror now, I feel my hands cramp around the steering wheel, then go slack. *I will know.* I rub a hand across my mouth.

The drive lies abandoned. So does the road. There is nobody here but myself.

Not yet.

I sink back into the seat as far as I can manage, moulding my body to the old fabric, making myself as invisible as I can.

Not long now.

Not long at all.

I am still sitting there, clutching the rifle, keeping an eye on the rear mirror, the top of the hollow, when I see it.

There seems to be something moving at the top of the road.

My eyes narrow. My knuckles turn white.

Wait.

Are those ... blue lights?

There is a car coming down the road. It is a police car.

I straighten. Has something happened? Anna, I think, a sudden surge of panic speeding through my body. Remember Jay's body, dangling from the chandelier. I watch the light closely. No, they are not going to her house. They are coming here.

Fuck.

That is the last thing I need. Tonight of all nights, I need the police as far away as they can be. The Doorman is not going to come as long as he sees blue lights flashing in the hollow.

A droplet of sweat falls into my eye. I blink. Wipe my face with my arm. The rifle in my hand. Fuck. I'm not allowed to have one. Hastily, I put it down. Already, the police car is driving past mine, up to the house. Holding my breath, I crouch down. They are not sounding their siren, but the blue light is flashing brightly through the hollow as they stop in front of the house. Someone gets out.

Fuck. Fuck, fuck, fuck. It's Angela. Bloody Angela.

Ensuring that the rifle is well out of sight, I get out of the car and throw the door shut behind me. Angela flinches as she turns around. I see that her hand goes to her baton. 'Detective Constable,' I call out as I walk towards her. 'What is the matter? Has something happened?'

I hear her release a breath. But her hand does not leave her hip. 'I'm on patrol.' She turns fully towards me. 'Sergeant said it might be good to check on you. Since you'd been to see us so much.'

Bloody now. *Of all nights, tonight is the one you finally decide to do something?*

'That's nice,' I say, lips twitching, forming a smooth smile. 'Thank you. I'm fine.'

Angela's jaw clenches. I see it clearly as the light passes over her face once more. 'You didn't sound fine to me. This past week.'

She takes a step towards me. With effort, I relax my mouth, pass a hand over it as the corners twitch up again. This has to be convincing. 'I'm fine. Really.' I laugh. Hope she doesn't spot the beheaded flowers. 'Goodness, how silly of me. Did I really cause such a fuss? I'm so sorry.'

Angela keeps walking until she is right in front of me. That is when I realise she did not only bring her baton. She also brought a gun. 'You are not silly, Caroline. Could I come in? Just for a cup of tea? A bit of a chat?'

I stare at her. She is so close now. Staring straight back. Her eyes are sharp. Fierce. Determined. Like this is personal.

'No, I don't think ...' I say. Race for an excuse. 'The house is in such a state, I would not want you to see that.'

'We can sit out on the porch,' Angela says, still searching my face. 'Looks fine to me.'

'It is a little dark for that, isn't it?'

'You didn't seem to mind a moment ago. Why were you sitting in your car?'

She has me pinned with her stare. She is taller than me, broader, with her uniform, her baton and gun. I feel the rage course through me again. Tonight of all nights. 'Is that illegal now?' I ask, my voice morphing into a hiss. 'What is this, Constable? An interrogation?'

'Not at all,' Angela says, not backing down. 'This is me being concerned. You don't seem to want me here. I wonder why that is.'

'It is late,' I say, not giving an inch either. 'And you cannot just come barging into people's houses.'

Her thumb glides along her baton, then digs deep into her belt. 'For seven days, you come rushing into the station. On the eighth, you want to tell me everything is all right?'

'Aye,' I say, firmly, passing a hand over my mouth.

'Then you are sure that there is absolutely nothing I can do for you? This is my job, Caroline. It is my job to help you.'

What a laugh. I almost do. But I need her out of here. 'I am absolutely sure that there is nothing you can do for me, Constable.'

Still, Angela is making no move to leave. None at all. 'That's fine,' she says. 'Nobody can be forced to accept help.'

I release a breath of relief.

'But it is my duty to protect you,' she goes on. The breath gets stuck in my throat. 'I will be patrolling the road tonight. Hopefully, you'll be able to get a good night's sleep. And whenever you are ready to talk to me, know that the Sergeant and I are here for you. Whatever it is. We can help you.'

I cannot believe what I'm hearing. 'No, listen,' I start, but all she does is turn around and walk back to her car. I follow her, desperation shooting through my voice. 'Listen, you don't have to do that, keeping you up all ...'

Angela does not even heed me. 'I cannot tell you what to do, Caroline,' she says as she gets into the car. 'Fortunately, neither can you.'

I rush to her open window. My mind is racing. There is something I need to say, anything, I'm racking my brain, but nothing will come out.

That is when a sound emits from her radio.

Both of us stare at it. Then I look back at her face.

She tears it out of its station, puts up the window, impatiently listening to the voice from the speaker. I cannot hear what they're saying.

But from the pained expression on hers, I know I have won.

Reluctantly, she puts down the window once more. 'That was the Inspector,' she says. She is biting her lip, staring out ahead, not looking at me. 'We've got a situation. He needs me.'

'Don't worry,' I say, relief flooding my body. My mouth twitches into a grin. 'I'm fine.'

She looks at me then. Again, as if this is personal. 'You can come to me any time. Whatever you need.'

What I need is for the Doorman to come to the door.

'Sure,' I say. *Leave* is what I think.

But Angela looks around the hollow once more, her blue lights cutting through the mass of black darkness. Her hands are gripping the steering wheel very tightly. Then she looks at the house, the porch. The flower beds. 'Everybody knows your story, you know that?' Angela asks abruptly. 'Everybody knows what happened to you. The parents, the teachers around here, they are using your story to scare their daughters. To make sure their little girls don't come home late, don't go out at night, don't open the door for strangers.' Her chest rises. Lowers. 'You are our bogeyman.'

My heart clenches. Angela is still looking at the house. 'That's why I became a policewoman. I wanted to be a poet, you know. Sit in York or in Paris or somewhere in some café and write pretty verses.' Her hand moves to the passenger seat, unwittingly, I think. There sits her small book, opened on a white page, a poem entitled 'protest'. Before she can touch it, however, she turns her eyes back to me. 'But then I realised what I really wanted was for my dad to stop telling me that story, with a hushed voice, as if it had somehow been *your* fault. Your fault for opening that door.'

I'm no longer breathing. Angela does not smile. 'I wanted him to stop telling it to my sister. And her to stop telling it to my niece.'

All she does is look at me with such force that I cannot move. 'It wasn't your fault.'

Something splits open inside of me. I can feel my heart, beating blood through my body. My chest lifts. As if it is the first breath I take. The first breath in nineteen years.

'I hope you know that,' Angela goes on. 'None of this was your fault. It isn't our fault what they do to us.'

Her voice breaks on the last word. She looks back out through the windshield.

'We deserve better stories,' she adds, under her breath.

Then she puts up the window.

I watch her drive off. Watch her for a long while, even when the blue lights have already disappeared. Shivering in the cold. But I'm not flayed.

We deserve better stories.

I get back into my car.

Putting the rifle once more on the passenger seat, I rest my hand on top of it. Look outside, at the hollow, the porch, the house.

The moon has wandered across the sky. It is behind the car now, throwing white light into the hollow in front of me. The house, the front porch. Whoever walks up to the door, I will see them.

All they have to do is come.

Time to end this bogeyman.

As I keep watch over the house, I glance into the rear mirror from time to time. Up at the top of the drive. Now that the police car is gone, it is dark again. There is nothing but the moonlight, the trees, their long shadows.

My eyes narrow. Wait. Isn't there a shadow, up at the top of the drive? Do I see a movement?

It could just be an animal. A fox. A bird. Crunching gravel. The whisper of trees. Rustling leaves.

Something is moving up there.

They are coming.

I shift. Sit up, lean forward to watch the mirror more closely. Laboured breathing. Watching for any sign of a silhouette appearing at the top of the drive, tall and dark and black.

My breath sounds loud in my ear, incredibly loud. Ever since I've come back to the car, it is like the air has turned shallower. I feel like I've trouble catching my breath. Like it's gone stale.

Opening the window an inch, I breathe and check the rear mirror again.

The moon shines brightly through the trunks of the trees. Their shadows are long. Laboured breathing. Sounds. Rustling. Leaves. Wind. I watch the mirror. Watching for them to come. Waiting. My vision blurs. Black spots smear across my eyes. I start, draw in a rushing breath, my vision clearing immediately. I realise that I've been holding my breath.

Wait.

If I stopped breathing, what were those noises?

Where did the laboured breaths come from?

The moment I have thought it, I see it.

A large, dark shadow. Rising in the mirror, filling the entire glass. A body, a head, limbs, a mouth. Not coming down the drive. Straightening up on the back seat.

The Doorman is in the car with me.

I scream.

I throw open the door, fall out of the car. Then I scramble to my feet and run towards the house. I race up the steps, push my body against the door. The keys slip through my sweaty fingers. I shout with panic. My heart is so loud I can't hear anything. My blood roars, roars as he is coming towards me, as the gravel is bursting under the Doorman's boots. I ram the key into the lock, turn it. Throw open the door. Slam it shut behind me, turn the key, once, twice, pull it out, run up the stairs. Into the bedroom, my parents' bedroom. I turn this key, too. It drops from my shaking hands. I don't pick it up. Run to the window. Look out. The roof of the porch below me, not far. The car, the hollow, the moonlight. The meadow, glistening silver.

Where are they?

I can't see them anywhere.

I shiver. Where are they? Already in front of the door, already stepping up to the bell?

Then why aren't they ringing it?

The Doorman was in the car. *In the car*. Right behind me. If I had not run like that ... If I had been only a little slower ... The Doorman a little quicker ...

Fuck. Fuck. It was their breath I heard. Their breath that turned the air stale. That I felt creeping up my neck.

Downstairs, the chimes are singing in the night. Was that the wind?

Was it the Doorman?

Ring the doorbell. Ring the goddamn bell so that I know you are out there.

Instead, I hear something different. Creaking wood. A light, swishing sound.

Steps on the staircase.

Steps on the fucking staircase.

Just like I imagined it. The Doorman, on their way to the bedroom, their hand sliding up the bannister, making that light sound. They are wearing gloves, but under the fabric, their hands have turned clammy with anticipation. Their mouth is filled with saliva as the bedroom door comes into view. I can hear the steps arrive at the top, on the landing. That is when the wood stops creaking. That is when all you hear is dull thuds on the grey carpet, soft and slow. And there is something else. I hear it even through the door.

I hear them breathe. Their breath isn't soft and slow.

It is excited.

My heart stops. Numbness spreads through me. Again. Everything turns bland and grey. Horror. Fury. It all freezes. Vanishes. As if this is happening to somebody else. I can feel myself turning cold.

There is deadly nightshade in my pocket.

Jay's body. One last decision.

At least it was his choice. At least he was in control.

No movement. No movement on the other side of the door. I don't move. They don't.

Then a whisper. A hand in the air.

Then a fist hits the bedroom door.

Knock, knock, knock.

And then a shoulder.

I scream again. I beg, I shout as I stumble backwards. The door bends as it is hit once more. Pushing open the window, I don't think, I don't hesitate. I jump out.

The porch roof breaks my fall. Pain shoots through my legs, up both of my knees. My left ankle twists and burns like it's been caught in a mantrap, steel teeth tearing at my flesh. Inside, I hear wood splinter. My heart hammers through the pain. I slide down the roof. With a loud bang, the door is torn from its hinges. I let myself drop from the roof to the ground. As I do, my ankle gives out. Another shout is ripped from my throat. I can't stand. I cannot stand.

So I crawl. I can't feel anything. On my hands and knees,

dragging my knees and wrists through the dirty soil, the dead flowers. Towards the car, as fast as I can. It's the only thing I see, the only thing I can focus on. If I can make it to the car, I can make it back to London. I can end this nightmare.

I hear steps thundering down the stairs. I think I do, when I'm halfway across the hollow. They're coming down the stairs. A window makes a screeching sound as it's opened, one of the back windows, they sound like that. I didn't lock them. The car. The car is so close. Come on, come *on*!

I reach the front door. Tear it open. Lug myself inside, up, my muscles screaming in protest, my left leg turning numb with pain. Thank God, thank God the key's still in the ignition. I turn it with a shaking hand. The engine roars when I hit the pedal. Thank God my right foot's still functional. I don't look for the Doorman. My body is spasming, my face. All I need to do is drive out of this hollow, down the road, onto the A684 and return to London. To Leyton. To safety. Numb, grey, cold safety.

And I do.

II. Truth

Chapter 9

OLIVER

Thank God she's home.

It is a clear autumn night. The air is cool, but the stars are all out. It is beautiful, even right here in London.

I watch the stars and think of her, upstairs in our flat. Finally, she's home. I put her to bed and now I am standing on the pavement, lighting a cigarette and looking up at the stars. They make me think of the time I had to have my wisdom teeth taken out. It was the first time that I had surgery. I didn't take well to the anaesthetic. When Mum drove me home, I threw up all over the back seat. I don't think they got rid of that smell before they got rid of the car.

Do you remember having your wisdom teeth removed? It hurts. You can't eat for a while. Mum made me soup. She was great. Tucked me into bed before she left to pick Dad up at the pub. I watched her drive off, and then I watched the stars from my window.

By the time they came back, it had started hurting. I guess

the anaesthetic was wearing off. They came in, put music on. They were taking dance classes together, and sometimes they practised downstairs in the living room, forehead to forehead, looking at each other like there was nobody else in the world. They wouldn't even notice when I watched.

I am telling you this so that you understand that they were happy. I remember thinking that one day I wanted to be just as happy with the woman I loved. Even happier, because for us, there would be no divorce. No packing of bags in the middle of the night, leaving without a word, going separate ways, moving away to cold cities on the coast.

I am telling you this so that you understand what Linn means to me.

That was just after I had finally got rid of my braces. Just before I dared to smile at her for the first time.

I mean, Linn. She wasn't the most beautiful. I didn't go for the most beautiful, I knew that would have been stupid. Like her friend Anna. That girl was stunning. Until she opened her mouth, that is, till you heard the way she spoke. Told you all you needed to know. An easy girl, that. She wouldn't be faithful. Never.

No. For me, it was Linn. She may have been plainer, but I knew she was the one I wanted. She was the one.

And I wasn't impatient, either. Already at an early age I knew that I wasn't exactly Tom Cruise. Or Brad Pitt, or whoever the favourite of the day was. Girls didn't go for me. They are merciless, women. They pretend they're not, but they are. Even more so than men. I joined the swimming team to build up a bit of muscle, a bit of frame, but still, I knew I wasn't the most attractive boy in town. Certainly not next to Jacob Mason. Then again, my dad wasn't exactly a ten, either. And still, Mum had noticed him. And I was patient. I didn't have to have my first girlfriend at fourteen. I could wait. If it was the right person, I could wait for them. Besides, Linn wasn't like the others.

Linn is the right person, believe me. I love her. I asked her to come back, and she has. Thank God she's back.

She looked pale and shaky, her ankle horribly swollen. Waiting for me on the doorstep when I came home. I didn't ask about it. Just hugged her close, then helped her upstairs. Helped her under the covers, where she belongs. All my adult life, I've taken care of this woman. It is difficult sometimes. Of course it is. I don't want to lie. But she's worth it.

We never needed many words, Linn and me. When we were teenagers, I kept my distance, too shy to do anything. It wasn't until we got to our A-levels that I realised I had to start acting or run the risk of missing my chance. I worked up the nerve to approach her on New Year's Eve, out there in the woods, after I'd had a few beers. Jacob gave me the idea, actually. Let's go get our New Year's Kiss, he said.

Dündar was with them. He always was. I'd been worried for a while that he and Linn were a thing, but after I'd watched them closely, I realised they were just friends. A blind man could see that Dündar wasn't interested in her. Maybe he was banging the easy girl. Who knows. All I knew was that Linn had nothing to do with that. She was still a virgin, I knew that, just like me. She was waiting for the right person, too.

And that night she kissed me.

I mean, can you imagine what that was like? Mum had just gone, and I didn't believe in anything any more; I'd even beaten up Colin Reed when he'd insulted her, called her a whore, rammed my fist into his face and felt the blood rush from his nose onto my skin. Could have ended badly for me if Reed would have had the balls to admit that he had taken a beating from someone like me. I was really far gone.

And then Linn kissed me, and everything made sense again. Everything had been worth it, all the waiting, all the concern about Dündar, every rejection I'd had to suffer from the girls at school, in Leeds, on holidays in Spain or Turkey. Like I wasn't even worth their attention.

I still can't believe she's back. That, once I've finished this cigarette, I can go up there and kiss her goodnight again. How lucky I am. I mean, do you realise how lucky I am that that woman ever became mine?

I was so happy that New Year's Eve, I felt like the entire world was made of powdery snow, carrying me home.

It wasn't until she told me about her university plans that the snow suddenly seemed to be melting down my neck. If she went to another university, we wouldn't see each other. I was due to go in for nursing; she talked about becoming a doctor, or a botanist even, an astronaut. If she became a doctor or an astronaut, she would meet all sorts of men who were more successful than me. I knew she would leave me. Women are like that. They will tell you it's about love, but it's not. And I get it. It's not a reproach, it's just biology.

As I stub out my cigarette, I remember how Linn laughed when I told her what I was worried about. She said that that didn't have to happen. When we went shopping for fragrances, I made sure to find out what her favourite was and ended up buying that one. I didn't care that it was for girls. All I cared about was her.

Taking out my keys, I unlock the front door and walk up the stairs, as quietly as I can manage. I don't want to wake her. Now that she is back, she needs her sleep.

At Jacob's party, the Friday after New Year's, a couple of people had noticed that I was using girls' perfume. Jay of course. And Dündar, or rather the easy girl. She made a joke about it. I don't believe she'd ever spoken to me before. I didn't know why she would start then. It seemed like I had done something to offend her, but I was sure it couldn't have been the perfume. It smelled so lovely, with its lavender fragrance. I remember it so clearly, even after nineteen years. If Linn loved lavender, I'd smell like lavender. Shame I can't wear it any more.

I tiptoe into the flat, the hallway. It is warm and cosy. Slowly, I take off my coat. I feel like I can hear rustling from the kitchen, the dining room.

And then I realised what had so offended her. Anna. I realised when I saw them kiss. Linn and Anna, at the party, out in the back. It wasn't just a single kiss like on New Year's Eve. Anna had Linn pressed up against the back wall, their hands roaming each other's bodies. They were kissing open-mouthed. They were laughing. Linn was moaning.

When I saw her back arch off the wall, when I saw her whisper something into Anna's ear and smile, I felt my heart stop beating.

She'd gone to the cinema with me. She'd picked out my perfume. We'd kissed. And there she was, drunk, so drunk, kissing not me, but Easy Girl.

I snuck off. Had a couple of drinks so that I'd work up the courage to ask her why she'd led me on like that when she'd always known what she wanted was a blonde Polish whore.

Carefully, I tuck my shoes into the rack, then open the door to the single room of our flat, with the open kitchen, the dining table, and the couch in front of the television. I smile when I see her standing in front of the oven. She should be in bed, I know, but when I see her making dinner wearing nothing but a sleep shirt, panties and an apron, I can't find it in me to complain.

Her panties. I remember pressing them to my face and breathing in her scent while she was gone.

'Sweet-O,' she says by way of greeting. 'I was famished.'

That she would dig out that old word. It reminds me of our childhoods. My voice sounds warm when I answer: 'I could have made you something, Linnsweet.'

She seems to be making pasta. The table is already set. I can see a burning candle. Blue, from Tesco. What I always buy.

'I'll change into something more comfortable,' I say and make for the bedroom. God, how lucky I am that this woman ever became mine.

Because you see, that night, when I'd finally drunk enough to work up the courage, she'd already left the party. It was still relatively early, but apparently, she had been very drunk.

I knew where she lived, though. Everybody knew Little Linny from Down-in-the-Dip.

I didn't tell anyone where I was going. Nobody would see me go there to laugh at me the next day for having fallen for a lesbo. I stopped at home to get a candle, and to pick some daisies in the woods around her house. Maybe she'd just been drunk. Maybe she still wanted me. After all, she hadn't gone to the cinema with Anna, had she? That had been me.

At the time, I didn't know I wasn't the only one who was on their way to the dip.

LINN

I'm back. Finally, I'm back.

GRAHAM

L ook here now. Look here!

LINN

I'm home.

OLIVER

Her parents weren't in. Their car wasn't there, at least. Good. I wouldn't have wanted to embarrass myself in front of Mr and Mrs Wilson. Bad enough that I'd met Jay Mason on the dirt road up to her house. Why wasn't he at his party? He'd driven Linn home, he said.

I almost sank my fist into his face then, just like with Reed. Imagined his skin splitting open, his nose breaking with a satisfying sound, blood rushing out.

Don't worry, Jacob said, spitting onto the ground, voice bitter, words slurred. She's not interested.

Not in you she's not, I thought, as I stood on her front porch, looking up at the house. As a last thought, I sprayed on more of my perfume. I had it with me, the perfume she'd picked for me. To remind her.

I rang the doorbell. Then I waited.

She didn't open up.

I could see she was in though. There was a light on in her

parents' bedroom. There was a silhouette moving behind the window.

And then I did something rather clever, if I might say so myself. When I rang again, I used their code.

Ding, ding, ding.

Everybody knew it was their signal. The mischief-makers and their games of knock, knock, ginger.

She opened up straightaway.

Her face fell the moment she saw it was me.

Still she let me in. She took me up to her parents' bedroom, stumbling up the stairs. She was giggling like a madwoman half the time, that's how drunk she was.

I tried talking to her once we were up there. Tried telling her that she was better off with me. That I loved her. But I realised it was hopeless. She was too drunk. Kept talking about Anna, about uni, about Anna.

You know, I was drunk, too. I was drunk, and she was so far out of it and she kept saying Anna's name like that, like a prayer. I was still wearing my bike gloves. She kept giggling and tried to light the candle I'd brought. Her hand wrapped around that candle ... She took my daisies off me, too, excited, her face glowing, as she said, *Wicked, they're Anna's favourite!*

That was when I realised I'd lost her. The love of my life. There was only way I could still have her.

It was really easy to push her down. She didn't even fight back. Just became rigid. She was wearing a dress, all I had to do was push up her skirts. She struggled a bit when I pulled down her panties, but they only had to go down to her knees. All that swimming really paid off.

Flowers for the Dead

You know what I still remember most acutely? How easy it was. When you've never seen it or done it, you think it is the most horrible thing, all tense and dangerous. But it took almost no effort. It wasn't hard. It was exciting. When she started shouting, all I did was push my fingers into her mouth, like I'd wanted to for years. She fell silent.

The only difficulty was that I couldn't get it up at first. Too much alcohol. That's why I used the candle to begin with. It was such a sight, watching her skin swallow that thin waxen thing, hearing her sob, feeling how easy that was. How powerful I could be. When she threw up because of me, when I could make her throw up again and again, until all that came out of her was retching and still I could make her body gag again, convulse under and around me, it felt incredible. I'd never felt anything like that before. I did get it up then.

I can feel myself turning hard in the bedroom as I change into my sweatpants. Thinking about it still makes me hard. Although it was not all fun. It was having her or driving to the train tracks to lie down on them. I knew I couldn't live without her. Knew she was the one. I'd waited so many years, never making a move on anybody else. I deserved this, and if I did not get it, I would kill myself.

Now it's different. Like last month, when I went to visit that intern. While she went into the kitchen to make tea, I undressed and lay down on the sofa, my penis already rigid. Her face when she came back in. Priceless. I know you might say it's not right, but let me tell you, she enjoyed it. Otherwise, wouldn't she have complained to someone?

Back then, though, I wasn't so suave. I don't know when

the bottle of perfume fell out of my pocket. When it broke. All I know is, when I'd come twice, Linn had chucked her guts up already, and the stench of vomit was almost as strong as the smell of lavender. I tried to clean up, mixing the shards of the perfume with the shards of the bottle she'd been drinking from. She didn't protest. She didn't shout. I knew I'd lost her, but at least I'd had her. I could live with that. That's something Easy Girl could never give her.

But then she didn't move at all. Linn didn't. I stumbled downstairs, panicking that she might be dead. You see, I knew I had done something illegal. I was crying, sobbing. And then I called the only person I could trust. The only one who'd understand.

I hear her shuffle with the cutlery in the kitchen while I put on a faded T-shirt from uni.

That's what changed my life for ever. That's when it happened. When I stood in Mr and Mrs Wilson's living room, crying, my gloved hands wrapped around their landline.

Graham picked up.

GRAHAM

I don't know what you're talking about. What he's talking about.

I'm not saying anything else.

OLIVER

Graham came round immediately. It was around midnight, I think. He found me crying out in the hollow. I told him everything, told him straight up. How Linn had led me on, how she belonged to me, what I had done. Did she fight you, he asked, did she say no?

That's when I realised that she hadn't. Not really. Not that I could remember. Cried, yeah, wriggled a bit, but nothing that could have broken my grip.

Maybe she liked it.

I told Graham I would have killed myself. He looked at me, one of his two boys for the Olympics, the quiet, the unassuming boy who'd never gone wrong before. The drunk boy.

Then he went upstairs to look at Linn and found her lying in her own vomit.

She wanted it, I said, when he came back down. She asked for it. She didn't say it, but she had asked for it, hadn't she?

His voice was rough when he spoke. Get out of here, he said. Get out.

And I did.

That would have been the end of it, too. I would have gone home, and Linn and I would have never seen each other again. If it hadn't been for her friends. Anna and Teoman.

How lucky I was.

They came to her house that night too, you see. I don't know why it was both of them. Anna had obviously been invited over for a date, but him? Maybe he was dropping her off. They were friends, I suppose.

When they found her, Graham was no longer there, and they immediately called 999. And they smelled it. Of course they did.

The lavender. My perfume.

I know because they told Graham. And because they came to my house that night.

Anna went right for my throat. Dündar was wild, but she was dangerous. She looked like she knew how to kill someone in the dark. She looked like she'd seen people shot dead in the open street and wasn't willing to let this pass.

That was my luck. My luck they came to my door to beat me senseless. Because then Graham had a reason to bring them in. I wasn't there in the room with them, of course. I was at the station. He had my photo taken, too, but he never developed that negative. He said he would keep this and if he ever heard of something similar again ...

Dündar and Anna, though, they didn't believe him. It wasn't good enough for them. So he told them that what they'd done to me was assault. If either of them was to be sentenced, they'd be kicked the hell out of this country and back to where they came from. That was before Poland joined the EU, you know. Thank God Turkey is still a long way away, and that it won't concern us now when it happens.

It was incredible how well it worked. They kicked up a fuss, sure. That's why Graham kept Dündar in the basement for a bit. But still, in the end, they didn't say anything. They tried talking to Linn, but by the time they got to her, it was too late: I'd already gone to her house, and brought her flowers, and she didn't want to hear anything about my being involved in this. Not the man who hadn't even been at the scene of the crime, not officially.

Do you realise how lucky I'd been? So very lucky. When Linn woke up and didn't remember anything, I realised I could go back to her, ring her doorbell, and we could start over. I realised all was not lost.

I'd got away with it.

And you see, that's what shocked me most, back then. That I got away with it. That you always get away with it. They tell you how bad it is, how wrong, but when you actually do it, they let you. They laugh at Sweden for *yes means yes* and let you do it. Everybody lets you. Men or women, doesn't matter.

That is what we were born for. We are men. Two hundred years ago, only the kings could afford to behave like this, the politicians, the higher-ups. Now, every man can be king. This is what democracy is all about. What used to belong only to kings now belongs to all of us. All you have to do is dare it.

That's not what Linn and I are all about, though. Some things are just meant to be. Back then, in the state she was in after that night, she wouldn't go away to uni on her own, I knew that. Jay gave me an alibi, we invented that story about my watch; in exchange, nobody mentioned that he'd been at her house. The ex-boyfriend who'd choked her, that wouldn't have looked good. He made me promise never to touch her again, but he didn't get it, did he? She would need someone to protect her. Not a girl. Not some Polish prostitute. No. Me.

And guess what?

She did.

I smile as I listen to her set the table in the other room. Still does. She just needed a little reminding.

GRAHAM

That's the thanks I get? I show you her file, I share all of my thoughts with you, and this is what I get in return? Baseless accusations? The coroner agreed, didn't he? Why don't you go ask him why he agreed? He thought it was plausible.

Dawson can say all he wants. Doesn't make it any truer. This is just one of your tricks. My word against his is what it is.

What do you mean, they've come forward? What do you mean, they're prepared to speak out?

What?

OLIVER

I didn't realise she was going to leave me until I spotted the suitcase under the grocery bags in the car, the night I was due to leave for Cornwall, for the conference. It is unforgivable that I didn't notice it any sooner, how upset she'd been. What my Linnsweet was thinking about. How she prepared her departure. I was so busy with my presentation, my very first keynote. I was so excited, working so hard, that I didn't realise what was going on. It was a major paediatrics conference, my favourite area. I love kids. If we'd already had kids, Linn would never have left.

Before I saw the suitcase, all I had noticed was that she would freeze sometimes when I touched her. She's no longer used to it, I thought. The past year, I have been travelling so much, for conferences and in-service trainings, and didn't complain about it either. I love Linn, but sometimes I felt like I was coming home from work only to spend my evening with another patient. It was just good to get a break sometimes.

Besides, it's normal, isn't it? Even girls like Linn, even they turn frigid at some point. Only natural, I suppose.

But the bags in the car, that wasn't natural. It meant I had to act quickly.

See, I could have talked it through with her, but that is not how it works. Do you think the intern would have sucked me off if I had asked her nicely? That is not how women work. They work differently than men. They like to gossip, to do things a roundabout way. It makes sense, biologically speaking, since they are weaker than men. That would not induce them to face a battle honestly and openly, would it?

So I knew there was no point talking to her about it. Sitting in that cab to the station, I thought about what I could do to remind Linn that she needed me. I don't blame her for forgetting; I really don't. We've both become complacent, I think, in our relationship. We could have both put in a little more effort. But now I had to remind her somehow.

GRAHAM

I did something for them. I did something for all five of them. They all needed me to lie for them. They needed for me to lie, for me to let the DNA evidence disappear.

What would have happened if I'd let it all come out? What would have happened to them, hmm? Linn would have had to see that she got assaulted because she'd led someone on; she'd probably have lost the court case, not having told him no, her life ruined for ever. Anna and Teoman, they might have had to leave the country. Jacob, he might even have become a suspect, what with their history and how he'd been the last to see her. Innocent or not, it would have shredded his reputation. And Oliver, his future would have been over. One mistake. One drunken mistake. After he'd waited for her for so long.

It was one mistake.

OLIVER

I didn't go to the conference. What was a keynote to my marriage?

First, I called the hotels she had browsed online, but when I ran out of options, I turned to the police officer who had always been there for me: I called Graham. All I wanted to know is what I could do to find her. If he had any pointers for me.

When he told me he'd seen her drive into town, I could not believe my luck.

I would never have expected her to go back there of all places. Never in a million years. But it made sense, in some ways. She didn't have friends to turn to, after all. Didn't need them, as long as she'd had me. I didn't encourage her to make any. Last time she'd had friends, they had almost taken her from me. Besides, it was much nicer to know that I had someone to come home to at night, sitting on the couch, waiting for me.

I took a cab to the closest car hire. Got a nice inconspicuous compact, black, nothing you'd notice. Then I took my things back to the flat, called in sick to the conference, and followed her north.

When I arrived, my first visit was to Graham. It was so good to see him again, our old coach. He has turned fat, yeah, but a man his age, he deserves his fat. I will never forget what he did for me. For all of us.

I told him Linn had left me. I said I would make some mischief, and for him not to worry about it. All I wanted was to make her come back. I wouldn't hurt her. Just a bit of fun.

He didn't look so chuffed about it at first, but then he told me Dündar was back as well, and I asked him whether he really wanted a man like that to fuck my wife on his turf? A man like Teoman Dündar, who thinks all women belong to him, anyway. That's just his culture, Graham reminded me. And he's right. He cannot escape his culture, Teoman Dündar. Neither can I. I'll always be too soft for my own good. That's what growing up in a Western snowflake democracy will do to you.

Graham did not want that. Besides, we were in the same boat, he and I, weren't we? Not that I needed to remind him, but if it became public knowledge that he had covered up such a crime, he would be done for, what with the current climate. He would be fired before he could even take a breath. So much for his pension plan.

So it was really quite easy. I went to the hollow at night and rang her doorbell.

Ding, ding, ding.

387

She knew what it meant. And I liked to remind her she was in danger. It's only true, isn't it? I mean, you can talk all you want about empowerment; fact remains, if you are a woman alone in a dark house, someone might come for you. I just wanted to remind her why she'd picked me over Easy Girl. Just wanted to remind her how much safer she would be at home. What I could do for her. Just in case she was checking her phone, I texted and e-mailed her, pretending to be in Cornwall. Making sure she knew she had a loving husband to return to.

I knew it would be a matter of escalation. That I had to come back and do it again. That I'd need to suggest to her in some way that the solution was to go back home, back to London. She wouldn't break into panic at first chance; no, Linn is not like that. It would take quite a bit of work to drive her to hysterics. Throwing the chimes against the bathroom window while she was in there, that was a lovely first touch. I had always hated those chimes, their soft cling-bing-cling. I had heard it all the while I was with her that night when her parents had gone out. Like a man speaking too softly. I put them back afterwards, making sure to leave no trace behind.

The night after, though, I messed up. Happy to admit it. I came to her house a little earlier, to settle in for the wait. That's when I saw them, through the kitchen window.

Linn and Easy Girl.

It made me mad. I drove back to the hotel, that secluded B&B down the A684, and got drunk off a bottle of gin. When I woke up after three hours having to piss like a horse, I drove by her house to at least leave her a reminder: a shattered bottle. I'd taken the label off the gin bottle, it looked a bit like Bacardi Breezer, that horrible stuff she had been drinking back then.

I was angry with myself for having messed it up; luckily, the next night, I got a priceless opportunity. When I snuck up to the house, I realised she was in the kitchen, washing up. She was standing right there, for everyone to see. Didn't she understand that she was making herself a target?

I crept up to the house. She wouldn't be able to see me, I knew, not with the lights on in the kitchen and the hollow completely dark. I'd tried it before. This would be fun.

I watched her as I breathed against the window. As I wrote DING. As she stumbled backwards and ran. It was so great to see her face. How that little joke really hit home. Rang the doorbell a few more times, standing on the porch, trying not to giggle.

And then I decided to have an even bigger laugh. She came home drunk the next night. I watched her sway as she came up the road; I was hidden amongst the trees, my car parked a bit further down in the woods. She was drunk from a date with Dündar, if Graham was to be believed.

This time, I didn't just ring the doorbell.

I came in.

GRAHAM

Now look here. Look here!

Did you really want me to destroy that boy's life? And hers? I mean, did you *see* her lying there, in her own vomit? No court would have sentenced him. It would have been her word against his, him a respectable, quiet, promising young swimmer, her a strange lass hanging out with foreigners, smoking and drinking and loitering where they shouldn't, ringing respectable people's doorbells till late into the night. Once the court learned how drunk she'd been, they would have seen that raising the issue of consent was laughable.

She wanted it, and now she was too ashamed to admit it, they would have thought. There's no way she could have told him no. She shouldn't have had that much to drink, they would have said. Accusing someone else of misconduct but drinking until chucking your guts up yourself? It wouldn't have made for a pretty picture. It would have destroyed her.

She wouldn't have had anyone. Not even Oliver would have stuck with her.

Antonia Luca agreed with me, if you want to know. She knew I'd gone out twice that night because we'd been sleeping with each other. She'd broken up with ... well, I wouldn't tell you, would I? It was someone at school. Just a kid. Disgusting. I'd found out, but I'd told her we could keep it between us. And that we could both get something out of it, right? Anyway, so I left her at midnight, an hour or so before Anna Bohacz's call came in.

Antonia made me tell her what had happened. She was badly shaken, but she agreed with me. I mean, not that she had a whole lot of choice, if she didn't want everybody to know she'd slept with Anvi Carling, one of the students entrusted to her.

Still, Antonia Luca never stopped feeling bad about it, I know. She never touched a student again, as far as I know. I think I'm the only one who's slept with her in a decade. Voluntarily, I mean. You know she goes to Leeds to book a hotel room and orders in young men, don't you? Boys, really. Girls maybe too, who knows these days? It's pathetic. And then I see her fiddling with that brochure in her office, for some dating website, as if she wasn't gone every Friday to amuse herself with what are practically still kids.

There was this teacher from Plymouth a few years ago; they met on holiday in the Dales, I think. They were both hiking or something. That was the first time I saw her without makeup. It was a Sunday morning and they were on their way to the bakery, walking hand in hand.

But it ended pretty quickly. I bet she told her lover what she'd done to Little Linny. Bloody stupid. Anyway, all I kept from that affair was that horrible PSYCHOLOGY TODAY mug. And the certain knowledge that she would keep quiet. She too thought Linny did not stand a chance in court, especially if she didn't remember anything. Fine, it was Antonia Luca who convinced me to show Linny her file, as if that could make up for some wrong she thought she'd done. But what good did it do? Linn just got it into that thick head of hers that she had been raped by a woman. A woman!

It only proved to me that I'd been right. In letting it end quietly. I knew I could save Anna Bohacz and Teoman Dündar, even Jacob Mason's reputation; and I knew I could save all of them the horrible embarrassment of such a trial, a trial that would mark them for ever. Linn most of all. She'd never recover from it.

How was I to know that he was going to come back?

OLIVER

It was so easy breaking in. Just pushed my fist through the back door and opened it. She was unconscious. It did something to me to see her lying there like that, slack, unmoving. It was so sexy. I had not thought of her as sexy in a long time.

I made sure she wouldn't choke on her own vomit. I wanted her alive and well. Then I carefully pulled off her jeans, took her panties, pulled the jeans back up and left.

What a trick. What a laugh. I snorted with laughter all the way on the drive back. To take off her panties. To take them with me. Genius!

But what happened next wasn't so funny.

When I came back the following night, I hid amongst the trees as always. I could see her car though no sign of Linn. What I did spot, however, was how she had reworked the garden. Dug up the flower beds. And while I was still watching, waiting for the right moment, I spotted Graham. Graham coming into the hollow, Graham walking up to the house.

C. K. Williams

Graham falling into that hole. Linn helping him inside. I watched it all. If Graham hadn't fallen before me, I would have missed it in the dark, I am certain. She had dug a hole in front of the porch. She had wanted to hurt me.

Me. Who'd taken care her of all of her adult life. Who'd held her during her nightmares, who'd changed and washed the sheets when she'd pissed herself, who'd scoured newspapers for funny headlines and supermarkets for her favourite foods and cinemas for films that were safe to watch.

I am still in the bedroom. From the noises emerging from the kitchen, I'd say she has stopped setting the table. In a moment, she might call my name for dinner. And I will still be thinking about how much that hurt – to think she would actually want to cause me injury.

To be fair, she didn't know it was me. The longer I thought about it, actually, the more endearing it became. She was so cute, my Linnsweet. Cat's got claws. That only made it more exciting.

Those *flowers*, though. Planting flowers in the barren beds like a petulant child. *Look here, I am not going anywhere.*

So, when I found the mantrap the following night, in the storm when lightning struck, because I got lucky and was on the lookout for traps, I had a brilliant idea.

Her begonias. Her pathetic begonias, always drooping their heads and losing petals. Throwing their pot into the trap felt great. Again, you see, I made sure no one came to any harm, and that nothing was destroyed, nothing of value, anyway. She could have got into real trouble if someone had stepped into that ancient thing. It might have ruined her for life. She

394

might have been convicted for bodily harm. I made sure it all went smoothly.

And told her this was my last warning. I had to return to London at some point, after all. Go back to work. So I changed the tone of my e-mails, asking her to come home. Even implying I might kill myself if she didn't.

Because, you see, life would be nothing without her. It's not easy being with Linn, it isn't, but I promised: till death do us part. It wouldn't be love if you gave up on the slightest hiccup, would it? And I love her. More than anything.

Lucky for me, Linn was waiting for me in her car the next night. Funny thing is, I wouldn't even have seen her if the constable hadn't come by. At the time, I was fuming. That useless dyke, with her baton and her emo nails and her ugly haircut. She'd only cut her hair like that to make a point, hadn't she, a point to men. *I want you to find me ugly.* Well, knock yourself out, but believe me, it's not your hair, it's your face that looks like your arse has been put in the wrong place. She almost ruined my plan by insisting she stay.

Furious, I went back up the road and phoned Graham as soon as the signal was strong enough. He called her back via his radio. He tried to tell me about Jacob Mason, too, sounded shaken, but I didn't care. Mason had killed himself because he'd lost his job and turned into an alcoholic who had no one left but his demented mother, not because of something that happened twenty bloody years ago. He kept quiet for his own sake as much as for mine.

Took me a moment to calm myself down, walking back to

the hollow. It was only when I saw Linn still standing there, watching that dyke get into the car, that I realised what a perfect opportunity this was. To give Linn the proper scare she needed.

So I snuck into the car while Linn was still watching the police car drive off. It was so exciting. Cowering down on the back seat, out of sight of the rear mirror. I only rose when I was sure she was looking into it. Had to stop myself grinning like a lunatic the entire time.

It worked like a charm. I followed her into the house. It was a good thing she had locked herself into the bedroom. I think no other room would have worked as well. When I knocked on the door, knock, knock, knock, and then started trying to break it down, I think she finally understood what I had been trying to say.

She took off with screeching tyres. Suddenly she didn't have to stick to the speed limit for once, a tic of hers that drives me mad, almost as mad as her ghost driving. I made a video of it. A gif. It looked really funny, how she sledded up the road.

And now she is back here. Now she is out there, in our kitchen. I feel a gentle smile pull at the corners of my mouth. Got her back in one week. How lucky I am. How lucky we are. This is meant to be.

I put a hand to my erection. Then I smooth down my shirt, put on a spray of fragrance, and walk back out to join her.

GRAHAM

Well, I couldn't know she was going to move away with him, could I? I couldn't know that, for fuck's sake! But even if I had, there were worse kids than Oliver Dawson. I mean, you should have seen him, he was crying and everything. One mistake.

And I mean, what did she lose? Of course it wasn't right, but objectively, what did she lose? Women are less ambitious than men, anyway. On average. Don't look at me like that, it's just biology. So she wasn't going to go off and become a fucking astronaut, was she? Our Little Linny, the girl stupid enough to get shit-faced and then open her door in the middle of the night? Not exactly astronaut material, right? She'd want children, that's what they end up wanting. Even if they pretend they want a career, when they turn thirty, all they think about is children. And that's *good*. Nothing against it. And she could have children with him, couldn't she? Unlike with that Anna lass. He had all the

397

right parts, and he'd provide for her, and he'd provide for a family.

She could have been *happy*. She *was* happy.

She still could be. As long as you keep quiet.

Think about it. Think about what will become of her. The last time she worked was, what, ten years ago? She has no qualifications, no job experience to speak of. You know what will happen when he leaves her, don't you? The food bank is the most harmless place she could end up. I'm not thinking the food bank, I'm thinking Soho, and I don't mean for a theatre visit.

But you can prevent it. If you keep quiet.

Otherwise, it's on you. It's you who will be destroying her life. By raking this all up again. You will send her to the food bank, to the brothel, when she might as well be happy. She could have all she needs, a man by her side and a couple of little ones and, sure, if she wants to, easing back into her job when the children are a bit older, maybe starting with some work experience and then going half-time. That could be her story. Just a normal story. She could have that with him. For fuck's sake, *she doesn't even remember*! She chose him. That was her choice.

You are greedy. Self-centred. All you wanted was the truth, at all costs. Now you got it.

Are you going to destroy her life with it? Do you really want to take all of this away from her?

It's on you now.

OLIVER

She's set the table beautifully. The candle is already lit and there is a vase on the table with a few daisies in it, so simple, really. Not my favourite kind of flower, but she wouldn't remember how she took them out of my hands that night, so I'm happy to forgive her. I smile warmly at her as we eat. Just like we sat here and had dinner a week ago, before she left me. Now she has come back. I am so grateful.

She doesn't say much, and neither do I. We don't have to constantly blabber like some couples. She's humming 'One Way or Another'. It makes me smile. Our song.

It's lovely, what she's made. Neither of us had any time to go for groceries, of course. I had to make sure to race back as fast as I could so that she wouldn't notice my absence. But we had some pesto left and a few nuts and pasta and it tastes great.

Then we go and watch TV. I'm not hard any more, but that's all right, too. We have plenty of time. When we go to bed. Or even better, tomorrow in the morning. I could wake her up like that. I could start when she is still asleep, lying limp and unmoving, not knowing what is happening to her until I am already well at it. Yes, that is a good idea. Like a reward. I didn't touch her in the house when she was lying there all limp and seductive, my own wife. I deserve to touch her like that now.

Tomorrow morning. It will be perfect.

And if she wants to, I can help her look for a new job, too. After the kids are born and taken care of. If she still wants a job, I'll help her. Encourage her even. Of course she should have a life of her own. It'll do her good. I might have been wrong there, trying to cut her off like that. Honest mistake.

Maybe we should go back up to Yorkshire together, actually. Go to Jacob's funeral. Go see his mum. Give her as much comfort as we can.

He was my best friend.

I realise it's true the moment I think it. He kept my secret. Even at the very end, he wouldn't betray me. We were best friends.

Yes, we should go to his funeral. Send him off properly. He deserves it.

When the *British Bake Off* is over, Linn says she wants to go to bed. I agree. While I brush my teeth, she changes into her pyjamas. Outside, there still seem to be a few people in front of the pub. Bit unusual, at this hour, but let them have their fun. When I emerge from the bathroom, I look at her, taking my time to do so. To appreciate how attractive I still find her, no matter what others might say. How attractive I find her again, after having seen her in her parents' house, rekindling an old flame. To think about how much I will enjoy pulling those trousers off her tomorrow morning, with her lying on her stomach, only down to her knees. It excites her when she does not have enough room to move. When she feels resistance as she wriggles. It's then, when I hear her breath hitch, that I really start enjoying it.

It is a nice thought to fall asleep to, her warm body next to mine.

It is dark when I wake up. I am a little confused at first. I do not usually wake up at night unless I've had a few pints and need to pee. Linn is still next to me, limp and lascivious, breathing regularly. I don't feel like I need to pee, either. Was there some racket outside, maybe, from the pub? Or did I have a bad dream? I feel like I dreamt of Jay.

Squinting, I look at my phone. It's 2.33 a.m. Groaning, I turn back around. Good thing that it is Sunday tomorrow. Means sleeping in. I don't even want to think about going back to work on Monday. Whenever I've had a holiday, even if it is just a week up north, I feel like retirement cannot come soon enough. It is not fair, how they make you rise at ungodly hours just because you work at a hospital. You have made it your life's work to help people, shouldn't that mean you get to sleep in?

I sink back into the mattress, closing my eyes once more. It's all right, though. Linn is back. My hand slinks across the mattress, towards her body. Her limp body. Maybe, now that I'm awake ... We don't have to wait for tomorrow.

Then I realise why I have woken up.
I realise what noise I heard.
The doorbell.
It is ringing.
Ding, ding, ding.

GRAHAM

What are you going to do?

OLIVER

I lie as still as I can. My heart is beating so quickly I feel like it will burst away from its muscles. It's impossible. I'm up here. She's up here. We're back together.

Could be the drunks from the pub. Could be coincidence.

Perspiration is collecting on my upper lip, under my armpits, between my legs. It's like I'm a rabbit, like a fox in a mad rush, a poacher, caught in that mantrap of hers. Like I stepped into it after all, iron clawing into my skin, tearing at my muscles.

The doorbell rings again.

Why is she not waking up? Why does she just continue sleeping? Can she not hear it? Smell it? It's like I am back at her house, smelling the vomit and the lavender, and hearing those horrible chimes.

Am I just imagining this?

Ding, ding, ding.

I had watched them, tapping it onto each other's hands.

404

Had watched the two of them tap it onto each other's skin, each other's bodies, as they kissed.

Ding, ding, ding.

A shout is ripped from my throat. I jump to my feet. I run downstairs, not thinking. All I know is I'll catch them. If they think they can still come between us, if they think this will scare me, I will prove them wrong.

By the time I throw the front door open, the street lies abandoned.

There is nobody there.

I stand in the moonlight. In the cold air. My breath is turning into little clouds of vapour as it leaves my mouth. I am shaking all over. Think of Jay's face in my dream, pale as death, his eyes wide open, staring right at me.

There is nobody here.

GRAHAM

She has left. Anvi Carling saw her drive out of town like a madwoman. 'She's gone,' Anvi said, 'so you leave Tony alone now, you hear me?'

Don't know what Anvi was doing out in the middle of the night, but I don't ask, do I? Or why she'd refer to Antonia Luca like that. But that's none of my business. She was dressed all proper when she came to see me at the station this morning, in that sari of hers, and a gentleman doesn't go asking indecent questions, does he now? It suits her well, that sari, hides the parts where she's, well, not in such good shape any more.

So Linn's gone.

She lied, didn't she? She didn't tell me back then how he rang her doorbell that night. She never told me about the expression she saw on her friends' faces, standing outside on the porch. And you'd believe her over me?

What? Oh, Antonia came to see me at the house last night. She looked horrible. Said all sorts of stupid things. That we

406

had to tell the truth. How stupid. Absolutely stupid. I told her she'd lose everything if it came out. Stark poverty, that's what was waiting for her. Do you think she could still practise if it turned out she'd told a lie like that? Not fucking likely.

I'm a counsellor, she said. It was my responsibility. I should have been there for her. If not to me, who else was Caroline supposed to turn to? But I was too ... I could not ...

I mean, Antonia never said anything, but I think it's happened to her, too, don't you? Something like what happened to Little Linny. That's why she couldn't talk about it, to anybody. That's why she went along with this in the first place.

But what do I know? All I know is she told me then she had been trying to help Linny. Giving her hints while she was here, so that she might find out herself. Like making me show her the file, like breaking her fucking doctor–patient confidentiality, talking about Jacob, Oliver, Teoman and Anna, Anna especially. And the way she kept suggesting that Linny go to a hotel. If Linn found out herself, then it would be out of our hands, she said. 'Finally,' she said, 'out of our hands.'

She also babbled something about the police who'd come to see her, asking questions. I thought she was just confused at the time. How wrong I was, wasn't I?

That's what you do, isn't it? Putting your nose where it doesn't belong and deciding in your righteous way what's wrong and what's right. You don't care about her at all, do you? All you care about is yourself. All you care about is getting on.

What? Oh, it was easy calming her down. It is. She's easily

flayed, Antonia Luca. Easy to threaten. All you have to do is shout a bit. She hates shouting. Makes her cry. It's so easy. Works with most people, women especially, I find. Seems to be a natural reaction. It's served me well in my time in the Force, especially as a superior. Makes everybody step in line, and you need them in line. There's a chain of command here. Of course we'd all prefer if it was all democratic and nice and all that, but that's not how you create a police force that works, is it? That protects people.

Didn't help with you, did it? Shouting.

Now, when Antonia Luca has left, I'm all alone at home, aren't I? All alone. I watch some TV, but I can't focus on it. It's like ... You know, I've been thinking about death a lot. About dying. It's only normal, isn't it? I'm closer to the end of life than its beginning, after all. Much closer. And you sit there and think about it and suddenly you get flayed. Like, to your core. There's nothing rational about it. It's pure and utter terror in my chest, sitting there, so heavy, making it hard to breathe. I can't breathe.

That's how I go to bed. That's how I lie down. I try and think of all the things I've achieved, all the lives I saved. But it doesn't matter. There's some things I never managed. Never found a wife to stay with me. Never had children. Grandchildren.

And then I think back on my life. You say what I did to Linn was wrong?

Then what about all the other things I did?

Do you mean to tell me they were all wrong? What gives you the right to look back on my life and spit on it? To make it all worthless? Make it all wrong?

So I lie there in bed and that's what I'm thinking about and that's why I can't go to sleep. I rarely can. It takes me hours of tossing and turning. It's even worse now that I've had to find Jacob Mason dangling from his front-room ceiling. I try to make do without, but after forty-five minutes, I fetch one of pills that Antonia Luca prescribed for me. To take just when I need them. I don't tell her I always need them. Half an hour and they'll have put me to sleep.

I've swallowed them and lain back down. I've closed my eyes and I've started breathing normally. Feeling the pillow under my head, the blanket over my body, my pyjamas on my skin.

That's when I hear it.

The doorbell.

Ding, ding, ding.

ANNA

I think I love you.

TEOMAN

I am not saying anything.

LINN

No one's more dangerous than the liar who lies to themselves.

GRAHAM

My doorbell rings, and I lie in bed and can't move.

She's gone. That means Oliver must have left, too, right? Isn't that what it means?

Then what does he want here? He told me that was what he'd do: play knock, knock, ginger with her. Nothing more. Just a harmless bit of fun, a little game. Like the mischief-makers used to play it.

He promised I'd never see them again.

Maybe he's come to say goodbye.

Maybe I'm just telling myself all this so that I'll get up and go down and face it.

My mind's a bit slow, my movements a little slurry, from the sleeping pill. I'm paggered, aren't I? As exhausted as I've ever been. Still, I manage to pull myself up and to my feet. I put on proper clothes. The doorbell rings again, but Oliver Dawson doesn't need to see me in my pyjamas, now does he?

I make it to the staircase. Remember two decades ago, when

Linny was a child, when Jacob was, teenagers, when the mischief-makers rang my doorbell in the middle of the night and thought I didn't know it was them. Thought not everybody knew it was them, when it rang like that.

It was clever of Oliver, clever of that boy. How he did it. How he used that. How he used Jacob Mason. Used me.

Poor Jacob Mason.

My steps sound heavy on the carpeted stairs as I make my way down to the front door. Staircase ends right in front of it, right there in the hallway. My vision's a bit blurry. I shake my head to clear it. But it doesn't seem to work, not really, my mind's still befuddled when I reach the bottom of the stairs. Shake my head again. My limbs. Bit better now.

Still, when I open the door, it's not Oliver.

It's Angela.

'Good evening, Detective Inspector,' she says. Proper lass, that. I see that she's not alone. She's got handcuffs with her.

As she puts them on me, I understand. With her chipped nails, that poor excuse for a haircut, that expression of grim satisfaction. Always reading that stupid poetry, Ella Wheeler Wilcox or what's her name, as if that book understood her or something. Always wanting to change things. And then all those calls she took in the break room, secretly, as if I didn't know she'd finally found some metrosexual city boy willing to stick it into her. That's what it is now, isn't it? That's what it will be from now on. Looking at lasses like that, who know nothing, spitting on my life, on all I've been taught and know, all I've done and achieved. That's what it will be from now on.

I don't put up a fuss. Haven't made a fuss, have I? You mark that down well. You mark that down, you hear me? I cooperated from the moment Angela rang my doorbell. You mark my words.

But you won't show that side of it, will you? Or they won't care, will they? The press won't. They're all snooping around for one kind of story right now, aren't they? And it's not my story. Not any more. That's what it'll be like from now on. They're rewriting the rules, but believe me, they won't be better rules. They'll just be helping different people. You're just helping yourself, aren't you?

What about her? Will you help her, Detective Sergeant Zwambe?

OLIVER

When I wake up the next morning, it is bright day already. Linn is no longer in bed. I can hear her rummaging in the kitchen. Bleary-eyed, I sit up. As I rub my tired lids, I remember my nightmare from last night. The doorbell, Jay Mason's face ... Then I stand up, throw water into my face and leave the bedroom.

Linn is all dressed already. I do not like to see that. I thought we might still go for it, but she is even wearing shoes and a jacket. Seems to be on her way out. 'Good morning, sleepy-head,' she says. 'Or should I say good day?' She laughs. A mischievous little laugh I have not heard in years. 'I've got to run, but I'll see you later.'

And she's out of the door.

Well, when she comes back. We will have plenty of time when she's back.

So I make breakfast, porridge and fruits and honey, I need to watch my diet, and then I watch some TV.

The thing is, she does not come back. Morning turns into noon turns into afternoon. I would text her, but I can't. She has a new number. Instead, I pace around the flat. I watch the match but can't really focus on it. Keep thinking of Jay's face. Think about going down to the pub, but I want to be here when she comes back. I cannot stand the thought that she may have taken off again.

Only when it is dark do I hear the key turn in our lock. It is evening by the time she returns. I stand up, relieved. There she is, coming in laughing. She is holding out a bunch of flowers to me. 'Look what I got you, Sweet-O. They're almost as lovely as the ones you sent me before you left for Cornwall.'

She smiles as she hands me the bouquet. It's very pretty, even with berries and all.

My flower girl. I laugh.

She's holding a bottle of red wine in her other hand. Pours herself a glass as she sits down at the table to sort through the mail while I return to the couch to watch some more TV. Her lips are red and glistening. I observe her closely for a while, but she seems perfectly normal. Taking a sip of her wine every now and again. Perfectly happy to sort through bills and play with the flowers on the table.

At some point, she comes over and brings me her wine. 'Do you want to finish it?' she says. 'I've had enough.' I put my arms around her waist, but she extricates herself with a smile, saying she needs to finish the paperwork. Taking a sip of the wine, I turn back to the TV. It's sweet, just like her lips.

At ten, it is utterly dark out. I wonder when she will join

me. We never turned on the lights, so there is only the TV and the candle burning on the kitchen table. My muscles feel strangely weak. Must have been sitting here for too long. Need to get up and stretch. Breathe properly. I yawn. Reach for the remote. Hit the OFF button.

Then she blows out the candle.

I don't know why. I just know I realise how dark it goes. Realise how my hands turn clammy.

Then the doorbell rings.

It rings three times.

I jump to my feet. I cannot see, but I can hear, the doorbell, fading out, and Linn's voice: 'What's wrong, Sweet-O? It's just the drunks from the pub.'

And then she laughs. Her mischievous little laughter.

Sweat trickles down my body. Down my neck, my back, my legs. I stumble towards the table, but my eyes haven't grown used to the dark yet. She does not seem to be there any more. I'm swaying on my feet, my muscles seizing, my lungs. I can't breathe. 'Can't you hear it?' I choke out.

'What?' Linn asks. 'Oliver, what's the matter?'

'The bell!' I bellow. My heart's beating so fast that I cannot help but bellow, like a stupid dog. 'You've got to hear it. You're lying.'

And suddenly her voice is very close. And very quiet. 'What bell, Oliver?'

I reach for her, struggling to breathe, but she is already gone. The sweat is running into my eyes now, making it even harder to see. They burn. My pulse is going so quickly it is all I can hear, hammering away in my ears.

Until it is her voice again, right next to my ear: 'Why would you hear a doorbell ring in the dark?'

Something dawns on me. I lash out but miss. The doorbell rings again.

Ding, ding, ding.

'Why?' Her voice in my ear. 'Why?' The pulse of my blood. 'Why?' The stench of my sweat. 'Why?' The stench of her blood.

She knows.

I cannot believe it. Cannot fathom it.

'You know,' I say into the sudden silence. 'You know.'

'Know what, Oliver?'

She's standing across from me. I can feel her presence. I lick my lips. Taste the strong red wine.

The wine.

'That it was me,' I say.

III. Justice

Chapter 10

LINN

Lavender. That was what was missing from the crime scene, from my parents' bedroom. There wasn't any lavender on the list in the file. There wasn't any lavender in the photos. And it made sense: Mum never put out more than one scent. It was always either rosemary and thyme *or* lavender, never the two at the same time. I told you this, didn't I? Yes, I see you nod. And the rosemary and thyme were in the photos, on the list. They were right there.

Still I *smelled* lavender. I know I did. It was the thing I'd always remembered about that night. That stench of lavender.

That meant the Doorman had brought it with him.

Remember how Jay said Oliver's perfume smelt like something out of a Chilcott catalogue? He would know, with the Chilcott pillows in his front room, the pouches of lavender they all come with.

It's funny, isn't it? It was never the daisies that struck me as odd. It wasn't even the candle. It was not what *was* there, but what wasn't. Just took me a while to realise.

I'm glad it was Mum who helped me solve it all. I hope she is somewhere where she can see me. I hope she knows. Hope they both know it was never their fault.

Miss Luca had smelled it too. It is even in her statement. And so had Teo and Anna. That is how they knew who'd been in the bedroom with me. Who'd done it.

God, Teo and Anna.

The train is moving smoothly beneath our feet, smoothly and swiftly. You wouldn't even know we were going 200 miles an hour if it didn't say so up on some screen. Anna's sitting next to me, in the seat by the window. Her hair looks whiter than I thought. She has her eyes closed.

On my other side, across the aisle, sits Teo. He's looking at me, at us. He's grinning, even though he looks tired. I don't know why I went a single day without it. Why I was so willing to believe Graham, to go along with it. Why we all were.

No, I do get it. It would have looked so bad for Jay, being the last who'd seen me. Besides, look at what it did to him.

By the way, thank you for showing me his letter. He tried telling me in the end. When he learned I was married to Oliver, he decided to leave me a final message, telling me the truth. Too bad that I only got to read a small part of it. Graham kept it to himself, of course. Forensics, my arse. You didn't get to see it till you'd arrested him, did you?

And I get Anna and Teo. For them, it was about everything. They were being threatened with deportation. Graham had done it before, when we'd broken into Bolton Castle, but this time, Jay and I weren't there to cover for them. And where would they have checked to see if what Graham said was true? There was no library in town, and the Internet was only something you talked about, not a place you actually went unless you were willing to pay by the minute and optimistic enough that the questions you had would be answered on some dubious webpage.

Teoman told me it took him one year to find out for sure that Anna and he could not have been expelled, at least not automatically, even if they had been convicted of assault. By that time, I was already gone. So was Anna. Off to uni, just like him. And this was the year 2001. He had only weeks ago been beaten by plain-clothes in Harehill, lying doubled up on the ground in Banstead Park between burning washing machines and wooden chairs. He did not trust the constabulary any more, not enough to take this to them.

'It doesn't matter,' he says now. 'I should have gone straight to the police. It was unforgivable.'

We're speaking quietly. He tells me how he started setting things on fire, trying to work his way up to a police station. He says he was lucky he got caught. Put him back on the right track.

We had to rush to catch the last train out of London, taking cabs to St Pancras from Leyton. Now he is not looking at me, fiddling with his sweater instead, merino wool. It is very soft. I take his hand and tap my fingers against his skin.

I went to see them, right after Graham and Miss Luca had shown me the file. When I had finally realised that they had been right. That the silhouette in my memory had not belonged to Miss Luca, or Jacob.

That if Jay didn't have an alibi, neither did Oliver.

Sitting in Teo's flat, on his parents' old couch, we made plans. About what to do next. How to make it right.

It's no surprise that we settled on a game of knock, knock, ginger.

We knew it was essential that Oliver would think I hadn't uncovered his identity. So I returned to the house. I got in my car. The original plan had been to drive off the moment I heard him ring the doorbell, so that he would see me go back. When I realised he was hiding in the car, I had to draw him away first. The access to the hollow was easiest from the bedroom, over the porch roof. I didn't mean to sprain my ankle, but improvisation can go wrong, too.

Anna and Teo had been in the garden the entire time. They watched Oliver drive off. They recorded it all.

Anna and Teo followed us to ring our doorbell together. What a laugh. How easily he admitted to it. We made an audio recording of it. Here it is, and some of his e-mails, in case they are helpful.

Teo is tapping my hand back now. I can't believe it took me so long to understand what Anna had been trying to say. 'Daisies and ...?' Lavender. I didn't let her finish. I was so convinced it could have been her. When she said she'd been furious, I made the facts fit my theory. I forgot that people don't normally come to your house to assault you when they are angry. No, they come to talk to you. Like she did.

Still, I really believed it could have been her. What a ludicrous thought. To think that I would fall for the same lie twice. But then, what would have been the alternative? To suspect Oliver? To think it could have been the man I married, the man who earned our living, the man I gave up everything for so that he could have the life he wanted …

It was unthinkable. Even though they always say that it's usually someone close to you. Even though my body had sometimes shirked his touch, even though it was not the first time I'd thrown up that morning … No, not him. Not Oliver.

Until I saw the list of flowers in the file.

I look at Anna. Her head's lying on my shoulder now, but her eyes are open. We are on our way across the Channel. I've always wanted to see Paris. I will be back for Jay's funeral, and to properly do up my parents' grave, of course, like I promised. Intertwining my hand with Anna's, I put my cheek to her head. She turns and kisses me on the mouth. 'Is that okay?' she whispers before she does, and I nod. That she would ask. Her lips on mine make my blood roar. And then we are both laughing, suddenly. Just like that.

You didn't need to know that last bit, did you? But I wanted to tell you so that you would know how happy we were, Detective Sergeant, before you had us stopped at the border.

I was just as shocked as you were when you told me. When I left my husband, he was in perfect health. Begging me not to leave him, yes. Saying that he couldn't live without me, over and over again. That he would end it all.

But he must have known he had lost me for good this time. He must have known there was no coming back from this.

And I'll be honest with you, absolutely honest: if he had killed himself, right there in our flat, I wouldn't have intervened. If, say, he would have taken a bottle of red wine and squeezed nightshade berries into it, downing it in one go, I simply would have stood there and watched. And once it had been over, I would have left without looking back.

But I didn't. I wasn't there.

What do you mean, why am I smiling? I am not smiling. My mouth twitches when I am under pressure.

What?

Oh, the Detective Inspector said that, didn't he? The same Detective Inspector who lied to our faces for almost twenty years?

You see, Detective Sergeant Zwambe, the point is, it is up to you now, isn't it? You know my story now. You have asked all of us to tell you everything that has happened, as if it was happening right in that moment. You have interrogated the Detective Inspector, Anna and myself, you have the recordings we made of Oliver. You have the e-mail he sent me, threatening to kill himself.

Teoman refused to say anything, but I am sure you understand; he has not had the best of experiences with the police. You found my file when Graham left it lying around in the archive; you latched on to the inconsistencies; you told Angela to watch us. You tried to help me, even though you know that only 7 per cent of all rape cases result in a conviction. You even found the dried nightshade in my pocket, took it off me. You were worried I would do something to myself, weren't you? Not to someone else. No no, you're better at reading

428

people than that. You are a very good detective. Next in line
for his job now that Graham is out of the way, I should think.
With Angela promoted to Sergeant, I wager?

Either way, now you know the whole story.

So you decide. You decide how this story ends. You decide
what story we deserve.

Tell me, Detective Sergeant: how does this story end?

THE FLOWER GIRL

You see, what I do is, I deliver flowers. You need a job, don't you, and at least you're outside sometimes, even though all you do is breathe in London's smog. Still, I can cycle a lot. I love cycling.

I don't actually like flowers, though. Most people who send them seem to be creeps. Either they're stalking someone or they don't care about a close relative enough to send them a proper gift for their birthday, or their anniversary, or even a funeral. Or they're liars. You'd be surprised how many men still send flowers both to their wives and their girlfriends, always at the same time. It's like there's an app or a secretary reminding them. Take my word for it: when someone sends you a bouquet of flowers, you better run. There's something they're hiding.

And you wouldn't believe what some people ask for. Just last week, I delivered a bouquet with deadly nightshade to a flat in Leyton. I repeat, *deadly nightshade*. Just because it's

Flowers for the Dead

called *Atropa belladonna* on our website doesn't make it any less dangerous. It comes with berries and all. Stupid. Make you lose faith in humanity, flowers do.

This morning, I've got another bouquet with *Atropa belladonna*, and for a funeral, too. People have no tact at all. Besides, deliveries to funerals can be really sad affairs, when you arrive and you stick around for a bit, smoking your cigarette, and see that almost nobody's coming to the ceremony. I sometimes stay then. Pay my respects. Costs you a hell of a lot of time, though.

That is why I'm glad that this time the delivery is for the wake, an hour or so before the service. I'm pretty hungry, and there is a Sainsbury's just around the corner (who doesn't live for cold pasta and bag of crisps for lunch?).

The sun's out as I approach the funeral home, even though it's chilly, making me wrap my scarf more tightly around my throat. My nail polish is badly chipped. Time to take off the blue, I think. Winter needs another colour.

Two people in mourning are standing outside the doors, a tall man in an elegant black suit and a blonde woman in a worn leather jacket. They are talking in lowered voices, standing close together, unconsciously turned towards each other, like old friends do.

I jump off my bike and ask them about the bouquet I am holding. The man – bloody hell, he has the darkest eyes I've ever seen – points me towards a room in the back of the funeral home.

I don't think I should go in there, I say.
No, you should, he says. *The widow is waiting for you.*

431

People are weird, that's what I told you. So I go in, step over the linoleum floors of the funeral home and into the small, bare room at the back, all white walls and grey floor, no windows, artificial light. A couple of candles in a corner, like an afterthought.

There's only one person in there. A very private wake, then. A woman, looking into an open casket. I think they're so freaky, open-casket wakes. Awkwardly standing in the door-frame, I clear my throat.

The widow turns around and smiles at me. Beckons me over. *Thank you so much,* she says, as I hand her the bouquet.

No problem, I answer. *I am so sorry for your loss.*

As I turn around and leave, I catch a glimpse inside the casket.

That's when I lose faith in humanity.

You would think it was because I catch the woman turn around, pull the deadly nightshade out of the bouquet, and place it inside the casket. You would think it was because I see her pick off the berries and press them onto his face, squishing black juice all over his pale skin.

But that's not it.

It is the body inside the casket. When I see it up close, that is when I lose faith in humanity.

It is a man. When I glance at his face, washed and embalmed, pale and peaceful, it takes me a moment to realise what is wrong with it.

He no longer has eyes.

In the empty sockets sit, sewn to the skin, two heads of lavender.

Fragrant dried lavender.

Acknowledgements

No book is made by one person only, not even the one who writes it. I would like to thank:

Thérèse Coen, wonder of an agent, without whom this book would never have seen the light of day, and even if it had, would not have done so in a presentable state. Thank you for persevering where I was about to give up. Thank you for believing in me when I was about to lose faith. Thank you for making this book happen.

Hannah Todd, for everything, most notably unwavering support, brainstorming that is productive *and* fun, enthusiasm especially for dark endings, a skilled editorial eye and the beginning of this novel, which simply would not be what it is without you, and that would make me very, very sad.

Katie Loughnane, for believing in the book so much that she would acquire it, and for all her thoughts on the next one to come. Thank you for championing this, Katie!

Everyone at Avon and One More Chapter, especially Sabah Khan, Molly Walker-Sharp and Helen Huthwaite for always welcoming me to drinks and dinner, whether in London or Harrogate. Thank you all for dedicating your time to books, and to their authors!

Lisa Pohlers, my tireless assistant, who says yes to every stupid request I put to her, who brainstorms and inspires and plots and is an all-around miracle.

Tony Russell for a keen eye and a precise copy-edit. And for the Barbour jacket!

Chris Foster, Sam Floyd and Muna Zubedi for invaluable advice on Yorkshire and dialects in the North.

All the unsung heroes of the publishing process. If you work in publishing, this is for you!

Each and every bookseller. Without you, there wouldn't be any books.

My students of the Novel Writing Workshop at the University of Bonn, who helped me plot and conceive the entire climax of this novel and are a never-ending source of inspiration, encouragement and support. *Auf die Zunft!*

Nicole Etherington of Hardman & Swainson for all her help with this project. Thank you for being a midwife to this baby!

Rebecca Solnit for writing *Men Explain Things to Me*, which helped me see what this book had to be about at its core.

My friends, always. There is nothing I would be able to do without you. *Ceci n'existe pas sans vous*. I would like to thank in particular Ina Habermann and Johannes Frohnhofen as well as Anne Küpperbusch. Also Lucy Seymour and Chris Foster for DEEN, as well as Elisabeth Lewerenz for Lewerenz & Lehnen.

My parents, Thomas Lehnen and Karin Surmann-Lehnen, for never treating their daughter any differently from her brothers.

My brothers, Nils Lehnen and Matthias Lehnen, for always supporting me, no matter how mad the idea – in fact, the crazier the idea, the more support was required (*and* provided!).

My boyfriend, Adrian Bolz, for loving me even though it isn't an easy thing to do.

Sir Arthur Conan Doyle as well as the makers of the BBC audio adaptations with Clive Merrison as Sherlock Holmes. Without you, it would never have occurred to me to write a crime novel.

Last, but very decidedly not least: The stranger who rang my doorbell seven years ago in the middle of the night one week after I'd moved to Bonn, living alone for the first time. Without you, this book would not exist.